SCANDAL WITH A PRINCE

By Nicole Burnham

Cover design by Patricia Schmitt
Edited by Valerie Susan Hayward
Edition: November 2013
ISBN: 978-0-984-7069-4-5

For more information or to subscribe to Nicole's newsletter, visit *www.nicoleburnham.com*

For Doug

CHAPTER ONE

Certain men possess voices so richly captivating, so drenched in sexuality, that they can bring a woman to her knees with a few simple syllables.

In a crowd of hundreds, it was the sound of one such voice that caught Megan's attention first.

Her stomach seized the instant her ears picked out the distinct timbre amongst the din of merry voices echoing through the packed rotunda of the newly-renovated Barcelona Grandspire Hotel. Around her, men and women went on sipping *cava* from crystal flutes as they discussed upcoming business deals or renovations to their vacation homes. Tuxedoed waiters continued their discreet circumnavigation of the room, gathering used hors d'oeuvre plates and refreshing drinks. On the surface, all appeared unchanged. It was a perfect late spring night in a perfect city, and thus far the hotel's grand reopening celebration was a resounding success.

Then she heard it again. Only three or four indistinguishable words, but they hit her gut with the same force as a sucker-punch from a male twice her size. A well-built male like Prince Stefano Barrali, whose third-in-line claim to the throne of Sarcaccia meant he enjoyed immeasurable wealth and connections without the pressures that usually accompanied them, while possessing the Mediterranean good looks and sultry charm that often did.

A few feet away from Megan, a gray-haired gentleman and his much younger wife cast subtle glances toward the hotel's side entrance, the one used when high-profile guests needed to make an inconspicuous arrival or exit. Megan resisted the urge to follow suit, but a breath later the overall volume in the lobby rose even as men tall enough to see over the crowd leaned closer to their companions to whisper into diamond-studded ears.

It's not possible. Not here, not on the biggest night of her career to date.

Without allowing her smile to drop or the cadence of her speech to change, skills honed by years of professional banter at events such as this, Megan continued her conversation with Mahmoud Said, the CEO of a large Egyptian telecommunications company, giving him an overview of the beachfront hotel's state-of-the-art conference and special event facilities. At the same time, she strained to catch the familiar sound once more. Perhaps the voice existed only in her mind, a stress-induced result of the months of work that had gone into tonight's soiree or a trick caused by the rotunda's domed roof.

No, even as Mahmoud asked a question about the hotel's business center, she accepted that she'd ceased imagining Stefano's flirtatious, luxuriant voice years ago. In all probability, the sound emanated from one of the televisions mounted over the bar in the cocktail lounge adjacent to the lobby. Though the bartender had been instructed to keep the sets muted in keeping with the formality of the night's celebration, with so many people crowding the lobby it wouldn't take much for a remote control to get bumped the wrong way or for a guest to assert herself and tune in to a report about a celebrity—or hot young royal—who caught her eye.

The Grandspire's manager, Ramon Beltran, circled through the crowd near Megan, patting shoulders, shaking hands, and accepting congratulations as he went, before he ascended the lobby's grand staircase to cascading applause. With a sweeping gesture, he sounded a ceremonial gong calling the guests to attention.

"Ladies and gentlemen," he announced as the reverberation faded, "thank you for attending our celebration tonight. We're honored to have so many friends and family of the Grandspire share this important evening. Dinner will now be served in the Gaudi Ballroom. I hope you enjoy both the meal and the view."

A pair of waiters opened the doors to reveal the ballroom's all-new floor to ceiling windows, which overlooked an immaculate beach and the Mediterranean Sea beyond. Modern tables topped with white-on-white orchids and Gaudi-inspired place settings filled the room. The resulting spike in conversation obliterated any chance Megan had of pinpointing the source of Stefano's voice.

Mahmoud excused himself to check on a friend, providing Megan the opportunity to conduct a discreet surveillance of the expansive marble lobby. Keeping her demeanor pleasant and professional, she scanned the faces of the well-heeled men in attendance, most of whom now escorted exquisitely gowned women past the lobby's large floral arrangements and into the ballroom.

The face that matched the voice didn't materialize. She exhaled, directing her nervous energy toward smoothing the silk fabric of the honey-colored cocktail dress she'd purchased especially for tonight, but her stomach remained unsettled.

At a signal from Ramon, Megan made her way against the tide of guests to encourage the attendees still clustered in the sunken bar area on the far side of the lobby to join the rest of the crowd in making their way to dinner. Progress was slow. All around her, air kisses were exchanged, lunches suggested, and holidays arranged as guests mingled. Gossip snaked its way through every conversation.

It was exactly the type of event where one expected to find Prince Stefano being courted by the movers and shakers of major corporations and high society, all of whom hoped that making inroads with the Barrali royal family would help them gain access to the family's vast financial and social network. However, as the Grandspire's head of business development, Megan had combed through the guest list for tonight's soiree more than once and Prince Stefano's name wasn't on it. It would not have escaped her notice.

As she descended the wide steps leading to the lounge area, Megan's gaze flicked to the bank of televisions mounted high over the sleek granite bar. Five soundless screens carried sporting events, but the sixth flashed the latest celebrity gossip. The bartender, a sociable young Catalan with a knack for attracting female attention, watched alongside a curvaceous blonde guest who gasped at the blaring announcement of a popular Spanish soap star's pregnancy with twins.

A sense of relief washed through Megan. That must've been it. It wouldn't be the first time Stefano spoke to her from a television.

The bartender glanced from the buxom blonde to Megan, shooting Megan a disarming *what can you do?* grin before fiddling with the remote to mute the sound and return the television to its usual sports station.

Megan arched a mischievous eyebrow at him, then at the blonde's back, before stretching her toes inside her new gold heels to release the tension of the last few hours. She couldn't blame herself for being on edge. Tonight's event was the culmination of five years of hard work. Given that investment of time and energy, together with a shortage of sleep this past week while the final preparations were made, she should've expected her nerves might get the better of her. She needed to take a cue from both the bartender and the guests lingering nearby and relax. The best way for her to showcase the refurbished hotel to the potential business clients in attendance would be to visibly enjoy the Grandspire herself—tonight's dinner, the art exhibition, the rooftop fireworks, all of it—and consider it a reward for a job well done. After all, she'd already booked eight major conferences and over two dozen smaller events for the coming months, enough to kick-start the hotel's income stream and gild her resume before she sought her next position.

Invigorated at the thought, she made her way to each of the seating areas in the lounge and introduced herself to those guests she didn't already know before directing them toward the ballroom. One by one, empty glasses filled the bar top as the partygoers progressed to dinner. However, a cluster of people remained near the fireplace, their attention riveted on a male seated in their center. Megan hated to interrupt, but couldn't see past those who were standing to identify the speaker. Only his highly polished shoes were visible between the high heels and wingtips of those surrounding him.

A man making his way toward the stairs glanced toward the fireplace when he thought no one was looking, though his partner, a woman whom Megan recognized as the owner of a major shipping company, stared openly, apparently unconcerned that others would notice her fascination with the conversation taking place.

The knot returned to Megan's stomach, twisting tighter than before. Everyone in attendance tonight was accustomed to the trappings of money and fame. Whoever sat near the fireplace held a special allure, even amongst the social elite, the kind often reserved for royalty. And *always* reserved for good-looking royalty.

A familiar rumble of laughter cut through the lounge, confirming her fear. Low, sexy, and even more inviting than Megan remembered, if such a thing were possible. Her knees softened and the floor seemed to sway beneath her.

After their last face-to-face meeting, she'd spent weeks trying to contact Stefano, using every means at her disposal, but now she needed nothing more than to escape. Seeing him in the flesh would make her want everything she knew she could never have, and she did not want to *want*. Especially not him.

Wanting Stefano could mean losing everything.

She took a step backward and started to turn away. She'd ask the bartender to send the group to dinner, then figure out how she could possibly avoid the prince for the rest of the evening so she could keep her attention where it needed to be: on work. Stefano's presence wouldn't distract her unless she let it.

"Megan." The telecommunications CEO she'd spoken with earlier appeared at her elbow, propelling her back toward the fireplace. "Have you had the opportunity to meet my guest? I didn't wish to say anything until I knew he'd arrived." Mahmoud's voice dropped to a whisper as he added, "You know these types. You cannot always count on them to appear when they say they will."

Before Megan could protest, the group parted in front of her to reveal a broad-shouldered man sitting on the far edge of the cocktail table, his face turned away as he laughed at a comment from a statuesque, cat-eyed brunette wearing the most arresting red gown Megan had ever seen.

Mahmoud cleared his throat. "Prince Stefano, may I present Megan Hallberg, the Grandspire's director of business development? Megan, this is Prince Stefano Barrali of Sarcaccia. His father and I have hosted a number of charity events together over the years, so I wanted Stefano to see the Grandspire's new facilities. I'm certain he'll give King Carlo a favorable report on the hotel's suitability for our future events."

The brunette tried to hide her disappointment at the interruption as Stefano spun around and stood in one easy motion. Megan's mouth went dry as sand. She'd forgotten how tall he was, how fluidly he moved. As Stefano stepped toward her, the memory of their first meeting returned in a rush that threatened to flatten her. He'd moved in that same easy manner when he'd approached her a decade ago, offering to carry a length of pipe for her as she struggled to maneuver it through an alley in the congested Venezuelan village where they both worked as volunteers. She'd joked that he was her hero when he'd hefted it onto one shoulder as if it were no heavier than a loaf of bread.

But there were changes in him, too. While the celebrity gossips frequently commented on Stefano's athleticism, his playful nature, and even his dimples, no report could accurately convey the ways he'd matured in the years since Megan had last seen him. Television and magazines failed to capture the masculine line of his shoulders as they filled his tuxedo jacket, the texture of the skin along his sunkissed cheekbones, or the utter charisma he exuded.

Megan forced herself not to flinch as he came within arm's reach. She hadn't thought it possible his appearance could improve over the years, but it had. He'd become broader, stronger, more confident...more *him*.

Of course, his most distinctive physical characteristic could never change. His eyes were a clear sea green with a distinct ring around each iris, as if Picasso himself had taken up a narrow paintbrush to edge the green in black. She remembered all too well the last time she'd looked into those eyes. She'd been twenty-two, as had Stefano. They each sported grubby clothes that evening, having worked the entire day to finish installing a water system, but they'd been unwilling to use a single precious moment to change, knowing it was their final night together before returning to their separate lives. Their *real* lives.

He'd threaded his long fingers through her hair as they stood on a secluded beach not far from the village. Even in the waning light of the setting sun, she'd seen the deep passion in those green eyes. "I will never, ever forget you," he'd whispered before pulling her into a heart-stopping, explosive kiss. "These have been the best days of my life."

It felt surreal to look into those same eyes now, knowing she'd been forgotten within weeks, perhaps even days, relegated to what would become a long, long line of disposable women. A decade's worth of women, starting with the one to whom he'd become engaged less than a month after leaving Venezuela. The one to whom he'd run, barefoot, across the palace courtyard in a photo that appeared around the world, intriguing even those who'd never heard of the Barrali royal family.

Yet she couldn't have forgotten Stefano Barrali, even if she'd wanted to forget. Emotion threatened to overwhelm her as he stood before her, reaching out to take the hand she extended as if she were on autopilot. Before he could speak, undoing her with his whiskey-rich voice, she managed a calm, "Prince Stefano, it's an honor to have you here at the Grandspire. I hope you're enjoying your time in Barcelona."

He wrapped his large hand around hers, the touch shaking her very center. Searching out any excuse to break eye contact, she glanced toward Mahmoud and thanked him for the introduction. It was an act of sheer self-preservation out of fear Stefano could see to her soul, revealing both the wild lust coursing through her and the secret she'd kept hidden for so long.

Twenty floors above them, in the expansive suite that served as Megan's residence while she worked on the hotel's revitalization, a young girl with sea-green eyes and the same dark, wavy hair as Stefano sat at a desk, under the supervision of Megan's parents, finishing her homework.

A young girl conceived that very night on the beach.

* * *

Megan Hallberg?

Adrenaline shot through Stefano at the mention of her name, propelling him to his feet. In the same instant, reason kicked in. After all these years, it was unlikely the same Megan Hallberg. Wouldn't she be married by now? Living somewhere in Minnesota, where she'd returned after they'd met during the gap year service project he'd pursued in Venezuela?

He turned, expecting to see a dour older woman he'd never before met, someone who'd fit the description of a director of business development for a major hotel, only to see a vital, sexy, alluring Megan.

His Megan.

Stefano's breath stilled at the sight of her.

He had no right to think of her as such. They'd shared nothing more than a brief, heady summer together, but after they'd left Venezuela—he to fulfill his military and royal obligations, she to finish her graduate degree—he frequently thought of her, and always in that way. *His.* There had been other women and other relationships, of course, but none like he'd enjoyed with Megan Hallberg. At twenty-two, how could he have appreciated the unique nature of the bond they'd forged in those few weeks together? The absolute freedom of those days in each other's company?

It likely wouldn't have worked between them—not in the real world, away from the isolation they'd experienced in South America—and they had both sensed it. Still, it was an easy fantasy to keep tucked away in a remote corner of his mind, one to be conjured forth on those days where he strained against his royal role.

He took in the sight of her, from her sweetly sculpted calves to her nipped waist and ripe bosom. Who knew reality would be so much better than the fantasy? The years had been good to Megan. Very good. Proper posture made her appear straighter and leaner than he remembered, but she still curved in all the right places. The ethereal color of her knee-length, cut-to-kill gown combined with the soft glow of the dimmed lounge lighting to make her blonde hair even more luminous than in his memory of those sun-filled, steamy days.

Then she met his gaze, firing his blood as if they'd never left that beach.

He approached to give her a warm kiss on each cheek, only to be stopped by her outstretched hand and formal tone. "Prince Stefano, it's an honor to have you here at the Grandspire. I hope you're enjoying your time in Barcelona."

He met her handshake, shocked she didn't remember him. Women always remembered him, and she had more reason than most. But as he studied the depths of Megan's soft blue eyes and felt the spark of her touch once more, he knew she did. She remembered it all.

Their attraction was still mutual. Still undeniable.

Megan turned her head to thank Mahmoud, who'd made the introduction, and Stefano saw his opportunity.

"Megan," he leaned in to drop a lingering kiss on her cheek, taking in the citrus and sunshine scent of her hair. "It's good to see you again. The Grandspire is stunning, but not as stunning as its head of business development."

He glanced past Megan to Mahmoud, who could not hide his surprise over Stefano's familiarity. "Megan and I met many years ago in South America on a volunteer project. She's one in a million." Capturing Megan's blue-eyed gaze once more, he said, "It was a memorable time, working there."

Her lower lip twitched. "Yes, memorable is the perfect word for it. It was a great learning experience for me."

Noticing for the first time that the lobby had emptied as guests transitioned to the ballroom, he pulled Megan's hand through his arm and guided her toward the stairs, hoping to put her at ease. "I haven't familiarized myself with the seating arrangements for dinner, but I would be honored if you'd join me. You likely know more about my life than you care to if you've seen a newspaper, but I'd love to hear how you came to Barcelona."

He'd also love to pick up where they left off. Megan clearly worked hard to attain such a position of responsibility. He'd been too young and too obsessed with his impending military training to realize the rarity of finding a woman of Megan's intelligence and beauty. The amazing chemistry they shared—chemistry he doubted time had dimmed—was rarer still.

Now he was old enough and experienced enough to appreciate a woman of her attributes. Damn if he wasn't going to make the most of the opportunity.

"Yes, I heard that you were engaged," she said as they made their way across the lobby. The group from the bar trailed in their wake, including Ilsa, the woman with whom he'd been chatting when Megan appeared, and his father's friend Mahmoud. "I'm sorry to hear it didn't work out."

Was she? Her tone made it difficult to tell. He certainly hadn't been sorry. Only sorry he'd become entangled in the first place.

She cleared her throat and added, "While I'd love to speak over dinner, Your Highness, I have a prior obligation. Part and parcel of the job, I'm afraid. But I hope you enjoy your meal. Our head chef has truly outdone himself." Megan slowed as they approached the entrance to the ballroom. Inside, hundreds of guests bantered happily, but he could only see Megan. There was a strength in her demeanor he didn't remember, one which spoke to a woman who'd developed an iron core. How had the years affected her, to change her this way? Was it simply the passing of time, or something else?

Slowly, she snaked her hand from where it rested in the crook of his arm, but not before he could catch the tips of her fingers. "Then perhaps you would meet me on the roof during the fireworks later. It would be a shame to miss this chance to catch up, don't you think?"

She blinked, considering. If he didn't know better, he'd think he read anxiety in her expression. But why?

"Of course, Your Highness. I'll look for you."

He let go of her fingertips, but not before capturing her gaze and murmuring, "And I for you."

CHAPTER TWO

Escape.

Megan needed to escape the ballroom before dinner finished or *she'd* be finished. She nodded in agreement as the Russian businessman beside her commented on the fine quality of the dining room's new chandeliers, then used the opportunity to glance over the man's shoulder and determine which of the ballroom's doors offered her the easiest out. Once her dinner companion finished his patter, Megan turned her focus to the podium and tucked her napkin to the side of her plate, waiting for a moment of applause so she could leave without being noticed.

She couldn't look at the table between hers and the podium—or the dark-haired guest seated alongside Mahmoud Said and smack in front of the speaker—much longer, not without having her manager or other coworkers notice her discomfort. They'd become a sort of family as they worked together on the hotel renovations. They'd see she wasn't herself tonight. Worse, Megan couldn't risk having Stefano corner her. She'd managed to hold it together when facing him in the lobby, but now that she'd had time to absorb the fact he was actually here in Barcelona, in the same room, breathing the same air, threatening everything she'd built for herself and her daughter Anna, she wasn't sure she'd appear so confident next time. She had too much at stake, and Stefano was a man used to getting everything he wanted.

A billion-dollar family fortune did that, even if the crown didn't.

"Please, my love," came a deep male voice close to her ear, "tell me I made your mouth water this evening."

At the hushed request, Megan twisted in her seat to face Santi, the hotel's head chef. He crouched behind her, his dark eyes sparkling with mischief as he scanned the room to assess the guests' satisfaction with his creations.

"Everyone's thrilled with your menu," she whispered back. "Of course my mouth is watering." Though not at the food—she'd hardly touched her dessert, enticing as it was—but at Stefano. It galled her that after all these years she found him both intimidating and exciting, and not necessarily in that order.

"Good, good. When the dinner plates came back to the kitchen, I feared the waiters had scraped them clean rather than the guests. The staff, they fear damage to my pride." Santi's accent thickened as he searched her face and added, "So tell me, why do you ignore my mandarin cake when I know it is your favorite? I come all the way from the kitchen to see your reaction, only to discover my beautiful dessert still sitting before you. It cannot be female concerns over fitting into your gown, because you are perfection tonight. Breathtaking."

She patted the older man's arm. Such a flirt, though he had a beloved wife and six children at home. "First, while I adore your mandarin cake, your chocolate is my favorite. And second, I ate far too much of the main course and need time to digest. You spoil me."

"Impossible. It was only halibut."

"No dish is 'only' with you, Santi. It's why you were hired."

Santi ignored the compliment and swirled a beefy hand in front of her face. "Your expression says that something is amiss. Tell me."

She shook off his words even as he said them. "You know better than that. It's only that duty calls before dessert. I need to ensure the fireworks team is ready before we send the guests upstairs."

Santi gave her an exaggerated look of doubt, then made her promise to meet with him in the next few days to share any comments she heard about the meal. "It's good for business to know what our guests desire," he explained quietly.

"It's also good for your ego."

He shrugged one shoulder, the casual gesture in contrast to the sudden serious-ness of his gaze, which traveled beyond her. "I was not expecting royalty tonight. But if I can satisfy him…well, again, it would be very good for business. It is good that he is here."

His words were a revelation. She needed to view Stefano much as Santi did, not as a powerful man to be feared or as the sexy father of her child to be desired, but as a business prospect.

"I'll get feedback once the speech is over, then meet you tomorrow afternoon to discuss everything." She grinned at the chef. "If it makes you feel better, why don't you send a few slices of leftover mandarin cake up to my suite? I'll enjoy it when this is all over, and you know Anna would be over the moon."

He waggled his eyebrows to indicate that he'd already done so. At that moment, the manager finished his dinner speech to thunderous applause, so Megan excused herself and slipped out the ballroom doors while Santi returned to the kitchen.

Once free of the dining room, she paused to inhale deeply of the lobby's fragrant blooms in an effort to clear her head and focus her energy on making the rest of the evening a success. She could dwell on her run-in with Stefano tomorrow. Resolved, she removed a stray cocktail napkin from one of the lobby tables, tossed it into the trash, then crossed to the elevator and punched the button for the roof deck. Halfway up, she bit back a curse and hit the button for the twentieth floor.

While she'd done what she could to protect herself, she needed to protect Anna.

The door to her suite flew open at the same time she slid her key card into the lock. A smiling face greeted her. "Mom!"

She couldn't help but laugh at Anna's exuberance. "What in the world are you doing?"

"I heard the elevator ding and figured it was you. Santi sent us a ton of dessert!" Anna let go of the door to race toward the suite's small kitchen. "Come see! Or did you have some already?"

Sure enough, the dark granite countertop was covered in beautifully plated slices of white cake topped with Santi's signature mandarin orange sauce and garnished with strawberries, raspberries, and blueberries. "Santi deserves a thank you note later," Megan informed her daughter.

"I know. I'll write one tomorrow morning." Anna climbed onto one of the barstools at the counter's edge and eyed the cake. She tucked her thick hair behind her ears, then looked up, her green eyes pleading. "Grandma said I could have a slice after I finish my homework, but it's going to take forever. Do you think I could have half a piece, since my homework's halfway done? It's not even due until Thursday. Please?"

"I'm not going to overrule Grandma," Megan said.

"Ha!" Bill Hallberg's voice came from the sitting area around the corner from the kitchen. "Told you, Anna."

"But Grandpa—"

"Oh, fine," Megan's mother, Joan Hallberg, said as she walked into the kitchen, waving a dismissive hand in her husband's direction. "Anna, since your mother's here, you may have a slice. But take it to the table."

"The coffee table?" In other words, where she could see the television while she ate.

"I suppose. But you'll need to take a slice for your grandfather, too. If you don't, he'll steal most of yours."

Beaming, Anna leapt from the stool, grabbed two forks, then dashed to the sitting area with a plate in each hand.

"You notice that she took the two biggest pieces, didn't you?" Megan said to her mother.

"She takes after her grandfather that way. It'll keep them happy." Joan frowned as she studied her daughter. Lowering her voice, she asked, "What's going on? I didn't expect you back here for hours. Well after we were in bed, at any rate."

Megan sucked in a lungful of air. After ensuring that Anna couldn't hear her, she said, "He's here."

"Who's—?" Joan's eyes widened as she realized only one man could elicit such a response from Megan. "You're kidding me. *Him?* Of all the nights and all the places in the world."

"That was my reaction."

"Oh, Megan." Hurt and worry creased her mother's brow. She reached out to rub Megan's shoulder. "You didn't see his name on the guest list?"

"Mahmoud Said brought him. Apparently Mahmoud works with King Carlo on charity projects and he wanted a member of the Barrali family to see the hotel's facilities."

"Have you spoken?"

"Only briefly and in public. But Mom? He remembered me."

The older woman dropped onto the barstool Anna just vacated, her eyes reflecting the same shock Megan felt at Stefano's familiar greeting.

"I know. I can't believe it, either," Megan continued. "He flirted with me. Asked me how I've been since Venezuela. Very lighthearted."

"Then he hasn't learned about Anna." Joan sighed. "Now is not the time, either."

"Definitely not." Megan bit her lip. "I know I promised Anna you'd take her to the roof for the fireworks, but I think it's too risky. If Anna sees me and the prince hears her refer to me as Mom—"

Joan reached across the counter to place her hand over Megan's. "Your dad and I will take her to the pool level to watch. We'll tell her the outdoor patio there will give us a better view than the roof. She won't have to try to see over the heads of all the adults and she can wear her pajamas if she wants."

"You don't think she'll argue?"

Joan shrugged. "If she balks, your father and I will say that since we're leaving tomorrow afternoon, we wanted to turn the fireworks display into a private goodbye party for the three of us. We'll make it sound like it's a big surprise for her. You know how kids are at this age. How you explain something is as important as what you explain."

"That's brilliant." Megan squeezed her mother's hand. "Devious, but brilliant. Thank you."

"I'm more worried about you than Anna. Be careful tonight, all right?"

Megan nodded, then let go of her mother's hand. She was about to call out a goodbye to Anna and her father when Anna came bounding back into the kitchen.

"Forgot the napkins!" Anna held out the front of her shirt, which bore a dollop of frosting. "Grandpa wouldn't let me lick it off."

"Good for Grandpa." Megan ruffled Anna's hair while Joan used a damp paper towel to clean up the spot. After all traces were gone, Megan told her daughter, "I have to go back to the party. It'll be very late when it ends, but I promise to look in on you, all right?"

"Okay." Anna foraged through a nearby cabinet for the napkins, but paused to smile at Megan. "Hey Mom?"

"Yes?"

"Your dress is really pretty. You look like a princess."

Megan's heart squeezed as she replied, "Thank you, sweetie."

Behind Anna, Joan put a hand over her mouth. Megan couldn't tell whether her mother was hiding an expression of dismay or of humor at Anna's compliment, so Megan focused on her daughter, reaching past her to locate the napkins.

She'd told Anna about Stefano last year, when Anna started asking pointed questions about her parentage. Thankfully, Anna hadn't latched onto any princess fantasies; she threw the term around as readily as any other girl her age and without thinking about the fact that had her biological parents married, she would be a princess. Anna had also been surprisingly understanding of the need to keep the information to herself. She'd asked occasional questions about Stefano over the weeks following that discussion, but they'd been asked in the same manner as other topics that piqued her curiosity on a daily basis, such as why her school colors were maroon and gold, or why Megan chose to buy fresh fruit at one stand rather than another. Eventually, she'd dropped the topic altogether. She was far more interested in her friends, her classes, and the impending visit from her grandparents.

Megan handed the napkins to Anna, who was still eyeing the dress. "My goal is to look like the type of person who can be trusted to handle organizing a big event, one like tonight's party, that might cost a company a lot of money. Think I accomplished that?"

"I guess," Anna replied, making a face. "I mean, you could wear jeans and I'd trust you. But maybe rich people trust someone who's dressed like they are?"

"I hadn't thought of it that way. I was thinking more along the lines of looking professional. But you may be right."

And perhaps that's why Stefano looked at her tonight with such interest. He'd been alone, far from his social circle, during their time in Venezuela. If he'd wanted companionship, he didn't have much choice but to grab any old girl, no matter what she wore or what the balance in her bank account. But once Stefano returned to Sarcaccia, he'd been surrounded by others like him. Wealthy businessmen like Mahmoud. Women dripping in jewels like that cat-eyed brunette in the red gown or his aristocratic ex-fiancée. The A-list actresses, catwalk models, and other females who'd entered and left his life in the years since his brief engagement ended.

Megan likely stood out in his memory because their encounter had been his one escapade at the lower end of the social scale. Well, that was fine. He'd made his choices in life and they hadn't included her. Or Anna. By keeping that thought firmly in mind, Megan figured she could coast through the rest of the evening.

"When you finish your cake—*and* your homework—Grandma and Grandpa have a surprise for you. So get to it."

Anna's eyes sparkled in delight before she returned to the sitting area with the napkins.

Megan did a quick check of her makeup in the bathroom, then returned to the kitchen to thank her mother once again for watching Anna for the evening.

"She's a piece of cake...so to speak. Your father and I don't get to see her often enough." Joan's voice dropped to a whisper as she walked Megan to the door of the suite. "You sure you'll be all right?"

Megan flashed her most confident smile. "Piece of cake."

* * *

If Stefano wanted to savor a romantic evening with Megan Hallberg, one that could fuel a thousand future erotic dreams, the setting couldn't be any better—or worse—than this.

Full moon low on the horizon? Check.

Warm Mediterranean breeze? Check.

Flowing *cava* and scattered trays of decadent dark chocolate-covered strawberries? Check.

Fireworks illuminating the sky with cascades of gold, green, blue and red? Check.

Local musicians playing in perfect time to the bursts of color? Check.

Whispered oohs and aahs from the gathered crowd? Check.

And that was the crux of the problem. The crowd. Dozens of CEOs, charity event organizers, and society mavens had monopolized every second of Megan's time over the last two hours. Whenever Stefano meandered closer to her, subtly moving through the rooftop crowd so he'd be in position to whisk Megan aside when the opportunity arose, another party guest captured her attention, gushing about the hotel's facilities and asking how soon they needed to call in order to reserve space for an upcoming event. After ensuring their booking needs were met, they lingered at her side to rave about the food, the beachfront setting, the modern facilities, even the lavender-scented shampoo provided in the guest rooms.

He wanted to be rid of them all.

The wicked part of him imagined shoving them all down the fire escape, even the musicians, leaving him alone under the stars with Megan, just as they'd been that night on the beach in Venezuela. The more imaginative—and pacifist—part of him wanted to encourage every last couple to take full advantage of the romantic views and luxurious bedding in their beachfront hotel suites. So few unattached guests were in attendance, they'd disperse quickly enough to pursue their own entertainments. All but Megan, whom he'd capture for himself.

The mere thought of holding her again made his body harden with desire.

First, however, he needed to take care of Ilsa, the dark-haired Dane who'd remained at his side most of the evening. There was no denying the woman's beauty. Even if Ilsa weren't wearing a body-hugging red gown, with her height and unusual, sensuous eyes she drew the attention of men as certainly as hummingbirds flocked to sweet-scented nectar in the midst of summer. Nor could he deny her intelligence. She was a witty, entertaining conversationalist, having completed a graduate degree in art history at the Sorbonne before moving to Barcelona to work at its contemporary art museum. But when Mahmoud politely inquired about the prince's interest in Ilsa, Stefano hadn't needed to engage in his usual conversational gymnastics to avoid the personal question. He'd been able to give his father's friend an unequivocal *no*. Ilsa was his sister's longtime best friend, the two women having been inseparable since they were assigned as boarding school roommates in Switzerland. Stefano would no more pursue Ilsa Jakobsen than, well, his own sister.

Beside him, Ilsa relaxed into one of the cushioned benches that skirted the Grandspire's rooftop deck, tilting her head back for a better view as the fireworks display reached its crescendo. Five giant bursts of gold opened like flowers, then separated to fall to the sea in a rain shower of glitter. Then, as a finale, a series of giant, spiraling fireworks were launched from barges at sea, their twisting shape mimicking the spires of La Sagrada Familia, Barcelona's famous Gaudi-designed cathedral that served as the inspiration for the Grandspire Hotel's name. The booming, original finish drew raucous cheers from the crowd.

As the last burst faded to smoke, Ilsa said, "No offense, Stef, but I believe this outshines the fireworks your father arranged for your last birthday party. I hope you're circumspect when you report back to King Carlo."

"No offense taken, because I agree." He glanced sideways at her. "We've been up here quite a while. You're warm enough, I hope?"

He'd fallen into the role of her protector soon after his arrival at the hotel. Stefano caught sight of Ilsa's familiar face across the lobby and waved in greeting only to witness her date, a renowned art expert who'd acquired the pieces on exhibit in the hotel lobby, drunkenly attempt to slide a hand under the rear straps of Ilsa's dress. Though Ilsa remained calm despite her date's increasingly aggressive behavior, Stefano immediately came to her aid, escorting her to the safety of the lounge where he could position himself between her and anyone entering the area.

It had dissuaded her date from continuing his misguided attempts at seduction during the cocktail hour, but only Stefano's watchful eye kept the pompous lout from humiliating Ilsa again during dinner. He'd kept her close ever since.

She laughed now. "You know I am. Much as you'd like to pretend I'm wearing your dinner jacket to stay warm, you know it's because you wanted to hide me."

"Not you. That dress. Or lack thereof."

She rolled her eyes in a manner reminiscent of his younger sister. "You're terrible."

"No, I'm male. And some males, as you discovered earlier tonight, are not gentlemen."

"Wish I could say that I discovered that only tonight."

"Wish I could say I didn't hear you say that," he retorted.

"Fine, fine," she muttered. "I should never have accompanied Raoul to this party. But I desperately wanted to see the art exhibit, so perhaps I'm as guilty of poor judgment as he is." Ilsa plucked a strawberry from the dessert tray set on the coffee table in front of them. After savoring a bite, she arched an eyebrow and said, "She doesn't like it when I talk to you. And she definitely doesn't like that you let me borrow your jacket."

Stefano frowned at the change of topic. "What are you talking about? Who?"

Ilsa tipped her head briefly in Megan's direction while keeping her eyes locked on his. "The blonde in the gold dress. The one you told Mahmoud you met in South America."

"Megan?"

Ilsa elbowed him. "Yes, *Megan*."

"I doubt she concerns herself with who speaks to me," Stefano said, giving his drink a lazy swirl. "If she does, it's only because she's working the crowd and hasn't had the chance to speak with me yet herself. It's her job to ensure I have a good time so I'll bring King Carlo's business to the hotel."

"That's not it." Ilsa shifted on the long bench, her casual gaze sweeping the crowd, which was beginning to dissipate now that the fireworks concluded. "She glances this way every so often. At first I thought it's because you're *you* and everyone is fascinated by royalty. But the longer the evening goes on, the more I doubt that's it. She's not in awe. She's curious about you and me."

Stefano bit back a smile. So he hadn't mistaken the frisson of sexual tension between them in the lounge earlier, despite the formal attitude Megan displayed on the surface. Good. To Ilsa, he said, "You're imagining things."

"I don't think so. And frankly, I believe you're interested in her, too. Don't pretend you're not." She stood and eased his jacket off her shoulders. "Take this back. I'm safe now—I haven't seen my so-called 'date' in nearly an hour, which means he's likely passed out in a potted plant somewhere—so I'm going to call it a night and ring a car service to take me home."

Stefano stood as well. "I'll escort you."

"And hand tomorrow's gossip headline to the paparazzi on a silver platter? I don't think so. You stay here. Conduct your business, make your father happy. I'll be fine. You don't need to be so overprotective."

He accepted the jacket she proffered without further argument, knowing she was likely right about the paparazzi—he'd seen the cameras outside the hotel when he arrived—then kissed her on both cheeks before promising to give her regards to the rest of his family.

Less than thirty seconds after Ilsa stepped into the elevator, Stefano reached his target. He smiled politely at the well-dressed man by Megan's side, a local politician wishing to thank her and the rest of the Grandspire management for preservation work the hotel completed on their stretch of Barcelona's beachfront, but in doing so Stefano made it clear he wanted to speak with Megan. Alone.

For ten long years he'd dreamed of this woman. Dreamed of how she'd look, how she'd sound. How she'd smell if he took her in his arms again. Now that she stood before him looking more luminous and sensual than in his wildest fantasies, he would not be denied.

Behind them, more guests meandered toward the elevators and stairwells, ready to call it a night. The politician cleared his throat, then excused himself to locate his wife. Stefano's hand instantly went to Megan's waist, claiming her before anyone else could approach.

"Hello again." He moved his hand up her back, leaving a healthy distance between their bodies so the action appeared more like a greeting between longtime friends than an attempt at seduction. He gazed straight into her eyes, then exerted enough pressure with his fingertips at the spot where the zipper of her dress met her bare back to ensure Megan understood his true intent.

He thrilled at her sharp intake of breath. Oh, yes. This would be a night to remember.

"You promised you'd look for me," he said. "You did not try very hard."

Chapter Three

If he only knew how long she'd looked for him last time they'd parted. *Weeks.*
Yet he could have found her anytime, both then and tonight. If he'd wanted
to, he would have. Even with romantic music filling the air and candles flickering
atop each of the rooftop tables, Stefano hadn't sought her out tonight until the
gorgeous woman with the cut-to-there red dress departed.

It wasn't so different than last time she and Stefano had been together; the
moment another woman captured his attention, Megan had been forgotten.

"I apologize, Your Highness." Megan forced her breathing to remain calm
despite the fact her lungs felt squeezed by an invisible force. She offered Prince
Stefano the same polite smile she'd given every other guest that evening. "Unfortunately, I've been busy. It's a big night for the hotel."

"I noticed." His fingertips brushed her zipper as he spoke. Whether it was
intentional or not, she couldn't tell. "Everyone is clamoring for your attention.
Still, I wanted to be certain you hadn't forgotten me."

Oh, most definitely intentional.

She paused, fumbling for the perfect response. For months she'd worked to
eliminate anything that might throw a monkey wrench into tonight's event. Week
after week had been spent poring over lists, holding staff meetings, making phone
calls, and inspecting every inch of the hotel property to ensure that everything
would go as planned. In the end, even those aspects of the evening Megan couldn't

control, such as the pleasantly warm Mediterranean breeze and clear night sky, fell exactly into place. She'd been overwhelmed by the enthusiasm guests showed for the refurbished hotel and its conference facilities, and she knew Ramon would be thrilled with the resulting increase in business.

Then there'd been Stefano.

Despite her best efforts, Megan's attention had remained fixed on the prince the entire night. While engaging in witty banter with the crème de la crème of European society, she'd privately simmered over the fact he'd spent the evening at one end of the rooftop deck in what appeared to be a rather intimate conversation with the dark-haired woman from the lounge, the one with the model-perfect body clad in a skin-tight, plunging red designer gown.

She'd told herself to consider his behavior one more checkmark on the list of things that were going according to plan, as Stefano's preoccupation with the woman kept him from seeking her out, but Megan's heart didn't want to follow her brain. She might not have seen Stefano in the flesh in a decade, but for the first time in her life she found herself jealous of another woman. Her heart took her right back to Venezuela, to the feeling of his strong, capable hands pulling her to him on that beach, holding her as if he never wanted to touch another woman in his life.

Which is why she couldn't bring herself to step away from Stefano's possessive arm now, even as the last of the guests wished each other good night and entered the elevator. Only a few waiters and the manager remained on the roof, clearing up the last of the glassware and double-checking the padded benches for forgotten items.

"As I recall, you made the same promise, Your Highness," Megan finally replied. "Yet you were also quite busy. I imagine there were many guests who wanted to meet you tonight."

In a voice low enough only she could hear, he said, "I realize it has been a long time, but you can call me Stefano, as you once did. 'Your Highness' feels rather formal, don't you think?"

"Prince Stefano!" A male voice boomed behind them. "I apologize for not welcoming you to the Grandspire before now, Your Highness, but I see that you are in good hands."

At the greeting, Megan shifted to see Ramon approaching. Stefano's hand dropped from her back as he turned to exchange the necessary pleasantries with the hotel manager, commenting on the building's modern decor and welcoming atmosphere. Behind them, two waiters quietly rolled a cart with used linens and glassware toward service elevator.

Megan kept her expression as professional as possible while the men spoke, in spite of her inner tumult. As much as she missed Stefano's warm touch at her back—craved it, even—she took the manager's timing as a sign. If she wanted to protect her daughter, let alone her own heart, she needed to keep her distance from Stefano. She might spend much of her day catering to the elite, but she wasn't one of them and didn't care to be. Her life with Anna was idyllic in every way that counted.

She'd be an idiot to linger alone under the stars with him, pretending to be something she wasn't, simply to satisfy a passing desire.

"Mahmoud Said assures me that your conference facilities are as well-designed as the Gaudi Ballroom," the prince said. "If that is the case, I imagine he and my father will be your guests again very soon."

"I'd be pleased to give you a private tour," Ramon said. "I realize it's late, so if you'd prefer another time, let me know what fits your schedule and I shall be at your disposal. I can provide you with an information package outlining our standard rates and array of services, but of course we're always happy to accommodate special requests."

Stefano shifted, his arm brushing against Megan's to send a jolt of awareness through her. "That's very kind of you. However, Ms. Hallberg—Megan—here is so efficient she's already made the same offer. We were just about to get started with the walk-through." His tone was relaxed as he added, "I know you must be anxious to get back to your family after such a long evening. Perhaps you'd be available tomorrow morning? I'm not due to fly home until noon. I'd be happy to pick up the information and pass it along to my father and his staff."

It was a polite response on the surface, but there was no mistaking the royal dismissal. Megan assumed Stefano and the rest of his family were skilled at such social maneuvering. It was the attitude of a man used to getting his way. Ramon's quick nod of acceptance only reinforced it. "I'm afraid I am already engaged through the lunch hour, but if you're agreeable, Megan could meet with you."

"A breakfast meeting would be perfect." Stefano glanced at Megan. "Could you make it at nine?"

"I'll hold a window table for you at the Jardín Alba," Ramon replied before Megan could respond. "It's on the mezzanine level and very quiet at that hour, so you won't be interrupted."

Megan scrambled for a means to protest, but the manager had already extended his business card. "Here's my contact information. If you have any questions or concerns, please feel free to call me day or night. The Grandspire would be honored to host the Barrali family."

Stefano slid the card into the inside pocket of his dinner jacket. "I'm sure my breakfast meeting with Megan will be quite informative. Thank you."

Stefano turned, but instead of brushing against Megan as he had before, he placed his hand on her lower back, then gestured toward the elevator with a flourish. "After you. I'm very much looking forward to the tour."

Megan nodded politely, more for the sake of her boss than for Stefano, then crossed the roof deck with Stefano's hand warming her skin through her thin dress. He didn't break contact until he punched the button to call the elevator.

"How kind of you to offer the tour, Megan," he said as they stood in front of the doors.

Megan glanced over her shoulder, only then realizing that Ramon wasn't with them, but had moved across the deck to rescue a forgotten wineglass from a planter ledge adjacent to the service elevator. She was about to suggest they invite Ramon to join them when the elevator doors opened. Stefano put one arm against the door to hold it while waving her inside with the other.

"I realize it's poor etiquette to contradict royalty, but I made no such offer," Megan said after the elevator doors closed. He stood within arm's reach of her in the enclosed space. The breadth of his shoulders and the way he held himself reminded her of a large, well-muscled cat waiting to pounce upon a mouse that'd mistakenly wandered into its lair. Instinct told her to keep to the far side of the elevator so she wouldn't fall prey to him, but would he read that retreat as fear?

And if he did, given that they'd parted in Venezuela on such casual terms, would he ask what caused her trepidation now?

She thought better of taking him to the now-empty business center with its rabbit warren of computer stations and instead punched the button for the floor just below the roof deck. It contained most of the hotel's larger conference rooms, including one with huge windows that faced both the beachfront and an adjacent high-rise condominium complex. If she took him there for his tour, Stefano might think twice before doing anything he wouldn't want to be seen in public. With the lights on in the conference rooms, anyone awake in the condominiums could see them.

"It is your job, isn't it?" he asked, making no effort to hide the desire lacing his tone. "To entice guests into staying?"

"For business, Your Highness."

He raised an eyebrow at her use of his title and took a step toward her. Her heart threatened to pound out of her chest, but instead of touching her, he reached past her hip to tap a small sign beside the elevator buttons. "But the hotel is also geared toward pleasure travelers, is it not? This, for instance, says there is a pool, spa, and outdoor patio."

"Yes, of course." No matter what, she would not take him there. Not if there was a wisp of a chance her parents could still be on that level with Anna. "Most luxury hotels do have those types of facilities."

The elevator stopped and the doors opened to an empty hallway. Megan stepped out ahead of Stefano, quickly making a left turn to lead him to the largest of the conference rooms. "All of our meeting rooms are on this floor. I'm taking you to the one we use for groups of a hundred or more, since it offers both a lovely view of the sea and all the latest audio visual—"

"I don't know what to make of you, Megan Hallberg."

Stefano stopped walking and leaned against the wall. When Megan stopped walking as well, he made a show of looking her up and down. The slow smile that spread across his face sent a wave of fire through her abdomen. And lower.

He was making this very, very difficult. "What do you mean?"

"Correct me if I'm wrong, but did we or did we not make wild, passionate love to each other once upon a time?"

The words were so unexpected she couldn't form a response. He reached out and grabbed her left wrist, pulling her toward him in the quiet hall. "I know you remember. I could see it in your eyes when you shook my hand in the lobby. You remember it all, don't you? How close we became that summer?"

Unable to trust her voice, she gave him a small nod. Wow, but the man was direct. More so at thirty-two than he'd been at twenty-two.

His tone softened. "Then why so formal? I meant it earlier when I said I wanted to catch up. Last I knew, you were going back to Minnesota to finish your graduate degree. I assumed you'd be happily married and settled in a nine-to-five job, living a busy life with a slew of children running through your kitchen on a daily basis. Never in a million years did I expect to see you here."

"Nor I you."

His fingers eased from her wrist to her hand, which he raised between them, near his heart. His index finger slid up her bare ring finger. "I want to know everything about you. What's happened to you since Venezuela. How you came to Barcelona. Everything." His fingers tightened around hers while his green eyes, so much like Anna's, searched her face. "I've thought of you often."

The words warmed her cheeks, but how could she believe him? To him, their encounter had been only that—a brief encounter—carrying none of the emotion it had for her. Though she'd been on the same page as Stefano when they left Venezuela, knowing they each had their own lives and that it was best they go their separate ways, she'd been young and naive to think he'd felt the same depth of passion she had during those heady days.

If he had, he wouldn't have ignored her attempts to contact him, let alone asked another woman to marry him less than a month later.

In one smooth motion, he pulled Megan into his arms, spinning her so her back was against the wall.

"Your Highness—"

"Stefano, please." His face was only inches from hers. He smelled of warm skin and masculine cologne mixed with a hint of *cava*. She closed her eyes against the rising wave of her own desire. Mustering what little remained of her willpower, she placed both palms against his chest to give herself space.

Big. Mistake. Even through his finely-tailored jacket and shirt, she could feel the hard lines of his chest and the rat-a-tat thump of his heart.

Near her ear, he whispered, "Tell me you've thought of me, too, Megan. Tell me you've slipped into bed at night imagining a moment like this, one where we could pick up where we left off." Even though he spoke English as well as she did, thanks to growing up with an American nanny, his Italian accent and lush voice sent her reeling. She had to stop this. Now.

"This isn't—"

Then his lips were on hers, hot and demanding, a veritable sexual weapon. Better than in her memory, better than in her dreams. Then, he'd been young and wild. He'd matured into a force of nature, intense and skilled, able to overwhelm her senses with the slightest touch of his strong hands, let alone his glorious mouth. He nipped at her lower lip, surprising her, and a whimper of longing escaped her. For a brief moment she realized it should mortify her, but the thought was forgotten as she kissed him back. He was right. She had spent nights lying awake, tossing in her bed, thinking of what it would be like to return to those days on the beach, making love to Stefano Barrali with the abandon of youth.

He pulled her tight against him, deepening their kiss and allowing her to feel his erection as he melded his body to hers. Just when she thought she could take no more, he shifted to kiss her neck, then the spot just below her ear he'd discovered all those years ago, the one that made her mad with want.

"Come to my suite," he whispered before his lips met hers once more, heating her to her core and sending her pulse into overdrive. Between kisses, he added, "We can take the stairs. It's only one flight down."

The world shifted around her as he whispered, "Please."

It would be so easy. Her parents and Anna weren't expecting her until late. Her parents likely wouldn't even be awake, let alone Anna. She and Stefano were alone. No one would ever know. It was the perfect opportunity to relive one of the best experiences of her life.

Better, judging from her body's reaction to his.

It would be wrong.

She squeezed her eyes shut, savoring the feel of his hot, talented mouth against her skin for a final moment before leaning back. Still trapped in the circle of his arms, she forced him to meet her gaze. "Stefano, I can't. Things are different for me now. Very different."

"You used my first name," he teased, running his fingers along the outside of her arm. With a wicked glint in his eye, he added, "And perhaps things are not so different. You want me as much as I want you."

"Believe me, I do. But…it's not so simple."

"It can be as simple—or as complex—as we choose."

Her gut twisted. Never in a million years had she imagined this moment, not like this. But now, facing Stefano, she knew what she had to do. "There's no easy way to say this. I wish I could've said it long ago, and I tried, I did. For months. But that night on the beach—"

"Was exactly what I told you then. A night I'd never forget."

She took another step backward, but it only gained her an inch. She was trapped between Stefano and the wall. "Especially for me."

Her serious tone finally seemed to register with him. His hands stilled. "What do you mean?"

"Stefano, I have a daughter. A wonderful, beautiful daughter named Anna."

"You have a baby?" His voice registered both surprise and resignation. "I see. You need to go home to your daughter, then."

She shook her head. "No, not a baby. Anna's in fourth grade."

"Fourth grade?" His eyes widened in shock, but Megan could tell he either hadn't made the connection or didn't want to. "That doesn't seem possible. That would make her—?"

Her jaw shook, but before he guessed at Anna's age, Megan managed to eke out the two words that needed to be said. "Our daughter."

CHAPTER FOUR

Stefano's stomach seized at her words. "What?"

He couldn't have heard Megan correctly, given the slight tremble in her voice. And if he hadn't misheard, perhaps she'd misspoken when using that word. *Our.*

Her gaze flicked to his arms in a silent request for space.

He let go, then took a step backward. The look in her eyes disturbed him as much as her words did. The adrenaline that pounded through his veins in anticipation of bedding the sexiest woman he'd been around in a long time stopped cold, leaving him ill at ease. "Clarify that last statement," he demanded.

This time Megan's voice didn't waver. "After we left Venezuela, I started the fall semester in Minnesota just as I'd planned. About six weeks into classes, I stopped by the student health center. I'd been feeling nauseous and run down for nearly a month and didn't seem to be getting better. I expected the nurse to tell me I picked up a virus or infection of some kind, given that we'd been working in rather filthy conditions. Instead, she informed me I was pregnant." Megan paused, searching his face. "I imagine my expression when given the news was close to the way you look now. Stunned and horrified and upset. It was the last thing I expected. We'd used protection, we were careful."

"Damn straight we were." He rarely swore, but he'd been overwhelmingly careful in that regard his entire life.

"When I asked the nurse if she was certain, I received a rather curt lecture on the failure rate of various contraceptives. I walked back to my apartment in such a state of disbelief that I detoured to a pharmacy so I could buy a home pregnancy test to confirm it. When it came back positive, I went and bought two more and waited an entire week before I took them, in case something I'd eaten or been around had caused a false result. Of course, those also came back positive and... well, I couldn't deny it any more."

Stef swiped a hand over his face but said nothing as he tried to process her words. His knee-jerk reaction was to deny paternity. It wouldn't be the first time a woman claimed he'd gotten her pregnant and not once had it been true. In both previous cases, he'd never dated the women, much less slept with them. But there wasn't a shred of insincerity in Megan's tone or manner, and the Megan he'd once known would never be so devious. It wasn't in her nature. And after all these years—particularly in this situation—what would be the point?

She held up a hand to stop him from speaking. "Before you ask the obvious question, she's definitely yours. There was no one else. Besides, you only need to look at Anna to know where she gets her DNA. She has your coloring. Your eyes. She even moves the way you do when she walks. It's eerie."

His chest clenched at her words. He had a *child*, a living, breathing child, and he had no part of the girl's life. He couldn't identify her if she stood in front of him. He didn't know her middle name, let alone the names of her teachers, her friends, or her pets. *If* she had any pets. He huffed out a breath, trying to ease the pain gripping his chest, the sensation that he'd been hit square in the heart with a sledgehammer.

"I'm so sorry, Stefano. This isn't the way I wanted to tell you," Megan added, her voice quiet.

"Obviously not." As he studied her, took in her serious expression and the regret in her eyes, his pain turned to anger. "Why didn't you tell me immediately?"

"I wanted to, but it wasn't that easy—"

"The words, 'I'm pregnant' come to mind. See? Easy." He worked his jaw, trying to rein in his temper, but the enormity of the situation didn't allow it. "Were you *ever* going to tell me? If I have a child, I have a right to know about it!"

"About her."

"Her!" he thundered.

At the look of alarm on Megan's face, he lowered his voice. "I doubt anyone is on this floor to hear. As you said, it consists of conference rooms."

"Still." She crossed her arms in front of her. "Would you like to go to a more private location to talk? I want to explain about Anna's—"

"*Now* you want to explain?" He hated the bite in his voice, but damn it, he was justified. No explanation could replace what had been willfully kept from him.

"I understand your anger." She held up her hands. "I'd be angry, too, if I were in your position. But it's not my fault and I would appreciate the chance to explain. Somewhere that allows me to tell you the full story without either of us being overheard. Please."

He shook his head in disgust. She'd hidden the girl for nearly a decade. There was no excuse for it.

And here he'd been dying to bed her again tonight.

"So my daughter, this Anna" —he paused, feeling the girl's name as it rolled off his tongue— "is here now, in Barcelona?"

Megan's lips thinned, as if she wanted to retort that Anna was *her* daughter, but thought better of the remark. After a moment's hesitation, she replied, "Of course. She lives with me."

"I want to see her."

"No." The answer was quick, decisive.

"If she's truly mine, I believe I'm entitled." How dare she refuse him?

"It's not that simple. As much as you may be entitled, I have to do what's best for her." A deep grinding sound emanated from down the hallway as the service elevator descended past their floor. She looked toward the sound, then back at him. "I'm sure I can find an empty room so we can sit down and discuss this without being disturbed."

"I have no wish to sit and talk." Not when he couldn't keep his words civil. How could she determine what was best for the child when she'd never even informed the father of the child's existence?

"But—"

"I learned long ago never to have a conversation when I'm…enraged." That was the most gentle word he could conjure for the emotional avalanche she'd triggered within him. "Give me twenty-four hours. Then we'll talk and resolve this situation."

"Resolve it? How does one *resolve*—?" Frown lines crisscrossed her brow. "Wait, aren't you scheduled to fly back to Sarcaccia tomorrow afternoon?"

"The flight goes when I say it goes. At least that I can control." He ground his teeth, then said, "For now, I'm going to bed. Alone."

"Stefano, wait—"

"Tomorrow!"

He spun on his heel and strode the length of the hallway, then slammed through the fire door to the stairwell and pounded down the stairs. He'd never walked away from a woman before, but it beat yelling at one.

How could she?

He jammed his room key into the door of his suite, noting as he entered that the digital clock on the thermostat indicated it was well after two a.m. He let out a sarcastic laugh as the door slammed shut behind him. He'd hoped to be wrapped up in Megan right now, her legs anchored around his waist, his hands exploring every inch of her alluring body, making the kind of passionate love he'd not made to a woman since, well, since Megan. Sex with complete and utter abandon. He'd expected to be drunk on it.

Instead, he was alone in his suite, trying to comprehend the fact that he had a child. One old enough to hold a conversation with him, to voice opinions, to tell him of her hopes and dreams. Perhaps old enough to talk back to him, as he'd started to talk back to his own parents at that age. Or maybe not. He had no way of knowing her personality, did he? For all he knew, she'd be the type who'd cuddle against him every night, begging for a bedtime story long after she was old enough to read on her own, simply because she liked his company.

The mental image of a child in bed brought him to a sick realization. Dear Lord, what if the girl had been injured or ill at some point? He'd visited enough children in enough hospitals over the years to know how badly those kids needed all the love and support they could get. Yet if his own daughter had been hospitalized and in desperate need, he wouldn't have known a thing. He could've been sitting on a yacht entertaining his father's business or political associates, laughing over glasses of Sarcaccian wine, completely oblivious to her pain.

He smacked a fist into the palm of this hand, galled all over again that Megan kept such a secret.

It wasn't simply that she'd denied her child. She'd denied *him*. How different might his life had been had he known? Would the fiasco of his engagement to Ariana even have occurred?

He ground his knuckles against his temple in frustration. He couldn't allow his mind to go down the path of what-ifs, especially where Ariana was concerned. He could only move forward. And as angry as he was at Megan, guilt gnawed at him for walking out on the very woman who'd borne his child, leaving her to find her way home alone in the middle of the night. He hoped she'd had the good sense to call a taxi or ask the hotel's car service to take her home so she'd be safe. It was too late for him to go back and rectify his mistake now.

He paced the suite's sitting area until his breathing steadied and his mind cleared, then paused near the floor-to-ceiling windows, finally taking a moment to look around the room Mahmoud reserved for him. As expected, it contained every luxury. A compact kitchen outfitted with the latest appliances and sleek granite countertops fronted the main room, which contained a glass-topped dining table, several designer chairs, and a chocolate-colored sofa crafted with clean, modern lines. A flat-screen television sat atop a gleaming art deco bureau. Beyond that, an en suite master bedroom boasted grass cloth wallpaper, fine art, and high-end linens, all of which appeared carefully chosen to create a serene escape from the hustle and bustle of the city.

He raked a hand through his hair as he turned to take in the view from the windows, studying the strip of distinctly Catalan shops, restaurants, nightclubs, and high-rise condominiums lining the beachfront. Judging from what he could see of the lighted interiors, the neighboring condos were designed to the same modern standards as the Grandspire.

He wondered if Megan lived in one of them. She must live very close to the hotel, he rationalized, given her job. Someone with her position needed to be on call at all hours. She might even live in the Grandspire itself; Mahmoud mentioned that the manager lived on site, perhaps the director of business development did, as well.

Facing the room again, he studied the space with new eyes. The Grandspire's suites were everything Mahmoud promised when he'd asked Stefano to take a look at the revitalized property. Its access to public transportation made it the perfect base for either a family or couple's vacation, while at the same time it provided the ideal setup for a traveling businessman craving both work-friendly amenities and options for evening relaxation. It was exactly the type of location Stefano's father, King Carlo, preferred for his functions. The entire city waited at the hotel doorstep, pulsing with life even at this late hour.

It was no place to raise a child.

He strode to the kitchen, intent on grabbing a cold bottle of water for his nightstand. On the way, he slammed a hand on the dining table with enough force to cause the centerpiece of fresh fruit to shudder, sending an orange rolling out of the bowl and across the table. As he replaced it, the fragrance of citrus reminded him that he'd promised to meet Megan for breakfast. A business breakfast.

Well, they certainly had business now.

CHAPTER FIVE

Given the late hour at which the festivities ended, few diners occupied the Grandspire's Jardín Alba restaurant at ten minutes past nine the next morning. Members of the waitstaff gathered in one corner, carafes of freshly-squeezed orange juice and hot coffee at hand, and conversed in low tones as they waited for more breakfast guests to arrive. The napkins had been laundered and folded, the silver polished, and even the exotic white flowers and greenery spilling from the central planter that served at the restaurant's focal point had been misted.

One guest in particular hadn't made an appearance. When Ramon Beltran stopped Megan outside the restaurant's entrance en route to his own meeting, he noted that it wouldn't be surprising for Prince Stefano to arrive a few minutes late and assured Megan that the breakfast would go well. Her sales folio contained a wealth of information on the hotel's special events options, she'd prepared for every possible question one might have about the Grandspire, and the manager had received nothing but positive feedback from guests on the new conference facilities. Mahmoud Said had been especially impressed, he said, which should work to Megan's advantage with the prince. Ramon even complimented Megan on her choice of dress, a soft yet professional cream-colored sheath in a style she knew flattered her figure.

"Don't look so worried. Enjoy yourself now that the grand reopening is behind us," he'd advised before leaving to catch a taxi to his own meeting. "Your passion sells the hotel like nothing else."

Megan refrained from informing him that selling the hotel was the least of her worries, let alone that "passion" was precisely what caused the etched lines between her brows this morning.

She took a sip from her water goblet before glancing at her wristwatch. It was convenient to believe that Stefano overslept or that he'd forgotten their appointment entirely, perhaps having only agreed to the meeting in order to pull her away from the manager the previous night. However, it was far more likely he'd chosen not to come at all given the anger vibrating through his body as he'd stalked out on their conversation last night. She couldn't blame him.

After an evening of *cava*, flirting, and hot, stolen kisses in an empty hotel hallway, no doubt he'd expected to have her in his bed. The way she reacted to his touch, it wasn't an unreasonable expectation. She'd *wanted* to be in his bed. Every caress of his lips against her skin, every breath she inhaled of his scent made her crave him all the more. No man set her very nerve endings to fire the way Stefano did, then or now. Judging from both his words and the intense need in his gaze as he'd trapped her against the wall, he felt the same.

Instead of a night of unbridled passion, he'd been smacked between the eyes with news that he'd fathered a child. But what else could she have done? Waiting until after they'd had a night of wild, passionate sex to say, "oh, by the way, you should know I had your baby" would've been far worse, at least from a moral point of view.

She groaned inwardly. Stupid morals.

Ten years ago, she'd tried every which way to contact him. Last night, when she finally had the opportunity...well, she should have handled things differently. She should've known that his manipulated tour of the conference site was a prelude to something more and told him about Anna the minute they'd been alone rather than trying to ignore his flirtation by discussing business. At least then she could've told him about their daughter in a caring and straightforward manner, rather than letting things progress to full-on, up-against-the wall, heated foreplay.

She inhaled deeply, attempting to block out the memory. As magical as those moments in his arms felt, and as physically right as they felt, the timing was completely wrong.

She blinked as she watched the restaurant door for a man who wouldn't come. Still, she couldn't leave, not for a while longer. She had to act as if she were here to do her job, as if she were waiting to start a meeting and the other party were experiencing nothing more serious than a traffic delay.

Give me twenty-four hours. Then we'll talk and resolve this situation.

What had he meant? Would he fight for visitation? Custody?

Her throat knotted. Visitation she could handle, so long as she had time to prepare Anna and the press knew nothing of it. As she'd explained to her concerned parents early this morning while they packed their bags, it might be good for Anna to know Stefano if that's what the prince wanted. Megan herself learned a lot about dealing with people from all walks of life by observing the way Stefano interacted with villagers, charity organizers, and government officials while they'd worked together in Venezuela. No matter what their background, rich or poor, young or old, people felt at ease within moments of meeting Stefano. Anna could benefit a great deal from spending time with him under the right circumstances.

But custody? Megan fiddled with her fork. No, demanding custody didn't make sense. Not only would a custody fight become public—and she would fight it with every fiber of her being—she'd be devastated by any such attempt and so would Anna. Stefano, for all his power, would never willfully separate a mother and child. Megan might not have seen him in a decade, but certain components of a man's personality didn't change. He'd always put the needs of a child, any child, before his own desires.

Still, he'd been deliberate in using the word *resolve*, which made her think he wanted more than simple visitation. Megan flipped the fork over and over between her fingers, trying to view the situation from Stefano's perspective, considering and discarding ideas before her breath stilled.

Could he have meant marriage?

As outlandish as the idea might be, it wasn't be out of the realm of possibility. Sarcaccia's royal family was known for clinging to its old country traditions. Stefano's siblings were unmarried and had no children, making Anna the only grandchild of the family's patriarch, King Carlo. Stefano might feel obligated to legitimize Anna both to adhere to tradition and to ensure his family's claim to the throne remained intact.

"No," Megan whispered to herself. She'd convince him it wasn't the best thing for any of them, for reasons that outweighed King Carlo's.

She quit fidgeting and returned her hands to her lap. As stressful as it might be, she had no choice but to wait for Stefano's explanation. It wouldn't help to have the waitstaff speculate on her odd behavior or to second-guess herself in the meantime. It had been the right decision to tell Stefano about Anna, even if the news hadn't been delivered at the time, manner, or place she'd intended.

At the muffled sound of applause rising from the cobblestoned street below, Megan turned toward the window. A guitar player performed outside a nearby bakery. His light, romantic tune drew a sizable crowd, happy to spend a few moments of their morning savoring the taste of fresh pastry while they listened. Megan couldn't help but smile at the scene. Since moving to Europe, she and Anna marveled at the skill of street performers. Some juggled, danced, or balanced on stilts while others wore heavy makeup and pretended to be statues. Her favorite were the balladeers who sang of love, family, and the richness of life.

Another round of applause echoed up from the street as the man played the last few notes of his song. The baker propped open the door to his shop using a triangle-shaped wedge, allowing the scent of fresh-baked bread to drift over the gathering. A father from the crowd handed his son two bills, one of which the child carefully placed into the guitar player's case before he skipped into the bakery. Others followed suit, dropping coins and bills into the case before either moving along or visiting the bakery. The guitarist smiled his thanks to each of them as he picked out chords to begin his next song.

Megan propped her chin in her hand as she viewed the scene. She'd planned to look for her next job in the United States, thinking that Anna might like the experience of attending an American high school, but perhaps staying in Europe wasn't such a bad idea. Anna could still spend a chunk of each summer in Minnesota with Megan's parents, but the cultural education that went hand-in-hand with living abroad was one which couldn't be duplicated.

Of course, it all depended on Stefano now. Would her life with Anna change now that the prince knew the truth? Or would things progress just as before?

"Megan."

Her attention whipped back to the restaurant at the sound of Stefano's voice. He stood less than three feet from the table, towering over her. He sported a crisp white shirt, open at the throat, well-cut charcoal slacks that emphasized both his height and muscular frame, and a pair of understated yet undoubtedly expensive black loafers. He was everything a modern royal should be, a man who exuded power and charisma, yet who dressed and moved with such a casual air he seemed relatable. Even his hair, wavy and lightly mussed, hit the sweet spot between contained and wild that stylists aspired to create for fashion shoots.

Before she could stand and greet him—wasn't that the etiquette when approached by a royal?—Stefano gestured for her to remain in her seat and pulled out the chair opposite hers at the small table. A waiter approached to fill their coffee cups and juice glasses and present them each with menus. While the young man wished them a good day and nervously described the restaurant's morning specials, Megan's heart beat double-time. How had Stefano approached without her sensing his presence? And how in the world, when his expression gave her no indication of what he felt for her, did he stir her emotions by doing nothing more than stating her name aloud?

Once the waiter left, Stefano made a pointed survey of the restaurant. An elderly couple who'd paid their bill set their napkins on the table and stood, the man circling the table to hold his wife's elbow as they prepared to depart. On the far side of the room, a suited businessman in his mid-thirties nursed a large cup of coffee while engrossed in paperwork, oblivious to Megan and Stefano's presence. A woman wearing a backpack and clutching a brochure for the city's open-top bus tour stood at the podium near the entrance, waiting as the host scanned the book for available dinner reservations. Otherwise, the room was empty.

Stefano's attention locked on Megan's face and one of his eyebrows hitched up, as if a conspiracy were being hatched. "It would seem no one is within earshot. Is that by design?"

"I imagine most guests are still sleeping or are ordering room service." She paused, trying to gauge his demeanor before adding, "Thank you for coming."

"I apologize for the delay. I was distracted last night and forgot to set my alarm."

Though the words could be interpreted as a dig, his tone didn't give that impression. "Please, I'm the one who should apologize. I'm so sorry about…well, I'm sorry about everything."

"I don't need an apology, Megan. Not at this point."

"All right." She scrunched her napkin in her lap, hoping he couldn't see her discomfort. But now what? She'd been so certain he wouldn't come to breakfast that she hadn't thought about what she'd say.

He'd said he needed twenty-four hours to think. Perhaps he expected her to honor his wish and stick to business this morning. Megan leaned to the side of the table and pulled the folio containing the Grandspire's group event options from her bag. She set it to one side of the table so Stefano could flip it open without hitting the glassware. "After you order, I'd be happy to go over the information for your father, if that's what—"

"No." He reached across the table and took the folio. "I'm going to open this and I'm going to appear to be reading it. I will ask you questions, which anyone observing us will assume are about the hotel. However, I have all the information I need for King Carlo and his staff. You and I will use this time to discuss our daughter. I don't want you to apologize. I don't want excuses. I want facts."

CHAPTER SIX

There was a hardness in Stefano's green eyes Megan had never seen before, which spurred her to a defensive answer. "Ask what you like. I have never lied to you and never will."

He leveled a doubtful look at her as he opened the folder and pulled out a map of the hotel's conference rooms. "You said you discovered you were pregnant about a month after returning home?"

"More like six weeks. But yes, when I was back at school."

"Why didn't you contact me?"

"I tried."

"Not hard enough." He ran his index finger over the map, then tapped it as if he'd asked about the setup of a particular room. "I didn't hear so much as a whisper from you."

No thanks to your staff.

She bit back the response and chose her words deliberately. "If you remember, we left things on a casual note. While you knew how to contact me if you wanted, I had no way to reach you directly. Only a number that connected me to a secretary named Dagmar." The woman she'd come to think of as Stefano's personal firewall, programmed to eliminate potential threats before they could infiltrate the palace network and gain access to the royal family.

What irked her is that she shouldn't have been seen as a threat.

He shrugged as if nothing Megan said surprised him. "Dagmar's retired now, but she used to be my personal secretary, which is why I gave you that number. She did everything—booked my travel, arranged my calendar, handled my correspondence—and yes, she fielded my calls."

"Even personal calls?"

"Yes. I'm forced to change cell phones frequently in order to keep the number confidential. I discovered long ago that it's easier to route calls through a secretary than it is to constantly update my phone number with acquaintances. Only my secretary and immediate family have it."

"Maybe easier for you. Not for me."

Frown lines puckered his brow. "Dagmar was discreet and efficient. If you called and gave her your name, it would have been routed directly to me. It's standard procedure for all my personal calls."

"Mine weren't."

He opened his mouth as if to argue, then looked past Megan and smiled as the waiter approached to take their orders and refill their coffee. Stefano asked for a spinach, tomato, and feta omelet with rye toast while Megan simply told the waiter to bring her usual order.

Once the waiter was out of hearing range, Stefano asked, "You eat here often?"

"I live in the hotel, so they know me well."

"Ah. I wondered, given your position here." He squinted at her, appearing to digest the information. His expression left her unsettled. "And what's the usual?"

"You won't believe me."

He circled his hand, encouraging her to tell him anyway.

"Spinach, tomato, and feta omelet. Rye toast."

That earned her another frown, but instead of commenting, he went back to the original topic. "Are you certain you spoke to Dagmar herself? Not someone who referred you to Dagmar?"

"At least four times, which is why I remember her name. She said, 'Thank you for your call. I have noted your information and Prince Stefano will contact you at his convenience.' Those were her exact words each time I phoned. It was as if I were talking to a recording."

"Dagmar was nothing if not consistent." He turned to a new page in the folio, keeping up the pretense of a business meeting. "And you gave her your full name?"

For Anna's sake, she fought to remain patient. "Of course I did. I told her that we'd been assigned to the same project group in Venezuela, thinking she could use that information to verify my identity if necessary. I told her it was important that you contact me and left her two different phone numbers and my e-mail address."

"Did you…I assume you didn't tell her what the call was about?"

How stupid did he think she was? "Only my parents know that you're Anna's father and they haven't breathed a word to a soul." Megan leaned forward, studying him across the table. "You're telling me that you never got my messages?"

"Never."

"I see." How could she phrase this without sounding jealous or catty? "I hate to point out the obvious, but you had another woman in your life by that time. Not only were you planning a wedding and dealing with intense press coverage, you were in the midst of your military training. Would you honestly have paid attention if you received a message from me during that period? Plus, it was ten years ago. Remembering a phone message from way back then would be—"

"Megan, I would have paid attention. I would have remembered." His gaze bored into hers. "I would have called."

She wanted to doubt him. Wanted to believe that her life would have been exactly the same had he actually been told of her attempts to contact him—after all, she and Anna were happy and healthy, and she'd landed a dream job in a dream city—but the steadfast look in Stefano's eyes told her he thought otherwise. If he'd received her messages, he believed everything would have been different. *Everything.*

Then his gaze dropped to her mouth. A shiver ran through her at the flash of desire that crossed his face before he stifled it.

He was quiet for a moment, then said, "You gave up trying."

She took a quick sip of her orange juice to gather her thoughts, then nodded. "When you didn't return my calls, I went online to see if there might be another way to contact you. That's how I learned of your engagement to Ariana Bassi. I was so busy with classes and morning sickness I hadn't even realized you'd gotten engaged. Once I read the news, I assumed that was the reason you hadn't returned my calls. I thought it best at that point not to upset your life."

Or her own. While Stefano's engagement hadn't been news in the United States, it was the talk of Europe. Photos splashed over the Internet showed Stefano racing across the palace courtyard, barefoot and bare-chested, to see Ariana the day after he'd returned from Venezuela. They'd become engaged soon afterward. Royal-watchers were mad for Stefano and his aristocratic bride-to-be, a Sarcaccian dressage rider with Olympic ambitions. The media speculated on everything from how long they'd been seeing each other to the most minute details of the planned wedding at Sarcaccia's grand cathedral, a ceremony scheduled to take place two months after Megan's due date.

If the media caught even a whisper of the fact that the royal groom had a secret two-month-old child, it would derail four lives: Megan's, Stefano's, Ariana's, and Anna's. Paparazzi would've been camped outside Megan's small, off-campus apartment in Minnesota within hours, hoping to cash in on the scandal. Once she'd shut down her computer and absorbed what she'd seen, she knew she wouldn't call again.

"Ah." Stefano looked stricken, as if he hadn't considered his engagement to be a factor. But how could he not?

"Stefano, think back to what was happening in your life then. If anyone had learned about Anna, it would've been a disaster."

Stefano scowled, but not before turning toward the window to hide his expression from the rest of the restaurant. "I wish you'd have persisted. Or tried to find another way to reach me. I would have wanted to know."

Could he not see reason? "Stefano—"

"It's all right. I understand why you didn't." He kept his gaze on the street, watching as the balladeer packed his guitar now that the morning bakery crowd had thinned. "You were likely right to keep the information to yourself after making so many attempts. The scandal would have been swift and certain. No child should start life under such a cloud of speculation. And it would only have gotten worse when my engagement ended."

Megan itched to ask what happened with the relationship but couldn't bring herself to pry. Press releases from both the Barrali and the Bassi families issued only three weeks before the wedding date stated that the couple decided to part amicably and that neither family would discuss the matter with the press. Despite Stefano and Ariana's requests for privacy, gossip about the couple continued to fill the media for months, only dissipating after Ariana eloped with a famous Argentinian polo player.

Had Stefano been heartbroken? Or relieved?

During the long nights Megan spent walking back and forth through her small apartment with a colicky baby, worrying about whether she'd be awake enough to make it through her next day of classes, she'd harbored a deep-down fantasy about Stefano picking up the phone and calling her to say he'd ended the relationship with Ariana because he missed what he and Megan shared in Venezuela.

Unsurprisingly, that call never came. Megan's mother advised her struggling daughter to simply love the child and trust that the rest would fall into place. She was right, of course. Anna outgrew the colic and Megan finished graduate school and landed a full-time job at the Minneapolis Convention Center. In the meantime, Stefano started to date other women—models, actresses, and women from well-connected European families. Megan's midnight fantasies eventually gave way to reality. She embraced her new career, her growing financial independence, and the ups and downs of life with an exuberant toddler. Then, the summer before Anna started kindergarten, Megan nabbed the position at the Grandspire, which turned out to be a dream come true.

Had Stefano actually called during those difficult weeks and months following Anna's birth, Megan suspected the relationship wouldn't have transcended its status as a brief, heady fling. She and Stefano were from two different worlds, as evidenced by her inability to contact him, if nothing else. His stratified circumstances weren't ideal for Megan, let alone for Anna.

He'd known it the entire time he'd been with her in South America. Otherwise, he wouldn't have been so anxious to see Ariana when he'd returned home.

Stefano faced her again, his demeanor back to the same easiness he exuded whenever he appeared in public, giving no sign that he was thinking of a long-ago broken engagement. "Let me ask the important questions, then. Anna is doing well?"

Megan nodded, unable to elaborate as their waiter approached the table with breakfast. The scent of freshly-made omelets and hot buttered toast filled the air as the young man set their meals before them. He arranged each plate with extra care, his posture rigid as he did so. Megan forced herself to stay quiet, though she was dying to offer him reassurance. He was clearly anxious to impress the prince. Sensing the waiter's nerves, Stefano set aside the hotel information folder to offer his compliments on the meal and the quick service. Once the waiter departed, Megan said, "That was kind of you. You have a talent for putting people at ease." People other than her.

"If I were really talented, they wouldn't be uneasy in the first place." Stefano gestured for Megan to go ahead and eat, urging her to tell him about Anna between bites. "You mentioned last night that she's in fourth grade?"

"Yes. She attends an international school here in Barcelona and loves it. Her teachers and classmates come from all over the world." Megan couldn't help but share Anna's enthusiasm for the school. "It's a unique experience. She has new stories to tell me every night about things that happened to her and her classmates—who did well on a spelling test, who told a funny joke, who brought what for lunch. She's taken field trips to several of the places she's studied in history class. Just last week her entire grade toured the monastery at Montserrat. And every summer she spends a few weeks in Minnesota with my parents, which allows her to see our extended family and become comfortable with living in the United States. The variety gives her a sense of independence that I love."

"It all sounds wonderful."

"It is." She gestured to the street, where the guitarist was busy unlocking a bike from a pole outside the bakery so he could ride on to his next stop. "In fact, just before you walked into the restaurant, I was watching the crowd surrounding that street musician and thinking about how fortunate Anna and I are to live here."

"By 'here' do you mean Barcelona in general or the Grandspire specifically?"

Megan paused with a slice of toast halfway to her mouth. Something in his tone set off her internal alarms. She returned the uneaten slice to her plate. "I meant Barcelona in general, but I've been lucky with the Grandspire, too. Anna and I have a two-bedroom suite on the twentieth floor. It allows us access to the hotel fitness center and pool and the location can't be beat. We're less than a mile from her school and within minutes we can be playing on the beach or sitting down at any of dozens of fantastic restaurants. We can even walk to our favorite fruit market, to the Gothic quarter, and to several museums. The list goes on and on. Why do you ask?"

Stefano lifted a forkful of omelet, taking his time to chew, swallow, and blot his mouth with a napkin before answering. "As wonderful as Anna's school may be, and as convenient as your living accommodations are to tourist attractions, I have to ask: Is a hotel really the best place to raise a child?"

CHAPTER SEVEN

No. No, no, no. Bile rose in Megan's throat. Stefano was actually questioning her ability to raise her daughter. But as a prelude to what?

How foolish she'd been to let her guard down when he asked about Anna.

Keeping her voice as level as she could manage, she asked, "What's your point?"

"No point." He set his napkin in his lap as casually as if they were discussing last night's fireworks display. "I simply want to know how my daughter is being raised."

His daughter? Technically, yes. But….

This couldn't be happening. Arguing for custody—if that was his intent—went against everything she believed about him. Megan balled her fist in her lap and counted backward from five, just as her mother urged her to do when she was a young girl and lost her temper with a playmate. Once Megan knew she could keep her tone restrained, she said, "My first instinct is to defend myself by asking who you are to judge my choices. As I recall, you made mention of your own upbringing more than once during our time in Venezuela, referring to your life in the palace as 'sanitary' and 'controlled.'"

"My upbringing is immaterial in this—"

"Please, let me finish." She couldn't allow him to argue her into a corner. The stakes were too high. "You said you didn't truly experience life until you were out of the palace during your gap year project. It offered you the opportunity to see the world as if you were a typical volunteer rather than a rich-as-sin prince.

That's what I want for Anna. I want her to experience all the world has to offer, at her own pace, and make friends from all walks of life. So if I need to defend my choices to you, well, there's my defense. As to living in a hotel, our suite is just as nice as the apartments in any of the condo buildings along the beachfront, which is where many of Anna's friends live. She can be at their homes within minutes." Megan took the folio from the side of the table, holding it in front of her so she'd appear to be going over the hotel information with Stefano. It also helped cover the fact her hands were shaking. "She's a bright, curious, and well-adjusted girl, Stefano. She's had the opportunity to see more of the world than I ever believed possible and she values what she's learned from experiencing other cultures. She's lived exactly the kind of life you'd want for her. She's healthy and she's happy. So am I."

He took a moment to absorb her words. She thought he'd acquiesce…until he opened his mouth. "But your job—"

"What about my job?" Her voice held more snap than she'd like, especially given that more guests were drifting into the restaurant, but a quick look around ensured that she hadn't been overheard. In a more rational voice, she asked, "What is your concern?"

He eyed her as if unsure what to make of her jumpiness. "Correct me if I'm wrong, but it's my understanding that work like yours, developing conference and event facilities, is transient in nature. Once a venue is up and running, with a stream of bookings to ensure future income, you move on. So even if Anna has all the benefits you claim, they're not permanent."

She took a deep breath and told herself that he was asking so many questions out of concern for a child rather than to attack her. "You're not wrong. It's rare in my industry to be in one place as long as I've been at the Grandspire. And I'll be leaving soon. A full-time sales force is taking over the bookings now that the facilities are complete." At his smug look, she continued, "However, I applied for this position when Anna was young specifically because the project was so extensive it would keep me in one location for several years. My success here sets me up to search for another position, one in which I hope to remain until Anna graduates from high school."

"But you don't know where?"

"Not yet. I'm looking for a situation that fits both my career goals and what I want for Anna." He didn't sound like he was asking out of curiosity about where she'd live, but accusing her of failing to plan ahead. She shut the folio, then smiled across the table as if they were nearing the end of a successful business meeting. "I know this is hitting you out of the blue, so I'm trying to be patient with your questions. But my job is no different than many others, across a number of industries. Every so often, I have to move. In fact, many other jobs would require me to travel for days or weeks at a time. This doesn't. I'm available for Anna whenever she needs me. So if you're insinuating that I'm not raising her properly, a child you don't even know—"

"That's the problem, isn't it?" His eyes shone as he leaned closer. "I don't know her."

His simple declaration left her stomach in knots.

"Maybe," she admitted.

Yes.

If he knew Anna, if he caught her sneaking a joyous cartwheel in one of the hotel hallways or witnessed the pride on her face when she earned an A on an exam, he wouldn't have doubts. Megan wouldn't be compelled to justify her parenting decisions as if arguing before judge and jury. Tears stung her eyes at the sight of the emotion in his, but she fought them back as yet another group entered the restaurant for breakfast.

"I can't know that she's happy, Megan. Hell, I don't even have a clue what she looks like." He glanced toward the new diners, who were being seated only a few tables away, then straightened slightly in his chair. Careful to keep their conversation discreet, he said, "Look, what's done is done. No matter what the circumstances, whatever the reason Dagmar failed to inform me of your calls— something I plan to investigate, by the way—all we can do is move forward. That's why I needed space last night, to come to terms with this and think of how best to move forward. That means getting to know Anna. You said no last night, but I think it's important that I meet her as soon as possible."

"I don't know if this is the best time for her." Everything was happening too fast. After years on their own, suddenly there would be another voice—a strong, male, and royal voice—in their lives. Perhaps for a weekend, perhaps on a regular basis, but either way, it would be a drastic change.

"If not now, then when? It won't get easier for any of us." He paused. "Does she know about me?"

Megan gave a slight nod.

His lower lip flinched in surprise. "Does she know I'm here in Barcelona?"

When Megan shook her head, Stefano exhaled. "What *have* you told her?"

Between sips of her coffee and bites of omelet, Megan explained briefly how Anna learned of her parentage. "It's not that I don't want you to meet her. I do. But knowing on a cerebral level that you're her father and having you physically show up in her life are entirely different things. Before I introduce you, I need to prepare her."

She couldn't believe she'd agreed so easily, and before talking to Anna, but how could Megan object when Stefano's request seemed so reasonable?

"All right," he said. "Talk to her tonight. We can have lunch tomorrow and keep it relaxed and informal. I don't want Anna to be frightened or uncomfortable."

"Tomorrow?" Megan swallowed hard. When he said as soon as possible, he meant it.

"I assume her wonderful school doesn't hold class on Sundays?" He flashed a wry grin, then popped the last bite of toast in his mouth. "I'm already in town. Staying a day or two longer won't raise any questions. My family and staff will assume I decided to extend the business trip through the weekend to visit with Ilsa. It wouldn't be unusual for me to arrange to see her or some of my other friends while I'm here. However, if I return to Sarcaccia and then make an unscheduled trip back to Barcelona, my family and staff will ask why. For the time being, I prefer we keep this to ourselves."

"Ilsa?" Was she supposed to know an Ilsa?

"I'm sorry. I assumed you were introduced at some point last night. Ilsa Jakobsen was the woman with me on the roof. You may have seen her in the bar when Mahmoud brought you over. Tall woman, red dress, hard to miss."

"Oh, yes. I remember her." *Hard to miss* was a colossal understatement. *Six-foot beacon of sexuality* would be a more apt description.

"Ilsa is my sister's best friend. Her date for last night's party was, shall we say, overly focused on the cocktail portion of the evening. I stayed close to her to ensure he wouldn't behave in a manner he'd later regret. Ilsa's like a younger sister to me. Family." He picked up his coffee cup. Seeing that it was empty, he set it back on its saucer. "In any event, I believe discretion is paramount and having friends like Ilsa in Barcelona provides a convenient excuse for me to stay."

The knot of tension that had twisted Megan's gut eased slightly. She wanted to attribute her relief entirely to Stefano's willingness to keep a meeting low-key and his desire to shield Anna from the public eye. However, a not-so-small part of her thrilled to learn he had zero romantic interest in the stunning brunette from the previous night. Knowing Stefano had watched over Ilsa because he worried for her safety reinforced Megan's opinion that the Stefano seated across the table from her now wasn't so different from the Stefano she'd met in Venezuela. Protective, sensitive, caring.

Truly, a prince.

"It feels odd talking about Anna when I don't even know what she looks like." Stefano's voice was quiet enough she had a hard time hearing him now that there were people chatting only a few tables away. "If I may ask…do you have a photo of her?"

The gentleness of the request tugged at her heartstrings. She supposed if they were going to meet tomorrow, showing him a photo today was the least she could do. "I don't think anyone would find it unusual if I handed you my phone during our meeting, do you?"

When he shook his head, she fished the phone from her bag, tapped the screen to bring up the pictures, then handed it to Stefano, trying to ignore the heat of his fingers as they brushed hers.

At his intake of breath, Megan smiled. "She's beautiful, isn't she? Her hair isn't quite as dark as yours, but it has your texture, very wavy and thick. And she has your eyes. Not just the color or the ring around the iris, but there's that same hint of mischievousness constantly lurking there. I have to watch it with her."

Stefano's attention remained riveted on the screen. "Is this recent?"

"Day before yesterday." She'd snapped it while Anna had been sitting at the kitchen counter showing off a batch of brownies she'd made with her grandparents. The late-afternoon sunlight streamed in through the suite's windows and hit Anna so perfectly Megan had pulled out her phone to capture the moment.

"I have a daughter." A mix of astonishment and joy tinged his words, as if he hadn't quite believed until that moment that Anna was real, and that she was his. He stared at the screen for a few more seconds before asking if he could look at the other pictures on the phone. As he flipped through them, smiling at some, carefully studying others, he asked, "Has she missed having a father? Or is there someone else who's been a male role model for her?"

The question left Stefano's mouth in a casual manner, but Megan wasn't fooled; he'd carefully considered it. Was his real concern for Anna and the influences she might have had over the last few years? Or was he attempting to determine whether Megan had any serious relationships in the last decade? Megan considered her answer just as carefully. "Anna saw a lot of my parents while I finished graduate school and worked at my first job in Minneapolis. She still sees them often and is quite close to my father."

"That's good." Stefano's gaze remained fixed on the phone. What Megan saw in his clouded expression revealed more than words could ever say.

"All these questions aren't really about Anna's upbringing, are they?" she asked softly. "You might not have seen me in years, but you knew me well enough then to believe that I'm a good parent. This is about you."

That drew his attention from the phone. "How so?"

"You feel cheated. You've missed out on her life, so now you want something to pick apart—her schooling, where she lives, whether or not she has a male role model—to feel as if you have something of value to contribute to her upbringing. Maybe to feel as if you haven't suffered a loss by not knowing her." His expression remained stoic as she spoke, making Megan more certain of herself with each word. She reached across the table to put her hand over his. "It's all right. It's human nature."

Stefano didn't respond. Instead, he slid the phone from his hand into Megan's, then shifted his gaze to indicate that their waiter was crossing the restaurant, heading for their table.

She pulled back and returned the phone to her handbag before picking up her fork to polish off the last few bites of her omelet as if they'd been discussing nothing more than the weather. As the waiter collected their plates and Megan signed for the meal, a large group of diners that included several high-profile guests who'd attended last night's event appeared at the entrance to the restaurant. No doubt they would ask to be seated close to the prince if they spotted him, which meant little time remained to discuss Anna.

Once they thanked the waiter and he returned to the kitchen, Stefano placed his folded napkin on the table and looked at Megan, his features unreadable. Instead of addressing her theory, he asked when he could speak with her next.

"I'm not sure. I need to talk to Anna first. Will you be staying at the hotel again tonight?"

"I've already extended my reservation." He circled the table, his movements smooth and controlled, to pull out her chair for her. Once she'd stood, he took the folio from the table. In a businesslike voice just loud enough for nearby diners to hear, he thanked her for the information on the hotel's facilities. He finished with, "I believe your business card is enclosed if I'd like to get in touch about booking a private event?"

At her nod, he angled his head so only she could see his lips and mouthed, "Tomorrow, then. Lunch."

CHAPTER EIGHT

She was right, damn it.

He'd entered the restaurant ready to launch an all-out assault, but within seconds Megan had completely disarmed him. The body-hugging dress that made her glow, the sweet smile as she'd watched the street performer, unaware that she herself was being watched, the open expression that said Stefano could ask her anything he wanted and expect an honest answer…she'd left him absolutely nothing to attack. And when she'd responded to his pointed questions with the observation that Stefano felt cheated, that he wanted to know he could contribute something to Anna's life, a life nearly ten years gone already, she'd pinpointed his deepest fear, realizing it before he'd done so himself. Her point was reinforced by the ebullient girl smiling at him from the screen of Megan's phone, holding out a plate of brownies with obvious pride at having baked them herself. His chest had constricted so powerfully at the sight of those large green eyes and flushed cheeks it was as if the air left not only his lungs, but the entire room.

He not only had a child, he had a child who didn't know him or need him. Apparently the mother of that child didn't need him either.

He leaned against the sofa cushions and stared out the windows of his hotel suite, unseeing. Anna was healthy and happy, unlike so many of the children he met during his years of public service. He'd never forget the faces of those kids, particularly one little boy with whom he'd played cards during a hospital visit when he was only a child himself. The boy died only days later, leaving Stefano shaken, but thankful for his own health and the health of his siblings.

He should be grateful to know Anna enjoyed what seemed to be an idyllic childhood.

Rather than feeling relief, it galled him that Megan could see things about him he couldn't always see for himself. At the same time, her simple observation made him want her all the more. He put his index finger and thumb to the bridge of his nose and closed his eyes against the conflicting emotions, attempting to process what had happened over breakfast.

Just twenty-four hours ago, he assumed he'd be spending this moment aboard his family's airplane, high amongst the clouds on the short flight to Sarcaccia. He'd planned to use the time to prepare notes for his upcoming meeting with the head of Sarcaccia's transportation department, making it clear which projects he felt needed immediate funding in order to draw more tourism to the island nation. Tourists didn't like renting cars, he'd argued more than once, and they would skip Sarcaccia in favor of other Mediterranean vacation spots if they were compelled to deal with both the cost and logistics of renting a vehicle. With enough tourists pouring money into the island, the updates to the current mass transit system would eventually pay for themselves. And the improvements wouldn't simply benefit those locals who made their living from tourism. The entire population would profit. The system upgrades would provide employment for several hundred engineers and construction workers in the short term. Then, once the upgrades were complete, it would allow for the opening of his country's new conference center, providing even more employment. Daily commuters would have more choices, roadway traffic would flow more smoothly, and parking wouldn't be such a hassle on the narrow, cobblestoned streets of Sarcaccia's congested city centers.

Now he wondered if he'd make the Monday meeting. No doubt if he called and asked for a delay, his father would hear about it. Once again, his parents would say nothing, but their disapproval would be apparent. None of King Carlo's children seemed able to satisfy their father's ambitions for them. The king worried they didn't care enough for their small country to ensure its future. Not because they didn't work hard, but because they hadn't worked hard *and* provided him with heirs. He'd view Stefano's extended stay in Barcelona as further evidence of his son's disregard for the country's future.

Stefano laughed aloud at the irony of it.

All he'd ever wanted was for his life to have meaning, a meaning derived from true accomplishment rather than his dumb luck at being born into the Barrali family. It was why he'd so loved the days he'd spent in Venezuela and why he'd grown to appreciate them more and more with each year that passed. Yes, he'd met Megan there. She'd shown him what was possible in a relationship; he'd learned that a woman could be attracted to him without caring a whit for his title or fortune. But Venezuela also gave him the chance to do soul-satisfying work out of the spotlight, where the months he spent digging a trench for a water line, moving pipe, and teaching villagers how to maintain their new water pumping and filtration systems weren't caught on camera. He was able to help people for the sake of helping, and he could do it on his own daily timetable rather than as part of some scheduled royal duty. If he wanted to spend an extra hour perfecting the water flow on a particular valve, he could do it. No keepers lingered at his side urging him on to the next event on his calendar. Seeing a young girl's face alight and knowing it was because he'd given that girl's family access to clean water, rather than because the girl had a prince visiting her village, made Stefano happier than he'd ever been.

To this day, it gave him a deep sense of fulfillment knowing that girl and her family would never again fight illnesses caused by contaminated water.

After Venezuela, he'd hoped military service would give him the same sense of accomplishment. He'd participated in a few sea rescues while part of a helicopter crew, but the satisfaction of a job well done was short lived, about as long as it took for the chopper to land. The subsequent news coverage felt awkward as he became the story, rather than his team or the people they'd rescued. He'd decided when he finished his service that he'd find a way to make a lasting contribution, something that would help hundreds, if not thousands, of people in a practical way, and in a manner that wouldn't necessarily become fodder for the evening news.

It was what drove him to focus on Sarcaccia's transportation system over the last few years. In it, he'd discovered a way to bolster his country's tourism industry and overall economy, but to do so out of the spotlight. While chopper rescues made for exciting television reports, transportation meetings did not. The pursuit brought him enormous satisfaction.

Yet those very efforts were often overlooked as his parents pushed him to find a woman they deemed suitable, one like Ariana, and to start a family. Only three or four months ago, his mother introduced him to yet another wealthy, single woman at a charity function. His mother mentioned at the time that while it was lovely Stefano wanted to improve the country's infrastructure there were hundreds of people qualified to undertake such a task, yet only he and his siblings could continue the royal line and ensure Sarcaccia's throne stayed in the Barrali family. He'd given his mother a pat response, as always, then flirted with the woman enough to satisfy his parents, but not so much as to lead the woman to believe in the possibility of a relationship.

Some days, he wasn't sure whether it was a good or a bad thing that his work wasn't recognized.

Stefano shoved off the hotel sofa, nabbing his phone from the corner table and punching in the number that would connect him directly to his father. Once his father's booming voice came on the line, Stefano let him know he was extending his stay in Barcelona another day to wrap up work and visit with friends, then quickly cut to news of Mahmoud. "He wishes you well," Stefano said. "His initial reports about the facilities at the Grandspire were accurate. I spent the morning with the director of business development getting the particulars, but I feel it would work well for any events you wish to host outside Sarcaccia."

His father followed up with questions about the hotel's exact location and airport accessibility while Stefano strolled through his suite, stopping near the windows. Now that Stefano had a chance to study the view in daylight, he was amazed by the early-season crowds on the beach enjoying the sunshine. It was a beautiful weekend day with high, fluffy clouds and a clear sky. He moved a step closer to watch a young family making their way along the planked walk that connected the hotel and the beach, but found himself distracted by the brilliant blue of the hotel pool, which occupied a rooftop deck that extended out from the side of the building several floors below his suite.

A woman in a bright red bikini swam the length of the pool underwater, popping up at the end nearest the diving board. After a few breaths, she stretched her arms overhead to grab the side of the board and hang from it, then walked her hands along the diving board's edge until she dangled from the very end. Her hair swept across her back like a wet curtain and one strap of her bikini appeared askew, but she didn't seem to care. The sight amused him. How many adults would do such a thing? Perhaps because the woman had the entire pool deck to herself, she felt free to horse around. Whoever she was, she was athletic enough to lift herself out of the water. From this vantage point he could see the outline of lean muscle in her back and arms. She looked as if she could hang from the board all afternoon.

As his father asked after Ilsa and Stefano told him a little about Ilsa's duties at the contemporary art museum, Stefano realized that the woman in the red bikini wasn't alone after all. A dark-haired young girl was also at the pool. She must've been standing close enough to the building that Stefano hadn't noticed her from his angle. She ran along the tiled edge, then abruptly slowed to a walk when she neared the diving board as if she'd been warned about running poolside. Moving with exaggerated slowness, the girl stepped onto the board and walked to the end, then leaned down cautiously, hands on her knees, to speak with the woman hanging from the end.

Using her body weight, the woman gave the board a bounce, making the girl laugh and feign falling into the water. A moment later, the girl executed a perfect dive over the bikini-clad woman and swam toward the opposite end of the pool. The woman turned, letting go of the board and following the girl with long, determined strokes, but not before Stefano caught sight of her face.

Megan. Meaning the girl in the striped yellow swimsuit now kicking water at Megan must be Anna. His mouth went bone dry.

"Will you attend dinner with us tomorrow night?" King Carlo asked, referring to the country's custom of inviting foreign dignitaries to the palace for Sunday dinner. "Your mother hopes the whole family will be there. The premier of Queensland is expected."

"I'm not sure if I can make it this week," Stefano replied, watching the pair pull themselves out of the pool. Though they seemed to have the same smile, Anna's skin and hair were darker than Megan's. He wished he could see the girl's face more clearly. "I have a lunch meeting tomorrow, so it depends on how that goes. I'll do my best."

"Your secretary didn't have anything on your calendar for tomorrow, so I couldn't tell when you'd planned to arrive," the king said. "Nothing until an appointment with the barber at the palace on Monday morning, then your transportation meeting."

"That's correct." He'd defer the haircut and possibly the transportation meeting, but the mention of his secretary reminded him of a more pressing issue. "By the way, I meant to ask you something. I know it was many years ago, but during the media circus surrounding my engagement, was Dagmar instructed to filter my personal calls more than usual?"

"What do you mean?"

The nonchalance in his father's voice seemed forced, but maybe that was Stefano's imagination. "She always kept me informed when I received calls from people who weren't my personal friends. You know, people I might meet in passing then who'd want a favor or who hoped to be invited to events at the palace. She would hand me a list of names and have me indicate which she should put through in the future and which she should gently attempt to dissuade. When everything happened with Ariana and there was so much attention on the family, was Dagmar told to be more aggressive about policing my calls than usual? Or not to bother me with the usual list?"

Now that Stefano thought about it, there should have been more calls than ever during that period, yet in hindsight, the volume of calls and mail hadn't seemed out of the ordinary. The only increase was for matters directly related to the wedding—tailors, caterers, security specialists—rather than from friends, acquaintances, or even the press.

"I certainly gave her no such instruction," King Carlo replied, though his decisive response made Stefano wonder if his father *knew* of such an order, whether or not he gave it. "Dagmar was quite capable. She knew how to separate the wheat from the chaff in order to protect you, especially during those times our family was under particularly intense scrutiny. When that happens, there can be thousands of phone calls a day to the palace lines."

He'd have guessed dozens, maybe hundreds, but thousands?

"That's the point of employing a good staff, Stefano. It keeps you from having to deal with non-vital tasks. If you recall, when you became engaged, you were starting your military training. That's where your focus needed to be." The king sighed. "I like your new secretary, but must say that I do miss Dagmar. She was a joy. Have you spoken with her recently? How is her health? Are her grandchildren doing well?"

Stefano allowed the change in subject, giving his father an innocuous answer about seeing Dagmar at a recent garden party where she'd been in high spirits, then finished the call with a promise to let his mother know about Sunday dinner once his travel plans became firm.

After setting the phone on the coffee table, he walked to the kitchen to make himself a cup of coffee. Though his body screamed for a nap after being awake most of the previous night, he wanted to be back on schedule so he'd be alert tomorrow. He punched the buttons on the coffeemaker, considering the phone call. His father's answer about Dagmar had been quick. Too quick. The king made it a habit to speak in measured words. Responding to questions about long-ago events warranted careful consideration. He'd also expected his father to ask what prompted Stefano's question since it wasn't typical to ask about decade-old phone calls, but he'd made no such inquiry.

The automatic brewer sizzled to life, sending an aromatic stream of French roast into a mug. Perhaps there had been far more calls to the palace than Stefano ever imagined. In keeping him from being distracted during those crazy, busy days—including being distracted by calls from Megan—his family and staff probably thought they were helping him. Keeping him from non-vital tasks, as his father put it.

He wondered what his father would think if he knew the true havoc that "help" wrought upon Stefano's life in this particular instance.

He sighed as he walked to the window cradling a cup of coffee he didn't particularly want. He hadn't lied when he'd told Megan he'd have returned her call. However, if he was honest with himself, he would've told Dagmar to winnow the calls had he known the volume was so overwhelming, and he likely wouldn't have thought to give her specific instructions regarding Megan.

Much as he'd like to attribute the botched messages to something sinister, an outside force that would excuse him from playing a part in what happened, he couldn't. It happened because of who he was. If he hadn't been born a Barrali, he'd have gotten the messages. Hell, he'd have gotten the call directly. He couldn't blame Megan for keeping Anna a secret, either. Again, if he hadn't been born a Barrali, there wouldn't have been a need.

He took a sip of the coffee, then set the cup on a nearby table. Megan and Anna had wrapped themselves in oversized white towels and were seated side by side on a lounge chair near the pool, chatting. They seemed happy, just as Megan claimed. He had to admit that the hotel wasn't such a bad place for them to live. Megan had no commute, meaning she could spend more time with her daughter. They had the world outside their door and the hotel pool offered them a safe, convenient place to relax and enjoy themselves.

He leaned against the glass to get a better look. Seeing Megan interact with Anna convinced him she'd done a good job raising her daughter. He didn't know the girl's personality—for all he knew, Anna could be rude and spoiled—but they gave the appearance of having a tight, comfortable bond.

He hadn't relaxed like that with his own parents since he was a child. Other than during occasional trips to Sicily, where his father's cousin owned a house that afforded them a measure of solitude for family vacations, they'd never been able to kick back and enjoy each other's company. Cameras were omnipresent, and any entertainment spots the Barralis frequented—whether an amusement park, a petting zoo, or a horse farm—used the royal family's appearance to boost their bottom line. Stefano didn't mind helping those businesses make money, especially since it helped the country as a whole, but he did mind the lack of private family time. His relationship with his parents simply wasn't the same as what he witnessed out his window.

Hell, even his family's Sunday dinners were public.

His phone buzzed. A quick peek showed a text from one of his older brothers, Prince Alessandro, asking if Stefano would make it to Sunday night dinner. Fabulous.

He should convince his siblings to take another family trip to Sicily. The house was still available to them should they want it and there was plenty of space. The property boasted a pool for afternoon swims, a fully outfitted kitchen for meals, and acres of land to keep any media at a distance. It might be just the thing his parents needed to know that their children still cared for them and wanted to spend time with them, despite the pressures and distractions that came with adulthood. How hard could it be to arrange a weekend's respite?

He smiled as Megan pulled Anna into her lap over the girl's protests. Anyone observing the pair would see that Anna was at the age where she enjoyed being close to her mother when they were alone, but demanded her independence if she thought anyone might be watching.

He wondered how Anna would handle their meeting tomorrow, assuming Megan didn't balk between now and then. Would Anna be frightened? Indifferent? Curious? So much depended on Megan and how she presented the idea to Anna.

For all he knew, they could be discussing it this very minute. If so, he hoped it was an easier discussion than those he'd shared with his own parents.

CHAPTER NINE

"You're sure you're okay with this?"

Megan studied Anna's face, trying to ensure her daughter was as nonplussed by meeting Stefano Barrali as she professed. True, Megan deliberately put Anna in a receptive mood with pool time, a fantastic lunch—allowing Anna the leftover cake from Santi despite the fact she wasn't quite done with her school project—and the promise she could go on a beach outing with her best friend late tomorrow afternoon. Still, shouldn't being told she'd be meeting her biological father, a man who happened to be a well-known prince, give Anna pause?

The whole idea certainly gave Megan pause.

"Mom." Anna allowed the fluffy pool towel to drop from her shoulders as she reached out to put her hands on Megan's pool-dampened cheeks. With exaggerated bossiness, she said, "He's a prince. Not a superhero or a god. Get it straight."

Megan leveled her with a look. "You're not as funny as you think you are."

"I get it from you."

"Don't try to kiss up," Megan said, rolling her eyes at the sarcasm in Anna's voice. "And please, let's keep the funny business tamped down during lunch."

"I know how to behave, Mom. Geez." Anna wrapped her towel around her shoulders once more.

"Good. Then I'll give him a call and tell him we're set."

Anna gazed across the pool deck while Megan retrieved her cell phone from under the magazine she'd brought outside. "Think he swims?"

"Definitely." The man looked sexier cutting through the waves in Venezuela as a rough-around-the-edges college kid than any of the men she'd seen gracing Barcelona's beaches over the last few years. Even now she could imagine the water beading on his chest and across the corded muscle of his arms as he waded out of the water, slicking his hair out of his eyes as he smiled at her.

Anna was wrong. The man was a god, just not the type Anna imagined.

"But we're not bringing him to the pool," Megan clarified. "Too many windows overlooking the deck. I think it's best you meet him for the first time in a quieter spot."

"Gotcha."

The reception desk put Megan's call through to the prince's suite. As she waited for it to ring, she wondered if he could see them now, assuming he was upstairs. She hadn't thought of it until this moment, but if he'd wanted to, he could've watched her and Anna the entire time they'd been swimming.

She pulled her towel tighter as his voice came over the line.

"It's me," she said simply. "I've made arrangements for lunch."

Without hesitation, he asked, "Where and when?"

"My suite at one, if that time works for you. I think that's where Anna would be most comfortable." Anna mouthed, *What are we gonna eat? Can I make something? Pleeease?* as Megan spoke, but Megan waved her away. Anna pulled a face, then dropped her towel to the deck and half-walked, half-skipped toward the diving board. "If you're seen knocking on my door, no one on the staff will question it. They'll assume it's business. And eating in my suite means we can speak freely."

When Stefano agreed, Megan gave him her suite number.

"Anything I should know beforehand?" Megan thought she detected trepidation in his tone as he added, "I'd like this to go as smoothly as possible."

"It's just lunch. Casual, like you suggested. Take your cues from Anna and you'll be fine." She hesitated, then asked, "Why? Is there anything you think *I* should know? You're not going to drop a bomb on us, like news you have seventeen other kids in various countries or that you've secretly enrolled Anna in clown college?"

Megan rubbed her temple. Why had she said that? As Anna had so bluntly stated, Megan wasn't funny.

Nerves. Chalk the idiotic attempt at comedy up to nerves.

"No, no bombs. Had enough of those this weekend." His laugh sounded genuine. "But you should know...you look smashing in red. Especially that red."

Before she could absorb his words, he said, "Tomorrow. One p.m." And hung up.

* * *

She answered the door wearing black.

The simply cut, sheer lace top contrasted with Megan's light skin and flaxen hair, while at the same time making her eyes appear more brilliant than ever. White slacks hugged her in all the right places.

Secretly, however, Stefano had hoped she'd wear red.

He rarely had trouble speaking to people—he'd been trained from birth to say the most diplomatic thing possible in any situation—but watching Megan sitting poolside in her bikini, seeing her bright smile from above as she'd first spoken to him about lunch, then observing the way she rubbed her forehead when she'd made the awful crack about clown college...well, he'd been momentarily smitten. He wanted her to know he was watching her, admiring her.

When he'd ended the call, he could swear her face turned as red as that delicious swimsuit.

Nevertheless, he should've kept the thought to himself.

"Prince Stefano, it's good to see you again. Please, come in." Megan stepped back from the door, holding it open and waving him inside. As she'd said, it would appear to anyone watching from the hallway—not that anyone wandered the twentieth floor hallway at noon on a Sunday—as if they were meeting to discuss business.

He entered, pausing once inside the narrow entry hall to allow her to lead the way into the rest of the suite. That's when he noticed she was barefoot. Bright red toenails peeked out where the hem of her slacks brushed the tops of her feet. When she closed the door, a woven red silk bracelet punctuated by tiny gold beads peeked out from under the cuff of her shirt. He couldn't help but smile. The toenails she could've painted days ago, but the bracelet was a deliberate choice, especially given its contrast with her basic black top. Had she worn it because of his comment?

"Why are you grinning?" Her voice was quiet, but filled with suspicion. "You look like the cat who ate the canary."

He shrugged. "Whatever you're cooking smells amazing."

She eyed him for a moment, as if weighing his response, then said, "Anna asked if she could make pizza. She's become obsessed with cooking lately. Mostly it's desserts, since that's what she wants to eat, but my mother taught her to make pizza dough. She does a competent job of it, too."

"In that case, I look forward to it."

He followed Megan to the kitchen, checking out the decor along the way. There was no mistaking the place for anything other than the hotel suite it was, but there were personal touches, too. Photos of Megan hugging Anna, a niche containing pottery he recognized as being made by a co-op near where they'd worked in Venezuela, and a small painted plaque declaring *You Have a Home in Minnesota* made the space unique.

When they reached the kitchen, all thoughts of the suite faded away. The girl he'd seen at the pool yesterday had her back to him and her hands fisted at her hips as she bent to peer in the window of an oven. Though dressed more casually than Megan, she'd clearly taken time with her appearance. Her denim shorts were topped by a white camisole, over which she wore a transparent sky blue top. Her thick, dark hair shone as if she'd spent a good deal of time going over it with a hairbrush. It hung off to one side, over her shoulder, as if she'd carefully arranged it there after looping it through a silver ponytail holder. Not a single strand was loose. When she bent further and splayed her hands across the top edge of the oven, he caught himself smiling at the sight of sparkly hot pink and robin's egg blue polish on alternating fingertips.

"Anna?"

At Megan's voice, the girl straightened and turned. A hard lump formed in Stefano's throat. Megan was right. This child had his green eyes, his darkly slashed eyebrows, even his forehead. God help him, but there was no mistaking that this child was his. She might be wearing feminine clothing and nail polish, but Stefano could tell she had his attitude without her having spoken a word.

God help Megan.

Anna assessed him with confidence. "Hello, Prince Stefano. Welcome to our home."

Then she curtsied. All the way to the kitchen floor.

"Honey, that's not what we discussed—"

"You don't need to do that," Stefano said at the same time. He wasn't sure whether to be embarrassed or to laugh.

Without a hint of sarcasm in her voice or expression, Anna asked, "Am I supposed to bow? Because I thought bowing was for boys."

"For a first meeting, I think a handshake will do." He reached across the granite countertop that separated the kitchen from the living space and waited. After few painful heartbeats, Anna stepped forward and clasped his hand with her own. Her grip was surprisingly firm for someone so small. "It's a pleasure to meet you, Prince Stefano."

He kept his smile steady. He couldn't quite believe he was shaking hands with his own daughter. "Why don't you call me Stefano? 'Prince Stefano' feels too formal."

Anna glanced at Megan, then back to him. "I'm not supposed to call adults by their first names. My mom's says it's a respect thing. Is Mr. Barrali okay? Or is that wrong, since you're a rich and famous prince and everything?"

Megan propped her forearms on the countertop and flashed Anna a warning look for the choice of words. "This is a bit of an unusual circumstance. It's fine with me if you call him Stefano while we're here in our apartment. But if you ever address him in public, go with Prince Stefano. Not Stefano. And definitely not Mr. Barrali."

"Sounds like a good compromise," Stefano said, hoping to alleviate the awkwardness of the situation. He'd spent more hours of his youth than he cared to remember being drilled on the finer points of etiquette, but this particular scenario was never addressed. He doubted there was a protocol guru in the world who knew the proper way to handle parent-child introductions.

"So you're, like, my father? For real?"

"I am." Seeing Anna in the flesh left no doubt.

Beside him, Megan shifted and cleared her throat. He imagined she was trying to steer Anna in a different direction, but he kept his focus on Anna, who quirked one side of her mouth as she studied him. "Can I ask a stupid question? Since you're my father and you're a prince, does that make me a princess? Or not really?"

"It's not a stupid question at all. The way royal titles work is complicated. But technically, no, because your mom and I aren't married, you're not a princess under the laws of my country." Keeping a straight face at the unexpected question proved difficult. He wasn't about to explain Sarcaccian legitimacy. He wanted to tell her that it was fine *not* to be a princess, but wasn't sure how a girl her age would view such a statement.

"Huh." Much to his surprise, Anna didn't seem bothered by the information. Rather, she appeared to weigh it in her mind as if she'd been handed the solution to a complex math problem and now wished to work it backward to be certain she understood.

He nodded toward the oven. "When I came to the door, I told your mother that whatever you're cooking smells amazing. Is that pizza?"

The question earned him a guarded smile. "My grandma was here last week and she taught me. But after I made it I figured you probably don't eat pizza, so it's okay if you want to order lunch instead. My mom does it all the time. We have menus." She gestured toward one of the kitchen drawers. "My grandma says that you can freeze pizza after it cools and it's still good, so I can eat it later. It won't get wasted."

She might take after him physically, but she had Megan's practical streak. Always thinking of a Plan B. He told Anna, "I don't eat pizza because no one ever offers. People assume I prefer fancy dishes with colorful sauces and radishes or cucumbers cut to look like flowers. Truth is, I'd much rather have pizza."

"No way."

The combination of hesitancy and surprise in her voice reminded him of how he'd sounded as a child on those rare occasions his parents allowed him something he was positive wouldn't be permitted. "It's true. Pizza is a treat for me. What kind of topping did you put on it?"

"On *them*. I made two. Wanna see?"

He circled the counter before crouching beside her to peek through the oven's window. Inside, a perfectly browned pizza occupied each of the two racks, their surfaces bubbling with cheese, green peppers, and mushrooms. He looked sideways at her, noting the satisfaction in her expression as she inspected her creations. "Did your mother tell you what to put on these?"

"No. Why? You don't like mushrooms, do you? I knew it." She stared at the pizza in dismay. "Well, I left half of one pizza plain, just in case. The mushrooms never even touched it, so you're safe if you still want it."

"No way." He took a risk in using her phrase, then gave her a gentle elbow to the side. "My favorite pizza is mushroom with green peppers."

She glanced at him and rolled her eyes. "You're only saying that to get me to like you."

"Like me or not, it's true. Maybe it's hereditary." Still crouched in front of the oven, he frowned over his shoulder at Megan. "Though apparently your mother and I like the same kind of omelets for breakfast."

"What can I say?" Megan spread her hands. "Anna and I have good taste. I told her to pick whatever she wanted from the fridge to put on the pizza."

"I like sausage, too," Stefano confided, giving Anna a sideways just-between-us look. "Do you have a sausage pizza hiding in there?"

When she shook her head and told him she couldn't stand sausage, he said, "I doubt the three of us could eat a third pizza, anyway."

"You haven't tried *my* pizza, so you never know."

"Think I'm about to find out."

"Timer says six seconds left, so…here goes!" She straightened, then pulled a pair of oven mitts from a nearby drawer and asked Megan to help her take out the pizza. Stefano sidled out of the narrow kitchen, watching as the pair removed the pizzas and made quick work of slicing them. When he noticed a festive-looking stack of napkins and plates at the counter's edge, he took them and went about setting the table.

He couldn't remember the last time he'd set a table, let alone with confetti-specked paper plates. It felt odd, but good.

"Oh, Stefano, I was going to use real plates," Megan said, glancing over at him from the kitchen. "Those were left over from one of Anna's class events. I can't imagine you'd—"

"I seem to recall the two of us eating off old, peeling plastic plates while sitting on a dirt floor in a family's shanty. I think I can handle paper."

That drew a cautious smile from her. "If it's fine with you, it's fine with me."

A few minutes later, as they ate the pizza, which was every bit as delicious as it smelled, along with a salad Megan prepared, Anna asked him what it was like to live in a palace.

He glanced at Megan before giving his answer. "Well, it's certainly beautiful. There are chandeliers in nearly every room, and Persian rugs so thick you can curl your toes in them. Since it was built in the days before electric heat, the fireplaces are so tall and wide you can walk into them." He tried to imagine what Anna would notice, were she to walk the palace's wide halls or sleep in its rooms. "The palace has gorgeous gardens on three sides. I played there all the time when I was a child. Then there's a parade ground in the front where tourists come to see equestrian demonstrations in the summer. There's also a giant clock tower beside the front gate that tolls every hour. When I was growing up, I would lie in bed at night and count the strikes, then listen for the last reverberation to fade away. I liked timing it, because the sound could change depending on the weather."

Her mouth dropped into an O. He could virtually see the wheels spinning in her mind, imagining life in a palace as if it were a fairy tale come true. "That sounds fantastic!"

"In many ways, it is. But have you ever heard the phrase, 'living in a fishbowl'?"

She hesitated. "Like, living underwater?"

"Not quite." He explained the meaning, then said, "Sometimes, it's like that for me. When I'm in the palace, I have very little privacy. I don't always control where I go, who I see, or even my own phone calls and e-mail. Everyone knows what I'm doing at all times."

"That must suck. Big time."

"Anna—" Megan's warning came despite the fact she'd just taken a bite of pizza.

"Not always. For instance, I don't have to clean anything or make my own bed. I don't even have to shop, because people who work at the palace bring me whatever I need. But can I tell you a secret?" At her nod, he said, "I don't mind making my own bed. And there are days I wish I could walk out my front door on a whim and shop the way you do. Not because I like to shop, but because it'd be fun to wander through a pedestrian shopping area and see the sights or stop for an ice cream without worrying about being watched or having my picture taken. I occasionally do it when I'm traveling, but it's rare while I'm at home. I'm usually recognized too quickly to have much time to myself. Living in the palace especially makes me appreciate times like this, when I can visit friends and eat whatever I want and be myself."

"Well, we're not your friends. We're your family." She paused, scrunching her nose. "Kind of. I mean, we're not really your family. But we *are* related, so I guess, well…you know what I mean."

"I do know what you mean." He kept his gaze fixed on Anna, but he could sense Megan's stillness as powerfully as a punch to the gut. He kept a smile in his voice as he whispered to Anna, "It's a little awkward meeting a parent for the first time when you're almost done with fourth grade, isn't it?"

"Totally awkward!" She picked a mushroom off the top of her pizza, popped it into her mouth, then shrugged. "But it's not a big deal, right? I mean, that you're my father. Not if no one knows."

He couldn't lie to her. "It won't be an easy secret to keep. I imagine someone will find out eventually, even if none of us say a word. Maybe not soon, but someday. Whether anyone knows or not, though, I do think it's a big deal to be your father. That's why I asked your mom if I could come to lunch today. I want to get to know you and I want you to get to know me."

She radiated skepticism as only a pre-teen could. "*You* want to get to know me?"

"I do."

"Huh." She took another bite of her pizza, contemplating that, then washed it down with a long sip of lemonade. Her plastic cup clunked against the tabletop as she set it down. "But I bet you never wanted kids. Like, if you didn't know I existed and a friend asked you if you wanted kids, you'd probably say no way. Right?"

Megan's voice was simultaneously chastising and understanding as she said, "Anna, honey, that's not really a fair question."

"I'd have said yes," Stefano replied. He suspected that Anna didn't really want to know his thoughts on becoming a parent, but whether he considered her a mistake. "Truth is, I've always wanted kids."

"But you don't have any. Other than me, I mean, and I don't count." There was no accusation in her tone. Her manner remained straightforward as she shook Parmesan cheese onto a fresh slice of pizza. "You aren't even married."

"No, I'm not married. But you *do* count. At least as far as I'm concerned."

That earned him a merry laugh. "If you want kids so much, how come you're not married? Most people who have kids get married."

This time Megan let the question go, though Stefano could feel Megan's uneasiness with both her daughter's blunt tone and the direction of the conversation. It didn't bother him as much as it might. Instead, he found himself drawn to Anna's straightforward nature.

"I'm not married because I haven't met the right person."

"In other words, my mom wasn't the right person."

CHAPTER TEN

She may have been.

He studied Anna for a moment, trying to determine whether her statement was one of hope, of accusation, or of simple fact. It was impossible to know, yet he suspected his response could make or break the girl's first impression of him. He knew it shouldn't matter—kids' opinions changed with the wind, and now that he knew of her existence, he planned to build a long-term relationship with her—yet he found he truly, deeply cared what Anna thought of him today.

"Your mom and I never had the chance to find out," he finally said. "Sometimes that happens in life. When it does, you do the best you can if you're fortunate enough to get a second chance. Your mom and I can't change the fact that I didn't know about you" —he shot a glance at Megan— "which wasn't anyone's fault. It just happened. But now that I do know, I'm here. That all right with you?"

She looked him up and down, as if she could read his mind by scrutinizing him, then gave a firm nod. A moment later, she said, "You know my mom made me see you today, right?"

Megan pinned her daughter with a glare. "Anna, you know that's not true."

Anna groaned. "Well she *would've* made me, but I said it was fine when she asked so she wouldn't *have* to make me. I wasn't sure if I'd like you or not, and I was afraid if I didn't then my mom would get all upset and everything would suck. Um, stink. But so far, this has been more fun than I thought it'd be. You're okay, Stefano."

Stefano bit back a teasing response, suspecting Anna might not appreciate it. "Glad to hear it."

"Me, too," Megan replied, turning to Anna to add, "though I wish you'd use more appropriate language, honey. We've talked about using 'sucks' more than once." She stood to clear the table, causing Anna to grab the final piece of pizza from the center of the table before her mother removed the tray. Stefano pushed back to help, but Megan waved for him to remain seated. "It's only a couple of plates and the salad. You and Anna keep talking."

He paused, ensuring she truly had it handled, then relaxed in the chair once more.

"That really was incredible pizza, Anna. Thank you." He gestured toward the slice still on her plate. "The crust was delicious and I could tell the mushrooms and peppers were fresh."

"Mom and I bought them yesterday afternoon at a market off La Rambla called La Boqueria. It's been around for hundreds of years. The stalls have fresh fish, eggs, veggies, spices, even soap and candles. There's a guy who makes pizza that's almost as good as mine, and one stall has a dozen different kinds of ham hanging from the ceiling, which is creepy but cool." She held her hands over her head as she spoke, as if showing off varieties of ham. "I didn't even know there was more than one kind of ham until we moved here. Oh, and there's a great place to get breakfast if you're at the market early. They cook it right in front of you and if you go more than once, they'll remember your name and what you ordered. My mom usually gets espresso and an omelet, but I like the toasted cheese sandwiches."

"I've heard of La Boqueria." The sprawling covered marketplace was a favorite of both tourists and locals. Photos of the lively vendors hawking their products regularly appeared in travel magazines. It struck him as a wonderful spot for strolling and people-watching. "Sounds like you visit fairly often."

"Tons. My favorite stall sells fruit juice smoothies. They sound boring, but they're not. The owners mash the fruit with ice in gigantic blenders early in the morning, then stack the smoothie cups in long rows by flavor so it looks like a rainbow." Her gestures became more expansive as she grew more and more excited by her own description. "My favorites are strawberry guava and banana coconut, but they have every flavor you can imagine. I swear, it'll make you hungry just looking at them!"

"Hearing you describe them makes me hungry and I just ate."

She crossed her arms over her chest and leaned back in her chair, a wicked smile slowly spreading across her face, as if she'd trapped him. "You should go with me. I'll show you all the best stuff, then we can have smoothies for dessert. Want to? It's not far."

Warmth spread through him. He'd love to have Anna show him the market, if only such a thing were possible. La Boqueria was a tourist mecca and the local media knew he was in town. Though he could sometimes negotiate public areas unrecognized while away from Sarcaccia, in this particular case he didn't stand a chance. "I appreciate that, Anna. Unfortunately—"

"Anna, you're going to the beach with Julia and her mom later this afternoon, remember?" Megan's interruption was so smooth, Stefano doubted Anna grasped that her request could be problematic. "But maybe another time."

"Oh, shoot!" Anna sprung from the table, eyes widening. "I totally forgot! Julia's mom called this morning while you were in the shower and asked if she could pick me up at two instead of three-thirty and I told her I thought that'd be fine."

Megan glanced at the oven's digital clock. "Anna, it's nearly two now. You're just remembering this?"

"It's okay. My stuff is packed."

Irritation flashed in Megan's eyes. "That doesn't make it okay. You have a guest—"

A triple chime sounded. Megan shook her head at Anna as she crossed the room to a small, wall-mounted intercom where the kitchen ended and the entry hall began. "Hello?"

"Good afternoon, Ms. Hallberg," the front desk clerk's voice came from the speaker. "I have Julia and Marta Pettite here for Anna. Should I send them up?"

Megan glanced toward Anna and Stefano, shooting daggers at her daughter. "Anna's already on her way down. If you could ask them to wait in the rotunda by the center table, she'll be there in just a minute. Save them the elevator ride."

"Will do."

She thanked him, then waved for Anna to grab her gear as she clicked off the speaker. As the girl scooted into one of the two bedrooms off the living area, Megan called, "Hurry! And next time, Anna, remember to give me my messages. I would've told you that you couldn't go until later."

"I will! Sorry!"

When Anna emerged from her room, Megan checked the bag for a swimsuit, towel, hat, and sunscreen. She pulled a few Euros from a drawer in the living room's bureau and tucked them into a zippered side pocket. "That's for water and a snack. Do you have your cell phone?"

She patted her pocket. "Yes, Mom."

"Okay. Hustle down and thank Julia's mother. Is she still bringing you home at six?"

"She said she'll call. We might go out to dinner on the way home because she says it's too hot to cook." Anna had the smarts to look sheepish. "If that's all right with you."

On an exhale, Megan replied, "All right. Whatever's easiest for Julia's mom. But if Mrs. Pettite doesn't call me, then I expect you to do it as soon as you know your plans. Understood?"

"Understood." Anna slung the straps of her beach bag over her shoulder and headed for the door, then spun around and beamed at Stefano. "Thanks for coming to lunch. That was cool. Think you'll be back here anytime soon?"

He couldn't help but return her impish grin. "If you'd like."

"Definitely! I will *so* take you shopping."

"In that case, it's a date." He'd figure out a way.

"Can you bring a picture of the clock tower when you come? Oooh, or pictures from inside your palace?"

"Anna!"

"Fine. I'm going, I'm going." She tilted her head back and rolled her eyes, then walked to the door with exaggerated footfalls as if belabored by her mother's chastisement. "Bye! Oh, and Stefano, you can take the leftover pizza if you want. It's okay with me."

Once the door clicked shut, Megan leaned her head back and stomped in a circle, mimicking Anna's march to the door. "Is this what you expected when you asked to meet her?"

"No. "He laughed at Megan's spot-on impression. "But I can't say I'm surprised, either. She's a pistol, isn't she?"

"That's a nice way of putting it. I would've said 'handful' rather than 'pistol.'" She moved to the sofa, eyeing him as she eased into one corner and folded her legs beneath her. Her red toenails peeked out over the sofa's edge. "Handful or not, I love her to pieces. I couldn't imagine my life without being caught in her whirlwind."

The description stunned him, momentarily catapulting him back to his own youth.

"What?"

"Nothing," he said, then corrected himself. "It's only…that's exactly the way my mother used to describe me. She told people I was like a whirlwind moving through the house. Not because I was messy, but because I was so active I wore out both her and the nanny." He could still picture the way his mother would sit on a garden bench and watch him whenever he could convince his siblings to join him in a race through the palace gardens. By mid-afternoon, his mother's eyes always drifted closed, yet Stefano would beg and beg her to wake up and watch him run. "When I came home during one of my college breaks, she said it had been too quiet without me around. She'd gotten used to finishing each day with the satisfaction of having survived a storm."

"Are you saying I have you to blame for my perpetual motion machine?"

"I suppose." He moved to take a spot beside Megan on the long beige sofa. There were bright orange throw pillows in the center which he moved aside so he could sit knee-to-knee with her. "I'm not handy in a kitchen, though. Her pizza really was quite good. Better than most restaurants serve, even in Sarcaccia or Italy. She has real talent."

Megan's face lit with pride. "That's all my mother. Anna loves cooking with her. My parents have come to Barcelona five times since I moved here, but they have yet to visit the Picasso Museum because my mother ends up spending so much time in the kitchen."

He felt a pang of jealousy. Cooking with Anna would make for an entertaining afternoon. How many of them had he missed? How many might there be left? "I bet she enjoys every second of it."

"I hope so. It's a long flight from Minnesota just to make pizza."

"True." A thought occurred to him. "Have you considered cooking lessons? There's a world-class culinary school right here in Barcelona. I know Anna's too young for a formal program, but I'm sure they offer classes for children. If they saw her talent—" The expression on Megan's face stopped him. "Bad idea?"

"She doesn't need cooking school."

He spread his hands wide. "Why not give it a try, if it's an option? I've heard that the facilities are spectacular. In fact, the head chef at the palace studied there, as have several other members of my family's staff. Anna would love it."

"I'm sure she would. But she doesn't need it."

"She doesn't *need* a lot of things. But if it interests her and it's within your capability to provide it, why wouldn't you?"

A bemused smile perked up the edges of her mouth. When Stefano asked what was so funny, she laughed as if she'd heard a terrific joke but Stefano had missed the punch line, making it all the funnier.

"Oh." He ran his hand along the back of the sofa, feeling the bumpy texture of the fabric's tight weave. He shouldn't make assumptions about what Megan could and couldn't provide. "Well, I'd certainly be happy to pay for the lessons."

That only made her laugh so hard she couldn't speak. A tear ran out the corner of one of her eyes, which she swiped away. He stared at her, befuddled, then spread his hands wide. "I give up. What's so funny?"

"What do you think?" she managed. "You're doing it again."

Ah. Now he understood. He relaxed into the cushions, his knee bumping against hers as he did so. "You think I'm trying to take over her parenting? Or, excuse me, 'contribute something of value' to her upbringing? Weren't those were your words yesterday when I questioned your parenting choices?"

"Good memory."

"That wasn't my intent. It's clear to me now that you've made good choices with her. I only want her to have the best, if the best is within reach."

"I realize that. But suggesting culinary lessons at the place your head chef studied after Anna served you pizza on a kiddie party plate? Tell me that's not hilarious." She leaned forward, the movement allowing him a breath of her light, citrusy perfume. "Look, I'm glad you care about her well being. The fact you didn't know she existed until this weekend, yet you feel compelled to ensure she's happy speaks volumes about the kind of man you are. And I deeply appreciate that. But she doesn't need to be handed everything on a silver platter to be happy. She's happy already."

"Cooking lessons aren't being handed everything on a silver platter." He held up a hand as she opened her mouth to argue. "But I understand your point. Cooking is off the table. So to speak."

That earned him another smile. "So to speak."

"Still, it doesn't mean I don't want to give her everything it's within my power to give. And by that, I don't mean material things. I mean experiences that will enrich her life and satisfy her intellectual curiosity. It's no different than what you said you did by accepting a job in Barcelona."

Megan sucked in a breath, making him wonder if he'd overstepped. "We need to take this slowly. She may have been fairly comfortable with you today, but there's going to be a period of adjustment for her."

"I know." He thought of the way Anna held her breath as he'd first tasted her pizza, waiting for his reaction, then trying to disguise her pride by looking down at her own slice when he'd complimented her. "I like her. A lot. Not simply because she's my daughter—or because she's yours—but for who she is. She's entertaining. And direct."

"Like when she asked you why you aren't married, despite the fact she knows better than to ask a question like that?" She screwed up her mouth. "It's tough sometimes, given her age, but she's been working on thinking first, speaking and acting second. I'm sorry if she offended you. I figured she'd have questions, but not precisely *those* questions."

Megan wrapped her hands around her knees as she spoke. The sun highlighted the beading in her red bracelet, making him think of that red bikini all over again. He wondered if he'd ever get that image out of his head.

He hoped not.

"She didn't offend me at all." He forced his gaze from Megan's hands and wrists to her face. "I'm afraid she gets any impetuousness from me, at least according to my parents."

"You must be joking. Calling you a whirlwind of activity, that I understand. Within five minutes of meeting you, I realized you couldn't stand to be still."

He frowned at her. "How so?"

"Whenever you found yourself with a free minute, you'd track down extra parts for a water pump or you'd jump to help someone else finish their project. You spent hours and hours playing stickball or soccer with the local kids rather than relax during your time off." Her eyes sparkled at the memory. "But impetuous? No. You always think before you speak or act."

"In public, and then only because the instinct was drummed out of me. Years of etiquette lessons, you know."

"Bet you'd have preferred cooking lessons." Her flirtatious smile sent a jolt of heat clear to his belly, then to his groin.

"No doubt." But right now, he wanted her. Her wit. Her warmth. Her passion.

Nothing was going to drum that instinct out of him.

He covered one of her hands with his own, exploring her soft skin, taking in the texture of the bones and joints beneath. Wondering at all her beautiful hands had accomplished, both at work and in her personal life with Anna. He expected her to pull away, but she remained motionless. "I can still be impetuous. For instance, it would be a shame not to take advantage of the fact that we're alone for the first time in a decade, with no one to see us, no one to hear us. Don't you think?"

He slowly circled one of her nails with the pad of his index finger, then raised her hand to his mouth, kissing the inside of her wrist where it peeked out from the cuff of her shirt. Still, she didn't pull away. She felt warm and alive, and he wanted her as never before. With his mouth still pressed to her wrist, he looked into her wide blue eyes and whispered, "We can do whatever we'd like."

CHAPTER ELEVEN

Impetuous. That was one word for what Stefano was doing to her wrist. Others came to mind first, each supplanting the other as the heat of his mouth seared into her very veins, coursing straight to her heart: *Divine. Sensuous. Rapturous.*

If this was what he could do to her wrist, what would his touch do to the rest of her?

Orgasmic.

Before the thought could settle, Megan turned her energy to keeping her breath even and her expression neutral. Mustering her most unaffected tone, she said, "You're a terrible flirt, you know. It's why you draw so much media attention." His skill at it also meant he likely wasn't fooled by her attempt at composure. He knew exactly what to say and do to make any woman swoon. Her most of all.

She should stop him now, before he detected the rapid thrum of her heartbeat against his lips, which remained pressed to her pulse point. She should be responsible, ask questions about what he expected from his relationship with Anna. Set some parameters.

She should *not* be thinking about the way the nerves in her wrist seemed connected to every other fiber in her body. Or the way he set them all to flame with nothing more than a quick caress of his mouth.

"This isn't flirting, Megan. Flirting is nothing more than banter intended to pass the time or to bolster the ego. I want far more than that."

Her heartbeat moved to her throat at his words. He was moving so fast…and yet, not. They'd shared a bond for years, even if he hadn't known the full extent of that bond. And he was a man used to getting what he wanted.

He moved her hand to rest on his shoulder as he eased his mouth along her arm in a slow, agonizing path, pausing to kiss the inside of her elbow through the sheer lace of her shirt. Her legs remained folded between them, serving as a final defense against his assault, but where he'd placed her hand on his shoulder, she betrayed herself by spreading her fingertips to explore the firm ridges of muscle hidden beneath his shirt.

Her hand felt as if it belonged there.

His voice low and sensuous, he said, "I've wanted more than flirting from you from the first day we met, but it took me too long to realize it. I want you. And I think you want me. Unless there's someone else?" His sea green eyes bewitched her as he studied her from beneath his dark lashes. "If there's another man in your life, tell me now."

She shook her head. With that small movement, something inside her cracked, as deeply and powerfully as ice splitting from a glacier. She slid her hand around the back of his neck and moved her knees out of the way so she could pull him toward her, so close she could feel the wash of his breath against her skin and smell the crisp, clean fabric of his shirt.

For a split second, fear enveloped her. She nearly drew back, but then his lips met hers, washing away everything but the sensation that this was right. He kissed her softly at first, sending waves of electric heat through every part of her, then more passionately as his hands came to frame her face. A murmur of pleasure escaped her, turning his kiss seductive, hungry, and full of the same pent-up need she'd felt from the moment she'd laid eyes on him in the cocktail lounge. He pulled her closer, the heat of his hands searing her skin through her thin top, warming her clear to her spine.

He smelled like heaven. Tasted better. All thought of parameters dissolved as his tongue flicked against hers. She pressed into him, craving more.

He eased her back against the sofa, deepening their kiss, tangling one hand in her hair as the other caressed her side in slow worship before cupping her breast. She welcomed his weight, reveling in the feeling of his large, hard body against her smaller one. When his thumb found her nipple through her top, she gasped.

He smiled against her mouth in response. "Still sends you?"

"Mmmm—" She melted in his hands, stunned that he remembered details she'd long ago let blur out of a sense of self-preservation.

He kissed her again, moving his thumb in a slow, tantalizing circle before easing back, teasing her, then starting all over. When his fingers finally found the top button of her blouse, she tore her mouth from his and put her hands to his shoulders. At his confused expression, she explained, "They're tricky. It's much faster if I do it."

"Be my guest." The flash of his wicked smile nearly did her in. "Because I plan to take the rest slowly."

He watched as she undid the tiny buttons one by one. When she unlooped the last one, he slipped his hands inside her blouse, spreading it wide, and tsked at the thin camisole underneath. "Sexy, but inconvenient."

Bending, he took her nipple into his mouth through the fabric. She closed her eyes, arching against him, burying her hands in his hair. In one swoop, he lifted her camisole and pulled it over her head. He murmured something unintelligible as he drank in the sight of her, admiring her as if he'd never seen a woman before, then his large hands spanned her waist and he shifted to lavish attention on her other breast.

Megan reached for the bottom of his shirt, tugging the crisp fabric free from his slacks, aching for the feel of his skin against hers. When he captured her hand to stop her, she felt she'd implode.

"Come with me," he stood, easing her from the sofa with him. Snaking one arm around her waist to pull her close, he raised an index finger to her lips, blotting away the moisture before tracing the outside of her mouth. "I want to be in your bed. Your sheets, your pillows."

Her very bones seemed to melt at the request. Only his grip held her steady. She pressed a kiss into the palm of his hand before meeting his gaze. "I want you there."

In one smooth, easy move, he lifted her and carried her to the bedroom, his mouth making love to hers until he set her in the middle of the bed. He looked down at her with unmasked desire as he unbuttoned the front of his shirt, then let it fall open as he worked at his cuffs. Her mouth went dry at the sight of his lean, muscled torso. He didn't have the build of a pampered prince; only a man who liked to test his physical limits could sculpt so perfect a body. She idly wondered what he'd done the last few years to keep himself so fit.

Not that it mattered a bit. She was about to reap the benefits of whatever trials he'd endured.

Unable to wait for him to finish, she shifted to the edge of the bed and unbuckled his belt, then took down his slacks, inch by inch, feeling emboldened enough to run her hands over his navy briefs and along his thighs as she went. Once free of his shirt, he kicked off his shoes and socks, then leaned over her and slid off her white slacks. He smiled at her thin, lace panties before he shucked them off, flicked them aside. And then they were chest to chest, skin to skin, heat to heat.

Never had she felt such overwhelming, all-encompassing want. More than when they'd been on the beach, full of young love and knowing it would be their last night together. More than in her most secretive, lust-filled dreams.

She could hardly breathe.

Pressing her arms over her head, he kissed a hot trail from her temple to the delicate spot on her neck that always drove her mad with desire. "You are so beautiful. *Bella.* My Megan."

He moved lower, his hands slowly caressing her shoulders, her sides, her stomach as his breath danced across her skin. At long last, his fingers reached to her core, finding the nub he sought at the same time his mouth came over her breast. She tilted her head back, sighing in pleasure as she braced her hands against the headboard. His hands and mouth worked magic, bringing her to the edge, easing back, then driving her mad as he brought her once more to the precipice.

"Please," she murmured, reaching for his shoulders with the intention of freeing him of his navy briefs. She lifted her head, tried to move him up to meet her kiss, but he ignored her. Instead, his head moved lower as he lifted one of her legs to his shoulder and angled his mouth against the spot his fingers had been for the briefest of tastes.

"Relax." His voice was thick as he interlaced the fingers of his free hand with hers. "Don't fight it. Let me love you."

Before she could protest, he entered her with his tongue. She bit her lip as he sucked, tasted, licked. His thumb returned to her most intimate spot, exerting just the right amount of pressure to send sparks ripping through her body. Her breath came in rapid, shallow bursts as she fought to retain control.

"Stef—"

"Let. Go."

At his whispered command, she shattered, arched, came.

He held her hips, continuing to drive her orgasm. She squeezed her eyes shut in an attempt to contain the explosion he'd caused. Stars danced on the back of her eyelids as she let her free hand drift down from the headboard. His hand found hers and captured it where he held her thigh.

Before she could recover fully, he planted a heated kiss to the inside of her hip, then moved to lie beside her, holding her legs wrapped tight around his waist as he kissed her cheek and whispered in unintelligible Italian. The rough skin of his jaw scraped her shoulder as he scattered kisses along her neck, then her collarbone. She buried her hands in his dark hair, reveling in the sensation of his skin pressed to hers while she slowly fell back to earth. As she caught her breath and her brain re-engaged, she rolled on top of him, looking for his discarded slacks, desperate to find a condom as quickly as possible so she could bring him to the same levels of ecstasy she'd just experienced.

If such a thing were possible.

"You're not going to believe this," he said when he realized her intent. "But your search will be in vain."

She stared down at him, noting the mix of concern and humor reflected in his eyes. "You don't have anything? *You?* As I recall, you even had a few with you on the beach. Not that they were all effective." At least one condom hadn't worked as expected.

"Contrary to published reports, I'm not in the habit of engaging in casual sex. So no, I don't have anything with me." He lifted an eyebrow. "Do you?"

"I might." As long as they hadn't expired. Condoms expired, didn't they? And wait…did he consider this casual sex?

One side of his mouth hitched up, his dimples pushing the thought from her mind. "You don't know?"

"Give me a sec." Reluctantly, she pushed from the bed. The cool air of the room sent a shiver along her spine as she crossed to her small en suite bathroom. She bent to search at the back of the drawer where she'd hidden the box from Anna's prying eyes.

Sheets rustled behind her. She turned to see that he'd angled himself for a view of her backside.

"You keep right on looking." His voice was sultry, seductive. Wicked. "I'll do the same."

She shouldn't be embarrassed after what he'd just done to her, right in broad daylight, but her face heated as she turned back to the vanity. She caught a glimpse of the box, grabbed it, then flipped it over as she returned to her bedroom to find the date stamp. Still good.

"Unopened, I see."

"Are you judging me?" As if having to search for protection wasn't enough to kill the mood already.

"No." He grabbed her waist and pulled her into bed beside him. After taking the box from her and setting it on the nightstand, he stroked an appreciative hand along her hip, then moved to her hipbone, her breast, and finally to cup her cheek, tipping her face so she met his gaze. "Believe me, I'm quite appreciative."

She bent to capture his mouth with hers, allowing her hands to drift to the waistband of his briefs, then to glide down over the firm muscle of his rear. She could starve, run marathons, and do more squats than an Olympic weightlifter and still not have that high and tight a butt.

It wasn't fair. And yet...

The thought was lost as he moved against her, the length of his cock pressing to her hip through his briefs as he returned her kiss. For long moments they remained like that, savoring the taste and feel of each other, until she could take no more. Easing her mouth from his, she stretched to remove his last bit of clothing, to feel the entirety of his glorious body against her own.

"Don't take this the wrong way," she murmured, admiring the sight of his broad chest and narrow waist as he grasped for a condom, "but you have improved with age."

He flashed the easy grin that made him a media darling. "Say that again in a couple of hours."

"Hours?"

He answered her with a searing kiss, one full of promise, then lifted her hips so she straddled him, his mouth still melded to hers. His hands locked around her waist, allowing him to enter her with such deliberate slowness she thought she'd die of sheer desire. He held still, waiting until she opened her eyes to see the need in his before he slid his hands up her back, freeing her to move with him in an exquisite rhythm.

"Stefano," she managed as she buried a groan in his shoulder, exhilarating in the taste of his warm skin as they matched each other move for move. He knew exactly how to drive her, to make her crave more and more and ever more. To make her forget everything but this moment.

"Tell me what you want." His breathing quickened near her ear as she clenched around him. "Tell me."

"You." *This.* Nothing in the world mattered beside the two of them, in this room, this bed, this moment. How many years had she savored the memory of their moonlit night together? How many ways had she fantasized about meeting him again, making love to him, having him bury himself inside her with yearning every bit as strong as her own? Yet the fantasies came nowhere close to what he did to her now. No one could imagine this.

Her muscles spasmed around his length, her thighs and calves wrapping tighter to trap him within her as his hands stroked her back and cupped her rear, urging her closer and closer to release. Never in her life had she gone to bed with a man on a whim. Never had making love felt as gratifying—and as terrifying—as it did in this moment, with this man. She sucked in a breath as she neared her peak. At the same moment, he lifted her, rolled her under him, then drove into her, deeper, faster, caging her hands over her head until she tilted over the edge, wave upon wave of sensation thrumming through her body. A moment later, he shuddered his own release, his lips pressed to her forehead as he fought to recapture his breath.

"Definitely better with age," he murmured as she drifted back to earth. She could only nod her agreement as he moved to her side, holding her firm against him. His hand drifted to her thigh, gently massaging the back of her leg with long, worshipful strokes.

"And you're definitely a flirt, no matter what you say," she managed. "But that's not a complaint."

She felt his smile against her temple at the same time his cell phone emitted a low buzz, the noise from somewhere on the floor startling her. His hand stilled on her thigh for a moment before he whispered, "Ignore it."

Then her bedside phone rang. She groaned and shifted to reach for it, but he grabbed her wrist and kissed her fingertips one by one. "Don't. You're occupied at the moment."

* * *

A second ring, then a third. "I need to look. It could be Anna."

Reluctantly, he released Megan, scooting to give her access to the small cordless phone perched on her nightstand. She peeked at the caller ID, blew out an exasperated breath, then picked up. In a surprisingly buoyant tone, she said, "Hi, honey. What's up?"

Stefano stretched to retrieve his own phone from the pocket of his slacks and listen to his voicemail. A call about tomorrow's meeting. He could return that later. An inquiry from his pilot about the flight schedule. A run-through of his week's schedule from his secretary. He shoved the phone back into the pocket as Megan wrapped up with Anna.

"She's leaving the beach in an hour to go to dinner," Megan said as she clicked off the phone and flipped over to face him. "Won't be back until after eight. She'll call when they leave the restaurant."

"Perfect." He punctuated the word by pulling her body back on top of his. He groaned with satisfaction as the curves of her breasts pressed against his chest, then swooped her hair out of the way so he could see her smile. "Because I desperately want to make love to you again."

"Already?"

"I did promise hours."

"You did." An enticing blush crept across her cheeks. "And I don't plan on answering the phone again."

"Then it's a promise I intend to keep." Hours wouldn't be enough. He had zero desire to untangle himself from her sheets, let alone from her, for days, weeks, months. He shifted so she could feel his cock against her thigh, watching her eyes as he did so, then raised his head and paused a breath's distance from her full, luscious lips.

"With your kind permission, of course," he ground out, eliciting a low moan of anticipation from Megan. Her eyes drifted closed as he completed the journey to meet her mouth with his own.

He took his time, deliberately, passionately, exploring every inch of her lavish body, memorizing each curve as he reveled in the silken texture of her skin. Finally, when he could take no more, he lifted her by the waist and seated her inch by inch, nearly coming undone as he watched the smoky desire filling her eyes transform to an all-out inferno. He made love to her again, guiding her movements as she rode him cautiously at first, as if testing his reaction, then with increasing abandon. The euphoria on her face as she spasmed around him, her head falling back as she cried out his name, brought him to the most explosive release of his life. Her fingers dug into his hypersensitized thighs. He covered her hands with his own to hold her in place, then closed his eyes as shudders wracked his body and his heart pounded in his ears.

This was the sin the biblical scholars wrote about, the tsunami of emotion and physical ecstasy they claimed could down a man. Well, he could be taken down. Blissfully. Everything in his being told him this was his destiny.

He could kick himself for letting Megan go the first time, for allowing himself to believe a life with Ariana was the proper course of action. How stupid he'd been. How *malleable*. His parents had known exactly what he'd do when they'd set him up with her.

At least the experience taught him to rely on his own gut instinct rather than bow to pressure from others, people who believed there was a right and a wrong choice for a prince in everything, even in the most personal of decisions.

A soft sigh escaped Megan's lips as she collapsed into him, spent. He savored her pulse pounding against his chest, thick and fast, then gradually slowing as she caught her breath. A few minutes later, he half-lifted, half-rolled her to his side and pulled her to spoon against him, which drew a long, soulful exhalation from her. Nuzzling her shoulder, he said, "That wasn't the sound of regret, I hope."

She threaded her fingers through his and squeezed. "No woman in her right mind—or body—would regret that."

"Good." They lay cocooned in her bed, neither willing to move. He relished the way her body melded to his and the cool glide of the sheets over their heated, intertwined limbs, and daydreamed about staying here forever, listening to her breathe, inhaling the sweet scent of her hair. Making love to her over and over, as long as his body could hold out.

It was vastly different than the last time he'd made love to her, yet in many ways their connection was the same. Improved, perhaps. They'd seen more of life's ups and downs and become stronger individuals as a result. From what he'd witnessed this weekend, she had more grit than any ten people. Just as adversity taught him to become his own man, it had taught her to become her own woman. What was it he'd thought when he'd first spoken to her in the bar?

Iron core. That was it. Megan possessed an iron core. But it existed in conjunction with a loving heart, the same one he'd seen when she worked with destitute families in Venezuela. It was evident in the way she looked at Anna or talked about the people with whom she lived and worked at the hotel, and even in the personal touches she'd added to her suite. The smart businesswoman who helped transform an outdated Barcelona hotel into a robust, thriving destination for social and business events was no different than the woman he'd seen joking with children as she'd taught them the basics of food and water safety.

A man would be lucky to have a woman like Megan in his life.

"I hope you didn't regret our time in Venezuela," he whispered, thinking back to their last night together. There'd been no soft sheets, no pillows, no time to luxuriate in their encounter afterward.

"No. Not for a second."

"Even when you learned you were pregnant?" It was a difficult question, but one he needed to ask.

He died a thousand small deaths as she contemplated her answer.

"I won't lie." She traced a line along his arm with one finger. "I worried about how I'd handle raising a child, especially since I knew she'd be born during my final semester. I wasn't about to drop out of school and risk both our futures. But I never once regretted being with you. Never. It was a wonderful, romantic memory to call upon whenever I faced a tough day."

His chest ached at her words, both with relief that their time together affected her the same way it had him and with the agony of knowing what it must've cost her on a day-to-day basis.

"I won't regret this today," she added, though her voice was thick with concern. "Not unless it somehow harms Anna. If that happens, I'm…well, I don't know what I'd do. I can't—I won't—do anything that hurts her. Do you understand?"

He buried a kiss in her hair. "I'd be an ass not to. Prioritizing Anna is what makes you such a good mother." If only his parents had done the same. They'd been overwhelmed with the needs of a country on the cusp of modernization, and in a sense had been parents to the entire population. Their own children had come second. Perhaps because in a way, the Barrali children needed their parents less than the country did.

It didn't make it easier for him.

He swept a stray curl behind Megan's ear. "I give you my word, here and now, that I will never hurt her. I'll protect her as if I'd raised her from birth, as if I'd known her name before she was born. No matter the price."

She pulled his hand to her lips and kissed the back of his knuckles. "Thank you for saying I'm a good mother. And thank you for your promise. It means more than you know."

He closed his eyes, forcing his breathing to stay steady in light of what he'd pledged. The price of failure might mean losing Megan—and Anna—forever.

A moment later, he said, "You must promise me something in return."

"Oh no. Now I'm in trouble. What promise *must* I make?" He could feel her light laughter as she shifted in the bed.

"If Anna ever decides to pursue culinary school, I'm paying for it."

She thwapped his leg. "Very funny."

"I'm serious." He caught her hand and held it against him while he took a quick nibble at the spot on her neck he knew made her crazy. "Speaking of which, I'm starving."

"It hasn't been that long since lunch."

"Check your bedside clock. Time flies when you're having fun. And somehow, I've worked up an appetite."

"Somehow." Amusement filled her voice as she wriggled to face him. Instantly, he missed the sensation of having his chest to her back and his cock nestled against the tight, smooth roundness of her backside. "Want me to order dinner for two?"

He raised an eyebrow. "Won't that raise questions? Given that you live here, I assume the entire staff knows your habits."

"As Anna so aptly noted, I have a drawer full of menus from the downstairs restaurants. We order dinner for two more often than I'd like to admit."

As if on cue, his stomach rumbled. "In that case, you likely know what tastes good. Order whatever you think I'd enjoy."

"Only if you select the wine."

That he could do. "There's a zinfandel on the first page of the room service menu that happens to be one of my favorites." When she referred to the wine by vintage, he nodded, then eased from the bed and strolled to the bathroom. He paused in the doorway, taking a moment to drink in the sight of her lying naked amongst the crumpled sheets. "Tell them to deliver in an hour."

At her confused frown, he flashed a smile designed to entice. "Join me in the shower in the meantime."

CHAPTER TWELVE

Precisely sixty minutes later, as Megan wrapped a towel around Stefano's waist and pressed a kiss to his torso to capture a particularly delectable-looking rivulet of water, a knock came at the door.

"This hotel has fantastic service," she commented, letting her fingers fall from the fold she'd created near his hipbone. She loved the slight curve of abdominal muscle right above that spot, having made her appreciation clear while they stood under the shower spray. "That's five-star timing."

"Want me to get it?" Stefano teased, grabbing at the ties to her robe as if to yank it from her body.

She rolled her eyes, then left him in the master bathroom as she strolled through her suite, fluffing her damp hair as she went. She hummed to herself. For the first time in weeks, she felt completely, totally relaxed.

Multiple orgasms did that to a girl. Especially when followed by a long, sultry massage in a steamy shower. The man certainly knew how to make good use of a retractable showerhead.

She sighed, then leaned against the door to ask the server to leave the food cart in the hallway. As she opened her mouth to speak, the knock came again.

"Room service," a familiar, thickly-accented male voice announced.

She backed away in surprise. "Santi?"

"*Si.*"

She crinkled her brow. Why would Santi himself deliver? Was there a staffing issue? A large conference was scheduled to begin in the hotel's new facilities tomorrow afternoon, with many of the participants arriving tonight; someone should have notified her if they were short waitstaff for room service deliveries.

She double-checked the coverage on her robe before opening the door. The head chef stood behind a rolling cart laden with covered platters, a basket of fresh bread, and two sets of silverware wrapped in perfectly rolled cloth napkins. But it was the sight of two wine glasses that put her on alert.

"Santi? What brings you here?"

"Your dinner, of course. I wished to tell Anna how much I liked her thank you note for the mandarin cake—she included a drawing of herself and your parents enjoying it—so I decided to make this particular delivery myself."

She pulled at the top of her robe, subtly making it clear she wasn't in a state to receive guests. "That's so kind of you. I'll let her know."

"She is not here?" His voice was so low she barely made out the words. "I saw her leave for the beach with a friend, but I thought she might have returned. This order, it is not for her, is it?"

Damn. "No."

"I should have known. She despises asparagus, even mine. This is for an adult, yes?" His dark eyebrows lifted. "Could it be a man?"

She shook her head at him. Santi hadn't raised six children without forming definite opinions on their love lives, and more than once he'd told her he considered her his seventh child. In a gentle, chastising tone, she whispered, "I say this with love...you're being nosy."

"Perhaps." His face softened as he rolled the cart into her entry hall, then lingered at her side. "Or perhaps it is simply worry."

"No need. I'm perfectly fine."

His dark gaze flicked toward her living area, then back to her, taking in her robe, wet hair, and makeup-free face. "I make note of what our guests order for room service, especially in the suites. For instance, I know who ordered this same zinfandel last night. And who did not place any food orders today, despite extending his stay. That same man could not tear his eyes from you the entire night of the fireworks celebration."

Against her will, her lower lip twitched. Santi noticed and placed a reassuring hand on her forearm. "Only I know, and I will say nothing. You deserve happiness in your life and I do not mean the kind one derives from a career or children. You deserve a grand romance." He whirled his hands in the air as if tossing a pizza and drew out the last two words. "But this man, he is a Casanova. You know? He plays with women. Be careful."

What would he think if she told him that Casanova wasn't so playful as to pack condoms? Instead, she leaned forward to give the burly man a kiss on the cheek. "You, Santi, are a dear. I promise, I'll be careful. Not that I'm confirming a single one of your crazy assumptions."

He let out a heavy sigh, as if resigned to watching a headstrong child learn a lesson the hard way. "In that case, I will say no more. Enjoy your meal and your evening."

She peeked under one of the lids. "If this tastes half as good as it smells, I'm in for a treat. Wait…is this other plate chocolate cake? You know I didn't order that."

"Occasional treats are good for the spirit," he said as he let himself out, "as long as you remember that long-term nourishment is more important."

So much for Santi's pledge to say no more.

Stefano joined her at the table a few minutes later. He'd replaced his towel with the hotel robe that she'd left hanging on the back of the bathroom door. The bright white of the robe contrasted sharply with his smooth olive skin and damp hair, making her desire his touch all over again.

Still, the atmosphere in the room seemed different than only moments before, when they'd shared an intimate shower. The spell was broken. Megan's trepidation about having Stefano in her and Anna's lives returned.

Damned Santi and his parental warnings.

Stefano must have sensed the change in her, because his mouth formed a grim line as he uncorked the wine, took the seat beside hers, then poured a half-glass for each of them.

After a few moments of silence, he said, "The call I received earlier was about an appointment I have tomorrow at noon in Sarcaccia. I'm scheduled to meet with the head of our country's transportation department to discuss progress on system upgrades."

A nice dry topic for dinner conversation. "Sounds important. Does this mean you're flying back tonight?"

He swirled the wine in his glass before taking a sip. "I had a voice mail from my pilot asking the same question. It's a quick flight, so I told him we'll go in the morning."

She wanted to know when he'd return to Barcelona, but knew better than to ask. Instead, she teased, "As long as you're not exhausted from your busy weekend."

"No. If anything, I feel rejuvenated." He scooted his chair closer to hers, handing her one of the silverware bundles before removing the domed covers from their dinner plates. He let out a low growl of approval as the scent of freshly-roasted chicken and steamed asparagus filled the room.

"Our head chef, Santi," she explained. "It's one of his specialties. I have no idea what he does to make it smell so divine. Something with lemon and his home-grown basil."

Stefano tapped his chicken once with the tines of his fork as he swallowed his first bite. "This is decadent. Did he also design the menu for the grand reopening celebration? The halibut that night was the best I've eaten. It's not an easy dish to pull off for such a large group."

"He did. Santi's a gem." An inquisitive one, but still a gem.

They spent the rest of the meal discussing Stefano's travels, both personal and professional, and the range of hotels and restaurants he'd had the opportunity to visit. Megan commented on the different management styles of the hotels with which she was familiar, noting when she'd visited some of the same locations.

When they finished their meal, she rolled the cart to the outside hallway and rang for pickup while Stefano carried the wine bottle to the coffee table. He made space for her beside him on the sofa. Once she was settled, he said, "The Grandspire is well-run, top to bottom. I haven't seen a single misstep during my entire stay. You must be proud of what you've accomplished here."

"I am. Though I can't take credit for the food."

He smiled at that, then his expression turned serious. "You mentioned at breakfast yesterday that your work here is nearly complete. When will you start looking for your next position?"

"Soon." She adjusted her robe so she could put her feet on the coffee table. "I haven't had much time to myself the last few weeks with the grand reopening, but I've put out a few feelers. Mostly in the United States, so Anna can see more of my parents. But I'm open to Europe, if the right school is available and the city has frequent flights to the U.S." Of course, with Stefano in Anna's life—for however long—staying in Europe would make visitation easier for him.

If Stefano stayed in her life. True, he'd appeared touched while looking at Anna's pictures on her phone and he'd seemed enchanted by Anna today. He'd said all the right things and acted as if he genuinely wanted to see his daughter again and get to know her better. But how would he feel in a week? In a year? Once he returned to his life in Sarcaccia and reality set in, would he be so anxious to do the hard work of building and maintaining a relationship? It wouldn't be easy to find gaps in his schedule that would allow for discreet visits. Even if he did, would he lose his fascination with his daughter? Children Anna's age could be trying at times, even in the best of circumstances, and who knew what Anna might be like as a teenager?

Of course…all that left aside whatever was happening between the two of them.

Stefano shifted on the sofa so he could pull Megan's legs across his lap. He smelled of her soap, her shampoo. Yet on his skin, the familiar formulas took on a different quality. More robust. Definitely more sexy. He rested one arm across the back of the sofa while his other hand settled high on her leg. She expected him to flirt, maybe suggest they return to the bedroom in what little time they had left. Instead, his demeanor remained serious.

"Do you mind if I see Anna again? I know I told her I'd visit, but I want you to be comfortable with it."

"No, I don't mind. In fact, I'd like it very much." She put her hand on his arm, keeping the touch firm rather than seductive. "But we'll have to be careful."

"I told you, I won't do anything to hurt her. I keep my commitments."

Like his broken engagement? She exhaled, wondering how that thought popped into her head. It was one more complication in what was already a complicated situation.

"I understand if you're worried I'll make promises to her I can't keep." His fingers flexed against her thigh. "I imagine every parent disappoints their children from time to time, but I'll endeavor not to disappoint mine. If I tell her I'm coming to visit, I'll find a way."

Megan had no doubt he believed every word he said. "I know that's what you want, but my concerns are broader than simply having you show up when you say you will. What happens when friends or relatives learn you're visiting her? Take tonight: If the reception desk sent Julia and Marta up rather than buzzing me first, there would have been some explaining to do. I don't think either of us are prepared for that. Anna definitely isn't."

Santi would raise questions, too, if Stefano appeared in Barcelona again. Worse, if Santi connected the dots and guessed that Stefano fathered Anna, she doubted the chef would be able to keep it to himself. He'd tell his wife, at the very least. From there, who knew where the information might go.

"Still," Megan continued, "if you want to visit her, I'm sure we can find a way to make it work."

"And you?" His voice was low, both sensuous and cautious. "I want to see you again."

She tried for a lighthearted answer. "Tough to see Anna without seeing me. The suite's not that big."

"You know what I mean."

She let her gaze fall to his long fingers, still splayed across the top of her leg. Anyone looking at the two of them sitting on the sofa would think she and Stefano were a passionate newlywed couple, unable to keep their hands off each other for the duration of a conversation; she knew better. "I don't know if that's wise."

Today had been a gift. A memory she'd cherish the rest of her life, just as she did the memory of their first encounter. But they both knew there was no future in it, not for the two of them. His life could never be hers. Even if she wanted to give up her freedom for a royal life—assuming the Barrali family would accept an American nobody from Minnesota as a romantic partner for their son—she couldn't force that life upon Anna. She wouldn't.

Stefano would soon realize the futility of it, too. While they'd be forever bound by Anna, eventually the romantic aspect of their relationship would end, and Megan's heart would break. She couldn't stare that heartbreak in the face every time Stefano wanted to spend time with their daughter. She definitely couldn't stand it if—when—the press discovered Anna's parentage, they also discovered that the fling hadn't ended at Anna's conception. The longer she let this go on, the greater the chance that could happen.

What would such a revelation do to Anna? Would she harbor dreams of them becoming a family and living in the palace in Sarcaccia, not realizing what that would truly mean? It was too big a risk to take.

"You're worried about what it will do to Anna if we're involved."

"I have to be."

He cupped her chin, tilting her face so she could see the determination in his expression. "I told you. I want more than flirting from you."

She smiled at that, hoping to hide the sadness practicality brought her. "What we did today went beyond flirting."

"I want to make up for what we lost in Venezuela." He caressed her cheek with his thumb, causing her stomach to do a slow flip-flop against her will.

"That's not possible."

"Anything we want is possible. We only need to want it." He moved his hands to her waist, then knelt on the floor between the coffee table and sofa and looked up at her. "Megan Hallberg, I want you to marry me. I want you to be my wife."

CHAPTER THIRTEEN

Megan's breath stilled in her lungs as she stared at Stefano, not quite believing what he'd said.

I want you to marry me.

The thought of marrying him made her giddy. Waking up next to him each morning, laughing together over coffee, spending weekends with Anna at the park…if only it could be. If only he hadn't been born a Barrali. If only it was something more than a fantasy. Still, it charmed her that he could dream of a fantasy life together.

A flinch of his hands at her waist made her realize he was waiting for her response.

"Well, when you said you could be impetuous, you meant it."

Crinkles appeared at the corners of his eyes. "Making love to you today was impetuous, but the feeling behind it was not. Nor is my proposal."

This was planned? She blinked in confusion. "Come again?"

"I've thought about it from the moment you told me about Anna."

The happy flip-flop of her stomach settled to lead. So *that's* why he proposed. Anna. She should've known. She forced a lighthearted tone to cover her emotional tumult. "I find it hard to believe you were considering marriage when you were so angry you left me in the hallway on the conference floor."

One side of his mouth hitched into a dimple-inducing smile. She suspected he knew exactly what that smile did to her.

"Maybe the thought came a moment after that," he admitted. "I was furious when you told me. It was a shock to learn I was a father and that you'd kept such a secret for so long. But once I understood that it wasn't intentional on your part, I realized all that we could have together. It makes such perfect sense, I haven't been able to think of anything else."

She glanced down at his strong hands, still encircling her waist as he knelt before her, then back to his bewitching eyes, trying to discern the truth in their depths. "You don't think that's impetuous?"

"Fast," he acknowledged, "but not impetuous. I've never been more certain of anything in my life."

He rose to sit beside her on the sofa and bracketed her hands with his. "You don't have to answer me now. In fact, you shouldn't. It's a big decision and you should take time to consider it."

As long as he'd taken to consider it?

"Living in the palace would mean a significant lifestyle change for you and for Anna. However, I can make arrangements to keep my block of rooms more private. The laws in Sarcaccia were recently changed to prevent paparazzi from following or photographing children, so Anna would have protections that aren't available in most other countries...protections I didn't even have as a child. There are dozens of high end hotels that would love to have someone of your expertise on staff and the country's new conference center will soon be hiring, so there are options for you if you wish to continue working. All it would take is a phone call or two for you to find the perfect position. The school system is excellent. Anna can study anything she wishes. Even—dare I say it—cooking."

Megan closed her eyes for a moment, overwhelmed by his grand plans. He'd thought through everything...everything except the real reason any couple should marry. "That's all very practical, but—"

"We have a connection, Megan. It's more than the fact we share a child. It's *us*. Time hasn't dimmed that spark. If anything, we're old enough now to understand how special it is. How rare and valuable."

She opened her eyes, intent on stopping him from uttering another word, but the heat in his gaze nearly made her say yes on the spot. Spending her life with this man—talking about each other's days over a glass of wine each evening, watching him with Anna, sharing her bed with him every night—would be a dream come true in so many ways. But it was only a dream. As he said, they shared a *spark*. A lasting, fulfilling marriage required more than a spark—no matter how hot that spark—even if he'd thought through the logistics of everything else. Logistics plus spark weren't good enough for her.

She wanted a marriage like the deeply passionate one her parents enjoyed. A marriage that would endure. A marriage built on love, trust, and mutual respect. Not a marriage built on hot sex during a college fling and a weekend in Barcelona.

Years spent raising Anna on her own taught her the importance of unconditional love. She wanted no less from a spouse. She wouldn't marry simply for convenience. In the end, it couldn't endure.

She pulled her hands from his and stood, needing space.

"I'll think about it, but I can't imagine an answer other than no."

"Why?"

She turned to face him from the opposite side of the coffee table, surprised that he sounded stunned by her response. "If you'd known I was pregnant before you proposed to Ariana, maybe things would be different. Maybe you and I would have taken that opportunity to reevaluate our relationship. Even so, I suspect things wouldn't have changed." She spread her hands wide. "We parted ways for a reason, Stefano. We knew we were from two different worlds, with completely different plans for our lives, and that nothing could come of it. I finished school, you went home to your military career and to a new relationship. As nostalgic as it may make us feel to look back a decade, let's be honest with ourselves. What we had was no more than a fling. A very hot fling, but a fling."

He leaned back on the sofa and folded his hands over the knot of his robe, his ease suggesting he'd expected her to say as much. "It was more than a fling to me, I just didn't know it at the time."

She started to speak, but he waved her off. "I learned over the years that what we shared emotionally was far more than what one experiences in a fling. I told you that I don't do casual sex. There's a reason. You changed me. Everyone I've dated since then has paled in comparison." A muscle in his jaw twitched as he spoke. "You still have that effect on me. And I think I have that effect on you. I'm not the only one who's not into casual sex."

"How would you know that?"

"*Bella*," the word came out as a tease, "you couldn't find the condoms. And when you did, it was an unused box."

She burned to point out that she had a young child and a full-time job. She lived in the very building where she worked. Casual sex couldn't be on the agenda, even if she wanted.

But…she didn't. The few men she'd dated over the years hadn't fired her blood the way Stefano did. Not enough to justify the risks a wild night in the sack would entail.

Even so, that wasn't a justification for marriage. He wouldn't have proposed to her if not for Anna. He couldn't love her, just as she couldn't possibly love him. Who fell in love in a weekend? Falling into *lust*, she could believe. That they had in spades. Seeing him on her sofa wearing nothing but a hotel robe and a mischievous, self-satisfied grin made her want to climb in his lap and wrap her legs around him all over again. If she succumbed to that temptation, she knew that in time, love was a possibility. For her.

For him? She suspected that if she spent a few days or weeks with him in his world, his fascination with her would wane.

She struggled to keep her voice level so he'd see things more clearly. "If what you say is true, if you truly believed we had a….a connection, then you could have found me any time you wanted." He hadn't, which told her exactly why he waxed poetic now. He discovered she'd borne his child. *That's* what changed him.

He shook his head as if he'd anticipated this argument, as well. "By the time I realized the enormity of what we shared, you were lost to me. Living and working on a different continent at best, married and settled at worst. It wouldn't have been right to phone out of the blue and interrupt your life, especially given how we left things." He waved in the direction of the windows. "Who'd think we'd find each other again in Spain, of all places? That we'd both be single and that we'd share a wonderful child? We've been given an opportunity here to right a wrong. To make a different decision than we did when we left Venezuela."

Megan's heart seemed to shrink in on itself as the words left Stefano's mouth. "No. What we've been given is a bubble. A place where nothing and no one can bother us, where we can enjoy each other—our connection—without the realities of the outside world. But bubbles are fragile, delicate things, Stefano. They don't last. No matter how much you may shield them, they eventually pop. Tomorrow, you'll head back to Sarcaccia and you'll realize that what we have isn't sustainable." She mimicked his wave toward the lights of the city, glittering to life now that night was falling. "Not out there."

And not as long as he saw marrying her as the *right* thing to do...tantamount to an obligation.

He shrugged. "I won't."

His confidence was infuriating. Sexy as all hell, but infuriating. "Then let me approach this another way. First, my life here is good. Very good. I have a fantastic career, one I built through hard work. I'm also free to come and go as I please. That can't be duplicated no matter who you call about employment or how you arrange your living quarters at the palace. Second, while I can pull off a night with dignitaries like I did for the grand reopening, I don't move in your circles on a day-to-day basis and frankly, I don't think I'd want to. That's what's expected of someone who lives in the palace and is part of the Sarcaccian royal family."

"But—"

She kept right on going, afraid if she didn't, she'd never say what he needed to hear. "Third, and most important, even if I wanted to get married and live in Sarcaccia with you, even if I wanted to take a stab at living a public life, even if marriage felt like the *right* thing for us to do" —she hoped he understood her choice of emphasis— "there's a third person involved. Doing what's best for Anna trumps anything I might want for myself."

Love being foremost on that priority list. Not that it was on offer.

He remained quiet for a moment after she finished. He leaned forward, putting his elbows to his knees and steepling his fingers to his chin. "May I speak now?"

She exhaled. "Go ahead."

"That's a long list of reasons to say no. They all boil down to the fact you don't trust me." It wasn't an accusation, but a statement of realization.

Megan bit back a groan. His light bulb moment was that she didn't trust him with her independence; in truth, she didn't trust him with her heart.

"How can I? I don't understand how you can trust yourself." She folded her arms over her stomach. "This is the first time we've seen each other in a decade. Even back then, we only spent a short time together. On top of that, you just discovered that you have a daughter. As in, less than forty-eight hours ago. How can you truly know what you want? What's *right?*"

"Because I do."

With that response, she let loose her penultimate argument, the one she'd been hoping never to reveal, but that he needed to address, for himself if not for her. "Did you know it the last time you asked a woman to marry you?"

CHAPTER FOURTEEN

Megan's outburst couldn't have shocked him more.

The air stilled between them. After all these years, the horrible sequence of events leading to the Ariana catastrophe still rankled. Tension squeezed Stefano's skull as he said, "I should explain that."

Her expression transformed from serious to exasperated, then from exasperated to apologetic in a matter of seconds. She forked her hands through her hair, finally flipping the air-dried strands so they fell down her back. "No, you don't have to. It's a private matter. I bring it up only so you can consider what—"

"I know I don't *have* to, but I need to. Not to the world, but to you. It's a huge part of why I know this" —he angled a finger toward Megan, then himself— "is right. Even if you distrust me so much you're standing on the opposite side of the table to talk."

Her gaze flicked to the table, then quickly back to him. Something in his choice of words bothered her. He could see it in her expression. But what?

"I'm trying to discuss this rationally," she finally replied, "but when I'm close to you it's distracting."

"A point in my column." He patted the empty space beside him. "Come. Sit. I'll tell you what happened so you can make a decision based on full information. Then I'll kiss you goodnight and return to my suite while you take all the time you need to think about my proposal."

"I suspect you'll say whatever it takes to get your way."

"Perhaps…if my way is right."

Her arms remained crossed, as if she needed to defend herself from him. "Have you ever been told that you're pushy, Your Highness?"

"Of course. It's part of the official prince job description. Lucky for you, I'm not half as pushy as the twins."

"From what I gather, that's not a high standard." Stefano's older brothers, Crown Prince Vittorio and Prince Alessandro, were known for their identical stubborn streaks as well as their identical looks. She took a few steps toward the sofa and held up her index finger. "I don't want details."

"I promise, only the highlights."

"Then go ahead." She sat on the opposite end of the sofa rather than the closer spot he'd indicated and folded her legs under her so he wouldn't pull her feet into his lap again. Not ideal, but he'd take it.

He settled in, mentally preparing for Megan's reaction to what would be the most embarrassing admission of his life, a truth only he and Ariana knew completely. "The wheels were put in motion before I left you in Venezuela, only I didn't know it. I didn't sleep a wink for those fifteen hours on the plane, even though we'd spent the previous night at the beach. Frankly, you were too much on my mind. When I landed, I expected to spend the next few days sleeping off the flight before reporting for military duty, but my parents had other plans."

"A welcome home party?"

"Only to someone with a sick sense of humor." Like his parents. "It was more of a welcome-to-your-royal-duty party…on no notice."

She grimaced. "Doesn't sound celebratory."

"No." He exhaled, suddenly as bone-tired as if he'd been transported back to that day. "The king and queen organized a massive charity event for the afternoon of my return, a garden party at the palace to raise money for our country's animal shelters. I was expected to attend and host a table of dignitaries. My parents also neglected to tell me that I'd be hosting that table with Ariana

Bassi. I didn't know until I sat down at the table and saw our names listed together in the program."

Frown lines puckered her brow. "Wouldn't you need time to prepare for an event like that? Or to discuss it with Ariana?"

Stefano shook his head. "Before Venezuela, I attended similar charity affairs a couple times a week. I functioned pretty well off the cuff by that point and my parents knew it. I didn't even think much of the pairing with Ariana at first. She was a close childhood friend and her parents are renowned for their philanthropic work with animals. However, it became clear to me—to both of us—during the few first minutes of the event that my parents arranged everything in the hopes we'd get together."

Megan surprised him by smiling. "Parents do like to see their children happy. Matchmaking has been known to accomplish that."

"True," he replied. "But matchmaking is about more than happiness where my parents are concerned. In fact, 'happiness' barely makes their priority list. When the Barrali line runs out, our government automatically dissolves and control of the country returns to Italy. No one in Sarcaccia wants that. We value our independence and our unique culture too much to become subjects of another country, even if it's what a treaty dictates."

She nodded, acknowledging Sarcaccia's well-known treaty with Italy. "You have a large family. Surely your parents aren't worried about grandchildren?"

"They're *always* worried. As were my father's parents and grandparents before him, I suspect." He eased closer to her, wanting to fill some of the empty space between them. "From the time my siblings and I were old enough to date, my parents stressed that it's our royal duty to wed and produce heirs, regardless of our personal feelings on the subject. Our forebears fought hard for independence. The people of Sarcaccia count on us to maintain it."

She smoothed her hands over her knees, sliding her robe so it covered her calves. "Even so, your parents' timing wasn't the best with you about to begin your military service."

"They were desperate. Their attempts to find spouses for my older brothers failed—I didn't learn of it until months later, but while I was in Venezuela, Alessandro threatened to move out of the palace if they refused to back off—so they decided to take a crack at me during the few days I'd be under their roof." He blew out an agitated breath. "My siblings encouraged it, since they liked Ariana and they knew it'd keep my parents from meddling in their lives. Guests saw the way my parents were watching me with Ariana and the gossip started. By the end of the afternoon, I felt as if I'd been tossed aboard a runaway train with no means to brake."

Megan pushed off the sofa without a word. For a split second, Stefano wondered what he'd said to upset her—he hadn't even gotten to the worst of it yet—but relaxed when she opened the refrigerator and withdrew two bottles of water. She handed him one cool bottle, then popped the lid on the other before taking her seat once more. "Certainly Ariana had something to say about all this?"

"She was as surprised as I was by the manner in which our co-hosting duties were being discussed at the party, as if we were an item. On the other hand, her parents were thrilled with the attention. Knowing my parents, I suspect they made Ariana's parents feel as though they were performing a service to their country by having her stand by my side at such a prestigious event."

"Ouch."

That was probably the best word to describe the entire afternoon. "Luckily, Ariana was a good sport. When no one was listening, she cracked jokes about being scouted as a brood mare due to her bloodlines."

One side of Megan's mouth lifted into a smile. "I think I like this woman."

He didn't point out that everyone liked Ariana. That had been the problem. Witty, poised, well-educated, beautiful…everyone in attendance considered her the perfect princess candidate. "The awkward setup and party gossip weren't the worst part of the day. That I could handle. It wasn't as if my parents hadn't tried to set me up before, even if it hadn't been done in such a public manner."

He set his unopened water bottle on the table, then waited until he caught Megan's gaze with his own before continuing. "Since press from across Europe attended the event, there was far more attention paid to the gossip than usual. The evening news carried a story portraying Ariana as my date and showed sensationalized photos of every moment we were together. For instance, when I stepped behind her to move a chair out of the way, a photo was snapped from an angle that hid the chair and made it look like I had my hands on her lower back. Worse, both of us had idiotic grins on our faces. It looked like we were smiling because I was grabbing her in a rather inappropriate manner, not because we were amused by the woman across the table who regaled us with stories about her dogs. Of course, *she* was cut out of the pictures."

"Of course."

"By morning, the entire country was mad with marriage gossip. One tabloid speculated that I'd come home early to be with her. Another ran a wild story saying she'd pined away while I was gone because we'd had a secret relationship for years. They reported that the palace would never have had us co-host a table unless we planned to wed. All nonsense, all with quotes from unnamed and so-called insider sources, but the lies sold papers and gave the newscasters something salacious to report. No one seemed able to resist a cooked-up story about a returning prince and a high society girl."

Megan's upper lip pinched. "Slow news day in Sarcaccia, huh?"

"That's one explanation." He was glad Megan could find humor in the situation. To this day the cascade of events boggled his mind. "My father woke me at five a.m. to warn me that I would be overwhelmed if I stepped outside the palace gates. Dozens of reporters had staked out the main entry. Apparently the media were set up outside Ariana's apartment before she even made it home from the party that night. She couldn't get into her building without running a gauntlet of cameras, so she called her parents from her car for help. They checked her into a hotel near the palace until security could be arranged. The press set up on the sidewalk outside the hotel within minutes of her arrival, essentially trapping her there."

"That's crazy." Megan's eyes widened as she finally grasped the enormity of the situation. "I had no idea. Gossip about European royalty doesn't exactly make headlines in the States. Not unless it's about the British, of course." Her tone made it clear that, though she realized the mess wasn't one of his own creation, she didn't see how he'd gone from overwhelmed party host to royal fiancé.

That part was hard to explain, even now.

"I couldn't quite believe it, either. I turned on the morning news to see for myself. I was stunned. The whole story was blown out of proportion. My father, on the other hand, seemed extraordinarily pleased with the coverage. Downright gleeful, in fact, and if you've ever watched an interview with my father, you know 'gleeful' isn't a word one associates with King Carlo. When he tried to convince me that the publicity was good for the country, I realized how carefully he'd orchestrated the whole thing. He'd even ensured that the press in attendance were those most likely to sensationalize the story. Given my level of exhaustion and the fact I was twenty-two and full of fire, I raged at him as I never had before and never have since. After hurling a few choice four-letter words his way, I stormed out of the palace in nothing but a pair of sweatpants and walked right past the gate guards and across the street to Ariana's hotel to make sure she was all right and to apologize for my abominable family."

"Ah." Megan sucked in her lower lip.

"Saw those photos, did you?" He wondered if anyone on the planet hadn't seen the shots. He'd looked a fool—barefoot, shirtless, unshaven, with pillow-flattened hair—and his lack of forethought gave the photographers everything they craved. In railing against the situation, he'd made it worse by tenfold. "I can only imagine what you thought."

The look on her face made it clear that he couldn't. Not unless his imagination went to murder.

CHAPTER FIFTEEN

"Well...I take it you weren't making an early morning run to see your lady love," she said, paraphrasing the caption that had appeared with several of the shots. Her tone was light, but the hastily-covered flash of pain in her eyes let him know that whether she considered their time in Venezuela was a fling or not, the photos wounded her deeply, and it was the kind of pain that came only after one experienced the all-consuming anger of betrayal.

It finally occurred to him that those shots had to be the first thing that popped up when she'd searched the Internet in her attempt to contact him. Back then, they were everywhere.

He fought the urge to reach across the sofa, pull her into his arms and tell her that now he understood, truly understood, how hard it must've been for her when she learned of her pregnancy, then discovered he'd become engaged. He doubted the act would be welcome at the moment. Less so when he finished his explanation.

"Not even close," he said. "The hotel doorman saw me coming and hustled me up to Ariana's suite, despite the fact I'd bloodied my feet on the courtyard gravel and looked like a vagrant."

He gritted his teeth for a moment, remembering how nauseated he'd felt when Mrs. Bassi opened the door, gave him a crisp nod, then left him alone with Ariana without comment. "Ariana was standing to the side of her hotel room window trying to see the reason for the sudden commotion without letting the photographers spot her. She was still wearing her dress from the afternoon before and looked completely overwhelmed by it all. At that moment, I realized what an idiot I'd been to do something so—dare I say it—*impetuous* by crossing the street, thinking I was going to somehow protect her with my presence."

Megan finished her water and crossed the room to set the empty bottle on the kitchen counter. "I take it she didn't throw you out?"

"No. It wasn't really an option, given the crush outside. We ordered room service and had breakfast while I bandaged my feet and tried to figure out how I was going to get back to the palace without making things worse."

"She must've been as cranky as you were," she said as she returned to the sitting area.

"She was." He let out a curt laugh. "But we bonded over the fact we'd allowed ourselves to be manipulated by our own parents. I finally made it back to the palace a few hours later, when my sister took pity on me and sent a car to the hotel's rear entrance so I could escape. I avoided my father for the rest of the day by shutting myself in my brother Alessandro's palace apartment and drinking obscene amounts of his Scotch. When I called Ariana that night to check on her, we ended up talking about our childhoods, the upbringing children of privilege have as opposed to the way the other ninety-nine percent of the world is raised—a difference that was made clear to me in Venezuela—and I ended up saying that we were good enough friends, we should just get married and make our families happy. At least we'd never torture our children the way our parents tortured us. And she said, 'Why not?'"

Megan's jaw slackened. "Why not? *That* was her answer?"

"Romantic, isn't it? Like a fairy tale." Unable to hold still any longer, he levered himself from his seat and paced. All these years later, his anger still burned. Not at his parents, or even at the situation, but at himself. His foolish, rash, rebellious young self. "I wasn't serious when I asked. I doubt she was when she accepted. If you call that an acceptance. We were young and incredibly reckless in many ways. But neither of us could take it back once it was said, and the next thing we knew, our parents arranged a press conference and we were standing in the palace drawing room answering questions about how much we had in common, how we'd attended school together as children, how she would continue to train for dressage competition even if she became a royal…all while flashbulbs blinded us. Ariana and I went through it in a daze."

He stopped pacing long enough to face Megan. "It wasn't until I left the palace a few days later to start my military training that I was able to think clearly and realize what a complete mess I'd made of my life. And of Ariana's."

Megan had the same pensive look as when she accused him of wanting to spoil Anna.

"What?" he asked.

"I suspect you *were* serious when you asked."

Hadn't she heard a word he'd said? "How could you—"

"Not because you were in love with her, but because you wanted to take control of the situation. Oh, you wanted to protect her, too. But even your need to protect those around you often boils down to a need for control. It's the same reason you stormed out of the palace and walked to Ariana's hotel. You didn't want your parents or even your duties as a royal to steer your private life. But the results of your actions weren't what you hoped."

He opened his mouth to argue, but thought better of it. Instead, he retrieved his water from the coffee table and took a long, slow drink. How could this woman, a woman who hadn't seen him in ages, make him question everything he believed about himself?

Worse, her observations could be right.

His parents had made a strong case for a marriage to Ariana. The two of them had much in common, her parents were well-respected and moved in the same circles as the royal family, and the country would greatly benefit. He'd known, on a common sense level, that it was a good match for him as a royal. But he'd wanted to dictate the terms. To *control* things.

Then—too late—he'd realized he felt no passion for Ariana, nor she for him. Common sense alone couldn't make a marriage. Damn his twenty-two year-old self.

He rolled the water bottle between his palms, contemplating how best to respond.

"Never thought of it like that?" Megan asked, her voice low.

"No. And I'm not saying it's true. It was a long time ago. Who knows anymore?"

"I do. You were born to a unique family, where virtually every move you make is public. You lack control in so many things, but you crave it like any other human being." She eased off the sofa and came to stand beside him. Gently, she put her hands to his chest, fanning her fingers before gazing up at him. "Do you remember when I told you about Anna and you said we'd talk in twenty-four hours? I mentioned that you had a flight home in the morning, and you said—"

"The flight goes when I say it goes," he repeated, surprised at her memory. "At least that I can control."

"When things aren't going the way you want, it's your first instinct."

"There wasn't anything wrong with asking for time," he argued. "I needed to cool off. It was the right thing to do."

"In that instance. But is it always?" Her hands dropped from his chest after giving him a firm pat, but she kept her face upturned to his. "As touched as I am that you proposed to me, I suspect it's for the same reason. To gain control of an uncontrollable situation."

He grinned at that, pointedly looking her up and down to emphasize the fact she wore nothing more than a hotel robe, one he could remove with a single flick of the wrist. "You don't think having the best sex of his life might drive a man to propose?"

"Perhaps." A blush tinged her cheeks. He could swear her eyes glistened before she looked down to the floor.

"Then think about it." He reached for her chin and tipped her face up to his once more. Her skin felt soft and supple beneath his fingertips. He could caress her face all day and never tire of it. "Ariana and I both knew we'd made a mistake. It took us a while to untangle it, but we did. I knew then that I'd never make that mistake again. I knew when I proposed to a woman, really proposed, it would have nothing to do with my parents or my duty to my country. It would have everything to do with the woman."

She covered his hands with her own, squeezed his fingers, then stepped back. Once again, she seemed to need physical space to think. He waited several painful seconds before she spoke. "I'm going to take that as a great compliment, Stefano, but everything you told me convinces me that a marriage between us could never be the dream you envision. The media went crazy over nothing more than an apparent date at a palace party. What will happen if they discover you fathered a child? I could never protect myself from that, let alone protect Anna. You'll want to control that story, but it can't be controlled. And that's setting aside any discussion of the obvious reasons people get married."

How could he convince her he'd never allow her to come to harm? That in this case, the risk would be worth the reward? "I learned what not to do from that experience. So did my family. My missteps with the press—and by missteps, I don't mean the fact I literally bloodied my feet—taught me how to handle myself in public better than years of parental lectures ever did. I can enjoy my life the way *I* want to enjoy it, but by making careful decisions rather than sprinting before I think. We only have to want it to make it work."

On the last sentence, she looked as stricken as if he'd hit her. "Megan?"

Before she could answer, chimes pealed from a small clock near the television, marking the passing of another hour. She squared her shoulders at the sound. In a tone more suited to discussion of a budget proposal than a marriage proposal, she said, "You've given me a lot to think about, but the answer is no."

Frustration boiled in his gut. Did she truly believe he'd asked on a whim? She should see that, given all that had happened between them, marriage was the most logical course of action.

And dammit, he meant it when he told her she was the best sex of his life. Never in his thirty-two years had a woman affected him as Megan did, either physically or emotionally. He'd tell her that, too, if it would make a difference.

But given that she'd accused him of saying whatever it might take to get his way, he doubted she'd believe it.

He studied her for a moment, but her planted feet, crossed arms, and resolute expression showed no signs of changing. He shot a pointed look at the clock. "How about if I change out of this robe, give you a very proper kiss goodnight before Anna returns, and promise to call? Would that be acceptable?"

Her nod was barely perceptible. His instinct was to tell her everything would work out, that he knew in his gut this was for the best. Instead, he turned toward the bedroom to retrieve his clothes. He *had* given her a lot to think about. Perhaps she needed time to analyze the pros and the cons herself so she could come to the same conclusion he did. She'd change her mind.

When he emerged from the bedroom, she stood staring sightlessly out the windows, uncharacteristic furrows etching her forehead. He flashed a grin when she twisted to face him, hoping to lighten her mood. "What are you doing next weekend?"

Her eyebrows arched in surprise. "I have no idea. I've been so busy with the grand reopening, I haven't thought about it."

"Let's spend Saturday together. You, me, and Anna. I'll stay at another hotel, one where no one will associate you with me. I'll call once I'm in town and we'll find a place to meet. It'll give me a chance to get to know Anna better and I'll show you how I've learned to deal with the media when I need to do so."

"The media?"

"There won't be any. Trust me."

He felt like a teenager finagling a date with the prom queen as he waited for her response. Thankfully, she nodded.

"Good. Then it's settled. In the meantime, think about what I said."

"Stefano—"

"What's the baseball phrase? Three strikes and you're out?" He couldn't resist. He reached for her waist and held her fast. The smell of her freshly-washed, warm skin combined with the scent that was uniquely hers, making him want to take her to the bedroom again. He smoothed her hair back from her face. "My first strike was leaving you in Venezuela. The second was being so young and naive as to believe I should satisfy my family's and my country's needs before my personal ones, and convincing myself that doing so would make everyone happy. I don't want to have a strike three. I want you in my life. I want Anna in my life. I want the home run. I want what's right for all of us."

She blinked. "Did you just use a baseball analogy?"

"I did. Did I get it wrong?"

"Not the analogy, no." He could see desire in her eyes, along with an internal battle that made her hold back.

Her gaze dropped to his chest and her hands followed. He stilled as she spread her fingers wide, sending a wave of heat through him. He could feel her breath against his neck as her hands moved to his arms. "All I can commit to is the weekend. And for Anna's sake, I'd prefer it if we don't let on that anything happened between us. All right?"

He leaned in and gave her a chaste kiss, resisting the urge to linger with his lips against hers. "Good night, Megan."

If he read her correctly, it would leave her wanting more.

CHAPTER SIXTEEN

Stretching nearly a mile from Plaça Catalunya to the Barcelona waterfront, where a statue of Christopher Columbus commemorated Spain's expedition to the New World, the wide boulevard known as La Rambla attracted both locals and tourists at all hours. During the day, tourists walked, maps in hand, as they searched for the side streets that would take them to the Gothic Quarter or one of the city's numerous museums. Street performers draped in metallic cloth positioned themselves atop painted silver boxes, motionlessly mimicking the Statue of Liberty or King Tut, waiting in silence for tips as music wafted over the crowd. Shoppers perused the flower stands, selecting the blooms that would grace their tables that evening. Artists hawked their wares, tour operators handed out pamphlets, and restaurateurs invited passersby to have a seat at their tables. In the meantime, groups of women paused for refreshments while shopping at one of the nearby department stores, purchased fresh vegetables at the local market, or picked up coffee on their way to work.

At night, as lights twinkled from high in the trees that framed the street's central cobblestone strip, families strolled, window shopping between stops for dinner and dessert. Jugglers and musicians practiced their craft while teenagers threaded skateboards through the crowd and lovers paused to steal kisses.

However, at seven a.m. on a Saturday, quiet reigned over most of the street. Catalans preferred to sleep in on weekends, so other than Megan and Anna, the only people about were those quietly preparing for the late morning onslaught of tourists. A street performer perched on an upside down milk crate, studying his cheekbones in a handheld mirror as he applied face paint. Behind him, a city employee hummed softly as he brushed a discarded candy wrapper into his long-handled dustpan. Down the street, a garbage collector heaved bags filled with the previous night's waste into his truck.

It was Megan's favorite time to explore the city, when the light breeze carried scents of fresh-baked bread and brewed coffee rather than rush hour car exhaust. This morning, however, the further she walked the more unsettled she became. She hoped she'd made the right decision in agreeing to meet Stefano.

She wasn't exaggerating when she'd accused the man of being pushy. That goodbye kiss he'd given her last weekend…oh, he'd known exactly what he was doing when he pulled away with only a slight touch of his lips to hers. He'd made her want. And wanting was the one thing that would sink her.

No woman in her right mind should want a prince. A prince could never, ever belong to anyone but the public, even if during those hours spent wrapped in her sheets, making love over and over, he'd made her feel as if they belonged to no one but each other.

He'd fallen to his knees and proposed to Megan claiming it was the "right" thing to do and that they shared a connection. That he'd had the best sex of his life. As much as hearing him say those words set her skin to flame, mind-blowing weekend sex wouldn't overcome the hurdles they'd face if they were to pursue a serious relationship, let alone a marriage.

He'd figured out that "right" wasn't enough reason to marry Ariana. He'd soon decide that amazing sex plus "right" wasn't enough, either.

A shame, because even a week later, she couldn't get the hours they'd spent together out of her mind. Nor could she forget that his engagement to Ariana was nothing like what she'd assumed for the last ten years, a love match made before he'd even arrived in Venezuela. He hadn't run half-naked in front of photographers because he was crazy in love. He'd done it because he'd been crazy with the need to protect someone and to throw off the shackles with which his family and duty held him.

The knowledge made her want him all the more, which made her equally crazy.

This is for Anna, she reminded herself as they made their way from the Plaça Catalunya bus stop toward La Boqueria. Anna should get to know her father, regardless of any feelings Megan might have for the man. Because as much as she tried not to, she definitely had feelings. Feelings that would go far deeper than lust or infatuation if she wasn't careful.

She smiled down at her daughter, who'd taken more time than usual styling her hair and choosing an outfit this morning, nearly making them late. Anna had quite the task ahead of her cleaning up the piles of clothing that now littered her bedroom floor. Megan wondered if it would get worse when Anna started middle school.

"It's an entirely different street at this time of day, isn't it?"

"I guess. But how come Stefano—um, Mr. Jones—couldn't meet us at our hotel?" Anna complained. "Is he going to be able to find us? It can get kinda crowded."

"There won't be many people this early. Besides, he's tall enough to see over any crowds, so I'm sure he'll be fine," Megan replied, ignoring Anna's first question.

They passed a quiet cafe, its lights off and outdoor tables empty save for the pigeons, then paused at one of Anna's regular stops on La Rambla, a small area in the cobblestoned center of the boulevard where an elderly Catalan woman sold birds. As the tiny, bent woman removed the overnight coverings from each of her cages, she made cooing noises to the winged creatures in greeting. Without fail, they singsonged back to her as they did every morning.

The sight of birds for sale in the middle of a city street never ceased to amaze Megan. She often wondered if the birds—as with the sketch artists and street performers—were a carryover from the medieval markets that stood on this same spot. She imagined the scene then wasn't so different, with local villagers arriving early each morning to hawk their wares or their talents.

A deep sense of calm spread through her. The timelessness of La Rambla felt incredibly grounding.

"I love that little blue one, Mom." Anna pointed to one of the cages, where a lively bird twittered to welcome the morning. "It's a parakeet, right?"

As Megan nodded, the bird woman smiled and waved Anna to the cage, then handed her a few pellets to drop into the parakeet's dish. Anna thanked the woman in Catalan, then stepped back to watch as the parakeet hopped to the bowl to sample the food. The vendor murmured her approval and patted Anna on the shoulder before moving to uncover the rest of her cages.

"It's too bad we can't have pets, Mom. I'd love to have this little guy in my room."

"Well, it's nice we can see them here." Without the maintenance. "It makes it special."

Anna shrugged, considering that. They thanked the woman once more for allowing Anna to feed the parakeet and wished her a successful day of sales before taking their leave. Three blocks later a subtle rise in volume hinted that they were near the entrance to the covered marketplace. As the only spot open at this hour, early risers came here to grab a quick breakfast or to socialize.

Megan only hoped they could pull off the socialize part without Stefano being recognized. Her stomach tightened with anxiety to think of him meeting her here. When he'd called earlier in the week, fresh from his economic meeting, he'd suggested breakfast at Anna's favorite spot and promised the outing would be without incident. "Believe it or not, I've done it before. You'll see. If we stay relaxed, we'll appear like any other tourists. No one will pay attention. But don't call me Stefano. Let's go with Mr. Jones."

"Jones?" She'd laughed aloud at the suggestion. Tall, dark, and Mediterranean…he looked like anything but a Jones.

"Trust me."

Megan had hung up the phone on a groan. The man was thick as a brick. He wanted to prove to her that he could protect her and Anna, not understanding that what she really needed was love. Deep, abiding, romantic love.

He'd put the proverbial cart before the horse. She wasn't about to explain it to him, though. If she did, could she ever trust it if he declared his undying love for her? She'd always suspect he said it simply to coerce her into a convenient-for-him marriage.

A moment later, Megan and Anna rounded the corner to Plaça de Sant Josep, where the public market sprawled under an expansive metal roof. Near the entrance, a knot of men unloaded crates from a line of vans while two others wheeled past them with fruit- and vegetable-laden dollies. A woman barely out of her teens sang to herself as she blew by carrying a massive stack of egg containers. Megan watched as the young woman darted around a man carrying a box stacked high with tomatoes, wondering at her skill in keeping the eggs from breaking. A few of the workers smiled in greeting or nodded in Megan and Anna's direction, a luxury they wouldn't have once the market filled with tourists and they were busy manning their stalls.

Once again, Megan's stomach signaled worry. How would they stay anonymous if everyone working in the market made eye contact? Who wouldn't recognize Prince Stefano Barrali when they saw him face to face?

"Keep your eyes open, Anna. We may have to—"

"I believe that woman was carrying our breakfast," a deep, familiar voice said at the same time.

Megan spun around to see Stefano, but not like she'd ever seen him before. He sported a fitted charcoal T-shirt, worn jeans with a battered black leather belt, and dark leather sandals. A slight but sexy growth of beard dotted his chin. Amber-tinted sunglasses with dark frames made it difficult to see his eyes, though when she leaned closer, she noted the amusement there. Above the light shades, a frayed Red Sox cap covered his dark, wavy hair.

"Good morning, Mr. Jones!" Anna emphasized the name as she looked him up and down, not bothering to hide her glee at his clothing choices. "You look, um—"

"Handsome," he finished. "That's the word you wanted, right?"

Anna pursed her mouth. "Uh…sure. We'll go with that."

Unless his own mother were to walk by, Megan couldn't imagine Stefano being recognized. The look was so...*not* royal. Even when he'd dressed in work clothes in Venezuela he'd had a regal presence, perhaps because everyone there knew he was a prince, whether or not they cared. Today he didn't ooze charisma in quite the same way. His entire bearing had changed, giving him the appearance of a streetwise athlete rather than that of a confident, stylish royal. Despite the fact he towered over most of the men bustling around them with market wares—and was, she had to admit, drop dead handsome—he managed to blend in.

"And you?" Stefano turned his dimpled grin on Megan. "Were you about to say handsome, too?"

Megan tried not to let him see that she was thinking exactly that. The stubble gave him a rough-around-the-edges aura that had her imagining what his cheek would feel like against her own. "I was about to point out that we're Twins fans, not Red Sox fans. But I'll forgive you this once."

"I'll keep that in mind." He glanced overhead to study the large, colorful sign adorning the entrance to Mercat St. Josep La Boqueria. "If this is any indication of what's under the roof, I suspect I'm in for a treat."

"Have you been inside yet?" Anna asked.

Stefano shook his head. "I was waiting for my tour guide. Should we explore first or go straight to breakfast?"

"Duh! Breakfast!" Anna grabbed Stefano by the crook of his arm and pulled him along. "You'd better be hungry."

"Of course." He gave Megan's arm a quick tweak so she'd follow. "Come on. A dash of espresso and you'll be fueled for the day. We have a lot on the agenda."

"If you say so." She kept her voice even, but inside, her heart raced against her will. A full day with Stefano sounded delightful, even if it held risk.

Maybe—if she were honest with herself—*especially* because it held risk, though she suspected that made her a less-than-responsible parent.

They wove their way through the first row of the market, stepping around crates as the stalls opened for the day. Attendants wiped down glass cases or arranged piles of fruit and vegetables into artful displays as they passed. "See the fruit juices?" Anna pointed out a stall where two women poured buckets of ice around rows of clear plastic cups filled with multicolored blended drinks. "I told you they're unbelievable."

"We'll come back and try some." He stopped walking and tipped his gaze toward a stall in front of them as the scent of warm buttered eggs and toast filled the air. Only a few stools were occupied at the polished wooden bar. "Please tell me that's where we're headed?"

"Yep, El Quim de la Boqueria," Anna beamed. "You're gonna love it."

Megan could only trail in their wake as they eagerly crossed the short distance to El Quim and slid into barstools, with Anna claiming the spot between the two adults. They were approached at once by a cook in short sleeves with a buzz cut and a small silver hoop in each ear. "Anna, Megan, so happy to see you!" He opened his arms wide. "And you brought me a guest this morning. But not your parents this time?"

"They left last weekend. This is Mr. Jones." Anna's voice was firm and direct. "And the two of us would like huevos con chipirones."

"You would?" The chef grinned at Anna before turning to Stefano for confirmation. "Mr. Jones?"

"That sounds delicious," Stefano agreed. "But I'll take mine with an espresso."

The chef nodded, not bothering to write down the order, then turned to Megan. "Could I entice you with huevos con gamba this morning?"

"Oh, why not?"

"Wonderful!" As he left to begin cooking, Stefano shot a look at Megan. "No espresso?"

"He knows that part," Anna said. "She doesn't have to tell him."

"Ah. I see." He made a show of studying Anna. "So what, exactly, are huevos con chip…what did you order again?"

Anna giggled. "Huevos con chipirones. Eggs with squid."

CHAPTER SEVENTEEN

His mouth dropped open in mock horror. "No wonder the cook wanted to double-check that order. You sure it won't make me sick? Because it will be a challenge to explore the city if I'm trying to keep my breakfast from making a return appearance."

Megan smiled at them both. "Sounds terrible, tastes like heaven. As long as you like squid."

"I do," he said over Anna's head. "Remember, I live on the waterfront. But squid for breakfast will be new."

The cook returned, handing espresso cups to Megan and Stefano and a glass of fresh-squeezed orange juice to Anna before moving back to the grill to tend to the eggs, humming as he went. At the same time, a group of twenty-something women approached the empty stools near Stefano. One asked him in clipped Catalan if the seats were free and he gestured for them to go ahead and sit. They dropped their bags and slid into the seats without a word or a second look.

Stefano took a sip of his espresso before turning to Megan with an I-told-you-so grin.

They spent the rest of their time at the counter enjoying their eggs, chatting off and on with the cook and planning the rest of their day. The group of women beside them ate quickly and left, then another group took the vacated seats and placed orders. As before, none of the patrons paid Stefano any attention. When they finished eating, Stefano left payment and a generous tip, then let Anna guide them through the market.

As the sun rose in the sky, the aisles of the market became increasingly crowded. Hunched women used wheeled carts both for balance and to carry their purchases, fishmongers handed locals paper-wrapped packages with the day's catch, and teenage girls in trendy clothes dodged up and down the rows, sipping fruit juice while giggling over the young male sales clerks and the packs of boys who walked through the market eyeing the candy and fruit drinks. Tourists soaked in the atmosphere while they oohed and aahed over the variety of cheeses, nuts, fruits, and vegetables on display. In spots, the congestion was so great Megan, Stefano, and Anna were forced to stop walking to allow others to pass. Mumbles of "excuse me" in a half-dozen languages could be heard through the crowd as shoppers jostled toward their targets.

Not a soul gave Stefano more than a passing look.

When they stopped at a narrow wooden stall so Megan could purchase her favorite milled soap, Stefano leaned in over her shoulder to take a sniff of the sage green bar cradled in her palm.

"Is this what's in your shower?" The question was asked in a voice so low only she could hear, yet the brush of his breath over her skin caused her face to heat, making her fear the clerk might infer the sexual nature of the comment without having heard it.

When Megan nodded, he asked the aproned clerk for two more bars.

The woman added them to Megan's bag while Anna walked to the side of the stall to look at a candle display. Megan withdrew her wallet to pay for the soap, but Stefano had already handed a bill to the clerk.

"The trick to being anonymous in a crowd is to choose a time and location where no one expects to see a celebrity and to act like everyone else," he murmured as the took the paper bag with the soap. "Locals are here now to shop for their dinner ingredients. The tourists are focused on the sights and smells of the market. No one knows I'm in town. No one has reason to look at me and wonder."

"It seems to be working." She angled her head so she could see his eyes through the light sunglasses. "Thank you for the soap. You didn't have to do that."

"What, buy some for my own shower?" His lenses couldn't hide the devilish sparkle in his eyes. "I happen to like it. Nice smell to the lather. And a nice slip."

She refused to think about him soaping up. Or about words like *slip*. "No, I meant pay for my bar. And for our breakfast. That was very nice of you."

He started to respond—the dimple in his cheek hinting at naughty thoughts—when Anna popped back around the corner holding a candle. "Can I get this one for my room, Mom? I brought my own money."

Megan reluctantly looked away from Stefano. "What do you think happens in a hotel when you leave a candle burning in your room?"

Anna twisted her mouth before ducking around the corner to put the candle back where she found it. When she rejoined them, she said, "I know, I know. It's major trouble if I set off a sprinkler. Oh, but look! Can I have one of those pepperoni samples?"

"Go ahead," Megan said, following Anna's line of sight across the aisle to a broad-shouldered, heavily-tattooed man sporting a flowered yellow apron and proffering a tray of cubed meats on toothpicks.

Stefano asked Anna to bring him one as the girl weaved her way through the swarm of people. He turned back to Megan, but the evocative moment they'd shared was gone.

For the best. Having Stefano lean over her shoulder with shower talk sent her pulse into the stratosphere, which inevitably sent her ability to maintain rational thought in the opposite direction.

"You know she'll find the spiciest sample possible for you, act like it's nothing, then watch for your reaction when you eat it?" Megan said.

"Exactly what I would've done at her age." Stefano reached into his back pocket and pulled out a small map of central Barcelona. "I didn't have time to look this over before you arrived. Do you know your way through the Gothic Quarter?"

"Enough to get to the chocolate museum," she replied as Anna returned with two cubes of meat on toothpicks. As predicted, without batting an eyelash she handed Stefano a dark-flecked piece Megan knew to be fiery hot.

He narrowed his eyes at her as he spun the toothpick containing the cube between them. "Did you also bring me a bottle of water?"

She deflated. "How'd you know?"

"Wasn't born yesterday." He handed her a few Euros so she could return to the counter for a bottle of water. "But that doesn't mean I won't eat it. I love spicy pepperoni."

They spent another half-hour strolling through the market, with Anna pointing out interesting items while bantering with Stefano as if he were a lifelong friend. Megan kept her input to a minimum, not trusting herself to join their chatter. Every time Stefano turned his dimpled smile in her direction or spoke in hushed tones, her insides tightened with a mixture of desire and frustration. When at long last they wended their way out of the marketplace to join the midday hustle and bustle of La Rambla, Stefano fell a half step behind Anna to join Megan.

"You're quiet."

"Letting you and Anna get to know each other." She forced lightness into her voice. "Seems to be going well."

"We have a lot of catching up to do." His hand grazed Megan's lower back as they turned onto a narrow, winding side street. "All of us do."

Anna spun around, walking backward on the cobblestones. "We can do it at the chocolate museum. You guys are slow!"

"We are not slow," Megan said at the same time Stefano dropped his hand from her back. "We're enjoying the scenery."

Stefano cast a glance upward. The stone buildings on either side of the alley soared high enough to partially block the sun, casting the storefronts and apartment doorways in alternating strips of shadow and light. Flowers tumbled from iron balconies on the upper floors, while further down the street a laundry line crossed over the gap between buildings. "The architecture here is spectacular. Most of these buildings are the same age as those on Sarcaccia."

Anna moved to walk between Megan and Stefano, unlooping a bright purple elastic from her wrist and pulling her hair into a ponytail as she studied the arches over each door. "Do the buildings there look the same?"

"For the most part. There are subtle differences, though. The balcony railings have different designs, and anything built in Sarcaccia from about 1200 to 1700 has elaborate carvings on the cornerstones." At Anna's baffled look, he moved to the street's edge and ran his hands over a large block anchoring the side of a pharmacy. "Like these. See how this stone on the building's corner has beveled edges, but a flat surface?"

"Sometimes they put the year or the store name on them, right?" Anna pointed to a bakery on the opposite corner with a brass plate adorning its edge. "Like that one."

Stefano nodded as they continued down the narrow cobblestoned street. "On Sarcaccia, it became a tradition for craftsmen to bid on the right to design cornerstones when a new building was erected. Stonemasons liked having a public place to showcase their best work, knowing it might get them future employment, and residents liked having unique designs on each building. Some are carved, some have metal plating. A few even have plaster decoration, but most of the plaster has worn away over time. Those that are left are protected under Plexiglass."

"I bet it's pretty," Anna said.

"It is. In the capital city, Cateri, there are even cornerstone tours where you walk building to building through the oldest part of town to learn about the different designs."

"That sounds cool!"

"I take it you've never been to Sarcaccia?" He glanced over Anna's head to Megan for confirmation. "Your mom says you've traveled quite a bit since you've lived here."

"No, but I've been to Italy. Oh, and to Corsica! Sarcaccia is near Corsica, right? I *loved* Corsica. Well, except the fact they speak French, which is totally confusing for me. We drove up into the mountains and then spent a couple days on the beach. The water was so blue, I could hardly believe it." Her eyes brightened as they exited onto a square dominated by a cathedral. Tourists filled the open space, some crouching to take photos of companions or the cathedral's towering spires while others consulted travel guides or maps.

"Sarcaccia is only ninety miles from Corsica. Same mountains, same beautiful blue water. But we speak Italian, which I consider the superior language." Stefano tilted his head to indicate the cathedral. "Shall we make a pit stop here on the way to the chocolate museum?"

"I'm hungry, but sure, if you want." Anna's tone indicated she was only saying yes to be polite.

"What, you think you're going to eat at the chocolate museum?" he teased.

"The museum tickets are chocolate bars. You'll see." Anna glanced at Megan as they made their way up the cathedral steps. "Can we go to Sarcaccia someday, Mom?"

Megan bit her lip and sent Anna a sideways look, hoping Anna would take the hint and keep her voice down. Now that they were surrounded by people again, she didn't want anyone glancing at Stefano, hearing *Sarcaccia*, and putting two and two together. "I'm sure we will at some point, sweetie. For today, let's enjoy Barcelona."

For the next few hours, they made their way through the Gothic Quarter, avoiding talk of Sarcaccia to focus on easy topics such as the gaggle of geese living in the cathedral's inner courtyard, Anna's classes and schoolmates, and the thick stone archways that covered the cobblestoned streets. At the chocolate museum, they lingered over the artisans' hand-crafted sculptures, oohing and aahing over the complexity of the displays before wending through Barcelona's narrow medieval streets to return to La Rambla. Street musicians and artists gave them an excuse to pause on a bench now and then. Stefano used those moments to ask Anna questions while Megan window-shopped under the pretense of giving father and daughter a chance to learn more about each other.

In reality, she needed to keep Stefano at arm's length. His easy manner and quick wit, no doubt honed by years of life in the public eye, worked wonders with Anna. By the time dusk fell, Stefano and Anna seemed as if they'd known each other for a lifetime rather than a week.

Megan had to give the man credit. Not only had he enchanted Anna, he'd enchanted her with his ability to move through the day as if he were any other man, one who didn't own an airplane or have a full staff at his beck and call. He'd even stopped at a kiosk to chat with the owner about the jewelry on display and purchase a simple leather bracelet for Anna. And he'd done it all without a soul recognizing him.

"Shall we call it a day?" Megan asked as she approached the bench where Stefano and Anna sat fascinated by a group of teens doing tricks on their skateboards. "Mr. Jones is probably pretty tired, Anna."

Anna twisted her new bracelet and glanced sideways at Stefano. A wicked glint lit her eyes. "Well…."

"We thought we could grab a light dinner from one of the kiosks and catch the Magic Fountain at nine," Stefano said. "Anna tells me it's fantastic. *Magical*, even. A must-see."

Megan frowned at Anna, then at Stefano. No, she shouldn't look at Stefano. He was temptation incarnate with his sexy jeans-and-T look and dusting of whiskers. Addressing Anna, she said, "You two have been conspiring against me."

"I wouldn't say conspiring," Stefano replied. He leaned back against the bench, stretching his muscular arms along the back and kicking his legs in front of him. It reminded her of the confident manner in which he'd leaned back on her sofa while urging her to marry him, all long, fluid limbs and enticing smile, while she'd tried to explain why it couldn't work.

"Then how would you describe it?"

"Conspiring has a negative connotation, which is why the common phrase is *conspiring against*. What we're doing is convincing you, since this is an activity you'd enjoy."

"You do love the fountain, Mom," Anna argued. "Please? It's almost eight already. If we want to go, we should get there before it's too crowded so we can stake out a spot on the grass, up close."

"I've never seen it." Stefano's voice dripped with mock pleading. "If I don't see it now, I might never have the opportunity—"

"You will so! You're coming back to visit me again!" Anna spun in the seat and landed a fake punch to Stefano's ribs, which sent him careening off the bench with a laugh.

"Fine, fine, I'll visit! But we're supposed to be convincing your mother to go tonight, not pointing out that we can go another time."

"Oh. Right."

Megan raised her hands in surrender. "We'll go. Before you two injure yourselves trying to *convince* me."

Anna leapt off the bench and high-fived Stefano. "Nice work, Mr. Jones. You're very convincing."

Megan rolled her eyes as father and daughter led the way, arm in arm. So much for semantics. Attending the fountain's water show might not be a negative, as Stefano put it when explaining *conspiring* versus *convincing*, but it was definitely dangerous.

CHAPTER EIGHTEEN

Stefano stole a look at Megan before drinking in the sight of his sleeping daughter. Half of Anna's hair remained captured atop her head in a bright purple ponytail holder while the rest hung in messy chunks over her face, which was planted just above Megan's left knee. Anna's expression as Megan rubbed her back was one of quiet bliss.

Damn if he wasn't jealous of a kid.

From the moment he'd spotted Megan in the crowd outside La Boqueria, a lopsided, half-awake smile on her face and her hair gleaming in the early morning light, he'd itched to touch her. He'd fought the urge to put his hand at the small of her back to guide her along the aisles as they'd wandered the market after breakfast, even going so far as walking with his hands in his pockets and keeping Anna between them to act as a buffer.

But then she'd paused to purchase a bar of soap and the fresh green scent, one forever intermingled in his mind with the heat of their shared shower, overrode his common sense. He'd leaned in close. He'd flirted. And when she'd spun to face him, he'd seen desire in her gaze.

If Anna hadn't returned to ask about the silly pink candle, he'd have kissed Megan then and there.

He'd managed the cathedral and the chocolate museum without giving in to her pull. It was easier outside the confines of the market, with its rich smells and romantic atmosphere. But there'd been a moment late in the afternoon when he'd caught a view of Megan from the side that made him ache. They'd offered to wait under a Gothic arch while Anna scampered across the street to drop a Euro in a musician's open violin case. The sun streamed between the buildings and through the stone arch at such an angle that it shone through Megan's soft blue irises, making them sparkle like crystal as she'd watched her daughter look both ways, then cross the narrow street.

Their daughter.

It was all he could do not to draw Megan close and kiss her on the forehead, just under the stray strands of hair twisting along her temple, and tell her how fortunate he felt. How amazing and miraculous it was that they shared this vivacious girl. How much he wanted to be with them—with *her*—and spend all his weekends this way. Instead, he'd turned away, allowing the moment to pass.

When they'd returned to La Rambla at dusk, tiny lights looped through the trees that grew down the center of the boulevard sparkled to life. The scent of roasting chestnuts floated through the air. Young adults gathered around tables in cafes on either side of the cobblestone street while lovers strolled past, arms around each other's waists. He saw Megan's gaze follow one young couple and thought of gently taking her hand in his—an easy, natural gesture given their surroundings—but she'd drifted away to admire a piece of art in a store window.

She wasn't playing hard to get, as other women he'd been with liked to do. Instead, she was doing exactly as she promised, allowing him the opportunity to spend time with his daughter.

So it was Anna's hand he held under the glittering treetop lights. It was for the best.

The more time he spent with Megan, the more impressed he became with all she'd accomplished. He'd known she was a strong, independent woman before he'd even spoken to her. When he first saw her walking in that alley in Venezuela, she'd been shouldering more pipe than most men would and doing it without complaint. She'd allowed him to help her, but she hadn't liked it. He could tell she wasn't the type who wanted to depend on others for anything.

If he pressured her now, she might view it as a challenge to her independence. But if he could keep his distance, let her see for herself that he could be a good father to Anna and a good partner for her, perhaps she'd reconsider his offer of marriage.

He had to give up control. Let her guide their relationship.

He also had to be patient. Patience, however, was hard to come by when Megan sat shoulder to shoulder with him in the near dark. As much as his brain told him to appeal to her logical side, his body craved an entirely different approach.

"She hasn't crashed like this since she was a little girl." Megan shifted so Anna's head rested more comfortably in her lap.

The three of them had selected spots in the grass near the fountain to wait for the show to start, with Anna asking Megan to sit in the middle, since that put Anna in a better position to see the fountain. But as more couples and families filled the open space around them, Anna put her head down for "just a sec" and was out.

"It's understandable. She woke up early and walked a long way today."

Stefano removed his amber sunglasses and propped them onto his tattered baseball hat so he could better see Megan. He could feel divots on either side of his nose as a result of wearing glasses for more than twelve hours and his leg muscles ached from sitting cross-legged. He wasn't used to being in the midst of such a crowd outdoors and hadn't counted on the discomfort of folding his legs under him. To buy space, he leaned back and propped his hands behind him.

"Think she'll wake up when it starts?" he asked.

"Hard to say. Maybe. It's all right if you'd like to call it a night." She leaned forward to study Stefano's face. Her eyes clouded and a small crease appeared between her brows. "You look tired, too."

"It's been a long day. Didn't think I looked that bad, though." He scrubbed a hand over his chin. "Maybe it's the beard. Makes me look like I haven't slept."

"I must say, this" —Megan reached up to touch the stubble covering his face— "is something else. I've never seen you with a five o'clock shadow. Even in Venezuela."

He froze as her warm fingers glided over his cheek and chin, then wondered if his sudden stillness alerted her to his intense reaction to her touch. If not, his desire must have shown in his eyes, for when she met his gaze with her own, she slowly withdrew her hand and lowered it to the grass.

At that moment, classical music blasted from speakers surrounding the fountain. Hundreds, if not thousands, of voices cheered as plumes of water sailed skyward in time to the music. The sight had to be spectacular, judging from the sounds of the crowd and the multitude of camera flashes, but he didn't dare look.

Megan sat motionless, her eyes turned toward him rather than the fountain. Despite the cacophony around them, Anna didn't stir.

In that moment, a sensation gripped his heart he'd never before experienced.

He didn't simply admire this woman. He loved her. He loved her strength. Her independence. Her open smile. Her ability to forgive the fact she'd been blocked from informing him about her pregnancy, and that he'd become engaged so soon after leaving her. And he especially loved her honesty, when she could've continued to keep Anna a secret. All of it spoke to the kind of woman she was. Unique in the world. Unique in his life.

He could never, ever let her go.

But he couldn't tell her, not until he was certain she felt the same. If he breathed a word, she'd think he was trying to manipulate her into marriage.

"No one has seen me like this," he finally said, running a hand over his face full of stubble. "Other than during field training, when I didn't have access to a razor for a few days, I haven't let it grow. I've certainly never been photographed with it."

A muscle jumped in her throat as she lowered her gaze to his mouth. "Good way to disguise yourself, then."

He was losing the battle now. His fingers curled in the grass as he grappled with his overwhelming need to kiss her. To show her, even if he couldn't tell her, how he felt. Perhaps, just once—

"Stefano? Is that you?"

Megan's eyes rose to his in a mix of surprise and concern. The voice had come from beyond Megan, beyond the middle-aged couple seated in the grass next to her. Shaken back to reality, he leaned forward, seeking out its source.

"It's me," the feminine voice came again. "Ilsa."

Then he spotted her sitting about fifteen or twenty feet away with a group of young women who, judging from their dress, were planning to spend the evening barhopping or dancing after the water show. When Ilsa saw he'd located her, she fanned her fingers in a small wave.

Cautiously, he glanced around. Everyone else's attention was riveted on the fountain. He looked back to Ilsa and smiled, then put a finger to his lips.

"Ilsa?" Megan hadn't moved. She seemed afraid to look. "The woman from the Grandspire party?"

"Yes."

"She recognized you?"

"She's known me for years." He shrugged. "But she also understands my need for privacy. She's been through this with my sister. She won't give me away to her friends."

"She said your name." Worry crept into Megan's voice.

"My first name only, and in a city where it's not uncommon. No one will make the connection." He hoped. He leaned forward to look past Megan again. The rest of Ilsa's group laughed as they held up their cell phones to snap video of the fountain, with its high, wild sprays and multicolored lights moving in time to the music. They seemed not to notice that Ilsa had spied a friend in the crowd. Ilsa gestured toward Megan, tilting her head as if to ask whether Megan was the woman she thought.

He gave a slight nod. It was useless to deny Megan's identity. Ilsa was too eagle-eyed by far. Not only had she picked out Megan from across the rooftop during the Grandspire fireworks and noted Megan's interest in Stefano, she'd recognized Stefano in a crowd with a day's worth of beard.

Ilsa smiled in acknowledgement then turned back to her friends.

"You think we're okay?" Megan asked quietly. She still hadn't turned around to look at Ilsa, as if afraid doing so would result in disaster. "Should we leave? *Can* we leave without being noticed?"

Stefano put his hand over hers, strictly for reassurance. "Like I said this morning, no one expects me here in Barcelona. No one is looking our way. We're fine."

His attention dropped to the still form in Megan's lap. "On the other hand, Anna hasn't moved a muscle in at least half an hour. If it would make you feel better to take her home, we can."

Megan assessed her daughter before looking back to Stefano. She shifted, but didn't withdraw her hand from beneath his. "We'll give her a few minutes. If she doesn't wake up, then we'll go, but we'll have been here long enough for you to tell her how much you enjoyed the fountain."

He smiled. "I'd like that."

"Me, too."

Megan didn't stir. Didn't look at the fountain. And he knew, knew in his deepest soul, that she desired him even if she refused to marry him. He could see it in the light blush creeping across her cheeks and the slight part of her supple lips. In the way her breathing changed whenever he touched her or smiled at her. At the same time, she didn't look at him in the same way other women did. It was as if she saw beyond the surface, beyond the royal title, to who he was as a man, and regarded him on that basis.

He threaded his fingers between hers and squeezed. He had to have her. No matter what it took, no matter how long he had to wait. He never considered himself a romantic, but what was their random meeting after ten years on the opposite side of the world if not destiny? In the soft glow and splash of the Magic Fountain, it certainly seemed possible.

Easing his head toward hers, he whispered, "Thank you."

"For what?"

"For a perfect day." He leaned in close enough to feel her warm breath mingle with his. Closing his eyes, he savored the moment before moving fractionally to kiss her cheek. He allowed his lips to linger against her skin for a half-beat longer than necessary for a proper thank you kiss before he pulled back, let go of her hand, and turned to watch the water arc toward the starlit sky.

He took deep satisfaction in the thready sound of her exhale before she said, "You're welcome."

CHAPTER NINETEEN

Megan wanted Stefano. Badly. Worse, the man knew it.

What he didn't know—what he could never know—was that she was falling in love with him. No, not *falling*. She feared she'd always loved him. Clandestine weekends spent together so he could make up for lost time with his daughter only served to show Megan that the dynamic, caring, utterly sexy man she'd met in Venezuela, the man she'd kept in her deepest fantasies for years, turned out to have matured into someone even better.

It killed her.

Which was why, as they made their way toward the parking lot that sat above one end of the Grandspire's beachfront boardwalk, Megan took care to keep a healthy physical distance between them.

It was the first time they felt safe being together on hotel property since he'd attended the grand reopening nearly two months ago. So far, aside from the emotional havoc it wreaked within Megan, his weekend visits had gone smoothly. The only blip occurred when Stefano's friend Ilsa had recognized them at the Magic Fountain during his first visit, but that was all it had been. A blip.

He'd even taken the chance he wouldn't be recognized and booked a commercial flight this weekend while his jet underwent maintenance. The change meant he couldn't send his travel bag to the airport with his pilot when checking out of his hotel, as had become his habit, but Megan offered her suite for storage and it hadn't been a problem. Stefano had his hotel's concierge deliver the bag while Stefano met Megan and Anna at the Parc del Laberint, an old Barcelona public area complete with a hedge maze and a country house that offered tours. Since Anna had never visited the maze, Stefano challenged her to a race from one section to the other as Megan watched from a nearby viewing area that allowed her to cheer their progress. After a relaxed picnic lunch in the park, they'd returned to the Grandspire so Anna could gather her things for an end-of-school celebratory sleepover at her friend Julia's apartment. Stefano planned to see Anna off, then retrieve his bag before heading to the airport.

Despite the alteration in what had become an easy routine, this weekend had been as trouble-free as all the others. Even now, as they strolled the boardwalk in the direction of the hotel parking lot, they appeared like any other family enjoying a sunny weekend. She'd chosen a simple sundress, while Stefano sported a plain white T-shirt, jeans, sunglasses, and his usual battered Red Sox baseball hat. Nothing about them stood out. If passersby glanced their direction, it was only to ensure Megan and Stefano had an eye on Anna, who'd run ahead to wait on the bench nearest the stairs to the parking lot. With as much gear as she carried for the sleepover, Anna looked like a runaway. Megan supposed she should've expected it when she allowed Anna to pack herself.

She sighed, thinking of how independent Anna had become in the last year. It was the age, Megan supposed. The girl seemed to be maturing in leaps and bounds. In no time at all, she'd be sending Anna off to college. At least it felt that way today, with another grade completed and summer upon them. Part of her loved seeing the changes in her daughter, while part wanted to grab Anna and hold on to her forever, to stop her from growing older so they could enjoy more time together.

"She prefers to do things on her own, doesn't she?" Stefano asked, as if reading Megan's mind.

"She does."

The weekend visits had worked to bring Anna and Stefano closer together, to the point that Stefano could now anticipate Anna's reaction to any given situation.

He knew her likes and dislikes, appreciated her creative mind, and had discerned at least a dozen ways to make his daughter laugh. When she'd turned ten on the first of June, he'd even resisted the impulse to buy Anna a pricey gift, instead taking her to her favorite ice cream parlor for sundaes. By the same token, Anna had grown completely comfortable with Stefano and loved their time together. Sometimes too much, as evidenced by the loud burp Anna let out as they'd left the park this afternoon and Stefano's resulting applause, but Megan supposed she could live with that. Allowing Anna to build an honest relationship with her father was important. He'd be an anchor for Anna in the coming years should she ever need him.

Megan decided that she even could live with wanting the man herself. As much as she never wanted to *want*, she reminded herself that she met gorgeous, desirable men in her professional life every day. She never dated them, no matter how strong the temptation, no matter how the men might flirt.

But oh, Stefano was a master at the game of flirtation. He had enough experience with women to know she desired him and he played that to the hilt, coming just-so-close to touching her back or brushing an arm against hers without actually doing it. Catching her eye and flashing those dimples whenever they shared a laugh. Speaking in double entendres he knew Anna wouldn't catch but Megan would, then continuing on in a completely innocent manner, as if he hadn't said anything the slightest bit risqué.

Giving her lingering goodbye kisses on the cheek when each weekend ended, but never attempting more intimate contact.

For days before he visited, she'd tell herself to regard him in the same light she did the attractive men who drifted through her professional life. No matter who they were, any desire she felt for those men eventually dulled over time by the simple fact they shared a business relationship; it was a pattern she'd learned to expect, which made it easier to resist their attempts at flirtation. The costs of not resisting were too high.

But over the last few weeks, Megan recognized that something more existed between her and Stefano, something far stronger than a case of lust. Something she couldn't resist in the way she'd resisted the other men whom she'd had the opportunity to date. When she first laid eyes on Stefano after a week apart, it was as if a switch flipped inside her, lighting her soul. It was more than the fact they shared Anna. It was in the flash of his genuine smile, the one that reached all the way to his eyes when he and Anna conspired against her, or tried to *convince* her, to engage in a particular activity. It was in his walk. His affable manner with shopkeepers and waiters. His quick and offbeat wit. Even—though she hated to admit it, even to herself—his instinct to protect everyone who entered his orbit.

Each hour they spent together brought out some new facet of his personality for her to appreciate. And each hour they spent together, it became harder and harder to resist—let alone hide—her growing feelings for him. She wasn't sure how many more of these so-called casual weekends she could take without having to physically sit on her hands to prevent herself from touching him.

On the other hand, he hadn't mentioned his marriage proposal in well over a month, meaning it was possible he'd changed his mind. In that case, maybe the situation would grow easier for her as time went on. They'd establish a visitation routine no different than that of other families with parents who lived separately.

As a bird swooped in front of them, then lit on a nearby trash receptacle, Stefano glanced sideways at Megan. Mischievous dimples deepened in his cheeks.

"Oh, no," she said. "I know that look and it's never good."

His smile widened. "While we were in the maze this morning, Anna asked me how old I was when I was allowed to have a computer of my own and whether I was allowed to keep it in my bedroom."

Megan harrumphed. "Well, you can guess why she asked that. What'd you say?"

Stefano pinched his lips as if considering his response. "Well, naturally I told her that in Sarcaccia, children may have computers whenever they want without having to ask their parents. I explained that the government pays for all the costs of—"

"You didn't!"

"Of course not." He chuckled. "I said, 'Anna, are you asking me because you've recently asked your mom if you could have a computer for your bedroom?' and she confessed that she had."

"Did she also tell you I said no on both counts?"

"I guessed that part. Little devil." He smiled in Anna's direction. She sat on a bench near the parking lot stairs with an over-the-top look of annoyance on her face meant to ridicule the adults for taking so long to make their way down the boardwalk. "I told her that you're a pretty good judge of when she should get certain privileges and that your word is the law."

"Thank you." Megan tipped her head and looked at Stefano. "Must say, I'm surprised you didn't offer to buy her the latest model with all the bells and whistles and have a professional set it up in her room, rationalizing that it's all in the name of education."

"Now who's the devil? You know I wouldn't do that." He sidestepped the distance between them and wrapped one arm around her shoulders in a friendly hug. The unexpected contact sent a flash of warmth through her from head to toe, probably exactly what Stefano intended. "Well, unless it meant she could take online cooking lessons."

"Wow. You really like to torture me," she replied as he released her, thankful she sounded like she was referring to cooking lessons.

"Are you shocked?"

Shocked wasn't the descriptor she'd use, but she arched an eyebrow in response.

At the same moment they approached the bench, a dark blue Audi sedan circled the parking lot before stopping near the top of the wooden stairs connecting it to the boardwalk. Anna popped off her seat and screened her eyes for a better look, then waved as the car door opened. Julia's mother, Marta, stepped out and waved in return.

Megan told Anna, "Mrs. Pettite will bring you back to the hotel tomorrow at noon. Be sure to thank her for inviting you."

"I will. Bye, Mom." She gave Megan a hug, then ran over to Stefano, who had stopped in the shade of a large palm tree where he'd be obscured from the parking lot. A smaller man might've been knocked over as Anna launched herself at his waist. "Bye, Stefano!"

"See you soon, *amore mia,*" he said, returning the hug. "Be good for your mother this week." He adjusted her backpack straps before she took off, her pell-mell run scattering a flock of birds that had gathered around a discarded baguette alongside the walkway.

Megan called out her thanks to Marta Pettite while Anna sprinted up the stairs, climbed into the back of the sedan, then collapsed in a fit of giggles with Julia. As Marta pulled out of the lot, Stefano took the seat Anna vacated and scooted to the side, inviting Megan to join him on the bench. "She's lucky to have such good friends. Does she spend the night away often?"

"Maybe once a month. Sometimes we have Julia or another of Anna's friends to our place. They love having breakfast at the hotel the next morning. Santi sends up waffles with chocolate sauce if he knows Anna has company." She couldn't keep the wistfulness from her voice as she added, "It'll be hard to give up those treats from Santi when we leave. Wherever we end up, I'll need to get Anna back here to visit."

"The man does make a fine meal," he agreed as he removed his sunglasses and set them atop the brim of his hat. "So does this mean you've started interviewing?"

"Not yet. Soon, though." She'd been too wrapped up in Stefano's reappearance in her life and follow-up calls from the grand reopening to actively pursue open positions, though she had several promising leads to pursue. But as she and Stefano sat side by side on the shaded bench, gazing out over the sun-drenched beach and the water beyond, part of her wondered, *would it be so bad to accept his offer?*

There were certainly positives to living and working in Sarcaccia. Working at one of the island's luxury hotels or, better yet, working on the development of a new conference center, especially one as modern and extensive as the facility being planned, would provide her the intellectual challenge she craved. Such a position would be long term, meaning Anna could finish her schooling in one location. Her parents would love to visit from Minnesota, since Sarcaccia offered plenty of activities for tourists and provided a good jumping-off point for trips through Italy, Monaco, and the south of France.

Then there was Stefano. Judging from everything she'd seen these last few weekends, he'd be a good husband—responsible, honest, dependable—and he'd do anything for Anna. He'd promised as much and she believed him.

But what about her? She needed more than Stefano's protection, more than job security. More than a marriage of convenience. Or did she? It would be so, so easy.

She breathed deeply, inhaling the warm salt air as if it had the ability to clarify her mind. No, she decided. Nothing easy ever paid off. She couldn't allow herself to succumb, no matter the temptation. In the long run, a marriage where the feelings were unbalanced wouldn't work. At least, that's what her brain said. For her heart, it was becoming an entirely different matter. More and more, she wondered if, maybe, he might love her in return. There were times when she'd catch a glimmer in his eye when he looked at her, a glimmer that made her believe he truly wanted her for her, not for Anna or out of a misguided sense of duty.

Then again, it might be wishful thinking…or simply convincing flirtation on his part. Never once had he said he loved her. He'd said they could *make it work*. He'd said it'd be the *right thing to do*. And what happened when Anna graduated high school and left for college? Would Stefano still feel he made the right decision in asking Megan to marry him?

If he was ever going to raise the topic again, it'd be now, when they were alone. If he didn't, well, she'd tell herself it was for the best.

"Have you considered Sarcaccia?" He surprised her again by putting his hand over hers, then running his strong fingers along her leaner ones to trace her knuckles. "I don't wish to pressure you—I promised I wouldn't—but my offer still stands. I meant it when I asked you to marry me."

The man could truly read her mind.

Though she couldn't say yes, she couldn't bring herself to say no, either. She kept her face turned toward the sand and waves, unwilling to let him read the conflicting emotion in her eyes. "I promised to think about it. I'm still thinking."

It wasn't the answer she wanted to give, but it was as honest as she could be.

"That's understandable." His hand stilled, but remained on hers. After a moment, he said, "I had a meeting earlier this week with the team doing the hiring for the new convention center. They've reached the point where they need a long-term director and have compiled a shortlist of possible candidates. They wanted to know if I was familiar with any of the names before they make contact. You were at the top of their list."

She turned in surprise. "Me? How?"

He shrugged. "You're rather good at what you do. I imagine someone recommended you."

She felt her smile falter.

"No, it wasn't me," he said. "My involvement with the conference center is primarily focused on the transportation improvements it requires. On the other hand, the committee knows I'm likely to have met some of the potential candidates in my travels. It makes sense for them to consult me before they begin the interview process, just as they'd consult anyone else who could give them insight into the candidates."

She wanted to believe him. But was this another situation where—when things weren't going his way—he'd taken action to control the situation? If so, it wasn't a move to share her life, but to orchestrate it.

"You don't believe me," he said.

"It's just…I can't fathom how they'd have gotten my name. It's not as if I'm local. And I certainly haven't dealt with anyone in Sarcaccia. I don't know anyone in the hotel or convention business there. Perhaps you mentioned me in passing or said something about your visit to the Grandspire?"

"Of course I told them about the Grandspire." He pulled his hand from hers and twisted on the bench to face her. His green eyes, usually so crystal clear, appeared darker and more serious behind his amber frames, though perhaps it was her imagination. "I've also told them about nearly two dozen other hotels and conference centers I've visited over the last few years. The developers want to take the best ideas from around the world and incorporate them into the new facility. I've done the same thing as I've studied transportation systems so we can make economically sensible upgrades to ours. But given the history you and I share, I did not mention you specifically. And they certainly don't know I'm with you this weekend."

Her heartbeat jumped at the phrase *I'm with you this weekend.* Only Stefano could make it sound so romantic and forbidden, even when nothing romantic had taken place.

"In any event," he continued, "I wanted you to be aware that you'll be receiving a call from the committee in the near future. I didn't want you to be caught off guard, given that my proposal is still on the table."

Hope welled inside her as he studied her face, waiting for her response. She wanted so badly to kiss those firm, gorgeous lips, to see his eyelids drift closed and feel his mouth against hers, hot with need. To hear him say he loved her. Not that they shared a connection or even that she was the best sex of his life. Not that they could make it work. Not that he was getting her a job. A job was something she could handle herself. A relationship required two people.

Only three words. They were all she needed to hear to tip her decision and pull her out of limbo. But she only wanted to hear them if he meant them with all his heart and soul.

Her heart felt as if it would beat out of her throat as he shifted closer, resting his arm on the bench behind her.

"You're still worried about the practicalities aside from your career, aren't you?" His brow creased into a frown. "Like how you might adjust to living in the palace? That's what's holding you back."

The bubble of hope inside her deflated. "Of course that's a concern. But" —she wracked her brain for a way to explain that he was missing the point without sounding needy— "there's a lot more to a successful marriage than...than practicalities."

"I'm aware of that."

"Then…wait a minute," she paused as a slow smile spread across his face. "What's with the grin? You look like a pool shark who's about to run the table."

"Because this means you *have* been considering my proposal. You haven't said anything in nearly two months, so I wasn't sure."

"It's the first time we've been alone in nearly two months," she pointed out. "And you haven't said anything, either."

"I see." His arm moved from the bench to her shoulder, his fingers grazing the tie to her sundress before pausing at the spot where she'd knotted it behind her neck. "I thought it best to give you space. But perhaps less space between us is in order if I wish to persuade you." He angled his head to look pointedly at the lean cotton strap. "Anyone told you that you look gorgeous in that dress?"

"You're teasing."

"This" —he leaned in so his lips grazed her cheekbone— "is no tease."

Her breath stilled as she felt him smile against her skin.

"You sure?" she managed. "Because I swear you're about to laugh at me."

"I'm quite sure." The brim of his baseball cap tipped at an angle that partially hid their faces from the beach, adding to the thrill of the forbidden. She willed herself to keep her wits about her, but when his mouth found hers, the desire she'd kept so carefully bottled up since the weekend they'd made love overwhelmed her. All she could think of was his kiss, his warmth, his fingers curling into the hair at the back of her head. The unfamiliar scratch of his stubble against her face along with the sweet familiarity of his tongue coaxing her to invite him in.

But was there love in his kiss? Her overloaded mind couldn't tell. Though on one level she knew she should pull back, desire drove her fingers to cross the short distance to his knees, gliding over the soft fabric to explore the corded muscles of his thighs.

"What else can I do to convince you?" he whispered before angling his mouth to deepen the kiss.

He tasted like pure bliss. Sunshine. Heat. The promise of utterly divine sex.

The barest hint of his cologne—or was it his soap?—tickled her senses, along with the scent that only belonged to him, the scent that had lingered in her pillowcase the night after they'd made love in her bed.

She could get lost in him. The frightening part was that the idea of surrender didn't frighten her as much as it should.

She eased away, though her fingertips remained on his shoulder. "Maybe we shouldn't do this here."

"Your suite isn't far."

"No, it wouldn't be—"

In her peripheral vision, she caught sight of a man moving along the beach. Instinct made her turn and look.

He held a long-lens camera to his eye. It pointed straight at them.

Chapter Twenty

The closer she and Stefano got to the hotel, the more fight-or-flight nausea roiled Megan's stomach.

"Smile and wave goodbye as if we're friends out for a Sunday afternoon stroll, then go inside," Stefano instructed as they rounded a stand of palm trees and low tropical plants bordering the hotel. He'd replaced his sunglasses and pulled the brim of his hat a little lower, but his voice sounded as if he hadn't a care in the world. "I'll be at your suite in a few minutes."

She did as he asked, then opened a side door and entered the air-conditioned hallway leading to the lobby. Only when the heavy glass door was firmly closed behind her did she dare turn and look. The man with the camera was nowhere in sight. Neither was Stefano.

Adrenaline pumped through her system double-time as she leaned against the cool interior wall. How could she be so stupid as to take a risk like that? The mystery man could have been a tourist or seaside bird-watcher. But more and more, she feared a member of the paparazzi finally recognized Stefano. If so, what had he photographed?

She closed her eyes and flexed her fingers in a quick effort to clear her brain. Only time would tell what images the man captured and where they'd appear. There was absolutely nothing she could do about it now.

Straightening her shoulders, she made her way down the hall and entered the expansive lobby, nodding to members of the staff and smiling at guests gathered in the rotunda area. Everything appeared normal. The bartender in the corner lounge was engaged in an animated conversation about soccer, bellboys whisked luggage trolleys to waiting guests, and the concierge scoured a book of restaurant menus for a young couple. Two children dodged in and out of the velvet rope that sectioned off the check-in area as their parents picked up room keys.

"Excuse me, Ms. Hallberg?"

Megan spun to see a young woman wearing a desk clerk's uniform cross the lobby toward her. "Yes. It's Cristina, right?"

"Yes." She'd only been working at the hotel a week and appeared pleased to be recognized. "Santi stopped by the desk about two hours ago and asked if I'd seen you. Did he find you?"

Strange for him to seek her out on a weekend. Unless there was a last-minute snag with the dining arrangements for a weekend event, he wouldn't. "No, I've been away. Did he say what it was about?"

"Only that if I saw you, I should tell you that he's looking for you." She pursed her lips, thinking. "He did seem preoccupied, but I couldn't say why."

"Thank you, Cristina. I'll call him in a few minutes."

"All right. Oh, and Ms. Hallberg? Great dress."

Unwilling to linger in the lobby, Megan thanked Cristina for the compliment, then took the elevator up to her floor. Within seconds of keying into her suite, a light knock came at the door. She opened it to admit Stefano.

"Well," she said once they were in her entry hall with the door closed. "That couldn't have been good."

"If it makes you feel any better, I didn't recognize the guy." He took off his sunglasses and ball cap and scrubbed a hand over his head, absently fixing the dark hair his hat had mussed. "I'm able to identify most of the photographers who are assigned to cover my family. He might've been a tourist snapping photos of the beachfront buildings."

"With that camera?"

"Unlikely," he admitted as they made their way toward the living area. "But I find a healthy dose of optimism the best way to handle these incidents."

"I suppose." She wanted to share Stefano's confidence, but her words sounded hollow. Another paparazzi photo of Stefano wouldn't affect his day-to-day life. To her, it could change everything.

He set his hat and sunglasses on the kitchen counter, then stepped toward her to take both her hands in his. His skin still held the warmth of the afternoon sun. "Optimism aside, here are the facts: He wasn't on my flight yesterday morning, nor was he at the park today. Neither of us noticed him when we were sitting on the bench looking out at the beach. Correct?"

"Correct."

Reassurance filled his voice as he continued, "That means Anna was long gone by the time he starting taking pictures. On top of that, I don't look like myself and the bench was partially shaded, so even with that lens, photographs taken from that distance will leave room for doubt. So *if* it was a paparazzo, and *if* his photos are published, I'll ignore them. No confirmation or denial from the palace means that they weren't worth comment, which means most people won't believe the man in the photo is me. It will end up being another celebrity tidbit that disappears into the ether."

She flexed her fingers in Stefano's as she studied his face, taking in the expressive black-ringed green eyes with tiny crinkles at the corners, the high, tanned cheekbones, and the firm line of his jaw. He was so strong, so sure, that she wanted to believe him. But how could anyone not see that the gorgeous, charismatic man before her was Stefano Barrali? If that lens was half as powerful as she suspected, someone who might not recognize him in passing on the street would look at the photos and say, *wow, Prince Stefano looks different with the stubble.* Not, *no way that's the prince.*

As he'd pointed out to her more than once, he wasn't recognized on the street because no one expected to see him, especially in casual dress. A tabloid photo trumpeting his name was an entirely different matter.

If she was snapped kissing the prince and publicly identified, what would it do to her career? To Anna?

Stefano grimaced at her worried expression.

"You're used to this," she countered. "I'm not. As much as I knew this was inevitable, I can't help worrying. I thought I'd have more time before having to deal with anything like this."

"I understand. In fact, I'd be surprised if you didn't worry. But I told you that I'd do everything in my power to ensure you and Anna aren't hurt. And I keep my promises." He raised her hand to his lips and pressed a warm kiss to the tips of her fingers one by one. "Speaking of which, we were in the middle of an important conversation when we were interrupted. I was trying to convince you of…something." He maintained eye contact as he moved his mouth to her wrist, a barely-banked fire lurking in his heavy-lidded gaze. "The car service won't be here for an hour, which gives us plenty of time to discuss my proposal. Ask me anything you want."

"Anything?" *Do you love me?*

"Anything. I want you to trust me." He grinned. "Though a single word from you could end the discussion so we can move on to other activities, if you prefer."

Yes.

The word popped into her head unbidden. She'd put off giving him a definitive answer for weeks now, unwilling to repeat her original response of, "I can't imagine an answer other than no" precisely because she *could* imagine it. She'd hoped some magic moment would push her one way or the other. The idea of marriage to Stefano seemed so monumental. Larger than the two of them. Yet deep in her soul, she knew she didn't belong with anyone else and never would. Fate, kismet, whatever it was that led him back to her after so many years, being with Stefano felt amazing both then and now. No other man stirred her this way, and though he didn't say the words she longed to hear, she suspected he felt the same about her.

But could it last?

It struck her then that *that* was why she'd procrastinated. She'd worried Stefano's visits would stop once they became inconvenient. He'd lose interest in her or in making them a true family. Real life in Sarcaccia would cause his enthusiasm for weekend trips to wane.

She'd wanted him to prove himself. After all her years alone, she didn't want risk being hurt. But would she hurt herself more by *not* taking a risk? If nothing else, being followed on the beach should teach her one thing: She couldn't live in limbo forever.

"Your brain is working too hard," he said, wrapping an arm around her waist and melding his body to hers.

That pulled a laugh from her. "I was thinking that these last few weekends have been wonderful."

"I told you we could make this work." Before she could argue with whether *make it work* was the proper standard for considering marriage, his gaze softened. "I know we're not exactly living in the real world. I can't hide under a baseball hat all the time and you can't hide our relationship from your coworkers, given that you live where you work. But what's important is that we make this work between *us*. You and me. If that happens, the rest will fall into place. I believe that with all my heart."

With that simple word, *us*, he addressed one of her biggest fears. Perhaps he did want her for her, and for what the two of them could be together, rather than because she was the mother of his child.

A plaintive beep sounded from one of the kitchen stools, where she'd dropped her handbag after returning from the beach. She ignored it and smoothed her hand over the front of Stefano's shirt, feeling the firm muscle and strong heartbeat beneath her fingertips.

Stefano was larger than life, yet so very human. If she chose the path he offered, which part would dictate her life? The prince or the man? She leaned into him, absorbing his heat as she touched her lips to the spot her fingers explored. All she had to do was say a single word and her world would change.

Take the leap. Trust him. Trust yourself. As Stefano said, the rest would fall into place.

She smiled against Stefano's chest, remembering that those were the exact words her mother used when Megan discovered she was pregnant with Anna. She'd tearfully informed her mother that she couldn't comprehend balancing motherhood, graduate school, and a career that hadn't even started. She'd never forget her mother's straightforward response.

Love the child. The rest will fall into place. Her mother repeated that mantra several times during Anna's bouts of colic. While there'd been a tough period of adjustment, eventually, her mother had been proven right. The rest had fallen into place. Now Megan couldn't imagine what life would've been like without Anna, nor did she want to.

It could be the same with Stefano, if she let it. She couldn't imagine life without him. Not anymore.

She swallowed hard. What she said in the next breath would change her life forever.

When Megan's cell phone emitted a second beep, Stefano pressed a soft kiss to her forehead. "I hate to say it, but should you get that in case it's Anna?"

Despite reminders, Anna probably forgot her toothbrush or pajamas. "Wouldn't be surprised. Her timing is terrible."

She reluctantly left his embrace to fetch her phone. She frowned at the screen, which displayed Ramon's office number. "It's the hotel manager."

Stefano gestured for her to take the call.

"Good afternoon, Megan," came the familiar voice. "I hate to interrupt your weekend, but are you on the premises?"

"Yes." He wouldn't need her in the hotel on a Sunday unless it was urgent. Perhaps Santi's attempt to locate her earlier was related. "Is there a problem?"

"No problem, but would you mind coming to my office? Mr. Gladwell is here from the UK and we have something important to discuss with you. Shouldn't take longer than ten or fifteen minutes."

"Of course." She glanced at Stefano, who had crossed the room to pull a large manila envelope from his overnight bag, which was tucked alongside the sofa. "But I'm not dressed for—"

"You're fine as you are. We'll see you shortly."

She clicked off the phone and set it on the countertop. So much for her conversation—and whatever else she'd been about to do—with Stefano.

"Trouble?" Stefano asked as he tapped the envelope against his palm.

"I don't think so. The hotel's owner is visiting from London." Her heart thrummed as she began to grasp the enormity of her next sentence. "He's in Ramon's office. They want to see me right away."

"Jack Gladwell owns the Grandspire, doesn't he?" Stefano didn't hide his surprise at her reference to the world-famous billionaire. "Were you expecting him?"

"Yes. And no. I mean, I've certainly never been invited to meet with him before. He usually swoops in and out without telling a soul. I'd hoped he'd attend the grand reopening, but his sister's wedding was the same weekend." Suddenly flustered, she swept a hand along her casual sundress and flip flops. "Ramon told me not to change, but I'll at least slip into slacks."

She took a step toward her bedroom, then stopped. "I'm sorry, Stefano. We were talking about—"

"Don't worry about it. I'll have my car service come now." He flipped the envelope so she couldn't see what was printed on the front. "From what I understand, Jack Gladwell isn't free with his time. We can talk next weekend."

She wanted to finish their conversation today, wherever it led. Another week would fray her last nerve. Plus, now she was curious about the contents of Stefano's envelope. She had the feeling it was meant for her.

"They said it'd only take ten or fifteen minutes, so figure thirty at the most. You're welcome to wait here." It was all she could do not to add a begging *please* to the end of the sentence. She wanted to spend the rest of her life with him. She'd be damned if she let a random cameraman or even a billionaire stop her from telling Stefano what she felt. She was ready to take the leap.

He turned to sit on the sofa, sliding the envelope back into his bag as he did so. "In that case, I'll see you in a half hour."

* * *

On first glance, few people would recognize Jack Gladwell as one of the richest, most business-savvy men in the world. With ruffled blond hair worn in a style slightly longer than was fashionable, tanned skin, and windburned cheeks, he looked as if he'd just stepped off a boat. A light coating of freckles dusted arms sufficiently muscular to haul crates or fishing lines with ease, and his casually untucked gray button-down shirt, jeans, and well-worn loafers added to his relaxed appearance.

However, on second glance, Jack Gladwell left no doubts about his abilities. His wide stance and straight spine betrayed the type of inner confidence a man gained only through experience and repeated, hard-won success. Despite his crooked smile, a sharp intelligence filled his gaze. He appeared able to size up a person in a few seconds and use that information to his advantage. As Megan entered Ramon's spacious office, Jack Gladwell stood near the panoramic window, seemingly oblivious to the stunning view behind him as he turned that assessing gaze toward Megan.

"Thanks for coming down on a Sunday, Megan," Ramon said, striding across his office to close the door behind her. "I'd like you to meet Jack Gladwell."

The British billionaire's light blue eyes danced with amusement as he approached her. He clasped Megan's hand in both of his and raised one eyebrow. "You changed clothes, didn't you?"

"I did," she admitted. "I couldn't bring myself to enter Ramon's office in an old sundress and flip flops. I hope you weren't waiting long."

"Not at all." He released her hand and gestured for her to take one of the two empty seats in front of Ramon's desk. Once she did, he took the other and turned it to face her. "I'll get right to the point, Megan. I have both good news and bad news to share with you."

Megan glanced at Ramon, who'd moved to stand behind Jack Gladwell, but he didn't appear concerned. In fact, he seemed to be holding back a smile.

"First, I'm afraid that Ramon will be leaving his position as manager of the Grandspire at the end of the summer," Jack said. "He's done excellent work here and I like to reward those who look after my financial interests. Therefore, I've asked him to join me in London, where he'll oversee my entire hotel business."

"That's terrific, though he'll be greatly missed here," she said. Ramon had worked hard with little credit to rebuild the Grandspire. The promotion was well-earned. "Having worked with him here the last few years, I can assure you that you'll be thrilled with your decision."

"I already am," Jack replied. "It's an entirely new position, created to ensure a consistently high level of quality across all twelve of my worldwide hotel properties. If anyone can keep a tight rein on such diverse locations, I believe it's Ramon."

She agreed. So why had she been called down?

Then the realization hit her: Jack Gladwell was restructuring his entire hotel division. She was going to be let go before she had the opportunity to leave on her own. She glanced to Ramon, then back to Jack once more, hoping her face didn't betray her emotions. "If that's the good news, what's the bad news?"

"That *is* the bad news, as it means I no longer have a manager at what has become my premier hotel property. Given the success of the Grandspire's revitalization, I'm quite particular about who will take Ramon's place. It's money in my pocket if I choose the right person and a great loss if I don't. Besides, it'd be a damned shame to see all Ramon's hard work go to waste. Don't you agree?"

"Of course." She smiled at Ramon. "We've learned a lot from him here."

"That's what I thought." He leaned forward, placing his elbows on his knees to look her in the eye. "Which is why I want you to take over the Grandspire, Megan. Are you up to the challenge?"

Megan's jaw felt as if it'd frozen shut. Jack Gladwell, one of the wealthiest, most powerful men in the world, had traveled to Spain to personally offer her a job running his highest-profile hotel? He hardly knew her.

He must have known what was going through her mind because he explained, "I realize that this comes from out of the blue, but Ramon has kept me apprised of your work here the last few years. I've looked over your reports as well as your conference bookings. You're astute when it comes to bringing in business and anticipating customer needs, and your staff adores you despite the fact you drive them hard. Ramon is confident you're the best choice for the position, as am I."

His praise made it difficult to find her voice. "I'm honored."

"So you'll take the job?"

No wonder Jack Gladwell was a billionaire. He spoke with the confidence of a man who always got what he wanted. "Do you need a decision today?"

The grin that spread over his tanned face surprised her. "Now that's the kind of response I'd hoped to hear." He turned to Ramon and said, "You told me she was smart."

At Ramon's shrug, Jack faced Megan again and said, "I like that you don't allow yourself to be railroaded into a quick decision."

"I wasn't aware I was being railroaded," she replied. Though of course she was.

"Let me know by Friday." He picked up a manila file folder from Ramon's desk and offered it to her. "This is a summary of your compensation package. I won't negotiate beyond this, so don't bother asking. You'll find it more than generous. In return, I expect you to remain as dedicated to the Grandspire as you have been since Ramon hired you. More so, if possible. I need people like you in my organization, Megan."

She accepted the folder without opening it. "Thank you, Mr. Gladwell."

He clapped his hands on his knees, then stood. "Call me Jack. And call me by Friday."

CHAPTER TWENTY-ONE

Megan kept the folder closed as she took the mezzanine stairs from Ramon's office down to the lobby. A month ago, every fiber of her being would've been overcome with the urge to whip open the folder and peruse its contents. An offer like Gladwell's was what she'd been working toward her whole life. Whatever the folder contained, it would mean security for her and Anna. She knew what Ramon's compensation had been as manager. She doubted Gladwell would offer her any less, especially given that she'd been with the Grandspire for several years already. She'd be able to sock away enough to cover Anna's college tuition without worrying about meeting her other expenses. Perhaps she could even afford to fly her parents here once in a while, rather than having them absorb the cost. But as wonderful as the financial security might be, the position itself meant more. She'd have the power to shape the Grandspire for years to come, she'd have Jack Gladwell's ear, and she'd have the ability to move to any job she wanted in the future.

It was a dream come true.

However, it would mean saying no to Stefano, which meant trading one dream for another. No matter what she did, the price would be steep.

She forced a smile as she approached an animated-looking group assembled near the bottom of the stairs, most of whom were studying city maps as they waited for the bus driver to pull around to the entry for the hotel's regular Sunday afternoon shopping tour. After giving one woman directions to the nearest restroom and promising that the bus would wait, Megan checked her watch. Still plenty of time before Stefano's driver arrived. As she passed the registration desk on her way to the main bank of elevators, she caught a glimpse of Cristina speaking to a guest.

"Shoot," Megan mumbled to herself, remembering that she'd promised to call Santi. She'd see what he needed after Stefano went to the airport. For what was normally her quietest day of the week, this Sunday was turning out to be quite eventful.

She exhaled, her mind racing a mile a minute as she traversed the spacious lobby. She couldn't tell Stefano about the job offer, not yet. She needed to contemplate it with no outside influence, even—perhaps especially—without Stefano's influence. He'd asked far too many questions about her job hunt already. She clutched the folder a little tighter. Perhaps the offer from Gladwell was the universe's way of stopping her from making a mistake, marrying a man who didn't love her back.

She punched the elevator button harder than necessary, frustrated with herself for allowing doubt to creep in where it shouldn't. Half an hour ago, she'd been ready to accept Stefano's proposal. When she saw Stefano, her gut would tell her what to do.

Hell, she knew without seeing him again what she'd do.

A long Saturday spent walking La Rambla and enjoying the Magic Fountain with Anna showed her that Stefano was everything she'd believed when they'd first met in Venezuela. She loved that man—self-assured, witty, caring, and, yes, sexy as all get-out—whether or not he wore a crown or lived in a royal palace. Being a royal was his circumstance, not his character. Circumstances could be adjusted, or you could adjust to the circumstances. But character didn't change. The weekends that followed their day on La Rambla only cemented her belief.

The rest will fall into place.

The lights over the doors ticked off the floors as an elevator approached. She'd never seen the numbers change so slowly. She needed to see Stefano, and she needed to see him *now*.

As she reached out to hit the button again, a beefy hand came to rest on her forearm. "Megan."

She turned to see a familiar face. "Santi. I was just about to call you." If "just about" meant a solid hour from now, after Stefano left for the airport.

"I have looked everywhere for you." The heavily-accented voice was hushed, breathless. She started at the rapid rise and fall of his chest. The man who never ran anywhere had apparently chased her across the lobby.

"What's wrong?" He appeared on the verge of collapse.

A family approached as the elevator doors opened to spill another large group into the lobby. Santi waved for the family to go ahead and take the free elevator, apparently needing to speak with her in private.

Once the crowd cleared, Megan said, "Now you're worrying me. The last time I saw you this serious, you had a banquet to serve and half your staff ill."

"This is worse. This is about you." His eyebrows puckered in concern. "Have you heard any...any news today?"

"News?" Had he somehow learned that she was being offered the manager's position? If so, why would he consider that to be bad news? "I don't think so."

He puffed out a breath through his nostrils. "Come with me."

Could no one tell her anything straight today? "Can it hold for an hour or so? I have someone waiting for me upstairs."

Stating that she had a guest in her suite only seemed to increase his agitation level. "I will be quick. Please, we should talk in my office."

He led her through a service door to the back hallway that connected the banquet rooms to the kitchen. Once in his domain, he wound his way through the cooking area at lightning speed, then past rows of stainless steel shelving and the hotel's two commercial dishwashers to his closet-sized office in the very back of the kitchen. Though small, the space was neat. Menus and order forms occupied bulletin boards on the walls. An apron hung on a corner rack and a photo of Santi's wife and children stood in a place of honor on his utilitarian desk. He opened the desk drawer and withdrew a page ripped from a newspaper, then held it out to her. "This was in yesterday's edition of *Última Celebridad*. Have you seen it?"

She took the clipping and scanned the article that dominated the top of the page. Her Spanish was far from perfect, but she gathered that it was an account of local soccer stars who'd engaged in a bar brawl after losing an important game to Real Madrid. The fight happened nearly a mile from the hotel. She quirked her mouth at Santi. "I don't get it. Were some of our employees involved?"

"No, no…not the article. The photo below it."

Her eye moved past the soccer news to the bottom of the page. There, in black and white, was a hazy photo of her sitting cross-legged on the grass with Anna's head in her lap. Beside her, Stefano was pulling off his sunglasses and smiling at her. It had been taken almost two months ago, the night they'd visited the Magic Fountain. She couldn't prevent her sharp intake of breath when she saw the caption. Roughly translated, it read: *Royal in Disguise! Secret Girlfriend Has Child!*

A paragraph-long blurb followed, speculating that the man in the photo was Prince Stefano Barrali, whose whereabouts during the weekend in question could not be verified. It went on to question the identity of the woman in the photo and her possible relationship to the prince.

She sat on the edge of Santi's desk to reread the paragraph. Though the caption could be read to indicate that Stefano fathered the mystery child, nothing in the paragraph itself indicated that, nor did Santi seem to have considered that possibility.

"I had no idea," she said. "This was several weeks ago. I didn't think anyone photographed us." She hadn't seen any cameras aimed their way. Nor was the shot taken from the direction where Ilsa and her companions were seated, snapping fountain photos with their phones.

But the published photo might explain the man on the beach. Given that this was yesterday's paper, someone could have figured out her identity and followed her today, hoping she'd lead to the prince. Or they might've followed Stefano from his hotel, hoping to discover his mystery woman. If so, there wasn't anything she could do about it now.

Besides, it wouldn't matter at all once she told Stefano yes. After that, it'd only be a matter of time before their relationship became public.

A busboy carried a tray of dishes past Santi's office. The chef cut behind Megan to close the door against the clattering of plates being loaded into the dishwasher. "My cousin works in advertising at the paper. When I saw this last night, I asked him off the record if he could find out how it was acquired. He said that a Belgian tourist was looking at her family photos after she returned home from vacation and noticed a man who appeared to be Prince Stefano in the background. She sold the photo to the paper, who cropped it to focus on you."

"This is all speculative," she said quietly as she continued to stare at the photo. "The photo was a fluke. The paper can't even say for sure that it's Stefano."

"The prince is difficult to identify," he admitted. "And Anna's face is also hard to see. But your face is very clear. This is a popular tabloid, Megan. Many of the employees read it while they're commuting to work on the bus or the metro. It will not be long before someone here identifies you, if they haven't already. I did."

"You are also the only person on the planet who knows he's visited me in my suite."

He ignored her comment, mumbling to himself as she continued to study the photo. "I hear things, you know. Things that make me think you are in trouble."

Her head whipped up. "What things?"

"I hear that you are out nearly every weekend. No one sees you come or go or knows where you are. I hear that Anna has not seen as much of her friends as usual." He waited a beat for drama before adding, "And I hear that Jack Gladwell is in the building today. It cannot be coincidence. The head of housekeeping insisted she saw him in Ramon's office—"

Megan shook her head at her friend. "Dear, dear Santi. I love you to death, but you are a worrywart. Mr. Gladwell is here, but I doubt a grainy black and white photo on the twentieth page of a gossip rag registers on his radar. He certainly didn't mention it."

Santi's eyes widened at her slip. "You have seen Jack Gladwell? In person? You spoke with him?"

"Yes. I met with him and Ramon." She held out the page. "But that's all I'm going to say, so please keep it to yourself. Here. I have to go."

He waved it off. "No, no. It is yours. I only wanted to warn you."

She let the page dangle between them a moment longer, then gave up and stuck it in the folder Jack Gladwell had handed her.

"Consider me duly warned." She couldn't help but give him a quick hug. The man was as close to a father as she had on this continent. "And thank you for your concern. You wouldn't be you if you weren't."

"You are welcome, always. I am sorry to have kept you." Santi stepped back, then closed his eyes and groaned. "The prince is in your suite now, isn't he?" He immediately waved his hands in front of his face as if dispelling a foul odor. "No, no. Say nothing. I do not wish to know."

"Someday we'll laugh about this over a bottle of wine," she assured him. "Then I'll tell you everything."

"Please, my child, some things…well, I can imagine." He shooed her out the door with a, "Go."

Chapter Twenty-Two

"Thirty-five minutes, not bad," Stefano said as Megan re-entered the suite and made her way through the entry hall toward the kitchen.

"I tried my best." She paused when she spotted him in the kitchen and arched one narrow eyebrow in curiosity. "You're cooking."

"Not cooking," he corrected, holding up the chef's knife and spinning it for her. "Slicing and dicing."

"My cantaloupe?"

"Okay, so I'm cubing it, rather than dicing it. But yes, your cantaloupe."

He wasn't used to being kept waiting, so he hadn't quite known what to do with himself. For the first few minutes after Megan left, he'd paced the room, wondering why Jack Gladwell was at the Grandspire. As one of the ten or twenty wealthiest individuals in the world and the owner of a conglomerate of companies in which he took an active interest, the man undoubtedly had a full schedule. If he wanted to see Megan, it was for a specific purpose. Was she receiving a promotion? A transfer? Any such offer coming from Gladwell himself meant a jump in both prestige and pay.

It also meant a tough decision for Megan, as if she wasn't facing a tough decision already. *If* that's what Gladwell wanted.

Finally, Stefano stopped pacing to make himself useful. He picked up a few of Anna's scattered belongings from the living area—a set of bright purple headphones, a book, her hair brush— and returned them to her bedroom, setting them neatly on her desk. He washed a glass and fork that had been left in the sink, then decided to prep the cantaloupe Megan purchased at the market that morning. The small kitchen and well-organized cabinets made finding a cutting board, knife, and bowl simple.

He thought activity would keep him from speculating on the topic of Megan's meeting. Unfortunately, since he was perfectly capable of slicing a cantaloupe and using his brain at the same time, he continued to turn it over in his mind. Soon, his thoughts turned to where things were headed with Megan when they'd been interrupted. He'd bet his entire yearly budget that she'd changed her mind about marriage. He could tell from the spread of her fingers across his chest as they talked. From the way she'd ignored her phone, despite the fact Anna might be on the line, so she could stay in his embrace. From the mix of desire, tenderness, and anticipation filling her soft blue eyes.

Yes, she had her doubts. What woman wouldn't when faced with marrying into his family? But she wanted to say yes. He felt it clear to his bones. He'd wanted her to deal with Anna first, knowing she wouldn't focus until she did. Instead, when he'd told her to answer her phone, she'd gotten Gladwell.

Now that she'd returned to the suite, as much as he itched to get right back to where they left off, he sensed that he needed to tread carefully and slowly. She was worth waiting for, if she had something else to work through first. He had to be certain that when she said yes, the commitment was rock solid, that she'd evaluated all the pros and cons and could agree with her eyes—and her heart—wide open. Anything less and she wouldn't be being true to herself.

"The meeting must have been important," he said casually as he tossed a section of the rind into the trash. "Did it go well?"

"I suspect everything Jack Gladwell wants is important, at least to him." She paused to remove her shoes and place them to the side of the countertop barstools, as if using the moment to gather her thoughts. "He congratulated me on the success of the grand reopening and the event bookings I've made. Apparently Ramon said nice things about me in his reports."

And she wondered how her name came up in Sarcaccia as a possible hire?

Stefano kept the thought to himself as he waited to see what else she'd say, but she walked past him to open the fridge and get herself a can of soda.

Certainly there was more to report. A multi-billionaire with investments all over the world wouldn't wait in the manager's office for Megan simply to tell her she did a good job. He tried again as he slid several chunks of cantaloupe from the cutting board into the bowl. "You've impressed Jack Gladwell. From what I know of him, he's not an easily impressed man."

A tinge of color spread over her cheeks. "You know him?"

"Not personally, but my parents have met him several times. He's heavily invested in Sarcaccia's wine industry."

"Oh." She held up a can of his favorite soda, but he shook his head. That's when he noticed that when she'd opened the refrigerator, she'd discreetly placed a thick folder on the opposite kitchen counter, tucking it beside the canisters of flour and sugar. She hadn't had the folder with her when she'd left. Whatever had been discussed during the meeting with Jack Gladwell, she wasn't ready to share it with him.

It shouldn't bother him—he certainly didn't share all the boring details of his work with her—but deep down, the sight of the folder unsettled him. Mostly because he suspected it contained more than boring details.

She took a seat at one of the barstools and sipped her drink as he finished cleaning up the cantaloupe. "I'm glad you waited for me. I promise, no more interruptions."

"Even if Anna calls?"

A wry smile lit her face. "I'll trust Marta to keep her occupied until you need to catch your flight. I want us to finish what we started. That is, if you're not too busy with your melon."

The spark in her eye reminded him of the first time they'd shared the sofa, the day he'd met Anna. The day they'd made love. The day she'd said no. Well, this time he meant to seal the deal. If she didn't want to discuss Gladwell, perhaps it was because she prioritized a marriage discussion.

Good.

"Before you say anything more, I have something to show you. I've been holding it all weekend." He covered the cantaloupe and placed it in the refrigerator, rinsed his hands at the sink, then walked to the sofa to retrieve the envelope from his bag.

Her expression made it clear she'd noticed the envelope when he'd pulled it out the first time. "I'm intrigued. What is it?"

"Open it and find out."

A quizzical look flitted over her face as she accepted it, slid her finger under the flap, then withdrew the sheaf of papers inside. He leaned against the counter and waited. After a moment, her eyes widened. "Stefano? What is this?"

"It's the information the committee is planning to give the candidates for the conference center position when they approach them. A complete job description, information on the center itself, and the proposed compensation package. I received a copy and thought it best to share it with you early."

She inhaled as she perused the top page. After she finished, she raised her eyes to his. They were filled with a confusion he didn't understand. "Why?"

He pulled out the stool beside hers and sat, wanting to be at her level. "Because your decision is tougher than any other candidate's. If you do decide to interview for the job, you'll be weighing all this, plus your relationship with me. Either way, I felt you needed time to know what you might be getting into." He paused. "Whatever decisions you make."

"It looks wonderful. Sounds wonderful." She set the papers on the countertop without reading further. "But I'm not sure I should be doing this right now."

"Why not?" he asked. The timing should be perfect. She could wrap up her work at the Grandspire and move to Sarcaccia on her own timetable. "The committee wants to start booking conferences soon, since the center is scheduled for completion in less than a year. You'd get in at exactly the right time to set the tone for the center and the type of events it hosts. It should be a great challenge, exactly what you said you wanted for your next position."

The more he'd read about the qualifications, the more convinced he'd become the position was right up her alley. And given the revenue she'd generated for the Grandspire, she should walk into the job, even without his recommendation. He'd seen the list of candidates and heard enough of the committee's discussions to know she'd blow them away during the interviews.

She took a long sip of her drink as he spoke, then set the can on the counter. Her shoulders were back, her entire body rigid, as if she were bracing for a punch. For the life of him, he couldn't imagine why presenting her with information on a job made her more tense than the conversation they'd begun earlier.

Patience wasn't his strong suit, but he waited until she was ready to speak. At long last, she met his gaze.

"Forget the job for the moment. I think we both know there's a bigger decision to be made here. Before I went downstairs, we were talking about something else." She angled her index finger between them. "I don't want a job—any job—to cloud that discussion. Like you said, it's about what works between you and me."

"Then let's talk." His confidence bolstered, he shifted enough so his knees bumped against hers. A smile lit her face as he did so, one that went all the way to her expressive eyes. Better yet, her expression was filled with the same barely-contained anticipation he felt.

It was a smile he knew he'd remember as long as he lived.

Softly, he asked, "Megan, do you love me?"

Her expression clouded. A heartbeat passed, then two. She straightened on her stool, her knees pulling away from contact with his. "Wait...*you're* asking me—" Her lower lip twitched. "Tell me, Stefano, why do you want to marry me?"

He frowned, unable to make sense of the sudden change within her. Surely by now, after the weeks they'd spent together, she'd know how she felt. But what was he supposed to say? If he professed his love for her now, would she believe him? Or accuse him of trying to control the situation, saying whatever it took to get his way?

"Is it because it's convenient, especially if I can be employed in Sarcaccia? Because of Anna?" Darkness edged into her voice as she added, "Or do you want to marry me because it's the *right* thing to do?"

"Megan, it's all of the above, and much, much more. I would hope that I've demonstrated that over the last two months." He wondered why his simple question spurred such a reaction. "But you didn't answer my question, and frankly, I think it's a very important one: Do you love me?"

He had to know. While he'd been raised with limited freedoms, she'd enjoyed autonomy. He couldn't ask her to change her life so drastically for anything but love. She had to know clear to her bones that she was making the right decision, and for the right reasons. He couldn't face another debacle like Ariana.

Losing Megan would pierce him in a way ending his relationship with Ariana hadn't and never could.

"Whether or not I love you isn't the point—"

It was the whole point. He tried a firmer approach. "What are you trying to tell me, Megan? Where is all this coming from?"

He caught the slight shake of her hands before she stood and planted them on her hips. "You want me to declare my love for you so you can say, 'Great, I have a palace apartment for you, I have a school for our child. And best of all, I have a job for you.' That's not what I want, Stefano."

"I thought we weren't talking about the job anymore." How, after all these years, did he not understand women? "So what is it, exactly, that you do want? Because right now, you're confusing the hell out of me."

"You *idiot!* I want you to marry me for me!"

Instantly, her face went red with embarrassment, as if she wished she could take back the outburst. When he remained silent, she pressed her palms together as if the action would keep her composed. "Look, I don't want you to marry me because it's convenient. Or because you're afraid that when the press gets wind of our relationship—which they will, eventually, whatever the nature of our relationship may be—that you need to protect me, and you can do it best if I'm under your wing."

He pushed off his stool and took a step toward her. She should know that after all that had happened with Ariana, he wouldn't propose out of convenience. He wasn't sure how in asking Megan the same question—if she wanted to marry him for *him*—he'd managed to shoot himself in the foot. On the other hand, the first part of her statement was *I want you to marry me*. And that was all he wanted, for the rest of his life. She only needed reassurance.

He was more than happy to give it to her.

Joy unfurled in his chest, so powerfully he couldn't stop the smile on his face. "Of course I want to marry you for you. When I brought up the job, I was simply trying to make your decision easier by ensuring your life in Sarcaccia *wouldn't* be all about being my wife. You can have a fantastic career if you want, your own identity separate from the royal family. And if protecting you and Anna is wrong… well, that would my responsibility as your husband."

Husband. He liked the way it rolled off his tongue when it came to Megan.

Megan didn't seem to agree. The smile he expected to light her face in response to his own failed to materialize.

"All that being said, it's *my* decision whether or not I take on that challenge." She eased away from the barstools, once again using physical distance to shut him out. "It's not something you can protect me from. And I don't want a job because you got it for me. I want a job I've earned and that I've chosen of my own free will. None of that has anything to do with marriage."

He gestured toward the envelope he'd given her, which lay on the granite countertop. "That's all this was. Information so you could make the decision that's best for you. I would never push you into a job. It wouldn't make sense. If you hated your job, how happy could you be? All I want is for you to be happy, whether you're my wife or not, whether you're working or not, though obviously I'd prefer it if being my wife made you happy."

She exhaled, visibly relenting. At that moment, his gaze snagged on the folder she'd brought back from her meeting. Again, seeing it tucked beside the kitchen canisters bothered him. When he faced her once more, he saw she'd noticed the direction of his gaze.

The air stilled between them. He knew then that his gut instinct about the folder was right. The physical space between them was the least of his problems. A gulf existed between them when it came to trust.

Without trust, they couldn't move forward.

"Tell me again what Gladwell wanted."

CHAPTER TWENTY-THREE

At her hesitation, he continued, "No. Let me guess. He made you an offer to stay on here at the Grandspire. Maybe with a raise, given the success of the revitalization. Or did he offer you another position, perhaps at one of his other properties? The man must own a dozen hotels. Then there are the casinos—"

"My meeting with Jack Gladwell has nothing to do with what we're discussing—"

"Oh, I think it does." Otherwise, she wouldn't have been so testy about the conference center job information he'd given her. She wouldn't have hidden the folder or avoided his question about how her meeting went. She'd have simply come back from her meeting and said, I love you, Stefano. I can't wait to spend the rest of my life with you.

He strode into the kitchen and grabbed the folder. The look of surprise, then dismay on Megan's face—and her subsequent attempt to school her features into a more neutral expression—reinforced his suspicions.

She didn't trust him. Not the way she should, given what he was asking of her. The joy that had spread through him only a moment before shriveled and died, leaving him hollow inside.

"There's a job offer in here, isn't there?"

She looked down for a moment before meeting his gaze once more. Too long a moment. "Yes, there's a job offer in there." She took a step toward the kitchen counter. "But it doesn't matter."

Before she could reach over the counter to take it away, he flipped open the folder. He knew he had no right to intrude in her private affairs in this way, but at this point, he had nothing to lose. He had to know what Jack Gladwell offered. Several sheets of fine stationery, the top page of which bore the logo for Gladwell's hotel conglomerate, filled the folder. A quick glance told Stefano that Megan was being offered the Grandspire's manager's position—and at an impressive salary—but what caught his attention was the smaller, ripped newspaper page sitting on top.

Oh, Megan. The words echoed like a whisper through his head. He set the folder on the table and held the page under the kitchen lights so he could see it clearly. It was a gritty, obviously zoomed-in photo taken at the Magic Fountain, one that showed him sitting with Anna and Megan.

He didn't speak Catalan, but he knew enough to get the gist of the headline, something about a disguised royal and a girlfriend with a child. His mouth went dry as dust as he stared at the photo. It was as if his past mistakes were repeating themselves. He couldn't allow what happened with Ariana to happen to Megan. "Did Jack Gladwell give you this?"

"No. One of my coworkers saw it and wanted me to know. But it's not important...if you read the paragraph below the picture, they say they don't even know if—"

"How can you say it's not important after all I went through with Ariana? Of course it's important!" Did she not grasp the ramifications?

She moved closer, rounding the counter to within arm's reach. Her voice was calm and reassuring. "Stefano, it's not the same."

No, it's not. Because this time, he was crazy in love. He was older and wiser and knew what that scrap of newspaper meant. And this time, there was a child involved.

The fact she hid such important information indicated issues were far bigger than the two of them. The risks if she didn't trust him were more grave than heartbreak.

His jaw ached, as if resisting what he knew had to be said. "The thing is, Megan, Ariana and her parents trusted my family enough to call and let us know what was happening. To tell us that the media tracked her and that she'd been forced to hide out in a hotel—"

Hands spread, Megan said, "But Stefano, you created the spectacle then. Your parents primed the media. Then, when they were watching, you gave them what they wanted by running across the courtyard half-dressed. You said it yourself: You were young and foolish. But there's no spectacle now. There was no reason for me to tell you about the photo because it doesn't matter."

"There will always be media—"

"Look, your life is what it is. You're going to get attention no matter what you do. You can't protect me from that. You can't even protect yourself from that, not entirely. But whether or not I can live with it is my decision. And that decision has to be based on—"

"There *are* things I can do to protect you. You just have to trust me. That's what this boils down to. But you don't."

"I do."

A sarcastic, barking laugh escaped him. He closed the folder and tapped it on the countertop as he stared at her. "This is what you call trust? Hiding this newspaper photo? Keeping the fact you have a job offer from me?"

She probably still didn't believe he hadn't put her name onto the shortlist for the conference center position, either.

Now it was her turn to look exasperated. "Stefano, I admit it. I didn't want you to see those, not yet. But not because I don't trust you. I didn't want them to weigh into our discussion of whether or not we should get married. Marriage shouldn't be about jobs. Or about what other people might think about our relationship, even if those opinions are broadcast on the evening news."

"I agree." So maybe *trust* wasn't the right word. But there had to be a certain level of openness. If there wasn't, it wouldn't work between them. It was bad enough he feared saying the words *I love you* to Megan might lead her to accuse him once more of saying anything to get his way.

He stared at her for a moment in silence.

After all these weeks, she still didn't grasp that he'd do anything for her. If she did, she'd have wanted him to know about the job offer, to have him be part of the discussion about what was best for her and Anna, and to ensure that no decision resulted in Megan or Anna being hurt. But she hadn't given him that benefit, despite the fact he'd done exactly that for her, showing her through his actions how he felt, and giving her all the time in the world to consider his marriage proposal.

He could tell from her body language that she wanted to say yes.

If she did, though, and she couldn't be open enough to make him part of the decision making where she and Anna were concerned, he could never be a true partner and husband to her. Worse, he couldn't protect them. One day, they would end up hurt.

From the moment he met Megan, he'd loved her sense of independence. Today, for the first time, he despised it for what that independence meant. No one could be that independent and married to royalty. But if that fierce sense of independence changed…well, she wouldn't be Megan any longer.

"All right," he acquiesced. "I suppose I can see things from your point of view." He set the folder on the counter and pushed it toward her. "You should hang on to this. I'm sorry I intruded. I shouldn't have. If you wanted to keep this to yourself, that's your call."

"Thank you."

He was about to prove to himself he could keep a promise—a promise he'd made in bed, in a hazy post-sex afterglow, but one he'd meant all the same—even if Megan never realized that's what he was doing.

"On the other subject we were discussing…I know you're having a hard time telling me what you need to say. So how about if I ease the burden?"

Anticipation made her mouth go soft. He took a step back, out of her reach, and squared his shoulders to draw up to his full height.

Dear God, this was going to be painful. He allowed a slow, reassuring smile to form.

"Given what Jack Gladwell is offering you, plus the fact it means Anna can stay in her current school, I understand that it's best if you stay here and take the job at the Grandspire. Not only are the people who work in this building like a family to you, you've been incredibly successful here. There's no reason not to take the next step up the ladder. With Gladwell as a mentor, your potential is limitless."

"What?" She faltered, then opened her mouth as if to argue.

He deliberately ignored her and forged ahead. Only years of training kept his tone upbeat, as if he were speaking to a foreign diplomat over dinner about an upcoming event they both planned to attend. "I'll endeavor to keep my life as separate from yours as possible to ensure your privacy. That way, you won't have to worry about more photos like this appearing in the paper. Sound good?"

Her eyes widened, then glimmered with tears. She blinked them back and shook her head. "Stefano, I didn't mean to—"

"There's nothing further to discuss where marriage is concerned, so don't worry about hurting my feelings. You were absolutely right to hesitate when I proposed. I understand that now." He felt his emotions harden, as if a shard of ice pierced his heart before expanding outward and encasing it. He embraced the sensation. He needed it if he were to ignore the stricken look on her face and get through the next few minutes. "I'm just grateful that you gave me the opportunity to get to know you and Anna better while you considered it. Like you said the morning we had breakfast in the Jardín Alba, you and Anna have built a fantastic life here. You're an amazing mother. And you'll be the best possible manager for the Grandspire. They're lucky to have you."

He couldn't change who he was, his nationality, his title, or the family into which he was born. He couldn't change the media or people's hunger for gossip. All he could do was choose how to handle the situation. He'd made some terrible mistakes in that regard in the past. Perhaps, in some small way, he was now righting those wrongs.

"You're misreading the entire situation." Her voice sounded hollow, as if she knew there was nothing she could do to change his mind but couldn't let go, either. "And Anna…Anna won't understand."

The hitch in her speech made it clear she was the one who didn't understand. One day, she would. And she'd be grateful he'd made the wise choice. It was the only choice that could keep both her and Anna safe.

He shrugged, as if it weren't a big deal. "Just tell her the truth, that it's wiser for you to stay in Barcelona while I stay in Sarcaccia. Let her know I'll continue to support her with every resource at my disposal—and by that, I mean emotionally as well as financially—and that I'll visit her here in Barcelona or anywhere else you choose when we both feel it's safe to do so and can arrange a private location."

He rounded the counter and kissed her forehead, just below a stray tendril of blonde hair, careful not to touch Megan with anything other than a quick press of his lips. "My car's going to be here any second. Let me know when it's a good time for me to visit again. And please tell Anna that I love her."

And I love you. Enough not to tell you, even if I thought you'd believe me.

Megan nodded, but he sensed it more than saw it. He grabbed his bag, then walked to the door without looking at her. It was abrupt, bordering on rude, but he couldn't let her think anything other than that he was oblivious to her suffering.

In truth, he couldn't bear to see her wounded expression as he left. But damn if he couldn't keep a promise.

CHAPTER TWENTY-FOUR

A fly buzzed against the window in front of Stefano, fighting to escape the confines of the palace library. He listened idly to the repeated thunk, thunk, thunk as the creature pummeled itself against the thick glass, unable to comprehend its inability to move out of the cool building and into the brilliant Sarcaccian sunshine.

He sympathized.

Stefano leaned back in his leather chair, straightening his legs under the centuries-old desk and yawning deeply. For the last five hours, he'd been reviewing the final plans for the island's transit system upgrades. It was a revolutionary, detailed system that required his full attention, but at the moment he couldn't give it.

Megan filled his mind.

There'd been no mistaking the confusion and frustration on her face when he accused her of not trusting him after she'd hidden the Grandspire job offer and the gossip page. But then he'd seen another emotion, one she tried to smother when he'd cut off her acceptance of his marriage proposal and claimed he understood her desire not to marry him.

She hadn't hidden the information because she didn't trust him. Not really. She'd hidden it because she loved him deeply and couldn't stand to have him worry. She loved him enough to marry him.

It both warmed and broke his heart.

He grimaced as the fly moved lower, then repeated its assault on the window. He'd made the only decision he could under the circumstances. There was nothing to second-guess.

He couldn't bear to see the woman he loved—and he loved her with every cell in his mind and body—at risk, even if she were willing to take that risk. Even if she did eventually learn to share information so he could protect her. He couldn't bear the haunted look in her eyes if something happened that put Anna in harm's way. He couldn't bear the thought of Anna being anything other than the bubbly, brilliant girl she was. But having to watch her every move and utterance the way he had during his own childhood would alter her personality, and not for the better.

He hadn't thought he was asking Megan to give up her independence. But in asking her to be open with him so he could protect her, that's exactly what he was doing.

The old cliché was agonizingly true: If you love something, set it free. If it comes back to you, it's yours. But since Megan couldn't come back to him—not without drastically changing her entire life and that of their daughter—it wasn't meant to be. Even if she had come to love him.

Insisting that she'd been right to turn down his proposal and stay at the Grandspire was as good a method as any to keep her safe.

Problem was, what now? It'd been two weeks since he'd set foot in Barcelona and still he felt unsettled. Restless. Trapped in a life he didn't want, but needed to live.

He watched the fly circle the spacious room, zooming past the stone fireplace and briefly lighting upon the back of a sofa before it flew in a zigzagged line toward another closed window.

A few months ago, he never would've rankled at spending a Saturday working. But while he'd made the transit system his passion the last few years, seeing his hard work come to fruition didn't give him the satisfaction he expected. He wanted to be in Barcelona, sitting at Megan's table, sharing the plans with her. Responding to her questions, listening to her ideas, seeing the glint in her eye as she noticed the timing of city bus routes during rush hour or the ease of connections from the airport to Sarcaccia's new conference center. Because she'd notice every detail.

Stefano shoved his fingers through his hair, elbows wide, then shook his head and adjusted his position at the desk. Once the transit plans were approved and construction on the system was underway, perhaps he'd find the joy again. He'd see firsthand the ways the Sarcaccians could benefit from the new system through construction employment, ease of city congestion, and quicker commutes from the suburbs into the city. People would have more housing options, rather than being stuck close to their jobs. Tourism would increase. The economy would thrive. As much as he craved Megan's approval, it was the citizens of Sarcaccia whom he was obliged to consider—first, last, and always—just as he always had.

The fly thunked against the window again. After two more failed tries, it spiraled down to rest on the wide sill as if recuperating for another attempt.

A knock sounded at the door, followed by his mother's gentle voice. "Are you busy, Stefano? Mind if we come in for a moment?"

He looked over his shoulder to see both of his parents enter the library—not waiting for his answer—and close the door behind them. Whatever they wanted, it was serious.

He gestured toward the sofa. "Have you eaten yet? I'm afraid I only have a pitcher of water—"

"We're fine, thank you," his father responded. King Carlo allowed his wife to sit first, then joined her on the sofa. They were an impressive pair, Stefano thought, perhaps more now that they were in their early sixties than when they were young. Queen Fabrizia jogged, biked, and attended yoga classes to stay fit, and it showed. Though she'd allowed wisps of gray to appear in her hair, she maintained a sleek, modern cut, one that suited her heart-shaped face. She easily looked a dozen years younger than her actual age, as did her husband. Despite a number of health scares over the years, King Carlo's ramrod-straight posture, firm jaw, and lean build combined to convince the world of his vitality. They each wore suits—hers an off-white, his a slim pinstriped gray—and carried themselves with a refined, self-possessed manner that left no doubt they were in charge of the expansive palace and all that surrounded it.

They didn't intimidate him as they once did, but he respected them and all they'd accomplished in their years ruling the country.

Stefano pushed away from the desk and crossed the room to the wall of windows overlooking the palace gardens. The early summer flowers were in full bloom, the trees verdant, the fountains shooting plumes of water skyward. It appeared a veritable paradise. "Since both of you are here, I assume you have something important to discuss?"

At their silence, he glanced behind him in time to see a look pass between them. His mother's lips thinned in consternation and she shook her head at her husband.

"What is it, Mother?"

She started to say something, stopped, then started again. "We don't wish to intrude, but we've noticed you haven't spent your weekends at home in quite some time. You've taken the plane, but haven't left a flight plan or word of your whereabouts with the staff. Then, when you arrive for Sunday dinner, you're barely attentive and hardly speak to our guests."

"I'm home now. And I was home last weekend, as well."

"Yet you lock yourself in the library or your apartment and speak to no one, not even the staff, until you appear for Sunday dinner, and you're no more sociable than you were before." She folded her hands in her lap. "Again, we don't want to intrude on your personal life, but is something amiss?"

"Are you seeing someone? Has it been causing problems?" King Carlo's tone held none of the queen's tentativeness. "If so, we should be informed. We realize you want your privacy, but you need to trust us for your own safety. The paparazzi can be aggressive, particularly when you're abroad. Your reputation—"

"Damn the reputation, Father." He shook his head and turned back toward the window. Funny, how his dad trumpeted safety, trust, and privacy. In a calmer voice, he said, "I apologize. I didn't mean that. In answer to your question, no, I'm not seeing anyone. Not at the moment. You have no call to worry."

Outside, a gardener pushed a wheelbarrow full of tree trimmings. Stefano couldn't imagine what the man found to shear. Every tree, every bush appeared immaculate. Not a leaf out of place. Stefano had spent hours upon hours running through the gardens as a child, often sneaking off to the far end of the property, where the trees and grass had been allowed to remain in their natural state. How had he not noticed the sterile nature of the garden as a whole before? Its lack of wildness the closer one moved to the palace itself?

Or was he merely chafing at the restrictions imposed on him now that his fortune of birth meant he couldn't have Megan?

"Your mother is concerned," the king continued. "As am I. You should extend us the courtesy of letting us know when you're traveling, even if you keep the details to yourself."

"Any further travel will be logged with my administrative assistant."

"Stefano." His mother's voice was soft, edging toward a plea.

He faced her, leaning to rest his hips on the wide windowsill. They *were* butting in where they didn't belong, but he appreciated that their curiosity about his personal life seemed mixed with genuine worry. They weren't perfect parents—far from it—but then again, who was?

Megan. A vision of her cradling Anna's head in her lap at the Magic Fountain flashed in his mind before he squelched it.

"I apologize if I've been rude. I've had a rough week. That's all."

Behind him, the fly resumed its pounding against the glass. His parents looked past him to track the insect's movements.

"That is huge," his mother breathed. "When we're done here, I'll call one of the staff to remove it."

"No need." Stefano spun and flipped the heavy metal locks at the base of the window. Time for the fly to get the sunshine it craved.

"Stefano, that must weigh fifty or sixty pounds. It hasn't been opened in years! Decades, more likely," his mother argued. "I'll call someone."

"It's only a fly, Fabrizia," the king said. "It'll die in a day or two and we can sweep it away."

Stefano ignored his father and pushed against the sides of the frame, driven by a sudden need to conquer the ancient mechanism. With a groan, the window gave bit by bit, chips of paint falling to the sill as it loosened in its chamber. He bent his knees, grabbed the handles mounted to the window's lowest edge, and lifted. It took nearly all his back and leg strength, but he managed to raise it to the height of his forehead. Outside, the gardener stopped pushing the wheelbarrow and scanned the building to search out the source of the sound. Within seconds, the fly looped down and out into the fresh air, heading past the gardener to freedom.

Stefano let the window slide back into place, then twisted the stiff metal locks to their usual position.

"If you were so desperate to be rid of it you could've swatted it. Would've been easier," his father said as Stefano faced them again. The twin vertical creases above the bridge of King Carlo's nose deepened. "I wish you'd tell us what's wrong. You're not yourself. Is it the transportation minister? Has he been—"

"It's not the transportation minister." He held up his hand to stop his father from making another guess. The gesture only irritated his father more, as King Carlo was unaccustomed to having his statements cut off.

Stefano strode from the windows to the room's center, taking the seat opposite his parents. They wanted to know? Fine.

"I'll tell you what's wrong. But" —he held up his index finger, daring to threaten the King and Queen of Sarcaccia— "what I'm about to say does not leave this room. Under any circumstances. If it does, suffice it to say it will have a negative impact on our Sunday dinner tradition."

His mother eased forward on the sofa but said nothing, her eyes fixed on his face, while the king crossed his arms over his chest in barely-contained annoyance and clamped his lips together. His eyes flashed fire.

"I've been taking the jet to Barcelona," he said. "Other than this week and last, I've gone every weekend since attending the reopening of the Grandspire with Mahmoud Said."

His mother's green eyes, so much like Anna's, widened. For the first time, he realized how much Anna resembled his mother. They had the same cheekbones, the same eyes, the same smile. He wondered if, in her youth, his mother had the same zest for life. He rather imagined she had...in some ways, she still did. His mother would fall apart when she met Anna. *If* she met Anna.

"Is the report true, then? The one about the woman who has a child?" his mother asked. "I saw it in the paper a few weeks ago, but there's been nothing since. Your father and I didn't want to pry. We'd hoped you would come to us if there was anything to the story."

That was a point in their favor, at least.

"Yes and no," he told her. "Yes, the report was true. But no, I'm no longer seeing her."

"Ah." His father's shoulders dropped and the furrows in his brow eased. He folded his hands in his lap and exhaled. "You do not sound happy, and I am sorry for that. I'm sure you had a great fondness for this woman if you were willing to see her despite the fact she's already a parent. But in the long run, I think you'll see that it's for the best. Such a relationship would be extremely difficult for someone in your position."

Rage simmered in Stefano's gut, but it wasn't the ignorance of his father's words that incensed him. It was the man's obvious relief. "You're right about the difficulties, Father, but it is *not* for the best. Not at all."

"You just need some time, son." His father's tone was dismissive. "There are plenty of women who are capable of making you happy. It is only a matter of time."

"No. There's only one woman." He knew his next sentence would change his life, and possibly Megan and Anna's, but it had to be said. "And that woman's child is my child, too."

CHAPTER TWENTY-FIVE

"Oh, Stefano." Crinkles appeared at the corners of his mother's eyes. She leaned toward him, placing her elbows on her knees and steepling her fingertips in front of her as she regarded him. He could feel her instinct to reach across the space between them and touch him, to offer comfort, but she resisted. "You're such a good man. From the time you were young, you've always felt such compassion for others, especially for children. I adore that about you. But feeling that this woman's child is somehow your responsibility—"

"It's not a *feeling*, Mother. She is mine."

His mother stared at him in silence, processing his words. She seemed not to breathe. She swallowed hard and straightened. When she glanced at her husband to gauge his reaction, her lower jaw trembled. Despite the gentle demeanor for which she was beloved, Queen Fabrizia was given to displays of emotion on only the rarest of occasions. His mother must be experiencing the same sense of shock he had upon hearing about Anna from Megan.

King Carlo merely raised one thick, well-groomed eyebrow. "Have you had a DNA test?"

"Ever practical, aren't you?" Stefano couldn't prevent the snarl that escaped him. "And no, I have done no such thing. There's no need."

King Carlo closed his eyes. Stefano suspected the man was counting backward from ten before speaking. When he did, his words were well-tempered. "Why do you believe this child is yours?"

"I know. If you saw her, you'd know, too." No DNA test would be necessary, even for his father, who was as cynical as they came.

"Truly?" The barely whispered question came from his mother.

"Truly."

"But…I can't believe this. A child?"

"Yes."

"I wish you'd told us as soon as you found out. How old is she?" A tentative smile tugged at the corner of his mother's lips as she asked the question, even as her eyes brimmed with unshed tears at the realization that she was, at long last, a grandmother. "You did say it's a girl?"

"Her name is Anna. She just turned ten and she's wonderful." He shot his father a quick look. "And before you ask, yes, I had an intimate relationship with the girl's mother then."

His mother angled her head, thinking back. The hint of joy he'd seen in her expression at learning she had a granddaughter faltered. "But that's when you and Ariana—"

She stopped abruptly when King Carlo patted her knee and stood. He moved to the rear of the sofa, then bracketed his wife's slender shoulders with his hands, giving her a light squeeze. Though the king's lips remained pressed in a tight line, Stefano would swear that if he could see into his father's skull, there would be wheels spinning so fast as to blur.

"May we ask the woman's name?" his father asked. "It wasn't in the newspaper piece your mother and I read."

Stefano flexed his fingers against the fabric of the chair. It pained him to tell his parents, knowing they'd want to speak with Megan. No doubt their minds would leap ahead to how they'd react in public if a reporter went digging and the story broke open. They'd want to craft a press release and coach Megan on how to handle herself.

But would they act in Megan and Anna's best interests? Or their own? He wanted to believe they'd consider those interests one and the same, but wasn't certain enough to take the chance.

"Again, between us" —he looked for each of his parents' nods of agreement— "her name is Megan Hallberg. She's an American I met in Venezuela. She now works at the Grandspire, which is how I ran in to her again. That's when I found out about Anna."

"You must have been caught completely off-guard," his father replied. His hands remained at the queen's shoulders, but the color had slowly leached from Queen Fabrizia's face. "Wait, if this was during the grand reopening....what did Mahmoud say? Does he know?"

"He doesn't know. No one knows." He fixed his father with a pointed look. "That's why I asked you about Dagmar and whether she'd ever been told to hold my calls or cull the list of messages. Megan was trying to reach me to let me know about the pregnancy."

"I see." His father absorbed that. "But she did not persist? Or send a message some other way?"

"She did, actually. She went on the Internet to try to find a way to contact me other than through Dagmar, since she suspected I wasn't getting her messages. That's when she learned of my engagement. At that point, she assumed I was intentionally disregarding the calls and thought it best to keep the news to herself."

His mother hissed in a breath. Stefano stared at her until she raised her eyes to his. What he saw there left him sick inside. "What is it, Mother? You look as though you're ready to pass out."

"Oh. Nothing. I'm simply...simply trying to imagine how you must've felt."

He didn't buy it. "You know the name Megan Hallberg" —his mother shook her head even as the words left his mouth— "...you *knew*...didn't you? And you kept it from me?"

"No! I had no idea!" His mother's jaw shook harder now.

"Then what *did* you know?" He hated the edge in his voice, but he'd never seen his mother like this. Even when she'd heard of her own mother's death in a car accident via the news, rather than from the police working the scene, she hadn't shown such raw emotion.

She reached to up to thread her fingers through King Carlo's. He looked as disturbed as Stefano. Whatever the queen knew, she hadn't shared any details with her husband.

"There was a Megan—back then, you have to understand that you had so many phone calls—and she was one of the callers I asked Dagmar to defer when we were trying to deal with wedding plans. I hadn't thought about it since, but once you said Hallberg…now I remember. But I didn't realize, Stefano. I would never do that—"

"Then why? You didn't even know her. You couldn't possibly know what she wanted."

"Everything was going so well for you. You and Ariana were engaged, which was my dream—and yes, I eventually realized that it was my dream, not yours—and you were about to start your military training." A single, flat tear slipped from the corner of her eye, but she didn't notice. Her entire being seemed devoted to telling her side of the story. "Then, the night before the press conference to announce the engagement, you had dinner with your father and me in our private apartment. Do you remember?"

"Of course." He'd finally apologized to his father for the argument they'd had the morning he'd stormed across the street to Ariana's hotel. He'd hoped never again to have such a stressful discussion with his parents.

"After we talked through the press conference, I asked about your time in Venezuela. What types of work you did, where you traveled, what kind of people you met. If you thought the experience was a valuable one. You mentioned a woman named Megan. You never said she was a girlfriend or that there was anything between you, but your expression told me she was special, and she was the only person you mentioned by name. When I saw that same name on Dagmar's list of calls soon afterward, I…well, that's when I suspected you might have had an affair with her. I didn't want you second-guessing your relationship with

Ariana. We had such a tight window while you were home to start the wedding planning. I didn't want you distracted by phone calls from someone I believed was inconsequential. And I didn't want anyone else to discover you'd had a fling so close to becoming engaged."

Stefano grit his teeth so hard his jaw ached. *Fling.* The word Megan herself had used when turning down his proposal.

As angry as he wanted to be with his mother, if Megan herself had argued that what they'd had was nothing more than a fling, how could he have expected his mother to believe otherwise?

"I am so sorry, Stefano. I had no idea." Remorse filled her voice. "I truly believed that deflecting the phone calls was harmless. That I was protecting both you and Ariana."

She shouldn't have interfered. She shouldn't have put Dagmar in such a terrible position. And, judging from King Carlo's guarded expression, she shouldn't be taking the fall for an action with which he agreed. That was assuming he hadn't taken the same action himself. Stefano wouldn't put it beyond his father to have approached Dagmar separately with a similar directive, asking that no calls from young women be put through unless they were strictly for business purposes.

It did no good to let his anger fester over something that happened a decade ago. He let out a long, purging breath, then reached across the space between them and gave his mother's hand a quick squeeze. "I forgive you."

It occurred to him then that, had he been more open with his parents, they'd have known he didn't need "protecting" from Megan. Not that he'd ever have told them about his romantic life, but the irony of the situation wasn't lost on him.

Finally, his father spoke. "I know it was a long time ago and it changes nothing, but did your...your encounter in Venezuela contribute to the end of your engagement?"

"No. Ariana had no idea. Frankly, she wouldn't have cared if she did."

His father tilted his head slightly, as if to ask, *then why did it end?*

Stefano forgot that they had no clue. He'd been so angry at himself for being manipulated and for—as Megan put it—taking rash actions in order to control the situation, that when he and Ariana made the decision to call off the wedding, he'd refused to tell his parents anything more than what was in the press release.

To this day, he could recite it word for word: *Prince Stefano and Ariana Bassi have mutually agreed to end their engagement. They have the deepest respect and admiration for each other and remain close friends. Therefore, they humbly request that the media honor their privacy and that of their families. No further statements will be forthcoming.*

He looked at his father and shrugged. "We didn't love each other. As much as I wanted to give you grandchildren and ensure the throne for the family, I couldn't marry a woman I didn't love. I wanted better for myself. I wanted better for Ariana. I was truly happy for her when she married."

"And what about you?" Though there was hope in his mother's voice, doubt lingered in her eyes as she asked the question. "What is going to make you happy?"

He stood, clarity coming to the jumbled, restless thoughts he'd had since leaving Megan. He could be happy—well, perhaps not happy so much as satisfied—if he could ensure Anna was happy. It's what Megan would want.

"Doing what's best for my child." And doing what he should've done for himself a long time ago.

"Will you bring her here?" King Carlo asked. "We would need to make arrangements for her security first, but it would allow her to receive the best education possible and access to all the—"

"No." He smiled to himself, resolved at last, while at the same time finding it humorous that his father suggested exactly the same course of action he'd initially proposed to Megan. How ludicrous it must have sounded to her then. "No, she already has the best of everything. In fact, I'll no longer be here, either."

His mother pushed off the sofa and approached him. "I know you're angry, even if you say we're forgiven. But you can't leave Sarcaccia."

"Oh, I'm not. But I *am* leaving the palace."

"No." The single word came from his father.

"Is that your desire? Or a command?" He met his father's iron gaze. Neither of them budged or spoke. Since the palace was constructed, royals lived within its walls until they married and had children. Often, they stayed until the eldest ascended the throne and their own offspring needed the space. But to his knowledge, the tradition wasn't law.

Finally, Stefano looked to his mother. "I'll let you know where to contact me as soon as I'm settled."

He crossed the library to his desk and neatly stacked his documents for later. A thought occurred to him, and he glanced up to take in his parents' horrified looks. "Have you considered taking a family vacation like the ones we took to Sicily when I was a child? We had so much freedom. There was time to relax, to enjoy each other's company, to be away from our round-the-clock public lives and have real family conversations. Not like our Sunday dinners, where we're surrounded by dignitaries."

"What?" His mother sounded confused. "You want to go to Sicily?"

"Not me, us. Maybe next year, in the spring, when the flowers are just beginning to bloom and we can go for walks or bicycle rides like we used to. I think it'd be very good for this family. Help us remember what's most important. Think about it."

With that, he strode out of the library, made a sharp left to jog down the palace's rear staircase, then pushed open the double doors to the gardens and the sunshine.

CHAPTER TWENTY-SIX

The text appeared on Megan's phone at one a.m.

In New Delhi airport. Flight to London with stop at BCN late tomorrow afternoon. Would a dinner invitation be considered railroading?

Though the number was blocked, she didn't need to ask who'd sent the text. She typed back a wish for a safe flight and asked Jack to call her at her Grandspire office when he landed in Barcelona so she could make a dinner reservation.

Megan then proceeded to toss and turn all night, her brain wrestling with her career dilemma even as her sheets became a tangle around her legs, but everything pointed to the same conclusion. She had to take the Grandspire job. No other offers would be forthcoming. It was her own damned fault. She'd been in such a funk during the last two weeks she'd hardly slept, let alone done the necessary follow-up for other possible positions.

Thank goodness Jack Gladwell took a last-minute trip to Nepal last Thursday, buying her another week until she was obligated to give him an answer. Not that it helped her in the least.

She rolled over and glanced at her bedside clock. Though it wasn't yet five in the morning, she tossed her sheets aside. May as well get up and face the day. When her feet hit the floor, she stifled a yawn.

After years of hard work at the Grandspire, she should be thrilled to be offered the position as manager. The pay and benefits were phenomenal, she and Anna loved Barcelona, and Anna would still be able to visit with Stefano. In fact, her life could continue much the way it had, but with a lot more financial and long-term job security. So why did it feel underwhelming?

Why had she put off accepting the job for nearly two weeks? Even with Jack Gladwell in Nepal, she could've left a message with his administrative assistant.

Because you fell in love with a prince, you idiot. Because saying yes to the Grandspire means saying no to a chance with Prince Charming and happily ever after.

She nabbed her toothbrush from its holder on the bathroom counter, squirted on the requisite amount of blue gel, then stared at herself in the mirror. Fatigue caused her own image to sway before her, spurring a flashback to her early days with Anna, when she'd walked her tiny apartment, exhausted, waiting for Stefano to call and tell her he wanted her. It'd been a pipe dream then, and it was a pipe dream now.

She ran a quick stream of water over her toothbrush before shoving it in her mouth.

Once the sun rose and she dropped off Anna for her first day of summer basketball camp, Megan would make the dinner call, then tell Jack Gladwell she'd waited to let him know she was accepting the position until she could speak to him personally.

Time to be a realist, Hallberg. Prince Charming only appears in fairy tales.

What man asked a woman to marry him, presented her with a pack of information on a potential job, then asked if *she* loved *him* without saying a word about whether he loved her?

Worse, what man then turned around and said he knew she didn't want to marry him—all evidence to the contrary—and that it was best if they *didn't* marry, all because she'd wanted to discuss marriage before letting him know about a job offer she had no intention of accepting or a grainy tabloid photo that no one corroborated?

A man who doesn't know what he wants. A man who doesn't truly love you in the first place.

She scrubbed her teeth harder than necessary, as if she could cleanse the thought from her mind.

Stefano had been right about one thing: No more photos or reports had appeared of the two of them. And with no palace confirmation of the prince's identity in that first, hazy photo, the story had disappeared. Life had continued on just as it had before Stefano's visits. Even Santi said nothing more. Their conversations centered on the usual topics of upcoming banquets, his wife and children, and the streak of beautiful weather Barcelona currently enjoyed.

On autopilot, Megan went through her Monday morning ritual of showering, applying makeup, and selecting an outfit before making her way to the kitchen to start a pot of coffee. As she poured freshly-ground coffee into the filter and breathed in the rich scent, she resolved to embrace her life as it was.

When she parted from Stefano the first time, she was alone and pregnant. She faced the prospect of juggling finals, a new baby, and job interviews, not to mention finding help with daycare during those first lean years. Now she had none of those concerns. She had everything she'd ever wanted in life, and Anna topped that list. They'd had a wonderful time selecting fresh strawberries at the market yesterday morning. She'd come home feeling happy and refreshed, despite the persistent feeling that Stefano should have been exploring the Saturday market with them.

Maybe she could make waffles for Anna this morning and top them with the berries, assuming the headache Anna developed last night was cured by a good night's sleep. Megan never prepared anything fancier than cereal on a weekday, so this would be a treat for them both. Cooking would occupy her mind until Anna was awake. Better that than thoughts of Stefano or Jack Gladwell.

As if on cue, a low groan came from Anna's room. Megan stilled, coffee pot in hand. "Anna?"

She heard nothing more, only the low hum of the suite's air conditioning.

"Anna? You awake? It's early, honey." Too early.

She set the coffee pot on its burner, flipped on the power switch to start the drip, then walked to Anna's door, which was cracked open about six inches. The light was off and the lump on the bed didn't move. She watched for a few seconds, but Anna didn't stir. Megan reached for the knob to pull the door closed, but paused.

No, this didn't feel right.

Carefully, she tiptoed into Anna's room and approached the bed. Anna's hair hung over her face, as usual. Megan reached to gently swipe it back. Her hand was still a few inches away when she felt the heat rolling off Anna in waves.

"Anna?" Megan looped Anna's hair behind her ear and pressed a hand to Anna's forehead. "Oh, honey, you're on fire."

"I don't feel good. My neck hurts," Anna whispered without opening her eyes. "A lot."

Megan crouched beside the bed. Anna had been a little warm last night, but Megan chalked it up to the fact that, after returning from the market, Anna spent the entire afternoon on the beach with friends. But this wasn't a case of too many hours spent in the sun. Megan couldn't remember ever feeling Anna so hot. "Your neck or your throat?"

"Neck. It hurts to move, Mommy."

Mommy? She hadn't been Mommy for several years. "Okay. Stay put and I'll get a thermometer."

She returned a few seconds later and a quick check confirmed what she feared, a dangerously high fever.

"Anna, I'm taking you to the doctor, all right? Can you get up?"

When Anna merely blinked, Megan said, "Never mind. I'll carry you to the elevator and we'll go straight to the car."

Anxiety knotted her insides as she peeled back Anna's covers and hefted her into her arms. She made her way through the living area, taking a moment to turn off the coffee pot with her elbow and loop her shoulder bag onto her arm before stepping into her shoes and hustling toward the elevator.

The closer Megan got to the car, the more she worried. Even when Anna had a bad case of the flu in third grade, she'd insisted she could get out of bed and take care of herself, though she only made it as far as the sofa. Then there was the time in first grade that Anna lied to her teacher about throwing up her lunch because she hadn't wanted to miss school.

Now Anna didn't care that she was being carried. She didn't even seem to notice. Worse, Megan could feel the heat of Anna's body through the girl's pajamas and her own blouse. It was like standing under a heat lamp.

Gently, Megan set Anna down beside the car, clicked it open, then eased Anna into the backseat and buckled the belt.

Anna's head rolled back. She groaned without opening her eyes. "Mom, that *hurts*."

"We're on our way to the hospital. You'll feel better soon, sweetie."

Anna mumbled what sounded like *yellow tires*, but when Megan asked what she'd said, Anna didn't answer.

Never in her life had Megan exited the parking garage or driven through the city so fast. She sent a prayer of thanks skyward that the predawn streets were empty and every streetlight went her way. As she pulled into the emergency entrance at the hospital, an orderly sitting on an outside bench crushed out his cigarette and approached the car. He took one look at Anna and called for assistance. First in Catalan, then in English when he realized Megan's Catalan was limited, he told her to take her car to the parking lot down the hill from the hospital and meet them in the emergency room. In the meantime, two nurses unbuckled Anna, moved her to a wheelchair, and whisked her into the hospital.

Megan's heart pounded against the walls of her ribcage so hard she thought it'd burst, and not from the exertion of sprinting back up the hill from the lot. The orderly's expression when he saw Anna was troubling enough, but the utter silence from Anna as the nurses wheeled her into the emergency room terrified her. This was no ordinary headache, nor was it a case of the flu.

As Megan passed through the sliding emergency room doors, a nurse approached to let her know that Anna was being evaluated in a nearby room and that Megan could join her daughter once the evaluation was complete. In the meantime, the staff needed Megan to complete paperwork for admission.

"Admission?" Megan asked in alarm. How could they know already that she needed to be admitted?

The nurse directed Megan to a seat in the waiting area. "When a child presents with a fever as high as your daughter's we admit them as a matter of policy. We'll get her situated, then you can join her."

Minutes felt like hours as Megan answered the necessary questions and inked her signature on a slew of forms, hoping against hope that a doctor would come out from the emergency wing to let her know that Anna had nothing more than a high fever and that they would soon get it under control. That the admission was nothing more than a precaution and Anna would be back to her normal, bouncy self soon.

No one came.

Megan clutched the clipboard in her lap and stared at the doors leading to the patient evaluation area. At long last, the same nurse who'd given her the paperwork came to collect it and waved Megan into a side room. As the older woman flipped through the pages on the clipboard, Megan asked, "Will I be able to see my daughter soon? It's been quite a while."

"The doctor will come in to speak with you in just a moment," the nurse said before ducking into the hallway and shutting the door behind her.

Megan sucked in air through her nostrils, willing herself to keep her composure despite the fact the nurse hadn't met her gaze, and despite the fact the woman moved her into a private room to speak with the doctor rather than ushering her into the area where Anna was being seen. In her experience, medical professionals were far more likely to be honest and give you the full picture when they knew you could handle the information. And now, more than ever, she needed information. For Anna's sake, she had to appear calm.

"Ms. Hallberg? I am Dr. Serrano."

She looked up to see a middle-aged, olive-skinned man with a serious, though thankfully not grim, demeanor. Forcing herself to keep an even tone, she said, "Yes. Please, call me Megan. You've seen Anna?"

"Yes." He closed the door before pulling a rolling stool from one corner so he could sit facing her. "I am afraid my accent is difficult for some to understand, so if my English does not make sense to you, please tell me. I can call the nurse back in to translate."

She forced a smile. Thank goodness she was used to Catalan accents. "Your English sounds fine to me. Please, go ahead."

He opened a file across his lap. "Your daughter has a very high fever, which can be dangerous in anyone but especially in a child her age. So" —he paused, as if searching his mind for the proper words— "I have given her medicine to help lower her fever and I asked for a test of her blood. The nursing staff is doing this now and I asked for a quick processing from our lab."

"All right." Though Megan had to concentrate to understand his words, there was a kindness and intelligence in his eyes that engendered trust. "Is she awake?"

"No, but for now, she is stable. Her fever is no worse than when she arrived. However, I am very concerned about her neck stiffness, her headache and her" —again, he struggled for the word— "her confusion. She was awake for a short time while I examined her, but she did not seem certain about where she is. She had difficulty answering basic questions. How long has she been this way?"

"Since about five, so a couple of hours now. I heard her moaning in her bedroom and went to check on her. I brought her here as soon as I took her temperature." She thought through everything Anna said since returning from the beach the previous afternoon. "She was tired last night and didn't want much dinner, but I assumed it was because we spent the morning walking through the marketplace, then she had a big lunch and spent the afternoon running around the beach with friends. She told me she was pretty worn out."

Dr. Serrano scribbled a note in Anna's file. "There was no confusion or fever when she returned from the beach?"

"She was a little warm and she did say she had a slight headache. It wasn't enough to worry me, and I didn't bother to take her temperature. Other than being more tired than usual, she seemed perfectly normal. Definitely no confusion."

"All right. It is very good that you brought her in."

Megan tried to remain patient as the doctor added more notes to Anna's file. Finally, he met her gaze. "Unfortunately, I suspect that Anna has meningitis, which is an inflammation of the" —he pointed to the back of his neck— "membrane around the brain and spinal cord. We must do a lumbar puncture to confirm the diagnosis and should have results shortly, but you will need to read and sign some forms first. Are you familiar with meningitis?"

No, no, no, her mind screamed, but she said, "Yes, I am."

Children died from meningitis. *Anna could die.*

CHAPTER TWENTY-SEVEN

Megan clenched her teeth against the thought and tried to focus on the doctor's words.

"Do you know of anyone with meningitis? Or with symptoms like Anna's? For instance, any of the friends she was with at the beach or any children from her school? Maybe from a camp, if she is in summer camp?"

When Megan shook her head, he exhaled. "Meningitis is very serious, yes? But fast treatment can prevent complications. This is why it is good you brought her here quickly. I wish for you to let me know right away if you learn of others with symptoms. They must get medical treatment immediately."

"Of course."

"I have a sheet with questions for you to answer. It will help us find the cause of Anna's illness and speed our treatment."

He handed her the permission form for the lumbar puncture and the questionnaire, then went on to explain the course of antibiotics he was starting for Anna. Thankfully, his English was solid whenever he spoke in medical terms. "We are moving her into a room upstairs. She will need more tests, including X-rays and a CAT scan, but I wish for her to be as comfortable as possible. Do you live near the hospital?"

When Megan nodded, he urged her to go home and pack a bag once she'd completed the questionnaire. He handed her another slip of paper. "This will be her room. It is on a pediatric floor. Until we determine the cause of her illness, she will need to be in isolation. However, there is a room beside hers that you can use. It has a window so you can see all that is happening with her. When she is awake and alert, she will be happy to see you there."

"Thank you." Her eyes filled with tears, but she willed them back. As frightened and upset as she was, it wouldn't do Anna a bit of good to cry. Not now.

Dr. Serrano's voice lost its businesslike tone as he said, "I do not wish to be… to intrude…but I know this is very hard. You may wish to call the father? Or someone else?"

"Maybe." Should she call Stefano? Her parents? Or wait for more information? "I don't know. Not yet. It's still very early in the morning."

He nodded in understanding. "Cell phones are not permitted inside the hospital, but you may use the phone at the nurse's desk on the pediatric floor anytime you wish. For now, Anna cannot have any visitors. Only parents in the next room until we know more."

Megan swallowed as the doctor stood. She looked up at him and asked, "Is there anything else I can do?"

"Not at the moment. The antibiotics must have time to work." Dr. Serrano put a hand on her arm for reassurance. "This will be a matter of days or weeks, not hours. Take care of yourself now so that you can be there for her when she is awake. In the meantime, we will do everything we can for her. I will let you know when results come from the lab. I want you to ask questions if you have them, whenever you have them."

"Thank you. I will." She liked this man. He seemed knowledgeable, caring, and—what she needed most right now—competent. "I'm sure I'll have plenty, I just…I need some time to absorb this."

"Anna is a strong girl. I am" —again, he seemed to struggle for the proper word— "optimistic. So we will hope for good news."

Once Dr. Serrano left, Megan bit her lip and forced herself to concentrate on the questionnaire. It was extensive, covering where Anna had been, what she'd eaten, what immunizations she'd had. After finishing, Megan handed it to the nurse and walked to the parking lot in a daze, realizing when she climbed into her car that her shoes didn't match. Not that it mattered.

The drive back to the hotel felt like an out-of-body experience, as if she were watching the rush hour traffic from afar rather than sitting in it, waiting for lights to change and cars to move.

Once in her suite, she packed a bag for herself in two minutes flat.

It wasn't until she entered Anna's empty bedroom and pulled her daughter's backpack from the closet that Megan allowed a tear to roll down her cheek without attempting to blink it back. She sat on the edge of Anna's bed and looked around the room as she tried to think through what to bring to the hospital. The bedsheets were askew and the room held the lingering scent of Anna's favorite strawberry lotion. A jeweled hairbrush rested on the room's small desk beside a pile of ponytail holders and a shell Anna had found on the beach.

Set off by itself, carefully displayed beside her alarm clock, was the small leather bracelet Stefano bought Anna from the street kiosk during their first Saturday outing.

Another tear followed the first. Then Megan couldn't stop.

* * *

Stefano woke with a start to unfamiliar surroundings. He blinked in the semi-darkness, attempting to separate the last vestiges of his dream from the reality around him.

Frequent business trips out of Sarcaccia meant he'd been in this situation before, lying on his back and taking few moments to figure out which city and hotel he was in and what was on his schedule for the day, but it'd never happened while wrapped in his own sheets, with the gray digital light of his own alarm clock beside the bed.

To his left, moonlight streamed in through wide, floor-to-ceiling windows overlooking the Mediterranean. City lights sparkled on hillsides that rose on either side of a softly lit marina, reminding him where he was. He pushed to a sitting position and took in the familiar panorama of Cateri's waterfront. Though he'd been asleep less than an hour, he smiled to himself in the dark.

New apartment. A new start. He'd brought only the essentials from the palace, limiting himself to toiletries, linens, a few days' worth of clothes, and his computer. He'd ordered a few basic pieces of furniture rather than peruse the selection in the palace's storage rooms, craving modernity over the centuries-old antiques with which he'd been raised.

Beautiful though it was, the spacious apartment wasn't his ideal. He'd much rather wake to find Megan beside him. But if he couldn't have her, at least he could have the gift she had given him—normalcy—and embrace it. It might take awhile for the people of Sarcaccia to accept that he lived outside the palace, perhaps longer for the paparazzi to get bored as they watched him come and go each day and decide they were better off covering other stories, but he knew in his gut this was where he wanted to be. In the new section of the city, rather than the medieval section his ancestors had settled, in an apartment any of his friends might own—all right, larger than most of his friends might own, since he'd purchased the entire top floor of the building—within walking distance of shops, cafes, art galleries, and the waterfront, rather than the age-old palace. He could even walk to the new convention center and the transportation hub currently under construction alongside it.

A muted light on the dresser across the room caught his eye, followed by a soft hum. Flinging back the sheets, he crossed the hardwood floor to retrieve his cell phone.

"Yes?"

His secretary's voice came over the line. "Your Highness, I'm sorry to disturb you at this hour, but you asked me to let you know immediately if I heard from Megan Hallberg. She called the palace and insists on speaking to you, despite the hour. The night answering service put her through to me. I have her on the other line."

"I'll take it. Thank you."

Adrenaline woke him fully as he waited. Finally, he heard the click of the connection. "Megan?"

"Hi, Stefano. I'm sorry to call so late."

The forced steadiness in her voice sent a chill along his spine and pricked the fine hairs at the back of his neck. "Something happened."

"Yes. It's Anna." Her voice cracked as she explained, "I'm with her at the hospital."

His world seemed to spin off its axis. "What's going on? Is it serious?"

The question was rote. He already knew the answer. Megan wouldn't call for a scraped knee or broken pinkie finger. Hell, she hadn't called at all since he'd left Barcelona. Their only contact had been via Anna, when he'd called to hear about her last day of school and Anna mentioned that Megan was in another room on a work phone call.

"It's serious." He sensed her steadying herself. "She was mumbling to herself when she woke up this morning. I went in to check on her and she wasn't herself. She had a high fever, complained of neck pain, and didn't seem able to hold a coherent thought. I brought her straight to the hospital and they admitted her."

Bile rose in his throat as he recognized the symptoms. How many times had he visited hospitals and heard stories from doctors and nurses about treating stubborn cases? He sat on the end of his bed, steadying himself for what he suspected would come next. "She has meningitis, doesn't she? That's what they think."

"Yes. The doctor suspected it when I first saw him this morning, but I just got the official diagnosis a few minutes ago." She paused, then on a deep breath said, "I know you're mad at me for hiding the job offer, Stefano, but…but I had to call you as soon as it was confirmed. There was an answering service at your number, so I insisted they let me talk to your secretary. I wasn't sure they would. She said you weren't at the palace—"

"I'm not." Stefano put a hand to his forehead and rubbed his thumb against his temple, as if by doing so he could will away what was happening to Anna.

"Mad, that is. Or at the palace. I told my assistant to let me know if you called, day or night."

"Thank you. I...Stefano, I don't know what to do. I've never been so scared in my life." On that, she broke, unable to stop him from hearing her tears. "I mean, she seemed fine last night when she went to sleep. A little run down, but nothing worrisome. Then she woke up in terrible shape. I didn't know what to think other than knowing I had to get her to the hospital. Wait. How...how did you know it was meningitis?"

Because when I was seven, I met a boy with meningitis who later died.

"I've spent a lot of time visiting pediatric wards and talking to doctors," he said. "Part and parcel of my job. Over the years, you see it all."

He pushed away the image that scarred his young soul to focus on Anna and what could be done in the here and now. "Who's treating her? What do they say?"

"His name is Dr. Serrano." She gave him information on the hospital and all the details of Anna's situation, everything from her current vital signs and bloodwork to the doctor's assessment of the infection raging through Anna's small body. Megan finished with a description of the course of drugs being used to treat her.

"Now I have to call my parents and tell them. They'll want to fly over, but since they were here last month I doubt they can afford another set of plane tickets." A feeble laugh escaped her. "I'll have to convince them that it's better for them to stay where they are. It's not like there's anything they can do. Anna's getting wonderful care, but now it's a matter of waiting to see how she responds to the drugs."

"Did Dr. Serrano give you any indication how long it'd be?"

"We'll know more in the next twenty-four to forty-eight hours." On an exhale, she said, "Watching her makes me feel so helpless, Stefano. I wish there was more I could do. I have a horrible feeling in my gut that I'm failing her."

"You're not. Hold tight and tell her I love her. I'll do what I can on this end."

"There's nothing to do, Stefano, not until we know if the drugs are working. But thank you."

He pinched the bridge of his nose. "Megan? I'm glad you called to tell me."

"I wouldn't dream of *not* telling you. Even if I know it's not something you want to hear."

"All the same...thank you. Keep me updated, all right?"

She promised, then hung up.

He dropped the cell phone to the bed and stared out the window for several minutes, wracking his brain for what he could possibly do. His gut instinct to control an uncontrollable situation, or so Megan would say.

Finally, he picked up the phone and started flipping through his contact list.

He might not have been there to assist at Anna's birth, but he'd be damned if he'd sit idly by and let her die.

CHAPTER TWENTY-EIGHT

Anna wasn't improving.

Thirty-six hours after she'd been admitted, fever still ravaged her body. She'd been conscious for a while, but that was nearly six hours ago. Megan had been permitted in the room, wearing scrubs and a mask as she leaned over the bed and talked softly to Anna, letting her know that the doctors were taking good care of her and that she'd be back to herself soon.

While she'd managed to display an upbeat attitude for Anna, even drawing a weak smile from her daughter, Megan felt like a liar. She had no more power over what was happening to Anna than she did over the sunrise and sunset.

It had taken everything in Megan's power not to cry when Anna's eyes drifted closed once more. Instead, she'd thanked the nurses for all they were doing and gave them space to work.

A nurse stuck her head into Megan's room. In broken English, she offered to bring Megan a cup of coffee from the cafeteria.

Megan thanked her but declined. She'd had so much coffee since her arrival her stomach ached. Or maybe that was stress. She'd hardly left the small room adjacent to Anna's. Though she deeply appreciated having the ability to monitor Anna, the four walls seemed to be closing in on her. Even the television mounted to the wall provided little distraction. The English news channel the nurse found for her after Megan gave up on a Spanish soap opera left her feeling maudlin. Stories about stock markets and foreign elections weren't exactly mood boosters.

Fingers interlaced, Megan stretched her arms in front of her, then over her head before pushing out of her chair to cross to the window. Anna was still out cold, lying on her back with an IV hooked up to one arm while monitors beside the bed ticked off her vital signs.

She swooped a hand over her head. She needed to call her parents and Stefano with an update soon, even if she had no real news to share. Her parents would offer their prayers and say what they could to make her feel better. But there'd be fear in their voices as they did so.

She had no idea about Stefano.

Though he'd been glad she'd called last night and had asked some pointed questions about Anna's condition, and had finished by saying he'd do what he could, he'd hung up on her soon after she'd said there was nothing to be done.

He said that he loved Anna. That was all she could ask.

You didn't trust him to love you.

Megan bit her lip. While Stefano both angered and hurt her when he walked out, the last thing she should be thinking of now was her relationship with the man. It wasn't that she didn't trust him when she'd kept the folder stashed away. She'd been scared. What if he'd seen the contents and thought she'd pursued the job without so much as considering a life with him? Or, worse, what if he'd panicked at the sight of the photo as Santi had and decided to stay away?

In the end, keeping the information from him caused precisely the result she feared.

She leaned her forehead against the cool glass that separated her from Anna. She shouldn't have been afraid of an open discussion with Stefano. He'd shown over these last couple of months that he'd care for her, he'd protect her, he'd encourage her in everything. True, he'd questioned some of her parenting decisions, but in the end, he'd listened and been willing to see things from her perspective. She should've trusted that he'd listen with an open mind when she explained how she'd gotten both the job offer and the photo. That they'd discuss the ramifications together.

She smiled, picturing the way Anna launched herself into his arms for a hug before going to her last sleepover at Julia's. Unabashed joy radiated from his face as well as from Anna's. She could only imagine how utterly enjoyable life under the same roof might've been for the three of them. And no doubt, during the times they were alone, she and Stefano would've had an off-the-charts sex life. The biggest risk she faced was that he might not love her as deeply as she loved him. But didn't every marriage carry that risk? There were never guarantees, in any marriage. She shouldn't have been scared.

On the other hand, the possibility she could lose Anna forever scared her all the way to her bones. She stared at the small, fragile body in the bed on the other side of the glass. With each passing minute Anna remained unconscious and feverish, that possibility became more and more real.

Dr. Serrano's low voice floated to her from the hallway, causing her to straighten. She couldn't understand his rapid-fire Catalan, but she gathered he was discussing Anna's case with the nurses. He'd visited Anna's room a half-hour ago, but left to take a phone call from another doctor before he could give Megan an update.

While she respected that Dr. Serrano had other patients and medical professionals who needed his attention, a selfish part of her wished he could've waited until after he'd shared what he planned to do next for Anna. The lack of information wore on her more as much as the lack of sleep.

At long last, the doctor rounded the corner and entered her room. He apologized for the delay in visiting her with an update, then gestured for Megan to take a seat so they could talk. Megan was too agitated and nervous to respond. Her jaw shook as she sent prayers skyward for Anna.

Once she was seated, Dr. Serrano dropped his clipboard on the bed, then sat beside it and leaned forward, his dark eyes filled with concern.

"She hasn't gotten any better, has she?"

"No, which is a bad sign. By now, the antibiotics should have had some effect. In fact, I'm becoming concerned about the potential for swelling around her brain." Megan's throat constricted as she absorbed the impact of Dr. Serrano's words. "However, I do have some good news."

"Yes?" She'd take anything at this point.

"There is a Canadian doctor—a Dr. Jenkins—who is the foremost authority in the world on bacterial meningitis. By good fortune he is at a medical conference in Madrid this week. I've spoken with him on the phone about Anna's case. He has some ideas about the next steps to take, though he would like to evaluate her himself first. We can have him here this evening with your permission. With his expertise" —he cringed slightly at his mangled pronunciation of the word— "I believe we can give Anna a fighting chance. More than a fighting chance."

How much did she adore Dr. Serrano right now? She shouldn't have begrudged him an instant of the time he took before he came in to update her. The man was an angel. "Anything that will help, you have my permission to do. And as soon as possible."

The doctor stood. "In that case, I will call him back right away."

"Thank you. From the bottom of my heart." She stood and clasped his hand. "I'm so grateful that you thought to call him and convince him to leave his conference to come see Anna."

"You are quite welcome," he replied. "However, Dr. Jenkins called me."

"He did?" Megan frowned as she released the doctor's hand. "But how could he—"

"A friend of yours knew of Anna's condition and called Dr. Jenkins asking for advice. When your friend mentioned that you live in Barcelona, the doctor called me and offered to come from Madrid if I wanted him to consult on Anna's case. I told him it would please me a great deal to have his assistance, but that I wished to speak with you first." Dr. Serrano raised an eyebrow. "Whoever your friend is, they must have a great deal of influence. That call for advice very well may save Anna's life."

Stefano. It couldn't be anyone else. Her heart swelled with gratitude.

"Even so, I really appreciate all you're doing for Anna. She's very lucky to have you."

The doctor smiled before leaving Megan alone once more, with only the drone of a television infomercial to keep her company. She returned to the window, but Anna appeared as she had all afternoon. Still, pale, and quiet.

Megan let out a ragged breath and told herself for the millionth time that afternoon that everything would be all right. Everything possible was being done to help Anna recover. Allowing herself to think otherwise wouldn't help Anna one iota.

Across the room, a low buzz came from her purse. After calling in sick to work again this morning—she couldn't bring herself to tell Ramon how bad things were with Anna, knowing he'd rush to the hospital and half the hotel staff would follow in his wake—she hadn't checked her cell phone. The messages were likely piling up. May as well distract herself dealing with them until Dr. Jenkins arrived. Rather than sit in the chair she'd occupied all day, she flopped on her back on the bed and thumbed the phone's power switch to reveal a new text message from her mother.

Thank you for tix. You shouldn't have. Will see you shortly.

Megan did a double take. Tickets? What tickets?

The message had to be meant for someone else. Her parents frequently enjoyed attending movies with the next door neighbors. Perhaps the neighbors bought tickets in an effort to get the Hallbergs' minds off their sick granddaughter. She'd bet anything the neighbors' phone number was right next to hers on her parents' speed dial.

As Megan started typing a response, a second message appeared on the screen.

Car service just arrived at the house. Flight in three hours. We'll be there tomorrow morning. Love you, sweetheart. Kiss Anna for us.

She paused with her thumbs over the screen. The message was definitely meant for her. But how in the world—?

Stefano. It had to be Stefano. He'd bought plane tickets for her parents so they could be by Anna's side.

She set the phone on the bed beside her after typing back a quick *see you soon*. She needed to call Stefano and thank him. She closed her eyes and pulled her sweater tighter around her shoulders as she thought through what she'd say. A simple thank you didn't cover it.

"Ms. Hallberg?" A soft voice came from the doorway. "Are you awake?"

Megan took a moment, then opened her eyes to see one of the nurses turning to tiptoe away. The angle of the sun had shifted. She must've fallen asleep. "Yes?"

The nurse spun back around. "I am sorry if I woke you. There is a Mr. Jones here who claims he is family? You said not to expect family visitors, but he asked me to find you—"

"Jones?" She blinked, dazed. It couldn't be. She pushed to a seated position. "Yes. Yes, let him in."

Skepticism clouded the nurse's features. "Only immediate family is permitted, you understand."

"He is immediate family." Megan used her index fingers to swipe the gumminess from her eyes. "Is he downstairs or up here at the nurses' station?"

A rich voice came from the doorway, gliding over her like a warm, comforting blanket. "I'm right here."

* * *

Megan looked like hell.

Black smudges marred the skin under her eyes, strands of hair fell from her loose ponytail, and her clothes looked as if she'd slept in them. She sat atop a hospital bed with its sheets perfectly in place, but its pillow mushed. A black sweater hung off the side of the bed and her cell phone rested face down near her hip.

She must've crumpled there in exhaustion, keeping herself available the instant Anna needed her.

Heaviness threatened to collapse his chest at the sight of her blinking at him. Never had she looked so beautiful. Stefano dropped his bag on the floor, then crossed the room in three steps to wrap her in an embrace.

Instantly, her arms came around him and she buried her face in his shoulder. "I'm so sorry. I'm so, so sorry."

He ran a hand over the back of her head, smoothing her hair. "Why are you sorry?"

"I don't know," she whispered into his shirt. "For Anna. For everything."

"No. Don't be sorry. It'll be all right." Still clasping the back of her head, he kissed the top of her hair. He wanted to say that he was sorry, too. Instead, he offered, "I called a doctor in Madrid who's offered to consult with Dr. Serrano if it will help."

She nodded against his shoulder, then slowly pulled back. Her eyes brimmed with tears, though she held them in check. "Dr. Serrano told me. When he said a friend of mine called a meningitis expert, I knew it had to be you. Thank you. And thank you for flying my parents here. I can't believe you did that."

He couldn't help but give her a small smile. He'd half expected her to accuse him of wanting to control the situation and tell him he shouldn't have made calls about Anna without consulting her first. But she didn't. She seemed genuinely grateful.

She frowned, then angled her head to look at his hat. "You got rid of the Red Sox."

"You said you liked the Twins. Does it look all right?"

She nodded, a smile pushing through her tears. "It's perfect for Mr. Jones. Suits his personality."

"Good." He eased back, his hands moving from her back to her arms. "So how's Anna doing?"

"Stable. But in this case, stable isn't good." She slipped from his embrace and stood, leading him to a window that separated her room from Anna's. He stood behind Megan and gazed through the glass.

"Dr. Jenkins should be here soon. He wants to examine her, then he and Dr. Serrano will decide what to do next."

"She looks so tiny." With her eyes closed and the covers pulled to the center of her torso, Anna was dwarfed by the bed. The sight of her brought Stefano right back to the hospital he'd visited with his mother when he was seven. Crisp white sheets, white walls, silver bed rails. Monitors flashing on either side of the bed. An IV bag hanging from a hook, its tube snaking down to a child's hand. The little boy whom he'd met then looked far better than Anna did now—he'd been alert and feeling well enough to play cards—and that boy succumbed to his infection only days later.

A masked nurse entered the room and glanced at the monitor, then put her fingers to Anna's wrist to double check the girl's pulse rate, yet his daughter remained immobile. He'd never seen Anna when she wasn't bouncing.

Never in his life had stillness caused him such fear.

"I'm scared to death," Megan whispered as the nurse departed, leaving Anna alone. "We can't lose her. We just can't."

We.

He put his hands on Megan's shoulders and squeezed, then slid his arms around her to pull her against him. He couldn't carry the horrible burden for her, but he could share it.

"We won't."

CHAPTER TWENTY-NINE

Gingerly, Stefano extracted one foot, then his arm, out from under Megan's slumbering form before twisting his way off the narrow hospital bed. He froze when she shifted a knee, drawing it closer to her body, but a beat later he realized she wouldn't wake.

It had taken nearly six hours from the time he'd entered her room, but he'd finally convinced Megan to lie down and rest, arguing that she needed to muster her energy for when Anna recovered. Dr. Jenkins and Dr. Serrano had spent copious amounts of time with Anna over the course of the evening. After analyzing a new lab report on the bacteria suspected of causing her meningitis, they opted for a different regimen of antibiotics combined with medications that would lower her fever and alleviate any pressure on her brain. The doctors seemed optimistic, but warned Megan that it could take a day or more to see results. While Dr. Jenkins had nodded to Stefano in acknowledgement of their long friendship—Stefano's family donated generously to a children's relief project the doctor founded—he knew from their earlier phone call that Stefano wanted to remain anonymous while at the hospital and refrained from addressing him directly.

Thankfully, Dr. Jenkins hadn't asked any personal questions during their phone call. Stefano suspected they'd come later, however. The nurses already wondered at his presence. Though they hadn't said anything since Megan claimed he was part of her immediate family, they'd looked at him askance. Anna wasn't listed as having a father in her medical records, Megan wore no wedding ring, and it was clear by the way Megan had fallen asleep cradled in his arms that he and Megan weren't siblings.

He leaned over the bed to adjust Megan's sweater—a necessity in the chilly hospital despite the bright summer sunshine outside—but resisted the urge to smooth her hair away from her face. As much as he wanted to stay and comfort her, he wondered at what point his presence would cause her pain.

After glancing through the window to ensure Anna looked as comfortable as possible, Stefano tiptoed into the bathroom with his overnight bag and eyed himself in the mirror. He'd thought Megan looked like hell when he arrived. Compared to her, he looked like muck dredged from the lowest levels of Barcelona's Besòs River. Not even when he'd been in the military and spent two weeks in the field, training in the rain and mud, had he looked this haggard.

Of course, he'd slept more than this during training.

After receiving Megan's call, he'd spent the rest of the night researching meningitis, trying to get a grip on what Anna faced and what the current protocols might be. He'd made phone calls and done what he could to get her help. He'd cancelled his appearances for the next day, claiming a migraine, and told his secretary to hold his calls and to do her best to fend off inquiries from his parents. Unwilling to use his own jet and alert anyone to his whereabouts, he'd booked a private flight to Barcelona. Once he secured a plane and pilot, he hadn't bothered to shower. He'd thrown on jeans, a T-shirt, and the Twins hat he'd ordered nearly a month before but hadn't yet worn for Megan. He'd packed only his toothbrush, deodorant, and one change of clothes, anxious to get off the ground as soon as possible.

He'd thought it the best decision at the time, but now his eyes appeared bloodshot and he was in desperate need of a shave and a shower. If—when—Anna awoke, he'd scare the daylights out of her. It was one thing to appear incognito, it was another to appear frightening.

He stifled a yawn as he rummaged through his bag for the toothbrush and toothpaste. He couldn't shower as long as Megan slept. One of them should remain alert and available in case anything changed with Anna. As long as no one got close enough to get a good whiff, he supposed he'd have to do without.

Probably a good thing he didn't have to worry about impressing Megan anymore.

A commotion from outside the room caught Stefano's attention as he finished brushing. Cautiously, he looked into the hallway for its source and spotted two nurses muttering in flustered Catalan. One was crawling under the sink behind the nurses' station while another handed her a stack of towels. A third nurse was on the phone, apparently arguing with maintenance over the time it would take to get help. She hung up and spread her arms wide as she looked at the other two nurses, her expression clearly indicating that for the time being, they were on their own.

Stefano stepped back into the room, checking first on Anna, then on Megan. Both were sound asleep. Figuring he may as well keep himself occupied, he approached the nurses' station to offer his help with what appeared to be a leak. He spoke no Catalan, but thankfully all three spoke English.

The nurse who'd been on the phone, a middle-aged woman who wasn't much taller than Anna, opened a cabinet alongside the sink. "Those are all the tools we have, I'm afraid. A hammer that's of no use at all and two wrenches. And some wire."

He shrugged. "We'll see what the problem is, then see what we need."

The nurse who'd been under the sink eased her way out. Her back was wet, so she left to change as Stefano crouched down, then slid in to see what caused the problem. The nurse who'd been cleaning up the mess handed him a flashlight and said, "It's Mr. Jones, isn't it? Please tell me you're a plumber."

He smiled to himself as he studied the pipes with the flashlight. "No, not a plumber. But I've done some work on water systems. Volunteer work when I was younger. I might be able to figure this out."

"I sure hope so." He heard her feet moving as he continued to study the pipe leading from the drain to the wall. "I need to go check on some patients, but Maria will be right here. Let her know what you need."

He assumed Maria was the nurse who'd lambasted the maintenance staff on the phone. A moment later, he was proven correct as he asked for a wrench and she bent to hand it to him.

"Do you know why it's leaking?"

He stretched to loosen the collar of a water filter that had been installed under the sink. "I think it's a simple case of either a weakened seal or a loose collar." Especially since the filter came off easily in his hands. He shimmied his way out from under the sink holding the filter. The seal looked fine, but the filter itself needed replacement. "More likely a loose collar."

The nurse immediately spied the brown filter and grimaced. "Let's change that. I'm sure I have another here."

As she rummaged in a nearby cabinet, Stefano poured the excess water from the filter container into a nearby bucket and disposed of the old filter.

"Got it," Maria said. She removed the packaging, then handed him the new filter. While he was under the sink with the replacement, she said, "Thank you. I know you must be terribly worried about Anna. It's kind of you to do this when you have her on your mind."

"This helps get her illness off my mind," he replied. "At least until the doctors have something new to report."

"Hopefully soon," she said. He could hear her ripping open a new roll of paper towels to clean the rest of the water that had run onto the floor.

"It's the worst feeling in the world not being able to help her," he said. "Meningitis can be so tricky. I knew a boy once" —he gave the filter collar a twist to lock it in place— "I thought he was going to be fine, but in the end, with meningitis…well, you've probably experienced plenty of difficult cases working here, so you're well aware of what can happen. So much is out of your control that it makes you want to help whenever it's an option. That volunteer work I said I did on water systems? The main reason I did it was because I never wanted to see a kid come down with a preventable illness when there are so many illnesses that aren't."

"I understand completely. It's why I became a nurse. Livia, too." Maria laughed. "She's the one who tried to fix the sink before you came out. She's a much better nurse than she is a plumber."

"She would've figured it out," Stefano said. He shone the flashlight around, ensuring nothing else under the sink appeared loose, then gave the filter a wiggle to ensure it was tight. As he was checking the seals, he heard a male voice asking where to put a bouquet of flowers and the nurse make an exclamation of surprise.

"Anna Hallberg, *sisplau*," the male added, to which the nurse responded in Catalan.

Stefano eased his way out from under the sink, glancing at the gigantic bouquet of flowers now on the nurses' station counter as he turned on the spigot. He bent and shone the flashlight underneath the sink, waiting for leakage, but there was none.

"Must've been the filter collar. It came off pretty easily and was wet on the outside. I think you're all set." He stood and handed her the flashlight, but couldn't take his eyes off the flowers. The arrangement was spectacular, yet completely appropriate for a young girl with its multitude of summery colors and a pink and turquoise Get Well Soon card printed in English.

Maria returned the flashlight to the cabinet. "Can you believe those?"

She didn't need to gesture to the flowers for him to know what she meant. "They're beautiful. Are they from the Grandspire?" The staff must've gotten together to send her an arrangement.

"The card says J.G," Maria said with a shrug. "Perhaps G is the Grandspire?"

"Good a guess as any." Though he'd bet his life it was Jack Gladwell. He tore his gaze away from the bouquet and told himself not to think about what it might mean. "I'm sure she'll love them."

She handed Stefano a paper towel so he could dry his hands, then offered to buy him a cup of coffee as thanks after she put the arrangement in Anna's room. "Our cafeteria blend is very good," she promised. "I can have them send it up."

"I'd much rather buy *you* coffee. Your staff is doing so much for Anna." He waved off her protests and said, "I'd planned to go there anyway to buy some for Megan, since my guess is that she'll be awake soon. Tell me what you want."

After taking her order, he left for the cafeteria, glad to have a purpose to occupy his mind, however modest that purpose might be.

* * *

Megan stood just inside the door to her room, using her shoulder to prop herself against the wall as Stefano offered to bring coffee back for the nurse. She hadn't heard all of the conversation between the two of them, but she'd heard enough to decide not to intrude. At first, she'd been amused by hearing him discuss water leaks and filters. On some level, she'd forgotten how capable he was despite his privileged upbringing. How he liked to fix things. How utterly ordinary he could be. It was part of his charm, part of how he related so well to anyone he met.

But then he'd started talking about the reason he'd gone to Venezuela. A boy with meningitis. A boy who hadn't made it.

As much as she felt sadness for the family of the boy who died all those years ago, she was moved even more by the realization that the child's death drove Stefano to far more than a gap year volunteer job. He'd said it to the nurse. *So much is out of your control.*

He wanted to help where he could. To *fix* things. To ensure no one around him was ever hurt.

And suddenly, everything about their relationship clicked into place.

She puffed out a breath and let her body sag against the wall as the nurses' station fell quiet once again. That was the promise Stefano had made to her, lying in bed that afternoon in her suite. He'd promised he'd never do anything that could hurt Anna. He'd protect her as if he'd raised her from birth. And he'd said he'd do it no matter the price.

She jammed her fingers into her hair. How could she not have seen it from his perspective? He'd said he brought her the information on the position in Sarcaccia so she could make an informed decision about marrying him. She'd blown it off, telling him she didn't want to discuss it. Neither had she wanted to discuss the offer from Gladwell. When he'd seen it—along with the photo snapped at the Magic Fountain—he'd accused her of not trusting him, of not allowing him to have the information he needed to protect her and Anna.

She should've known he'd never marry her if he believed that marriage could possibly result in either of them being hurt, and he believed she'd be hurt if she didn't allow him to protect her. Turning down a great job offer and having one's photograph run in a newspaper also ran that risk.

A groan escaped her. If Stefano had that promise on his mind, no wonder he'd suddenly changed his mind about marriage and acted as if he knew she was planning to turn him down, saying it was for the best. In truth, after seeing the contents of that folder, he probably couldn't envision a life in which they could be together without Anna being hurt.

What must that decision have cost him?

She allowed her hands to drop to her sides as she stared ahead sightlessly. How stupid she'd been. Stefano was willing to accept her, warts and all. He'd forgiven her for keeping Anna a secret. Even if it wasn't her fault, it was a huge secret to have kept. He'd made amazing, passionate love to her. He'd given her space to consider his proposal. Given up weekends of glamorous parties and soirees with gorgeous, worldly women like Ilsa to chase a giggling prepubescent girl through a hedge maze.

He'd done everything under the sun to earn her trust. And while he hadn't said he loved her, his actions had shown it. Right down to showing up at the hospital to support her when she needed it and tapping his network of friends and acquaintances in order to save Anna's life.

A flash of movement in Anna's room caught Megan's attention, causing her to move to the window that separated their rooms. Dr. Serrano was in with Anna again, listening to her chest with his stethoscope. Megan waited, hoping to see a sign the doctor was satisfied with what he observed. For now, however, it was tough to discern anything. He had his back to her and was leaning over the bed, completely blocking her view of Anna.

"You're awake," Stefano's luxuriant voice soothed her anxiety as he walked up behind her. Judging from the wonderful smell of freshly brewed coffee that entered the room with him, he'd been true to his word to the nurse.

"And you brought me coffee," she said, turning toward him. He held a steaming coffee cup in each hand. A brown paper bag dangled from beneath one of the cups. "That officially makes it my best morning here yet."

A wry smile lit his face as he handed her one of the large cups. Despite the growth of beard and shadows under his eyes that came from a lack of sleep, his grin set her heart racing. He held his own cup of coffee and the paper bag, which he switched to the hand that was now free of her cup. "I brought croissants, too. Not the healthiest choice, but it's all that was available this early. I figured you could use some fortification."

"You are a prince," she whispered, but he still shushed her as he shook open the bag so she could select one.

His gaze moved past her to the window. "Any word?"

"Not yet. I'm trying to be patient." She took a sip of the coffee, which was surprisingly flavorful this morning, then turned back toward Anna. Dr. Serrano appeared to be taking Anna's pulse, though his position still blocked Megan's view of her daughter.

"I suppose that's all we can do." Stefano gestured for her to take a seat in the room's sole chair. "Come on. Have breakfast. It'll kill a few minutes, at least."

Reluctantly, she left the window and took the proffered seat. Leaning back, she closed her eyes and allowed the aroma of the coffee to refresh her brain to the extent it could.

"Now there's a look of ecstasy," Stefano said.

"It's a look of exhaustion," she mumbled.

"Funny...this is the third time we've had breakfast together, yet this is the first time we've spent the night together beforehand." When she cracked an eye, he added, "It's not how I envisioned it."

"Please tell me you're not flirting with me."

She meant it to be teasing, but an expression of loss and confusion passed over his face before he stifled it and replied with a lighthearted, "Never."

He stood abruptly and went to the window.

She fumbled for a way to diffuse the tension that suddenly seemed to fill the air. "Stefano, you know—"

"She's awake." Stefano's face seemed to light from the inside as he grinned. "Really awake this time. Megan, come here...I think she's talking."

CHAPTER THIRTY

Megan was at the window before Stefano finished speaking. Dr. Serrano was holding up his fingers and Anna was telling him how many there were. "Oh my gosh, Stefano! She *is* talking!"

Both of them remained riveted on the scene before them. After another minute of chatting with Anna, Dr. Serrano reached down and patted Anna's arm, then turned and saw them watching from the window. When he gestured that he'd come speak with them in a moment, Megan thought she'd burst.

"The antibiotics must be working," she said as Dr. Serrano stood beside Anna's bed, scribbling notes in his file while Anna closed her eyes and drifted back to sleep. "Let's hope."

"Do you want to talk to the doctor in private?"

"Don't be silly. She's your daughter, too." Even if no one else knew it.

He responded by giving her a quick, one-armed hug in silent thanks, releasing her before Dr. Serrano entered their room.

"As you can see, the news is good," he said in his heavy accent as he removed the mask he'd worn into Anna's room. Though his words filled Megan with relief, the doctor's tone remained professional. "Her fever has come down in the last few hours. She's very tired and needs her sleep, but she is able to answer questions clearly. She could tell me her name and address, she could count backwards from ten, she could tell how many fingers I showed her. She even noticed the flowers on the stand beside her bed. Best of all, she could tell me some of what she was doing the day before she was admitted. She even said, 'I wish hospitals let people wear real clothes because I look stupid.' So her sense of humor is intact. Those are all very good signs."

Megan exhaled for what felt like the first time in days. "That's very, very good to hear."

"She is not" —he glanced at the ceiling for a moment, as if drawing the words from an invisible source— "not out of the woods. She still has a fever and she is very weak. But the new course of antibiotics seems to be working."

"Thank you, Dr. Serrano," Stefano said. He sounded as relieved as Megan felt. "We appreciate the long hours you've spent with Anna."

"Anything for my youngest patients. I understand from Dr. Jenkins that you were the friend who called him." The doctor smiled as he shook hands with Stefano. "Thank you for doing so, Mr. Jones. His input was helpful and I was pleased to have him here yesterday. He left earlier this morning to return to Madrid, but gave me his contact information to keep him updated."

"He'll be thrilled to hear about her progress," Stefano replied.

Megan glanced toward the window. Anna's eyes remained closed. "How soon can I go in again?"

"Whenever she wakes. I would like her to sleep undisturbed as much as possible. Be sure to scrub up first, just to be safe." He removed the stethoscope from around his neck and tucked it into his pocket. "I will call Dr. Jenkins to give him the news, then I will be off for a few hours. Dr. Santos will check on her throughout the day, then I will be back tonight. If you need anything at all, let Dr. Santos know. She's been updated on Anna's case. The nurses are here to help, too."

Megan thanked Dr. Serrano once more, then let him go. The man had to be exhausted, perhaps even more exhausted than she. To her surprise, Stefano walked to the door and closed it behind the doctor.

"Come here," he said. He opened his arms, inviting Megan to fall into his embrace. "She's going to be all right. By the time your parents get here in a few hours, she may even be able to tell them hello."

"I hope so." She allowed herself to relax against him, wrapping her arms around his waist as he cradled her head to the spot where his strong, broad shoulder met the base of his neck. His pulse beat there, a strong, steady thrum against her cheek. "As he said, she's not out of the woods yet. But I'm feeling very positive."

"Me, too. I have to be." His lips pressed to the top of her head as he murmured into her hair, "I love her so much." Then so quietly she could barely hear it, "So much."

The admission nearly felled Megan. She knew, deep in her soul, that he'd meant it for her, too. His palm spread across her back, warming her through her shirt, even as his other hand kept her head tucked against him.

Tentatively, she moved her lips to where Stefano's pulse beat, just above his collarbone at the base of his throat. At the intimate contact, his breathing became shallower, more heated. His fingers flexed against her back, then slid lower. Neither of them could mistake this for an embrace driven solely by relief. Not anymore.

His mouth moved lower, kissing her forehead, her cheek, and then—as she shifted to allow him access—her lips. He didn't pretend to want gentleness. His kiss was hard, rough as the whiskers dotting his jaw, filled with need. She responded with the same hunger, opening to him, encouraging him to touch and feel and taste every part of her. To give him what he needed, even if he refused to acknowledge to himself that he did, in fact, need it.

Suddenly, his hands went lax against her back. Once again, it was as if he could read her mind. He eased his mouth away from hers. "We shouldn't. No matter how good this feels, we—"

"The nurses aren't going to come in." Though as she said it, she realized that they very well could walk right into Anna's room and see them through the window.

"It's not that."

He took a step back. Slowly, he moved his hands to her shoulders, then down her arms, until only their fingertips touched. Sounds drifted to them from the hallway: a mop bucket being rolled by a maintenance worker, a phone ringing, the distant ping of an elevator. With a sigh, he broke contact.

He scrubbed a hand from his forehead to his chin, a blend of sadness and frustration darkening his face as he looked at her.

"I know," she admitted.

"Do you? Can you understand?"

"The last thing you're afraid of is the nurses. You're far more afraid of what's outside the hospital walls. That's what makes you afraid to love me. And" —her chest tightened as she said the words— "I think you do. Love me."

Stefano's mouth opened as if he wanted to argue, but she reached to cover his lips with her index finger. "I know why you're doing what you're doing. Why you essentially took back your marriage proposal. Why you're dying to kiss me now but feel it's wrong."

He brushed her hand aside. "You're not—"

"You promised me that you'd never hurt Anna. And I know you keep your promises. But Stefano, that's an *impossible* promise. At least in this situation. You can't stop living your life for fear you'll get hurt, or that someone around you might get hurt."

A muscle jumped in his jaw as he considered her words. "Megan, you know my situation is different than most. You're guaranteed *to* get hurt if you're in my life. You have an unbelievable job offer right here, working with people who care about you. Even Jack Gladwell—"

"There are no guarantees with anything. Ever." She didn't want to discuss Jack or the Grandspire. Instead, she gestured toward the window, toward what really mattered in her life. "If there were guarantees, a perfectly healthy girl wouldn't suddenly be lying there so sick she could die. There weren't guarantees the antibiotics would work, either. *Nothing* is guaranteed."

His jaw continued to work for a moment as he looked at her, then at the floor, then back at her. "It's impossible."

What a stubborn, stubborn man. She loved him so much she could burst, and simultaneously wanted to throttle him.

"Stefano—"

"No." He waved her off. "No discussion. In time, you'll see that I'm right about this. And now that Anna's fever has broken, I should go before Dr. Serrano or the nurses realize who I am. It's only a matter of time. As it is, my secretary will soon have difficulty holding off inquiries regarding my whereabouts."

For the first time since he'd arrived, Megan wondered how he'd explained his absence from the palace. Since it was the middle of the week, this was clearly no weekend jaunt to visit friends. He must've missed a number of engagements. "Does your family know where you are?"

"In bed with a terrible migraine and not to be disturbed on doctor's orders. At least as long as my secretary can convince them of that fact."

"And do you have a plan to sneak back into the palace?" He must feel a teenager sneaking back into the house after a night out, but on a grander scale.

His mouth lifted into a half-smile. "I'm not worried about that part."

She hated to let him go—her entire being wanted to convince him that what they had wasn't impossible—but she knew from his rigid stance and the determined set of his eyes there would be no dissuading him. Not today. "All right. Do what you need to do. I'll keep you updated on Anna's progress as best I can. My parents will be upset that they missed you."

"One of these days, I'll meet them. I promise. And sooner rather than later."

He started to leave, but paused near the door and frowned as if forgetting something. He strode past Megan to the small table beside the bed, grabbed the pad and pen resting there, and scribbled a note. He turned and handed it to her. "Use this. It's my direct line."

"Is this your cell phone number?" The number he'd said only his parents and secretary had?

He withdrew a small phone from his pants pocket. "This very one. I should've given it to you weeks ago. I don't want you to go through anyone else ever again to reach me. Call when you know anything. I want every detail."

"I will. I promise." She folded the paper and held it to her heart as he snagged his bag from the floor, then disappeared from the room without a backward glance.

* * *

"Mom, Stefano was here, wasn't he?"

Megan put down the book she'd been reading to Anna—an activity they hadn't done in years, but it kept Anna from complaining about the taste of hospital gelatin—and said, "I think you're still confused, honey. Are you talking about Mr. Jones?"

Anna's eyes widened for a moment, then a grin perked up her face. At long last, color—healthy color, rather than the burn of fever—was finding its way to her cheeks. The sight sent a wave of happiness washing over Megan. "Yes."

"Well…Mr. Jones was here to visit. He left a few days ago, just before Grandma and Grandpa arrived."

Anna pursed her lips and nodded, as if she'd just been handed a secret code and was about to embark on a grand adventure. "I wish I could've talked to him. But I'm glad he came."

"Me, too. He loves you, sweetie. He's called the nurses' station every day since he left to check on you. He even brought a doctor here to work with Dr. Serrano. The two of them worked together to choose the medicine that helped make you better."

"But I still feel cruddy," she complained.

"I know." If Anna only knew how sick she'd really been…it was for the best for now that she didn't. "But if you finish the gelatin and crackers, the nurses said your IV can come out."

"Good, because I hate it. Needles are gross." She grimaced at the half-eaten cup of amber-colored gelatin. "Do I have to eat it all?"

"Give it a try. If not, you can try again later."

She ate another teaspoonful, then pushed it away. "I'll try in a minute."

"Whenever you're ready." Megan picked up the book again, but Anna had other ideas.

"Mom, you know Marco from my class?"

Marco? She set the book aside and wracked her brain for a Marco from Anna's class list. "Oh, do you mean Marco Carbone?"

"Yeah. Can you let him know I'm in the hospital, but tell him I'm okay?"

"Of course, honey." Megan smoothed back a stray strand of Anna's hair. The girl needed a shower as soon as she was able. "Do you want me to let anyone else know? Like Julia or your other friends?"

Anna shook her head, but stopped as if the movement caused pain. "Marco will tell everyone."

"All right." Megan adjusted the pillow so Anna could relax against it while remaining upright. "I didn't realize that you and Marco were friends."

"We are." Anna picked up her spoon, but set it down without trying the gelatin again. "Um…he's kinda my boyfriend."

At *ten?* Megan bit back her first response, then said, "I see. You didn't tell me that."

"It's no big deal."

Good. And thank goodness her parents decided to go to the hospital cafeteria for lunch, because this wasn't a conversation she wanted them to hear. Megan waited a moment before asking, "What kinds of things do you and Marco do if you're boyfriend and girlfriend?" They certainly hadn't gone on a date or done anything together outside of school, not that there'd even been school for a few weeks now.

"The usual stuff." When Anna failed to elaborate, Megan circled her hand, urging Anna to continue. "You know. We sit together in the cafeteria at lunchtime and we try to get on the same team when we play dodgeball or soccer in gym class. And he's, like, the first person I'm supposed to text about things. Stuff like that. I don't want him to think I'm ignoring him because I haven't texted him in a while. I mean, because it's summer, so really all we do is text."

Megan couldn't help but smile at that. "His number's on the class roster at home. When I check in at home again, I'll let him know." When the time was right, she'd ply Anna with more questions about how she ended up with "kinda" a boyfriend and what that meant.

Anna exhaled and settled deeper into her pillow. Megan resumed reading, but only made it a few paragraphs before Anna asked, "Is Mr. Jones your boyfriend now?"

Megan carefully kept her smile in place, though the question struck her like a knife to the heart. Ever since Stefano walked out of the apartment, she'd been in agony. Watching him leave the hospital after refusing to acknowledge his feelings for her felt even worse. "No."

"Do you like him?"

"Of course I do, but things are a little different for adults. We don't have dodgeball teams."

Anna seemed to digest this. In a matter of fact tone, she said, "He hasn't asked you out, has he? You know that you can ask him out if you like him. It doesn't matter who asks anymore."

Megan stifled a laugh. "I'm aware."

"You should think about it. He might be too chicken to ask you, but I think he likes you. Sometimes guys don't want to be the one to ask."

Not if they already asked once and the answer took so long he decided it was impossible.

Megan forced back the thought as she leaned forward and tucked the sheets tighter around her daughter, then tweaked her nose. "I think you need to focus on getting better. Anything else is a waste of your energy."

Anna giggled, then glanced toward the door. "The nurses can't hear me, Mom." Despite her assertion, she lowered her voice. "But if you married him someday, wouldn't it be incredible? Not just because we'd get to live in a castle—I mean, castles are cool and all—but I bet it has space like Grandma and Grandpa's house in Minnesota, so we could have a dog. Wouldn't a dog be great? And I really like Mr. Jones. He'd be an awesome dad. Like, a real dad in our house, instead of a dad who visits."

Now she was really glad her parents went to the cafeteria.

Megan started to speak, but before she could get out the first syllable Anna added, "I know you're going to tell me it's silly, and I shouldn't get focused on it or anything, but it's fun to think about what it might be like, isn't it?"

"It's not silly," Megan said on a sigh. "We all like to daydream about living in a fairy tale. It's human nature."

"Do you?"

"Sometimes," she admitted. She leaned forward and smoothed the sheet covering Anna's upper body. "Right now, though, you need to have some real dreams. Sleepytime dreams. Your body still needs rest so you can get out of the hospital and enjoy your summer."

"Then school again. Somewhere." She let out a monster yawn before asking, "Do you know where we're going yet?"

"No. But there's still time before I need to get you registered." Some. "In fact, as soon as you go to sleep, I have a call to make about a job."

"Is it a good one?"

"It could be."

"Okay." One side of her mouth hooked up as she turned to her side and closed her eyes. "I hope it's somewhere sunny."

"I'll do my best."

She ran her palm over Anna's hair, tossed the half-eaten gelatin cup, then left the room with the image of Anna's trusting smile warming her heart.

CHAPTER THIRTY-ONE

Never in her life had Megan turned down a job offer.

For the first few years after she'd graduated, she'd been thrilled to have a job, period. Then, when she'd been offered the business development position at the Grandspire, she hadn't bothered to interview anywhere else. The warm welcome she'd received from Ramon and the rest of the staff was the stuff of her dreams. They'd made her feel part of the hotel and the city. They'd given her a home and gave Anna the same love they lavished on their own children.

Even as she stepped out of the white Mercedes taxi and smoothed her hands down the front of her favorite navy suit, Megan found it hard to believe she'd actually turned down her second job offer from the Grandspire. Jack Gladwell was likely the only person more stunned than she. When she'd hung up the phone after thanking him for the job offer, his patience, and for the generous bouquet he'd sent Anna while her daughter was in the hospital, she'd fully expected to be sick to her stomach. Instead, her veins thrummed with a burst of energy, as if she'd just stepped off a Venezuelan zipline platform to soar over the jungle canopy and enjoy a view only the hovering birds usually experienced. It was, in a word, exhilarating.

After she'd left her parents and Anna in the suite and boarded the flight to Sarcaccia this morning, however, doubts crept in. This risk wasn't Megan's alone to take, no matter how right it felt. There was Anna to consider. Though Anna had only been out of the hospital a few days and had several weeks of summer vacation left—time which she should be using to fully recover—Anna was already asking when she'd know about school.

Megan blinked in the bright sunlight before ascending the wide steps into the Ristorante Villa Enrica, a picturesque white stucco building clinging to a cliffside above the Mediterranean Sea, and told herself not to think about the Grandspire and the what-ifs. She needed only to concentrate on today's job interview. If she didn't get this position, she'd need to start her job hunt from scratch and hope she landed a position quickly enough to register Anna for school.

But if she did get the job...well, she had no idea what would happen then, either. She'd said it herself: There were no guarantees with anything. Ever.

A pale blonde in a smartly tailored black dress topped with a matching jacket approached, her heels clicking on the tile floor of the cliffside restaurant. A warm smile lit her face as she extended her hand in greeting. "Ms. Hallberg, welcome to Sarcaccia. I'm Natalie Costa. It's a pleasure to meet you in person. I trust you had a good flight?"

Megan replied with the appropriate niceties. She'd felt comfortable speaking with Natalie during their phone calls—though she'd pictured someone named Natalie Costa as having coloring closer to Stefano's—but her pulse pounded overtime as they walked toward the rear of the elegant restaurant. Natalie mentioned during their last call that they'd hold the interview in a private room over lunch and that Megan should bring her appetite.

"I hope you've allowed yourself a few hours to explore the island after our meeting today," Natalie said as they passed through the main dining room. "It's a beautiful country."

"Especially with the weather as glorious as it is," Megan agreed. "I admit, I've wanted to visit Sarcaccia from the first time I saw pictures of the beaches and mountains. It's far prettier in person."

That drew a smile from Natalie. "I grew up in Denmark and never imagined I'd leave, but then I met my husband." She shrugged. "I had my doubts about moving to Sarcaccia to be near his family, but from the moment I walked into our first apartment in Cateri, the island became my home."

That explained the contrast between Natalie's fair complexion and locally common last name. "I'm sure it was a difficult decision."

"For love, it wasn't so difficult. Especially since he bribed me here with the promise of a sea view." She indicated a set of oversized glass doors set into the restaurant's rear wall. "As you can see, it is quite an enticement."

Megan stepped out the restaurant's large glass doors and bit back a sigh as warm wind caressed her face and the scent of flowers in bloom washed over her. A wide stone stairway led to a stone patio that ran the entire length of the restaurant's lower level and offered a panoramic view of the sea. The early afternoon sun made the water sparkle as if thousands of diamonds had been cast upon its surface. In the distance, a pleasure boat made its way out to sea, headed north toward Corsica and beyond. A half-dozen small fishing boats, each holding two or three occupants, were visible within a half-mile of the shore.

As if wishing to make itself worthy of its postcard view, the restaurant patio itself was a feast for the eyes. Rustic wood tables of varying sizes filled the area, each topped with wide white umbrellas that kept the feeling light and airy while protecting diners from the sun's harshest rays. Pink, red, and white flowers spilled from oversized urns spaced out along the wall at the patio's edge. Natalie led Megan down the stairs and to the patio's walled edge. Shielding her eyes, the taller woman pointed along the coastline to the north. "See the long white building just south of the grand marina?"

"That's the new conference center?" The modern structure was spectacular, even from this distance, with large windows facing the sea from underneath a roof that swooped in a manner reminiscent of a wind-filled sail.

"It is." Natalie went on to point out the location of several large waterfront hotels, most of which were undergoing refurbishment in anticipation of new business, then to describe the planned transportation connections from the airport, bus terminals, and medieval city center, which was a tourist favorite. "Once finished, the conference center will be easily accessible from anywhere in Europe. All that's left to do is to complete the interior, hire a staff, and start marketing it to potential clients."

"Well, if that's all," Megan said, amused. "I look forward to hearing more details on your plans."

"The members of the committee are looking forward to meeting you. They should be gathering in the private dining room now. I've also invited a few representatives from the transportation sector and the adjacent hotels in case you have questions about where they stand with their development plans. I want you to understand the full scope of the project and its role in the country's economy."

Natalie turned to lead Megan from the patio wall toward an area set further back, shaded by the restaurant itself. "We'll be meeting here, just off the patio." As she paused to secure an umbrella that threatened to blow loose, she added, "I must say, you've come highly recommended. When I learned of your work at the Grandspire, I put you at the top of our candidate list. Not only have you generated buzz for the hotel throughout Europe, I understand the grand reopening was quite the event. I admit, I'm jealous of those who attended."

"Thank you," she replied, reaching to help Natalie lock the umbrella in place. "A lot of work went into making the night a success. We wanted guests to walk away knowing what to expect if they wished to host an event or conference in the hotel, then to share that knowledge in their professional and social circles."

"Which is exactly what Mahmoud Said did with us," she said on a smile.

"Mahmoud?" Not Stefano?

"We consulted with his company on the communications plan for the conference center. He has a high opinion of your work and insisted we contact you when we were ready to interview for the position." They finished securing the umbrella and continued across the wide patio as Natalie spoke. "He claimed that anyone who met you would want to book events with you because you're one of the most organized, personable people he's had the opportunity to meet."

Megan bit the inside of her lip to keep her jaw from dropping. She had the feeling she'd gained the confidence of the wealthy Egyptian CEO, but not to that extent. While Mahmoud was a sociable man, she'd never known him to be effusive. "That's very kind of him to say. I'll be sure to thank him later."

One more check in the *Stefano was right, you were wrong column*. She should have trusted him when he said he hadn't been the one to give the committee her name.

"He's not your only fan." Natalie lowered her voice. "Before we go in, I did receive a second recommendation for you, though it was off the record."

"Oh?" she managed to sound casual, despite the unease rising within her.

Natalie paused outside the door leading to the restaurant's private room. "I'm very close to my cousin, who works in Barcelona and was a guest at your grand reopening. When I mentioned that I would be interviewing candidates for the conference center, she immediately mentioned your name and asked if I'd heard of you. She was blown away by the Grandspire's operations. She also said she thought you'd fit in well in Sarcaccia and would be an asset to our country. My cousin's best friend is a member of Sarcaccia's royal family, so she's spent a great deal of time here and knows the country well."

Megan felt the look of disbelief cross her face, but knew trying to hide it would prove futile. "Your cousin wouldn't happen to be Ilsa Jakobsen, would she?"

Though the two women had different coloring, Ilsa was Danish, like Natalie, and equally tall. Stefano mentioned that Ilsa lived in Barcelona and had been room-mates with his sister. Now that she studied Natalie, she could see the resemblance in the tilt of their eyes and the manner in which they walked.

Natalie grinned. "One and the same. You met her, then?"

"Actually, no, though I did notice her at the party and we have a mutual friend." Not that Megan would identify the mutual friend.

"Ilsa is *always* noticed at parties." Natalie shot her a knowing look. "As you might guess, she's invited to many."

Megan liked Natalie more and more every minute. "I'm surprised she recommended me, given that we weren't introduced."

Natalie moved toward the door. "She was impressed by the party and by all she heard about you. I'm sure you'll impress the committee, as well. Come on in. They should be ready."

Megan was still pondering Ilsa's possible motive for recommending her when she stepped into the sunny room. A group of well-dressed men and women mingled near a table set for ten. She recognized the head of Sarcaccia's tourism bureau from its website and was introduced to the woman nearest the door, who headed the conference center's hiring committee. As Megan turned to meet representatives from two local hotels, a door at the far end of the room opened to admit a late arrival, one who instantly drew the attention of the entire room, just as he'd drawn the attention of everyone in the bar when he'd first come to the Grandspire.

And then she heard his voice, an unmistakable, rich tone that unraveled her soul.

Natalie leaned closer to Megan. "Ah, and here's our transportation guru. I believe that you've met Prince Stefano Barrali?"

* * *

The swiftly-concealed shock on Megan's face mirrored the emotion simmering through Stefano as he crossed the room.

She's really here.

Stefano had done a double take when perusing his e-mail this morning. While both lunch and dinner with the committee were on his schedule, he hadn't known which two candidates the committee would be interviewing. Not until he'd read Natalie Costa's e-mail, confirming his availability to answer any transportation questions and stating that it was her hope they'd only need to conduct these two interviews to land the perfect hire.

The entire drive from the palace to the restaurant, trepidation clogged his throat. *She'll have cancelled. There was a mistake with the names. Natalie will call to inform me of her error at any moment.* But no call came. And now, as he traversed the room while shaking hands with committee members at the same time Natalie moved toward him with Megan at her side, making introductions along the way, the lump in his throat grew.

The pale, hollow look of exhaustion and fear that clung to Megan in the hospital was gone, replaced by the vibrant, smiling face he'd come to love. Her cheeks were rosy, her expression bright with life, and her hair shone as it did the night he'd seen her in that gorgeous, honey-colored gown at the Grandspire reception. A navy suit with a light blue blouse complimented her eyes to perfection. It wasn't his opinion alone. Every male in the room looked at her with admiration, and that admiration wasn't strictly of the professional sort.

Welcome to the world of hot-blooded Sarcaccian men, Megan.

He could only hope the other men in the room didn't feel the same electricity he did when he looked at her.

"Prince Stefano," Natalie greeted him with a broad smile. "Thank you for making time in your schedule. Mahmoud Said mentioned that you met Ms. Hallberg at the Grandspire?"

"I did." He turned to Megan, whose stance radiated confidence even as trepidation lurked in the depths of her blue eyes. "It's a pleasure to see you again."

"And you as well."

She extended her hand, but instead of shaking it, he raised it for the briefest brush of his lips. He shot her a questioning look, one he hoped she understood. Though her eyes widened fractionally, her expression revealed nothing about whether her decision to interview was due to him, the job itself, or both. "Thank you for coming to Sarcaccia."

"Shall we be seated for lunch?" Natalie asked, corralling the group. "We'd like to get to know you better, Megan."

For the next hour, after asking a few general questions about Megan's background, Natalie and the other committee members discussed the construction of the center, the planned technologies, the center's current budget, and the types of events they anticipated hosting. The hotel representatives discussed their facilities and plans for coordinating with the new center. Megan gave input where appropriate and asked all the right questions, demonstrating her knowledge of both the new facility and its importance to the country's economy. Finally, Stefano was asked to give an overview of the country's transportation upgrades. He managed to sound professional, though he wondered if others at the table could see his emotions written on his face. He wanted nothing more than to pull Megan aside and ask her when she'd decided to interview for the position and, more importantly, why.

Had Jack Gladwell changed his mind? If the bastard hired someone else while Anna was in the hospital....

No, he wouldn't have. From the moment Stefano opened the folder with the job offer, he knew Gladwell was determined to hire Megan, and Gladwell wasn't the type to change his mind. And the flowers he'd sent to the hospital meant that Megan was on his mind a full two weeks after the offer had been extended.

He was dying to know what happened.

Laughter filled the room as one of the hotel managers described a fiasco involving a sick bird that had made its way into his hotel's lobby. The sound of Megan's distinctive, lilting laughter illuminated his soul. What did it matter if Jack Gladwell rescinded his offer or not? Megan was here. He could tell from the subtle looks shared amongst the committee that they liked her. She'd get an offer, he was certain.

He wanted to kiss her into oblivion and beg her to stay. To tell her he couldn't promise her a life of complete privacy, but he could promise her his undying devotion and love. On the other hand, he knew he wouldn't. It wouldn't be safe for her or for Anna. And frankly, he knew the job here, while challenging, wouldn't give her the paycheck Jack Gladwell could afford. If she wanted the best for Anna, she should accept that position rather than this one.

The waiters cleared the last of the luncheon plates, signaling the end of their interview time. Natalie handed her empty glass to a waiter, then leaned forward to address Megan directly. "You accomplished a great deal at the Grandspire. I hope it's not improper of me to mention, but you were fairly young to take on such a huge task. I'm sure it was quite intimidating. If we were to offer you this position, it would be even more substantial and would have a higher profile. This isn't simply one hotel in a chain, it's our country's center for business. Our economy will be greatly impacted by its success or failure. What have you learned from your experience at the Grandspire that makes you believe you'd be a success here? Do you have any concerns when it comes to that success?"

Megan's eyes lit at the question. "I won't lie. I was scared witless when I accepted the Grandspire job. But I was also more excited by it than by anything I'd experienced to that point. I like a challenge. But what I learned from the experience there is that it's not all about me. I built a family at the Grandspire, and as with any family, we all have our strengths and weaknesses. It takes getting to know your family to know who is best at which tasks. If someone is talented but struggling with their role, perhaps that role needs to be adjusted. Perhaps the person needs more education or training to meet the challenge. But to do that, you need a foundation built on mutual trust. That's what created the success at the Grandspire."

Megan's gaze took in the committee members one by one, lingering on Stefano before she turned back to Natalie. "When an undertaking is larger than life, even when it seems impossible, trusting those around you makes facing that challenge a lot of fun and ultimately, very rewarding. That trust enables you to leave your fear at the door and work with the belief that everything will fall into place."

A muscle twitched in Stefano's jaw. Megan meant for him to understand the deeper meaning of her statement.

She hadn't come for the job. She'd come for him. And she wanted him to trust *her*.

Natalie consulted her notes, then said, "In that case, we're about done here. You should know that we have one more candidate for the position, whom we'll be interviewing later today. However, if we were to offer this position to you, would you take it? Or are you considering other offers?"

"Technically, that's two questions" —Megan's full lips twitched in amusement, but her voice remained serious— "but they have one answer. This is the offer I want. It gives me a chance to help develop a brand-new facility and put my own mark on it, and that's rare in this business. In fact, I turned down a very good offer when I learned that this position was available. It was a risk, but I couldn't ask for anything better than a life and a career here in Sarcaccia. It's a risk I was willing to take."

That earned Megan a satisfied nod from Natalie, who pushed back from the table to stand. "Thank you. You've given us a great deal to discuss. We'll make our decision by tomorrow, so expect to hear from me soon."

A flurry of activity ensued as the committee members' chairs squeaked back from the table, though Stefano sat riveted, his heart in his throat. He watched as Megan made the rounds, shaking committee members' hands and thanking them for their time. Only when two men beside him began whispering about how the other job candidate would compare did Stefano shake himself to the present.

She turned down Gladwell.

Still, no matter how well she'd done today, as she'd told him in the hospital, there were no guarantees in life. Ever. The other candidate was solid, too. Megan could be hunting for a job again just as Anna was about to start a new school year.

Without speaking to those seated near him, he shoved back from the table and threaded his way through the room, determination propelling him forward. Trying to reach her in the crowded room reminded him of his thwarted attempts to get her alone on the Grandspire roof the night of the fireworks. He couldn't be so patient this time. He was only a few feet from Megan when Natalie signaled that she'd escort Megan to the front of the restaurant.

"I can call a taxi for you, if you like," Natalie offered, pulling a cell phone from her handbag. "Are you headed to the airport?"

"My flight's not for a few hours." Her gaze flashed past Natalie to Stefano, then back again. "But a taxi to the city center would be great."

"I'm heading that direction," Stefano said, inserting himself in the conversation. "I'd be happy to give you a ride."

"Your Highness?" The room quieted at the shock in Natalie's voice.

Stefano's eyes didn't leave Megan as he said to Natalie, "I'll be back before the next interview. In the meantime, I'll show Megan what Sarcaccia has to offer."

He imagined tongues would wag the moment he left the room. It was a risk he had to take. He had to know what she was thinking.

His heart leapt at the mixture of hope and surprise that passed over Megan's face before she squelched it in favor of a more professional demeanor. "If you think that's possible, Your Highness, I'd love it."

Chapter Thirty-Two

"You know, the polite thing to do when visiting is to call first."

"Who says I wasn't planning to call when I finished the interview?"

Megan settled back against the soft leather seat of Stefano's car. She hadn't expected him to drive a plain sedan. Something more along the lines of a Ferrari or perhaps a James Bond-type Aston Martin seemed more suited to a wealthy bachelor prince wishing to hug the curves of Sarcaccia's mountain roads. Then again, she hadn't considered that he'd drive himself at all.

His laughter echoed through the car. "Of course you were."

"I wasn't told you'd be there," she replied. When Natalie said the interview would consist of the committee plus a few representatives from the hotel and transportation sectors, the words 'one of whom is royal' weren't spoken. She stole a sideways glance at Stefano. "I also had no idea Mahmoud Said recommended me for the job. Or that Natalie Costa is a cousin of Ilsa Jakobsen's. Did you?"

"I did." His hands glided over the steering wheel as they turned from the hotel's tiny parking lot onto the two-lane highway skirting the cliffside, heading toward the marina and modern hotels she'd spotted earlier from the restaurant patio. No other cars were on the road, it was only the two of them, the warm air, and the sunshine.

"You didn't say anything," she pointed out as she rolled down the window a crack to enjoy the seaside air.

"I needed you to trust me when I said I wasn't the one who gave the committee your name. I wanted you to know that, for once in my life, I wasn't trying to control the situation."

She smiled at that. "And I interviewed for the conference center job without telling you because I needed you to trust *me*."

"Trust you to…what?" His eyes went to the rearview mirror. He squinted as if searching for something before focusing once more on the road ahead. "Make a stupid decision and turn down a great job in a place you love? A place that's perfect for Anna?"

"No. I needed you to trust me to make the choice to come here even if you've convinced yourself that the situation is impossible."

"Because if people trust each other, anything is possible?"

She grinned at his mimicry of her interview answer and raised a finger in the air as if she were a schoolteacher. "That was only part of what I said. I also said that everyone needs to understand each others' roles and adjust accordingly."

His gaze flicked to the rearview mirror once more before he cut to the left, taking a rutted road off the highway. Her fingers curled around the armrest as her purse bumped off her lap.

"Even I know this isn't the way to the marina or to central Cateri." She drew in a sharp breath as the car skirted the side of the cliff. The road looked more suited to sheep or horses than vehicles. "One wrong turn will take us into the sea."

"Hang on. You'll see where we're going." The car jostled downhill for a few hundred yards until they reached a flat area set into the side of the cliff that offered just enough room to park two or three cars. Stacked stones framed the end of the space and separated it from a small beach. Stefano rolled to a stop and cut the engine.

"I'm not dressed for this," she noted.

"Me, either. But no one followed us, we're completely shielded from view, and I thought you might want privacy."

"With you? On Sarcaccia?"

"With me. On a beach."

"Impossible," she teased.

"Being on a beach with me, or the privacy?"

"You tell me."

That drew a slow, sexy smile from him, one that made her pulse jump. He opened his car door and signaled for her to do the same. "Come on."

She followed him to the front of the car. He extended a hand as she approached the stacked stones, helping her to step over them, then brushed off the top so she could sit without ruining her suit. The breeze was light here, with the cliffs protecting them, yet it was enough to keep the air cool and comfortable. Better yet, the water in the cove was calm. The waves lapped the shore in such a gentle rhythm even a child could wade out without fear of being pulled under. How Stefano found this hideaway, she couldn't imagine. "This is gorgeous."

"One of my favorite places. I don't come here often. I'm too afraid it'll be discovered. One of my sister's boyfriends brought her here once." He tilted his head, as if remembering. "I gather the relationship didn't end well, but she loved the spot. She says it's the only place on the planet she can feel completely alone and safe. The narrow road and the angle from the cliff don't allow for anyone to photograph this spot from a distance, and no one can approach without being heard."

Megan could understand why he kept the location secret. Which reminded her....

"Last time we looked out at the waves together, a photographer did snap a picture of us." She pulled off her heels and sank her toes in the sand. "I don't know if you've looked, but as far as I can tell nothing has shown up anywhere yet."

"No." He sat atop the stone wall beside her, his shoulder inches from hers, and looked out to the sea. "Nor will it."

"How do you know?"

"I purchased them."

She turned her head slowly to study him. "You…really? How?"

A tight smile played at the edge of his mouth. "I spotted the same man in the airport that afternoon, waiting to board my plane. He was actively trying *not* to look at me, even when I walked right in front of him. I knew then he had to be a paparazzo. He went through the boarding line before me and I managed to see his ticket while he was standing in front of me on the jetway. As soon as I got back to the palace, I gave his name to my assistant. She tracked him down and offered to buy the photos for a rather outrageous sum, stipulating that she would only do so if he signed a contract guaranteeing they were on an exclusive basis." He gave a sarcastic grunt. "Having Barrali money comes in handy now and then. It's the Barrali fame that's a pain."

She put her hand over his. Softly, she asked, "Is it? I'm not so sure."

He looked down at her hand, but made no move to take it. "If I weren't a Barrali, we never would have been separated. We would have raised Anna together. My entire life—*our* entire lives—would have been vastly different. So yes, I'd call that a pain. I also think that, because I'm a Barrali, it's for the best if we keep things as they are. I need you to understand that. I can't have you or Anna put in harm's way. Or pull you into a life you weren't meant to live."

"If you weren't a Barrali, we might never have met." She spun on the stone to face him, waiting until he looked her in the eye before continuing. "You might never have gone to Venezuela. I wouldn't have had Anna, and I certainly wouldn't be sitting on a beach with you right now. If you weren't a Barrali, Anna very likely would've died in the hospital. Your *fame*, as it were, meant you had the connections to bring in a terrific doctor."

He opened his mouth to argue, but she continued, "Most of all, if you weren't a Barrali, you wouldn't be *you*. You're protective, strong, and unbelievably confident, yet you have a heart of gold. All of those things are a product of your upbringing. I heard what you said to the nurse about meeting that child with meningitis. That's part of who you are, deep at your core. I was so sure I wouldn't fit into your world that it blinded me to the fact that I love you for *you*. All of you. When I hid the job offer and the newspaper photo from you, it wasn't because I didn't trust you."

He raised an eyebrow in skepticism. "You didn't trust me when I proposed to you."

"No, I didn't," she admitted. "Like I said then, I didn't think you knew what you wanted. I'd just seen you after years apart, I'd just learned the truth about Ariana, and it was a lot to absorb. But after we spent more time together, I grew to love and trust you. I saw that you were the man I fell for in Venezuela and so much more. I'd decided to accept your proposal and I didn't want anything to get in the way."

"You were scared I'd tell you not to come to Sarcaccia if I knew about Gladwell. Especially after we'd just been seen by a photographer."

"I didn't want it to weigh into the discussion because I'd made up my mind. But yes, I was probably scared of what you'd say. Same thing with the newspaper photo. So I did exactly what I'd accused you of doing whenever you wanted things to go your way. I took control. I stuck it over by the sugar canister in the kitchen so you wouldn't know. And it ended up blowing up in my face." As it probably should have. She should've been open with him.

"And now?"

She lifted a shoulder, then let it drop. "Frankly, I'm still scared. I'm scared you won't want me here. Or that if I'm here, you won't want to marry me. I'm scared that even if you do, I might fail at being what you'd need me to be as the wife of a prince."

Her fingers tightened over his hand as she finished, "But I'm sure that this is where I belong, even if I don't land the conference center job. As long as we can be open with each other—if you can trust me to tell you when newspapers print silly photos, and I can trust you with the task of protecting Anna and me—we'll be fine. Even if it means finding a job at one of the hotels or having to live in a palace with little privacy and a lot of expectations."

"Sure enough to turn down Gladwell? I still think that was foolish. His offer was more than generous. And he's Jack-freaking-Gladwell. He's one of the most powerful men in the world. Think of the opportunities you'd have working for him."

She grinned at both his statement and his use of the word *freaking*, which sounded completely out of character given his lush Sarcaccian accent. "Jack Gladwell doesn't have nearly as much to offer me as you do."

He was silent for a few long, painful moments before saying, "In that case, I'm afraid I have some bad news for you. It may alter your plans."

His dour tone sent her stomach plummeting. She'd been sure she'd handled the interview well. The committee members seemed happy with her responses and she'd felt a genuine friendliness in the atmosphere. Natalie, in particular, seemed anxious to hire her. So what had happened?

Or did he truly not love her? Was he going to stick to his guns regarding marriage?

"Go on," she urged when he said nothing more.

"I hate to tell you this" —he reached up to tuck her hair behind her ear, leaving the palm of his hand to cup the side of her head— "but if you accept the job, which I am quite sure you'll be offered—"

"How could you know—"

"—you won't be living in the palace."

His tone remained serious, but a glimmer in his eyes led her to say, "No?"

"You have the option of getting your own apartment, of course. My guess is that the committee will be so anxious to have you that you could negotiate a stipend to cover the cost. But I'd much prefer you live with me. In my home."

"Live with you?" She felt her jaw go slack as she processed the second part of what he'd said. "Wait…in your…did you say home?"

"More of an apartment," he clarified. "When you received the offer from Jack Gladwell and I returned to Sarcaccia, the palace felt suffocating. I decided it was high time I moved out."

She stared at him in stunned silence. No one moved out of the palace, not the children of the monarch, at least. She'd read enough about Sarcaccia over the years since Anna's birth to know that much about its traditions.

"I don't believe it," she said. "That's…that's not done!"

A self-satisfied grin tugged at the corners of his mouth. "Being with you showed me how much I value my independence. The best times in my life have been when I've been away from the palace and its strictures. When we volunteered in Venezuela, when I was in the military, and especially when I was with you in Barcelona. I could be myself."

"In disguise," she pointed out. "That's the antithesis of being yourself."

Laughter erupted from him. "In disguise, when necessary. But still myself, the man I truly am on the inside. When I couldn't have you in my life because you'd be working for Gladwell—or so I thought—I decided I had to be true to myself if I ever wanted to be happy. While I can never get away from the media completely, or from my role in the royal family, being away from the palace will give me space."

"I take up space. So does Anna."

"There's plenty," he assured her. "It's the top floor of a gorgeous old building, but it's been completely modernized on the inside. There's a doorman, underground parking, and four large en suite bedrooms. The international school is a half-mile away and there's an enclosed park out back if one would like to, say, walk a dog or play ball. Oh, and there's an ocean view. You might like it. In fact, I'll admit that when I bought it, my first thought was that you'd love it. It even has one of the decorative cornerstones I told Anna about the day we explored the Gothic Quarter."

"It sounds like heaven." Especially if she shared it with Stefano.

"In that case, I have an important question to ask." His other hand came up to frame her face, the intensity in his gaze making her dizzy. She knew with a certainty that he was going to propose. For real, this time.

And this time, she'd give the answer she knew would make them both deliriously happy.

"Would you, Megan Hallberg, consent to" —he paused dramatically, then raised an eyebrow— "owning a dog with me?"

For a split second, she was taken aback, but soon laughter spilled from her with such intensity that tears sprang to her eyes and rolled down her cheeks. "A dog?" she choked out. "Why yes, Stefano Barrali, I will consent to owning a dog with you. I'm sure it'll make Anna very, very happy."

"Will it make *you* happy?"

She nodded. How could she ever live without this man? "It will."

He leaned in to brush his lips against hers, the slight touch sending a shiver of satisfaction through her. She expected him to kiss her again as she leaned forward and moved her hands to his thighs, but instead, he eased back and said, "Perhaps we should do things in the proper order. Marriage first, then the dog? It should be raised by two loving parents. If not, there'd be a scandal. Sarcaccia's an old-fashioned country that way."

She punched his chest. "You're miserable, you know that?"

"Only without you." His thumbs caressed her cheeks, wiping away her tears. "I love you, Megan. With all my heart and soul."

A deep sigh escaped her as she looked into his brilliant green eyes—so much like Anna's—and absorbed the depths of emotion there. "It took you long enough to tell me. That's all I wanted to hear the day Gladwell offered me the job. All I wanted to hear when you proposed marriage in the first place."

He grimaced and leaned his forehead against hers. "I was so worried you'd think I was trying to manipulate you into marriage, I didn't want to say the words. I'm an idiot."

"Yes, you are. A *royal* idiot. But you're also sexy, intelligent, controlling, impetuous, witty, and—if I may say so—mind-blowing in bed. You've shown me that you love me, even if you haven't said it. And I love you. The whole package."

He shifted to study her face. "Does that mean you'll marry me?"

"Yes." Her toes curled in the sand as she added, "Absolutely. And as soon as possible, for the dog's sake."

"Good. I want this to be done properly." A devilish glint lit his eyes. "Speaking of done properly, we have the beach to ourselves here. It's amazing what can be done properly, given a few minutes on a private beach."

"Minutes? What happened to hours?" With a not-so-subtle yank, she pulled his shirttail from his slacks, then slid her hands underneath to caress his bare skin.

"Hours. Days. Years." He shrugged. "You decide."

This time, when his hot mouth met hers, there was no hesitation, no doubt, only the promise of a long, happy, thrilling future together.

Thank you for reading *Scandal With a Prince*. If you enjoyed this book, please consider leaving a review at your favorite bookseller or book club website.

Learn about Nicole's upcoming releases and get special insider perks by subscribing to her e-newsletter at *www.nicoleburnham.com*

Nicole is also on Facebook at *www.facebook.com/NicoleBurnhamBooks* and on Twitter @nicoleburnham

Read on for an excerpt of Nicole's next Royal Scandals book, *Honeymoon With a Prince.*

Honeymoon With a Prince
By Nicole Burnham

Kelly Chase woke with a start, nearly knocking over her daiquiri as she flung her hand to the right, in the direction from which she could've sworn she'd heard the low *whunk* of design books slamming into the floor.

She blinked when the sounds of rolling surf and distant laughter reminded her she was nowhere near the office. While her heartbeat slowed to its normal rhythm, she cursed herself for trying to ruin a perfectly good honeymoon by dreaming about work.

Then again, her friends accused her of ruining a perfectly good honeymoon by opting to take it without the groom.

Having barely rescued the daiquiri, Kelly pushed herself to a seated position, righted her sunglasses, and took a long, fortifying sip of the sweet pink drink. Before her, a cerulean sea spread out as far as the eye could see, its surface glittering in the late afternoon sunshine. Small boats bobbed along on the waves, some carrying fishermen back to shore after a day of work, while others served as floating escapes for those who wished to relax away the summer undisturbed.

Satisfied that all was as it should be, Kelly stretched back on her lounger and closed her eyes. Rays from the sun seemed to warm her from the inside out, lifting her mood, making her feel unencumbered and free.

No matter what friends and family said, this trip was absolutely the right decision.

Since her presumed groom was a first-class jerk, boarding the plane alone yesterday for the overnight flight to Europe seemed the perfectly logical thing to do and not ruinous at all. She'd wanted to visit the idyllic Mediterranean island of Sarcaccia since she'd first heard of the place. Even if none of her friends could accompany her on short notice—either that or they didn't want to, given that she'd dumped her fiancé ten days before the wedding—she wasn't about to let the airline ticket and rented villa go to waste.

Besides, not only had she paid all the deposits for the trip out of her own hard-earned cash, she'd put in countless pushups, crunches, and treadmill miles while living on salad, egg whites, and veggies over the last three months, all so she'd look good in her wedding photos and the pricey bikini she now sported. She wasn't about to let *that* go to waste.

The breeze picked up, ruffling Kelly's hair and cooling her skin just enough to make her drowsy again. She'd earned this nap, in this chair, on this beach, even if she did end up dreaming about work. And frankly, dreaming about work wouldn't be so bad—she'd never been afraid of hard work, since it gave her life a purpose—if she hadn't sold her business for the presumed groom.

The thought of oh-so-perfect Ted Robards and all his promises made her mutter aloud, "Arrogant jackass."

Woof.

The unexpected sound was so deep and close to her ear that Kelly launched from her chair, carried by the warm blast of dog breath that signaled a sizable beast. This time, she did knock over the daiquiri.

Her heart threatened to pound out of her chest as her feet hit the sand and she whirled to look behind her. A dog the color of rich, dark chocolate and with roughly the size and build of a German Shepherd sat at the head of her chair. A dark tongue hung from between pointed teeth, bouncing up and down as he panted.

"Hello," she addressed the creature, who seemed perfectly harmless aside from his massive build. His strong shoulders and lean frame didn't budge as she stared at him. It was as if he'd been trained to sit in that particular spot until commanded to do otherwise. "You surprised me. Would your bark happen to sound like a thick stack of books hitting the floor?"

The dog cocked his head as if he understood. He was gorgeous, all restrained muscle and shiny fur. Though she'd grown up with dogs and loved them to pieces, she'd never seen one quite like this. His eyes were a surprising blue and his nose long and lean, ending in a wet black snout. When she put a hand on the arm of her lounger, allowing the big boy to come close and sniff, then nuzzle, she discovered his short coat was soft as the fuzz on a newborn kitten.

"My goodness, but you're beautiful." Once he seemed comfortable enough with her, she scratched his triangular ears, which stood at attention, then moved her hand down his neck to feel for a collar. Nothing. Despite the lack of identification, the dog seemed well-loved. His weight was healthy, his eyes clear, and his coat neat, especially given that he was at the beach. She scanned the chairs nearby. Most were unoccupied, since the majority of beachgoers who'd arrived early in the morning to claim their spots had now left for the day. Of the few that remained, none appeared be searching for a dog.

"You're welcome to stay here if you like," she said as she cautiously resumed her seat in the lounger. Hoping he knew a few basic commands, she urged him to lie down beside her. He stepped forward, so he was at her hip, then sat once more and cocked his head, as if waiting for instruction.

Using one of the hand gestures she'd used for her own pets when she was a kid, she urged, "Down."

No dice. She tried a few different gestures. Different commands. Still no luck.

"Oh, come on. The least you can do is lie down like a good boy after causing me to lose a very expensive drink. Bar service on this beach is infrequent and not at all reasonably priced."

He scooted closer, then rested his head on her thigh. His gaze shifted to meet Kelly's in a not-so-subtle hint.

"You" —she rubbed circles behind the dog's ears— "sure know how to kiss up. Do you do this with your owner, too? I bet you do."

The dog let out a low, happy whine of satisfaction, then promptly turned around and stuck his butt in her lap.

"You've gotta be kidding me," she murmured, but since the dog seemed hungry for attention—or a good scratch—she obliged. "You'd better not have picked up any fleas in this sand."

As the dog shifted to get closer to Kelly, she discovered he was wet under the uppermost layer of his coat, close to the skin. She glanced toward the water, wondering if that's where his owner might be. A white boat, about the right size to carry four to six people out for a day of fishing, approached the tiny local marina about a hundred yards down the beach from her. From this vantage point, Kelly couldn't tell how many people might be on board or if they were looking for a dog, but she didn't pick up any unusual vibes. Another two men stood at the walk-up bar where the dock met the beach, but given that they'd passed her a few times earlier that afternoon carrying beer bottles and large bowls of appetizers with no sign of a dog at their heels, she doubted the big boy was theirs. Behind the bar, a walkway leading to a set of six boat slips stood empty. Five boats were docked and covered for the day. She assumed the vacant slot belonged to the white boat.

She glanced in the other direction, toward the parking lot and the cliffs that framed the beach, but nothing indicated the dog had come from there, either.

The dog let out another low moan and shoved its rump harder against Kelly's hand.

"You're incorrigible," she complained, though she continued to give the dog attention. After a few minutes, he let out a deep, throaty groan, then flopped in the sand beside her, turning so his head rested on the lounge chair near her hip. Though his body went lax, his eyes remained open, scanning the area as if watching over her.

Soon someone would miss this dog. Wouldn't they?

Keeping one hand tucked into his short fur, she leaned back in the lounger and waited. Soon the sun would dip low enough to cool the air and chase the last of the beachgoers home. If she couldn't find the owner by then, she supposed she'd need to call the local police. There had to be some type of animal control organization on the island. Hopefully they'd find the owner and not send the boy to the pound.

She couldn't bear that thought.

"You're fine with me," she whispered. It felt reassuring having a dog to keep her company after all the upheaval of the last few weeks. He likely needed love, just as she had. She most certainly wasn't going to let down this sweet dog the way Ted—the liar—had done to her.

As if he understood, the dog pushed himself out of the sand and climbed into the lounger beside her, shoving Kelly to the very edge as he squeezed against her with an *oomph*.

Kelly laughed, but allowed him to take over the space. "I bet your owner doesn't let you do this on the sofa at home, huh, boy?"

He let out a whiny grumble in response, then plunked his head on her shoulder.

It wasn't her idea of a honeymoon cuddle, but she had to admit it was infinitely better than sharing her chair with Ted.

With any luck, she'd never see him again.

* * *

Massimo Barrali held a hand over his eyes, shielding them against the glare of the setting sun as he walked the beach. Somewhere, likely jumping in and out of the surf, he'd eventually find his dog.

He only hoped he wouldn't find the crazy thing in trouble. Gaspare wasn't exactly a people dog; he'd been trained to protect Massimo and—though he was never aggressive—preferred not to associate with most other humans. Water, on the other hand, did strange things to Gaspare. While Sarcaccian Shepherds were bred to work with livestock and thrived on running through the rough terrain of the island's high country, Gaspare seemed more at home frolicking in any body of water to which he could gain access. The ocean, lakes, even—on one memorable occasion—the fountain behind the royal palace. It was the one situation in which Gaspare's rigorous training failed.

Massimo's gaze traveled from the surf toward the seaside bar, where two men nursed beers and chatted with the bartender, to the large storage locker beyond it. A lifeguard busied himself dragging lounge chairs from the incoming tide and stashing them in the wooden structure so they'd be protected overnight. Beyond the lifeguard, a family trudged toward the steps leading to one of the private villas that lined this section of beach. Towels were draped over their shoulders, the father carried a small cooler, and the teenaged son and daughter elbowed each other as they walked. Despite signs that the beach was emptying for the night, the dog didn't materialize.

Since Massimo couldn't call for Gaspare without drawing attention to himself, he turned from the dock and made his way along the shore in the direction opposite the bar, toward the parking lot. Gaspare was an intelligent dog. Perhaps he'd simply gone to the car, knowing it was time to head home.

Massimo swore to himself as he strode along the beach, his mood becoming blacker by the moment. It was his own fault, of course. He should've known Gaspare would leap overboard and doggie-paddle the last two hundred meters to shore. The beast had been itching to swim from the moment he'd realized Massimo was driving him to the boat dock for a spur-of-the-moment fishing excursion this morning. Unfortunately, Gaspare's wild jump angered a group of nearby fishermen, who'd been compelled to yank their lines as the dog approached. Massimo had to spend several minutes soothing their tempers. He couldn't have them telling their friends—or the media—that Prince Massimo and his dog ruined their afternoon catch. Unfortunately, during the time Massimo spent making nice with the fishermen, he'd lost track of Gaspare.

Next time, he'd come alone. Despite humoring his parents' suggestion that he always have Gaspare along as security when he spent time outdoors by himself, no good came of bringing the dog fishing. Then again, he'd rather have Gaspare for company than anyone else.

A wave rushed up the beach and over Massimo's feet as he made his way along the firm sand at the water's edge. A few lounge chairs remained on this section of the beach, but only one appeared occupied. A pair of long, lean legs stretched up from the lounger's footrest toward an extremely firm, round backside clad in a tiny pink bikini. The woman lay on her side, showing off a hip perfectly curved for a man's hand, seemingly oblivious to the fact she was the last remaining person on the beach. Normally pink wasn't his favorite color—he'd always had a strong preference for bright red or a sexy, not-so-innocent white when it came to bikinis—but given what this woman looked like from the waist down and the fact he had to pass her to reach the parking lot, he suspected he was about to discover the wonders of pink.

As he moved closer, what he saw from the waist up wasn't bad, either. A shoulder rounded with just enough muscle to be firm without being hard. A long, elegant neck. A tangle of shiny, reddish-brown hair exactly the color of the palace's infernal afternoon tea twisted on top of the woman's head.

Then he heard the moan.

He paused, stunned. Only one creature on Earth made that sound, and then only in one instance. Gaspare. Getting his butt scratched. Something the dog never allowed any human to do other than Massimo and—on rare occasions—Massimo's sister, Sophia.

Who in the world was this woman, and what had she done to his dog?

He covered the stretch of sand that separated them in quick steps. When he came to the base of the chair, he drank in the sight of Gaspare's large body wedged alongside the woman's. Sure enough, she had one arm stretched to rub his dog's backside. Gaspare's head was tipped back in ecstasy. And no wonder... even with her eyes covered by a pair of large sunglasses, the woman in the chair looked better from the front than from the back. She gave no indication she'd seen him approach; he got the impression her eyes were closed.

Gaspare, on the other hand, let out another moan and wiggled closer to the woman, deliberately ignoring Massimo.

"You are unbelievable, you nutty dog. Did your owner send you away for excessive cuddling?" she said just loud enough for Massimo to hear. So, an American. And the soft voice was every bit as sexy as the woman.

A slow smile spread across his face. *Good dog.*

ABOUT THE AUTHOR

Nicole Burnham is the RITA-award winning author of over a dozen romance novels, most featuring modern-day royalty. She has lived and traveled all over the world, absorbing different cultures and visiting the opulent palaces and lush gardens that inspired the Royal Scandals series. *All About Romance* declares, "Nicole Burnham gives life to a fictional kingdom and monarchy that feel as though they could be real" and "gosh darn it, Nicole Burnham is *good*....readers should definitely check her out."

Nicole currently lives in Boston. She enjoys yoga, games at Fenway Park, taking her dog for long walks, and reading the many romance novels on her bookshelves. Most of all, she loves writing stories about far-off countries, deliciously powerful heroes, and passionate heroines for her readers.

You can read more about Nicole and sign up for her popular e-newsletter at her website, *www.nicoleburnham.com.* She's also on Facebook at *www.facebook.com/NicoleBurnhamBooks* and on Twitter @nicoleburnham.